A VICTORIAN SPECTATOR

Uncollected Writings of R.H. Hutton

A VICTORIAN SPECTATOR

Uncollected Writings of R.H. Hutton

Edited with an Introduction by
Robert H. Tener and Malcolm Woodfield

The Bristol Press

This book is for Jean

First published 1989 by The Bristol Press.
Paperback edition published 1991

The Bristol Press is an imprint of
Bristol Classical Press
226 North Street
Bedminster
Bristol BS3 1JD

Jacket photograph from the original frontispiece of *Brief Literary Criticisms*,
1906. By permission of the Syndics of Cambridge University Library.

ISBN 1-85399-028-0 (hbk)
ISBN 1-85399-183-X (pbk)

A CIP catalogue record for this book is available from the British Library.

Printed and bound in the UK by Billings and Sons Ltd, Worcester.

Contents

Preface

We have attempted in this selection of Richard Holt Hutton's uncollected writings to choose articles that suggest something of the quality and range of his work over the many years of his connection with the *Spectator*. We have tried to reproduce his articles as accurately as possible, even to preserving his punctuation. Hutton was a careful proofreader; only half a dozen corrections had to be made. Since both editors shared the labour of editing this volume, both share the responsibility for the finished work.

For many years we have been in receipt of unstinted kindness from successive editors of the *Spectator* and from members of its staff. Our gratitude to them can scarcely be put into words.

Our edition would not have materialised had it not been for the generosity of the University of Buckingham which made it possible for Malcolm Woodfield to spend some time in Calgary planning the collection with Robert Tener. For this help the two editors are deeply grateful.

A work of this sort inevitably involves an editor in seeking aid from others more knowledgeable than he, so we take pleasure in thanking the following for help generously given: Barry Baldwin, Bill Blackburn, Robert Carnie, David Oakleaf, Janis Svilpis and George Wing. Barbara MacLeod bravely faced the task of typing the entire document. And Kim Richardson and Michael Bird of the Bristol Classical Press proved to be exacting but kindly editors.

Finally, we thank the Editor and Mr Charles Seaton of the *Spectator* for their many kindnesses over the years.

Hutton's Life and Writings

'What are your historical Facts; still more your biographical?
Wilt thou know a Man ... by stringing-together beadrolls of what
thou namest Facts?'
                    – Thomas Carlyle, *Sartor Resartus*, Book II, Ch. X.

If not the major post-Romantic critic of the Nineteenth Century, Richard
Holt Hutton is at least the greatest reviewer of the Victorian Age. As
John Morley remarked at the time of Hutton's death, Hutton had a wider
range than even Matthew Arnold who was, like Hutton, a critic of
literature, politics, society, and religion. In more than 6,000 articles,
essays, and reviews published over half a century, Hutton appraised a
huge number of contemporary figures, books, and ideas, whereas Arnold
on principle largely refrained from reviewing his fellow Victorian writers.
Like Arnold, Hutton wrote on Continental and American authors, but
his great strength lay in his assessments of Carlyle, Clough, George Eliot,
Newman, Tennyson, Trollope, and Wordsworth – and Matthew Arnold.
And he wrote on a host of other matters as well: on political, educational,
and ecclesiastical affairs; on currents of philosophical and theological
thought; and on the warfare of science and religion. In the latter capacity,
he was perhaps the greatest lay preacher of his age.

Hutton was born in Leeds on June 2, 1826, the third son and fifth
child of Mill Hill Chapel's Dr. Joseph Hutton, and grandson of another
Joseph Hutton, the Unitarian minister of Eustace Street Chapel in
Dublin, the city where Richard's father had been born. Richard was
always proud of his Irish ancestry but equally proud of his Yorkshire birth,
believing that these were the sources of his lively imagination and his
sturdy sense of reality.

In 1835 the Rev. Dr. Hutton moved his family to London so that his
sons could receive a better education than Leeds afforded. As
Dissenters, Unitarians were excluded from the ancient Anglican
foundations of Oxford and Cambridge. University College, London, was
established for the benefit of such Dissenters, and non-Christians as well.
Richard first attended the school connected with the College, then the
College itself. Here, under Augustus De Morgan, George Long, and

Henry Malden, Hutton studied Mathematics, Natural Philosophy, Greek, and Latin, taking prizes or certificates of honour in every class, and winning the highest award the College bestowed when he graduated in 1845, the Flaherty Scholarship in Mathematics and Natural Philosophy.

After a dreary year of reading law, Hutton spent the winter of 1846-47 tutoring James Martineau's son, Russell, at Heidelberg, where Hutton met Frederick William Robertson, who was later to become a famous Brighton preacher. (Robertson it was who first implanted in the young Unitarian's mind the possibility of belief in the Incarnation, though it was F.D. Maurice in the later 1850s who brought this to fruition.) During his stay in Germany Hutton resolved to abandon the law and to take up the Unitarian ministry. For this purpose he entered Manchester New College in the Autumn of 1847 where Martineau and John James Tayler were his mentors. So impressed was Hutton by Martineau that he spent the winter of 1848-49 with him and his family in Berlin, the two men reading philosophy together under the guidance of Trendelenberg and others. Between 1848 and 1851 he attempted (except during this studious interval) to gain a permanent congregation but failed; his sermons were too learned. In the meantime, in 1849, he took his examinations for the M.A. at University College, capturing the Gold Medal for Political Economy, Logic, and Mental and Moral Philosophy. In October, 1849, he was appointed Vice-Principal and Chaplain of University Hall, the just-established residence for Presbyterian (Unitarian) students at the College. Arthur Hugh Clough was the Principal. Hutton's stay was brief, as it was, too, in Manchester the following year where he taught school. Then at the end of June, 1851, he married Anne Mary Roscoe, sister of William Caldwell Roscoe whom Hutton had met at University College and who, though short-lived, was to become a fine literary critic. In November, 1851, Hutton was invited to help edit the *Inquirer*, a Unitarian weekly newspaper, but this position he was forced by illness to relinquish in mid-summer, 1852, along with the Principalship of University Hall, a post to which he succeeded when Clough the previous Christmas was asked to resign. Severe inflammation of the lungs sent Hutton to Barbados in October. He and his wife caught yellow fever soon after their arrival; he recovered, but on December 20th Mary died.

Believing that he must spare his voice (he had lost the use of a lung), Hutton now turned to editing as his profession. From 1853 to 1855 he edited the *Inquirer* and the Unitarian quarterly, the *Prospective Review* (to which he had contributed since 1847). From 1855 when he helped to found it to 1862 he co-edited the *National Review* with his closest friend, Walter Bagehot, whom he had met at University College in 1842; together they made it one of the great Victorian quarterlies. From 1857 to 1861 he was literary editor of the *Economist*, in the meantime in 1858 marrying, according to the rites of the Established Church, Eliza Roscoe, Mary's cousin. (Hutton was rapidly gravitating towards Anglicanism.) In 1860 he edited William Caldwell Roscoe's *Poems and Essays* in two volumes. The following year came the great opportunity of his life.

Near the end of January, 1861, Meredith White Townsend bought the *Spectator*, a Liberal weekly which had declined since the death in 1858 of its founder, Robert Stephen Rintoul. Townsend had been highly successful in conducting the *Friend of India* near Calcutta, but ill health had forced his return to England. Having soon recovered, he set about vigorously to restore the *Spectator*, but shortly realized he could not do it alone. He had heard about Hutton while still in India, and now through Bagehot secured an interview. As an afterthought, when Hutton was part-way down the stairs, he offered Hutton a joint-proprietorship, and thus in June Hutton joined him as literary editor.

Together the two men threw immense energy into improving their paper. Each on an average wrote four articles a week besides sharing the three pages of short paragraphs summarizing the news which prefaced each issue. Townsend, the political editor, only occasionally wrote book reviews, but Hutton regularly produced two political articles a week besides writing for and supervising the "Books" department. At first their support of the North in the American Civil War caused a serious drop in the paper's circulation, but by 1865 the victory of the Federal cause vindicated the editors' position, and the *Spectator* thereafter went on from strength to strength. At the time of Hutton's death thirty years later the *Spectator* was the leading weekly in the British Empire.

In the early days of the partnership Hutton was forced to supplement his income. For several years he was an examiner in Political Economy for the University of London, was from 1858 to 1865 Professor of Mathematics in Bedford College, and in 1865 contributed a series of political portraits to the newly established *Pall Mall Gazette*, reprinted in 1866 as *Studies in Parliament*. From then on, however, he experienced growing financial security.

And growing recognition, too, as a writer and thinker. In 1869 he was invited to be a founding member of the Metaphysical Society, thus becoming personally acquainted with Gladstone and Tennyson, Huxley and Tyndall, Ruskin and Manning, and many other leading Victorians. (In the *Nineteenth Century* in August, 1885, after the Society's dissolution, he wrote a brilliant account of a typical meeting.) In 1871 with the publication of his major work, the two volumes of *Essays Theological and Literary*, largely drawn from the *National Review*, he was accepted into the Athenaeum. In 1875 he was appointed to a Royal Commission on vivisection. In 1878 he was invited to produce the English Men of Letters volume on Sir Walter Scott, only the second title in this famous series.

Bagehot had died in 1877, and Hutton set about to widen the fame of his friend by editing his works which he accomplished in three collections: *Literary Studies* (1879), *Biographical Studies* (1880), and *Economic Studies* (1881). In 1887 he brought together several of his own essays published in various journals in *Modern Guides of English Thought*, in 1891 he published his book on Cardinal Newman (a man he is said to have hero-worshipped), and finally in 1894 he produced the two-volumes of *Contemporary Thought and Thinkers* containing articles and reviews that had previously appeared in the *Spectator*.

The final nine years of Hutton's life were darkened by personal tragedy. In 1888 as a result of a carriage accident his wife lapsed into a deep depression from which she never emerged. She would play chess with him, but apart from "Hello" and "Goodbye" never spoke to him again. He insisted on caring for her at home and therefore had to curtail nearly all of his social activities though he continued to attend to his duties at the office. Even that became increasingly difficult as illness attacked him more and more seriously in the 1890's. Then on February 9, 1897, Eliza Hutton died, and on June 26th he made his last contribution to the *Spectator*. On the 9th of September, after several weeks of coma, he, too, passed away.

Note

Information about Hutton's life will be found in *The Dictionary of National Biography*; Mrs. Russell Barrington's *Life of Walter Bagehot* (London, 1914); J. Drummond and C.B. Upton's *Life and Letters of James Martineau*, 2 vols (London, 1902); Robert Tener's three articles on Hutton's editorial career in *Victorian Periodicals Newsletter*, 1974, 1975; and in *The Wellesley Index to Victorian Periodicals* (Toronto, 1979), III, 135-46. We have also benefited from private information from the late Professor J.H. Hutton.

A Victorian Spectator

To most readers of English literature, the *Spectator* is an important eighteenth century journal of literature and criticism. But there was an equally important and possibly more influential Victorian *Spectator*. Its joint editor and proprietor was R.H. Hutton, "who, in the eyes of the present generation," wrote a contemporary, "represents the *Spectator*. His individuality it is which we find impressed upon every page of the review." Another wrote simply: "In fact, Mr. Hutton is the *Spectator*."[1] To a Victorian, "no English journal wields a stronger influence over thoughtful men," and to a modern historian, Owen Chadwick, "Hutton turned the *Spectator* into the most revealing guide to the progress of the English mind."[2]

With one exception, all the pieces in this selection are from the *Spectator*. Each is reprinted in full, and none has been reprinted before; indeed this is the first selection of Hutton's work since a posthumous and unscholarly selection, *Brief Literary Criticisms*, was edited by Hutton's niece in 1906. In some sense it is, then, the case that, as Philip Davis has written, Hutton is the "unjustly neglected Victorian critic."[3] Paradoxically, on the other hand, most Victorian scholars concur in this. In the Routledge "Critical Heritage" series, which has for some twenty years been reprinting the contemporary criticism of major writers, essays and reviews by Hutton appear in almost *all* the volumes of nineteenth century writers. Within these volumes, Hutton is often a "major" figure: his essay on Hawthorne is the longest in that volume, while the volume on Hardy contains five pieces by Hutton – no other critic is nearly so well represented. Many of these writers appreciated Hutton's work: when the *British Quarterly Review* published Hutton's "The Poetry of Matthew Arnold," Arnold wrote to its editor to say, "Hutton has written an estimate of my poems far more careful, graver and abler than any which has yet appeared;" George Eliot was so pleased with Hutton's review of *Romola* that she broke firm rule and wrote to him about it, "you have seized with a fulness which I had hardly hoped my book could suggest, what it was in my effort to express" in the novel; Trollope wrote, "of all the critics of my work he has been the most observant, and generally the most eulogistic."[4]

This could hardly be called "neglect." Hutton's work has also been noticed by many modern scholars: Rosemary Ashton calls him George Eliot's most acute Victorian critic, Philip Davis calls him Wordsworth's best critic; when J.B. Schneewind came to add a bibliography of Victorian reviews to his selected essays of John Stuart Mill, Hutton is one of only three critics cited (mentioning his series of reviews in the *Spectator*), and in a bibliography of Tennyson, Douglas Bush included only two Victorian critics, one of whom was Hutton.[5]

Hutton's work has been neglected in so far as it has received very little sophisticated critical attention as an independent and whole body of work. It is difficult to add to the body of canonical writers, and Hutton did not welcome or facilitate the possibility: he forebade publication of a biography, he wrote voluminously but anonymously, in a form which was fragmented and, though retrievable, also ephemeral: Hutton, in effect, forfeited his own identity in being wholly identified with a newspaper, a disembodied "spectator." Most of his huge body of work has been identified or, at least, attributed, only in the later twentieth century, often on the basis of internal evidence. The notes to the present selection are used to present some of this evidence. This essay is intended to introduce Hutton as editor and critic, and especially to define his work with reference to that of three contemporaries with whom he was most deeply concerned and who are less "neglected:" Matthew Arnold, J.H. Newman, and George Eliot.

Hutton was a published writer for exactly half a century. His first review was published in 1847 and his last in 1897. His editorial and reviewing career began with the quarterly *Prospective Review* and the weekly *Inquirer*, both of which he wrote for and helped edit until the mid-1850s. He then helped to found and edit the quarterly *National Review* (with Walter Bagehot), while also writing for the quarterly *North British Review* and the weeklies, the *Economist* and the *Saturday Review*. The progress of Hutton's editorial career shows him moving from journals which are explicitly linked to religious movements (the two Unitarian journals with which he began), to ones which have more tenuous religious affiliations, to journals which are apparently secular. This parallels Hutton's religious journey from the Unitarianism of James Martineau through the Broad Church movement of F.D. Maurice, to a High Anglicanism influenced by John Henry Newman. Nevertheless, Hutton's own writing was divided between theology, literature, and politics. It was, however, Bagehot's appointment as chief editor of the *Economist* which Hutton, writing to Clough, felt would "prevent any chance of an improving position at the Economist, and perhaps curtail my general *influence* in the politics, which I should not like."[6] It was the promise of such influence which took Hutton to the *Spectator* in 1861.

The journal had been founded by R.S. Rintoul in 1828 and bought by Meredith Townsend in 1861. After only a few months Townsend realized that he needed both financial and editorial help, and offered a half share to Hutton, thus beginning what later editors felt to be an "apostolic succession." Hutton, however, remained at his desk until 1897, and it is to this period and this periodical that the pieces reprinted here belong.

By 1861 journalism was part of an expanding business in which the products of literature were potentially as much a commodity as cotton was to the textile trade. As an industry the press grew rapidly after the removal of trade restrictions in the 1850s and 1860s. These and other changes, such as advances in production, newsgathering, and information technology, had their most dramatic effect on the daily press in London and the provinces. These changes also affected, however, the weekly "literary" journal, as they did every specialized periodical: in London alone an astonishing 115 periodicals were *launched* in 1859.[7] Indeed, the weekly review was influenced by the publishing trade in general to a far greater extent than was the quarterly review. The literary content of the latter tended to be essayistic, reflective, and not necessarily concerned with contemporary literature or even with the books ostensibly under review. The quarterly reviewer was not above inventing books on subjects to which he wished to address himself.[8] The weekly reviewer was directly concerned with those products which the publishing trade thought it worthwhile to issue, even if his indirect concerns were more personal.

The press was not only a growth industry in the second half of the nineteenth century but also a competitive one. Journals came and went, were bought up and killed off, but there were four "intellectual" weeklies (the category to which the *Spectator* belongs) which were particularly important, not only in terms of the length of their survival but also in terms of their circulation, their influence, and the stature of their contributors. These were the *Athenaeum*, the *Academy*, the *Saturday Review*, and the *Spectator*.

Of the four, the first and last were by far the oldest, both having been established in 1828. The *Athenaeum* had deteriorated since 1853 under the editorship of Hepworth Dixon. The *Spectator*, on the other hand, had received new impetus in 1861 when R.H. Hutton joined Meredith Townsend as new joint editor and proprietor. The two other journals, by contrast, were new ventures and were influential by virtue of their very newness as well as their high quality. The arrival of the *Saturday Review* in 1855 caused an enormous intellectual and commercial stir amongst the weeklies. In terms of circulation the journal was a spectacular success and as a result most of its rivals for the weekly intellectual readership had to drop their prices in the late 1850s. In terms of intellectual tone and content it was both elitist and flippant, at the same time serious and dismissive. The *Saturday Review* writers policed the world of letters and politics, but they were not regarded as either law-makers or final judges: their reviews were arresting but recorded few lasting convictions. The *Academy*, founded in 1869, was consciously addressed to the group of like-minded intellectuals referred to by its title. Though it was by no means a friend to Matthew Arnold, it appealed to the Arnoldian man of culture. Its scope was European; indeed its form was taken by its founder, Charles Appleton, from European models.

In commercial terms, Hutton's *Spectator* had to find and satisfy a demand within this market, and to define itself in contrast to the tone and content of, in particular, the *Saturday Review* and, later, the *Academy*. However, behind and around the commercial pressures on the form and content of the weekly review of literature lie the intellectual influences imposed on and by the reviewer himself. Hutton's anonymous though widely-known editorial "we" expressed the reconciliation of his personal interests (as a professing Christian, for example) and the obligations deriving from his role (as professional editor). An examination of Hutton's personal interests will reveal how weekly reviewing becomes an integral part of an intellectual life and part of a general movement which set itself to find a language and a meaning for the immediately-contemporary analysis of literature and thought. This movement is specifically non-Arnoldian in its audience, its language, and its literary interests, especially in paying attention to the form most frequently presented to the weekly reviewer, and the one which Arnold most obviously neglected: the novel.

In 1893 the *Spectator*'s political rival, the Tory *Speaker*, carried a series of articles on the British press in the course of which the writer rather grudgingly allowed that "bit by bit the conviction has been forced upon us that if English journalism has a chief he is to be found in Mr. Hutton."[9] Though the basis of this judgement was Hutton's position as an editor, his staple literary production was the weekly review. He almost always, even in his longer essays, dealt with the contemporary in literature and thought and rarely wrote retrospective or historical essays. While paying homage to the accepted canonical hierarchy of writers, Hutton would not write about Shakespeare, Chaucer, or Milton unless, exceptionally, an occasion presented itself. Two such notable exceptions are included in this selection in the form of essays on Johnson and on *Clarissa*. Hutton's writings on literature are considerable, yet this prodigious output was actually surpassed by his production of political leaders and reviews. Shortly after he joined Townsend the two changed the format of the journal from that of a weekly newspaper to that of a weekly review of "Politics, Literature, Theology and Art." It was previously entitled a journal of "News, Politics, Literature and Science."

Now the "News of the Week" section was written in a narrative form which suggested that it was one man's version of political events. Moreover, the replacement of Science by Theology in the main title must be attributed to Hutton's influence. Indeed, a contemporary wrote of the change in editorial interest: "Religion had never been prominent in the journal, but Hutton at once began to preach, and he preached to a great and listening and picked audience until he died."

The audience who read Hutton were middle-class liberal intellectuals. This readership was to become an easy target for the fin-de-siècle journalist anxious to dissociate himself from Victorian complacency as he saw it. So to the later observers of the scene this readership was "a public sheltered in leafy rectories and snug villas from the headlong decisions and rowdy activity of the world." Another late-Victorian describes the *Spectator* readers as "gentle souls, fond of flowers and birds...middle-aged and declining gracefully to a future existence for which they were fully prepared," who "looked askance at a Huxley traveling rough-shod over their dearest orthodoxies." Several such writers describe how this flock of simpletons would look forward to the "repose and refreshment of a Saturday evening" when R.H. Hutton would make everything all right again.[10]

Hutton himself, however, was not regarded even by these writers as a representative of the type which constituted his readership. Although Hutton did, eventually, join that bastion of the Establishment, the Athenaeum Club, he was never part of the Oxbridge High Table set (his religious affiliations having originally denied him access). Similarly, he never moved in social or political high society, despite being on quite intimate terms with Gladstone — until, to Hutton's great regret, the *Spectator* editor (and son, let us not forget, of an Irish Unitarian) opposed the Liberal Prime Minister over Home Rule for Ireland, permanently crippling the Liberal Party in the process. He wrote to Gladstone: "I can hardly tell you how difficult my work as a journalist has become to me, since I felt compelled to take a different view from yours on the Irish question. Instead of enjoying it as I used to, it has become all duty work ever since."[11] Typically, this personal note is kept scrupulously out of the newspaper where Hutton is, as it were, impersonally "compelled" by his convictions, political, religious, and cultural. Not that Hutton was any radical, although his concern for "ordered freedom" included siding — almost alone amongst British newspaper editors — with the American North, championing women's access to professional and educational rights, and waging a career-long campaign against vivisection.

The caricatured gentility of his readers stands in sharp contrast to the embattled Hutton portrayed in contemporary accounts. The

Academy described Hutton as "the Invisible David of the *Spectator*" (invisible, that is, in contrast to the visibility of the reviewer who signed his work), yet in spite of considerable admiration of Hutton's fighting qualities, writers of the end of the century saw his writing as defensive and reactionary. The *Dial* reviewer described Hutton as "entrenched behind a barricade of prejudices" from which he conducted "a skilfully defensive campaign" against the forces of secularization.[12] A writer in the *Athenaeum* (April 22, 1899) described Hutton's life thus:

> Throughout a period of great intellectual ferment, Mr. Hutton stood forward as the champion of spirit against the assaults of Materialism, and as the champion of Christianity against Agnosticism and Scepticism.... Mr. Hutton was one of those who faced the first onslaughts; he protested that spirit was an element in the universe at least as real and at least as potent as matter. (p. 489)

The portrait threatens, as intended, to overreach itself in showing Hutton resisting the forces of secularization with the weapon of the weekly review, and risks bathos in opposing his "protest" and the "onslaught." The account is true in suggesting that the common concern in all Hutton's work is with the relation of the subject under discussion to the beliefs of the age. Yet it would be wrong to suggest that he was reactionary. When the writer says Hutton "stood forward," he means to suggest that Hutton is in the forefront of current debate, not that he is backward-looking. That word "Agnosticism," for example, was first published and given currency by Hutton (in a review reprinted below, "Pope Huxley," *Spectator*, January 29, 1870) because the old-fashioned denunciation of "Atheism," with its associations of sin and immorality, made no sense in the mid-nineteenth century where doubt struggled centrally with fundamentally new intellectual issues and where faith had to be reconciled with post-Kantian epistemology.[13] Hutton wrestled with the problem of doubt and, like the angel with Jacob, gave it Huxley's new name as a new age dawned and absolute victory was no longer conceivable. "The concern of educated Victorians," wrote Owen Chadwick, "with the fundamental questions of human life, is not better illustrated than by the wide influence of Hutton's *Spectator*.... Hutton's mind is a noble illustration of a new Christian attitude towards belief. It was sympathetic because it knew what it was about."[14] Hutton is, as the final words of the *Athenaeum*'s judgement suggest, a "realist" in dealing with contemporary thought. The writings of Newman were, as I shall discuss later, particularly important in enabling Hutton to address in a complex way the question of "realism" in both artistic and religious expression.

Hutton makes it clear in one of the first reviews he wrote for the *Spectator* that his concerns were going to be, in practice and on principle, the wants of his generation even if they contradicted his own desires and convictions. We might take the review reprinted in this selection, "Mr. Grote on the Abuses of Newspaper Criticism" (*Spectator*, June 29, 1861), as the manifesto of the new editor. He wrote: "Criticism must have at least enough of the creative power it deals with to feel completely its spell and fascination. And this is not got by critical habits: it is got by long apprenticeship to uncritical habits; by readiness of sympathy and flexibility of taste."[15] Hutton thus places himself in an interpretative tradition which includes both the "criticism" of biblical exegesis and also the "creative power" of George Eliot.

Hutton's "flexibility of taste" is not, of course, matched by flexibility of belief, so that his subject-matter is broad and diverse but his interests and convictions consistent and even narrow. Hutton's notion of "flexibility" is quite different from Arnold's, and it is the limitation of the Arnoldian canon and clerisy which Hutton aims to go beyond. He continues:

> the only criticism which is really likely to be useful on the minor works of every-day literature is that which has been trained and disciplined in worthier studies. Here is the mistake of the cut-and-dried man of culture. He goes about with the secret of having learned to appreciate the "grand style." He has lived in Homer till he can recall the roll of that many-sounding sea.... When first fortune compels him to deal with the daily literary efforts of ordinary Englishmen, he chooses such as are more or less connected with his real admirations.... And no doubt it is a trial to men steeped in the culture of the noblest literature of the world, to appreciate fairly the ephemeral productions of a busy generation. It seems beneath them, and the more they trample it beneath them, the less are they competent to detect its higher tendencies. But still the critic who allows this feeling to grow upon him abdicates his true office. Unless he can enter into the wants of his generation, he has no business to pretend to direct its thoughts.

Hutton is offering, especially in that final sentence, a powerful rebuttal of Matthew Arnold while laying down principles of weekly reviewing in deliberate contrast to those of other intellectual journals. Mark Pattison was to describe the *Academy* in 1870, when he was its editor and proprietor, as:

> a journal which should systematically survey the European literary and scientific movement as a whole, and pass judgement upon books...from a cosmopolitan point of view; a journal in

which only permanent works of taste and real additions to knowledge should be taken into account, and in which the honesty and competence of the reviewer should be vouched for by his signature.[16]

Hutton's intentions contradicted all these: his method is consciously occasional, not "systematic" or holistic; his main interest is English writing; his work resists the progress of scientific materialism; his work is "provincial" rather than "cosmopolitan;" he sees his task more as that of describing the present importance of passing ideas than as that of judging with the eyes of posterity; last, he has complex reasons for preferring the plural editorial "we" in journals (though he distrusted anonymity in fiction) to the subjective "I." For Hutton, only the fragmented form of the weekly review provided a way of making sense of the "real" nature of life in the second half of the nineteenth century. What began as a necessity became a virtue in that the weekly reviewer's placing of the part before the whole seemed to him the only available mode of knowing what secular life was like, and in thus making sense of life he was resisting the most dangerous product of secularization, namely the belief that life made no sense. The weekly review was both peculiarly apt for the tendencies of his time, and a means at the same moment of resisting those tendencies. These tendencies and characteristics of the age are often Hutton's real interest, and he places his authors and their works in relation to the *Zeitgeist*, and judges whether or not they resist or travel with that stream of tendency.

Matthew Arnold's "On Translating Homer" had just been published when what I have called Hutton's "manifesto" was produced in 1861. Arnold is clearly the type behind Hutton's "cut-and-dried man of culture," and Arnold's leisured criticism is contrasted with "the ephemeral productions of a busy generation." Hutton's notion of "entering into" the wants of his generation almost ensures his own disappearance, while Arnold's critical pose and his concentration on the essay form to be republished in book form ensured the elevation of the office of the critic over the importance of the weekly text. This failure to "enter into" Hutton also finds in Arnold's literary criticism: "for a critic, he remains too much himself.... His head is too clearly lifted above his subject to permit him to enter into it with full sympathy" (see "Mr. Arnold's Last Words on Translating Homer," reprinted in this volume). Arnold's interests, as he stated privately and publicly, consciously excluded consideration of the contemporary: he wrote, explaining the exceptional status of his late essay on Tolstoy, "in general I do not write about the literary performances of living contemporaries or con-temporaries only recently dead," and argues in "The Function of Criticism at the Present Time" for the need of "the English critic" to "dwell on foreign thought" if he is to learn and propagate the best that is known and thought in the world.[17]

The seven articles reprinted in this volume represent part of an appreciation of Arnold's work, often acutely critical of it, which Hutton continued for most of his career. Not only do they form the most important critique of Arnold by one of his contemporaries, they also help define for us Hutton's own position. The contrast drawn in the cutting and sarcastic "An Intellectual Angel" is meant to oppose Hutton's method and character with those of Arnold: "There are two ways of getting at almost all true discriminations, — the mode of calm and leisurely intellectual survey, and the mode of upward- labouring faith, — by the clue of pure thought, and by the clue of moral sympathy, — by the practice of an intellectual gymnastic, and by tracking home the higher instincts of the spirit." The occasion for the essay is Arnold's attack on English cultural and political philistinism, "My Countrymen," and Hutton largely agrees with the analysis of "the blunders of the great middle-class." But Hutton disapproves of the position from which Arnold makes his criticism, the language he uses, the detachment he cultivates: "others have convicted them of the same blunders from a far less elevated and yet far more hopeful position in the very midst of that zone of prejudice and custom-blinded intelligence, by the mere force of that genuine sympathy with freedom which overpowers, even without dispelling, the cautious fears of selfish conservatism." This "zone" is where Hutton feels he works. He regards Arnold, however, as a paradoxically detached dogmatist, "the angelic doctor of our times" in whom "the dogmatism which is natural to the temperament of the earnest practical zealot is in him perverted into alliance with the temperament of the calm, purely contemplative thinker." This detachment from the actual is nicely caught by Hutton in the 1866 review "Get Geist," in which he contrasts Arnold's teaching with "the great practical explosion of *Ungeist*" in the form of the Hyde Park Riots: "While the outer mind of London," he begins, "has been fermenting all the week with the turmoil of the Hyde Park Riot, the inner mind of London has been travailing still more patiently with the birth of a new intellectual obligation — 'to get Geist' — cast upon it by our greatest intellectual seer." That piece also should remind the reader that each of these reviews has an occasion and a context, is part of a newspaper issue and the political and cultural issues the journal as a whole addresses.

Arnold is, as Hutton portrays him, "angelic" in speaking from a great height, and Hutton develops the comparison into a nicely Hebraic analogy:

If we, the "dim common populations," get a blessing from Mr. Arnold at all, it will only be as Jacob obtained it from the angel

who wrestled with him "till the breaking of the day." He has no
spontaneous blessing to bestow on the class whose culture he
despises; and as that culture begins to light up their sky he would
only find a reason in it for leaving them, — "let me go, for the day
breaketh." ("An Intellectual Angel")

Hutton sets himself the task of bringing Arnold down to earth with
"upward-labouring faith," and holding him there while the day of popular
culture dawns. It is, Hutton implies, popular culture (including both the
novel and unselfconscious religion) which will translate the Philistines
and be renamed Israel, rather than the self-consciously high culture of
Arnoldian Hebraism. Only believe, Hutton seems to say, and the age is
not the dreary wilderness in which Arnold, in the last words of "The
Function of Criticism," sees himself dying.

Arnold is, of course, a decidedly secular angel, whose messages are
therefore to Hutton "useless but beautiful." This combination of
dogmatism with contemplation, and of spirituality with Godlessness, is
what interests Hutton:

> Mr. Arnold engaged in the delivery of one of these messages is
> really a subject for artistic study. The unquestionable truth of
> the matter, the condescending grace of the manner, the serene
> indifference to practical results, the dogmatism without faith, the
> didacticism without earnestness, the irony without pain, the
> beauty without love which mark the message, are all equally
> remarkable.

Having turned Arnold into a subject for artistic study, Hutton offers a
characterization intended also to typify the age as one of dogmatism
without faith, and of other such fragmentations and "perversions" of
characteristics which were perceived as having once been "naturally"
whole.

Hutton suggests in a late (1886) essay on Arnold and J.H. Newman
that Arnold came under Newman's influence in Oxford in the 1840s and
yet belongs to the following generation, when Emerson, Froude and
Chambers's *Vestiges of Creation* were in vogue though the limits of
"certain premature scientific assumptions" were not yet laid down. For
Hutton, Arnold remained caught between two worlds, or rather caught
between the world and the other-worldliness of Newman, a combination
of literature and dogma which produced a prophet without a religion,
crying in the wilderness. He cultivated, says Hutton, a secular stoicism
"which magnifies self-dependence, and regards serene calm, not
passionate worship, as the highest type of the moral life."[18]

Hutton objects in particular to the cultivation by Arnold of this
detachment and self-dependence. In "Mr. Arnold's New Poems" he

ingeniously suggests that Arnold's fondness for quoting and revising his own words shows the "really characteristic pleasure which Mr. Arnold takes in falling back, as it were, on himself." In "An Intellectual Angel," however, Hutton more seriously denounces the notion that such detached self-dependence offers privileged insights for the few who can cultivate it: "he regards the power of seeing things as they are as the monopoly of a class; and indeed, arrived at as he arrived at it, it must always be the monopoly of a class" ("An Intellectual Angel"). Hutton also finds fault with the very notion of self-cultivation. When he suggests that Arnold's fragmented intellectual character and delivery is "a subject for artistic study," he is not being merely sarcastic, but consciously implying that Arnold's position is a pose, an aesthetic concern claiming moral force. In the closing words of "Mr. Arnold on the Enemies of Culture" (reprinted below) the implication that Arnold is self-dramatizing is made explicit; Arnold's idea of culture, says Hutton, produces not progress but "self-consciousness, moral affectation, aesthetic melodrama."

In that striking last phrase, Hutton opposes Arnold to the "inwardness" he admires in George Eliot and attacks Arnold's self-consciousness, his creation of his own dramatic "persona" out of the personae of intellectual luminaries:

> When he praises Dean Stanley's wisdom and sweetness, and Mr. Jowett's moral unction, and Spinoza's "beatific vision," as a critic, he does well. But anyone attempting to subdue his own ruggedness from an aesthetic perception of the beauty of Dean Stanley's sweeter wisdom, or to attain unction because he sees that Mr. Jowett's unction is a real beauty of his character, or to reach a "beatific vision" of his own because it added something to the richness and serenity of the great Pantheist's philosophic calm, would only fall into conscious affectations.

The difference between Arnold and Hutton here is between their conceptions of human character and the source and purpose of moral authority. Their differences find expression in their modes of reading literature, of finding value in the literary construction of "character," but they are rooted in contrasting religious beliefs or, more precisely, in Hutton's refusal to accept, with Arnold, that culture goes beyond religion. Arnold argues in *Literature and Dogma* that one can derive from Christ's teaching, as from the teaching of Stanley, Jowett, or Spinoza, a "secret" and a "method" — namely, "the breaking the sway of what is commonly called oneself...and the proof of this is that it has the characters of life in the highest degree — the sense of going right, hitting the mark, succeeding."[19] This, suggests Hutton, is a gospel of secular success for the nineteenth century — "Blessed are the pure in heart, for they shall succeed."[20] For Arnold, St. Paul's injunction to "seek those things which are above" means "identifying yourself with Christ by attachment, so that you enter into his feelings and live with his life." Such a translation of oneself into another body implies a secular notion of individuality, a relative self which can lose, because it never "really" possesses, its identity. The change brought about in such an individual by such a belief would be attributable to the feeling of sympathy with Christ, not to Christ himself. It would be comparable to the changes brought about by feeling "sympathetic" to the characteristics of Stanley or Jowett: the sympathy is with those elements of oneself which one "finds" there. For Arnold, seeking "things above," whether it be spiritual or literary "high work" (since for Arnold they are identical), results in feeling like a Christian; for Hutton Christ is the *cause* and motive of seeking "things above." Hutton similarly criticizes Arnold in a long essay on the poetry reprinted in Hutton's *Literary Essays* for trying to define himself in terms of Wordsworth's "sweet calm," Goethe's "wide and luminous view" and Sophocles's ability to "see life steadily and see it whole." He argues that Arnold took from Goethe and Wordsworth "a style of clear heroic egotism" but does not "borrow from either of them the *characteristic motive and individuality* which in them justifies that style."[21] Moreover, it is the Arnoldian character of Sophocles which Hutton elsewhere (in "Mr. Arnold on the Modern Element in Literature," reprinted below) devastatingly denies to Arnold himself: "Mr. Arnold himself only sees life steadily at the cost of seeing it whole. He sees little bits of it with very perfect vision indeed, but his power of integrating life by his imagination—we apologize for a pedantic and detestable word—is not large." The connections between literature and religion are vital—as he says at the end of the same review, "the poet who can 'adequately' see our modern life at once 'steadily' and 'whole' would necessarily rest upon a much deeper and more mysterious faith than that of Sophocles." Again, the 1867 review of Arnold's poetry reprinted in this volume describes the view of the growth of Christianity embodied in the poem "Obermann Once More," as teaching that "Christ was the occasion, not the cause, of this great reaction." That distinction is crucial for Hutton. His whole defence against materialism focused on the materialist's attribution of physical cause to spiritual effect. His attack on Arnold is directed to Arnold's attempt to claim motive and purpose for progress where there is only expression. For Hutton, the causes of human activity—whether political or cultural—lie elsewhere. It might be said that all Hutton's writing and reading is, in a complex sense, "occasional"—not merely in being published in journals and dependent on whatever happens to be published, but in resting on a belief that all human activity, including authorship, is divinely authorized.

Hutton's emphasis on Arnold's failure to "integrate" both himself and the cultural differences he perceives suggests contrasts with Hutton's critical aim and method of integrating an author's expression into the body of the author's work, and integrating that work into the story of the world. Where he characterizes Arnold's work as *melodrama*, we might characterize Hutton's as *narrative*, with all the meaning that term has taken on in more recent critical and ethical debate.[22] Hutton looks for the story, the character, and the plot, behind a work of art or a line of poetry. His criticism is itself a narrative, broken into many pieces and spread over half a century of writing, but achieving a consistent wholeness nevertheless. Where Arnold, in the 1853 Preface to his own *Poems*, characterizes the age as one in which "the dialogue of the mind with itself has commenced," Hutton was trying to make narrative connections and construct personalities.[23] Matthew Arnold, on the other hand, failed in Hutton's view because he went no further than ranking the subjects of his criticism. Hutton wrote of Arnold's criticism of literature:

> He will tell you whether a poet is "sane and clear," or stormy and fervent; whether he is "rapid" and "noble," or loquacious and quaint;...whether a descriptive writer has "distinction" of style, or is admirable only for his vivacity; but he rarely goes to the individual heart of any of the subjects of his criticism;—he describes their style and class, but not their personality in that class; he *ranks* his men, but does not portray them; hardly even seems to find much interest in the *individual* roots of their character.[24]

As Julia Wedgwood wrote, Hutton, by contrast, had "hardly any sense of rank in literature."[25] This is not wholly true—he does not dispute the Victorian canon (Homer, Chaucer, Shakespeare, Scott), and he does have writers to whom he returns when he is able—Wordsworth, Newman, Tennyson, George Eliot. But he also tries to "characterize" writing and writers. The manner of Hutton's reading and characterization is nowhere clearer than in the comment he makes in the course of the essay on John Stuart Mill reprinted in this volume; undoubtedly, he says,

> ...this great uniformity of style and want of individual touches,—read, for instance, through the three thick volumes of "Dissertations and Discussions," and hardly anywhere will you stop and say, 'There is the very man,'—make it more difficult to appreciate Mr. Mill's individual genius than it usually is in the case of men who have so powerfully influenced the thought of their day.

We might call this sort of reading, which "finds" the man incarnate in the words, a hermeneutic of recognition: "Ecce Homo!"

Hutton's hermeneutic practice is further allied to his purpose of reading with a sympathetic and "integrating" imagination. He says in the review, reprinted in this volume, of Henry James's *Tales*: "In all these stories there is the same bent for discovering and analysing, not the harmonies, but the discords, of the world. Mr. Henry James loves torsos." We might say that Hutton hated torsos but loved bodies, the whole articulated life. His criticism abounds in "embodiments" and re-membering. He writes of Browning: "His imaginations, instead of *embodying* themselves in his poetry, only divulge themselves in it" (Hutton's italics). Elsewhere, he writes of Scott in one of the two books Hutton wrote (the other having been a study of Newman): "his imagination was one of *distinct embodiment*" (Hutton's italics).[26] Often his criticisms of other readers are for their failure fully to imagine another's embodiment and history, while his work is often marked by his migration into another's life and work. Most notable is his work on George Eliot, though his essay on "Johnsonese Poetry," in this volume, is also remarkable in the same respect — his comments are true to Johnson while being, perhaps by being, unlike Hutton: "No one ever realized more deeply, that life is disappointment; no one ever realized more deeply, that disappointment itself may be life, and a noble life, too." Hutton's sympathy, however, was bounded by the body of his own self and its convictions — it had its limits. The essay here on Walter Pater, "The Cultus of Impressionability," tries to be sympathetic: "the tendency of Mr. Pater's study, for all who read it with sympathy...." Hutton's effort, however, to incarnate Pater's voice, the most disembodied of Victorian critical voices, crumbles before "the impression of a man glorying in his susceptibility, hugging himself...recording every shade of namby-pamby tenderness in his unreal passion...enshrining himself in his aesthetic exclusiveness of feeling as a god in the golden cloud of Olympus." Self-consciousness, exclusivity and "unreality" (to which I shall return) are the great sins to Hutton (along with, his words might imply, hugging one's own image or acts of "Greek love," as homosexuality was encoded). He tries to achieve the reverse effect himself, largely by trying to portray the characters of his subjects, and defining those characters in relation to one another and as if in constant dialogue by repeated contrast and comparison: so, in essays presented here, Browning is compared to Tennyson, Swinburne to Shelley, and Henry James to Clough. This is a marked quality in Hutton's criticism, and places minds in dialogue with each other to counter Arnold's sense that the dialogue of the mind with itself is the dominant Victorian mode.

What we have called Hutton's hermeneutics of recognition is closely allied with his constant repetition, his adoption and codification of particular lines, his close scrutiny of texts and his comparison of variations and recensions. His reading, especially when one considers the pressure of time under which he laboured, is astonishingly attentive to style and revisions. One of his most important essays on Wordsworth is a comparison of early and later Wordsworth ("Wordsworth's Two Styles," *Modern Review*, July 1882, pp. 525-38), and the review "Arnold's New Poems" in this volume consists largely of such scrutiny. "We feel now," says Hutton in the latter piece, "towards some of Arnold's poems as we might towards friends who had two or three different bodies, and who were fond of trying the permutations and combinations of bodies in which they could appear to us." It would not be stretching the point to relate this to the Victorian debate about materialism and personal identity as well as to hermeneutic concerns: in other words, to the two questions, "What is a body?" and "What is a text?" which are both being asked in, for instance, Strauss's *Life of Jesus*.

When Arnold proposes touchstones of "poetry of the very highest quality," he expressly refuses to define the "mark and accent" of this quality except to say that they are "in the matter and substance of the poetry...in its manner and style."[27] He implies that the source of their excellence cannot be told, cannot be narrated. Hutton, by contrast, primarily asks himself in his reviews to define the character of the poetry he quotes. This is not only because it enables him as a reviewer to be more pointed, but because he places a particular importance on language and on the meaning contained in its style. For some indication of this importance and of his purpose in quoting and analysing texts, we might look to his 1876 "Preface" to the second edition (London, 1877) of his own *Theological Essays*, in which he writes:

> Is not the deed or sign, the action or the smile or frown by which a moral or spiritual truth is illustrated, an essential element in the truth itself? Might not our Lord's own sentence on the woman taken in adultery — "Let him that is without sin amongst you cast the first stone" — if uttered by a cynic, by a disbeliever in human virtue, have been turned into a sneer at the radical rottenness of human nature — an argument for universal tolerance of sin founded on universal despair — instead of what it was, an argument for universal tenderness and sympathy, with self-abhorrence, founded on the consciousness of universal weakness and temptation? (pp. xi-xii)

This is the moral equivalent and authority for Hutton's "flexibility of taste" in literature, and in both fields his search for meaning concentrates on character, on the character of words and of their speaker. His reviews, in common with most, relied heavily on quotation and he seems to have seen his role as one who supplies "signs" which illustrate the texts rather than using, as Arnold does, the texts to illustrate his arguments. Hutton supplies what he takes to be the "action" and "character" behind a text, or (as the writer of his obituary in *The Times* put it) he delineates "the moral atmosphere wherein a writer moved and dwelt" (September 11, 1897, p. 6). This attempt to delineate the "moral atmosphere" of a writer and to penetrate his or her mind was not popular with many reviewers or with Arnold himself. G.H. Lewes complained that it was the influence of German aesthetic criticism which led reviewers to try to penetrate "the special genius of the writer." Lewes wrote: "The critic is never easy until he has shifted his ground. He is not content with the work as it presents itself. He endeavours to get behind it, beneath it, into the depths of the soul which produced it. He is not satisfied with what the artist has given, he wants to know what he meant."[28] Hutton was frequently accused of inferring more from a text than was justified by what the artist had given. Leslie Stephen, reviewing a collection of Hutton's work in 1871, criticizes an essay on Shelley for its attempt to "squeeze more out of a metaphor than it will naturally produce." He concludes: "If all other men see less than they ought, Mr. Hutton is inclined to see more than really exists." In a similar vein, Arnold's publisher Alexander Macmillan wrote to him complaining that Hutton's review of *Essays in Criticism* "has Hutton's fault of seeing round and over you too much." Arnold himself thought another review of Hutton's had his "fault of seeing so very far into a millstone."[29] This latter comment was in response to Hutton's pursuit of the validity of Arnold's worship of Goethe:

> He worships Goethe for that steady and constant recognition of limitation which was the intellectual rather than the poetical side of his mind.... [He shows] a deficiency in sympathies lying beyond the intellectual sphere.... What Goethe called the 'daemonic' in himself,...he prefers to ignore, yet it is often (as in Shelley) the essence of poetry.[30]

Arnold's reaction, expressed in a letter to his mother, is instructive:

> The *Spectator* is very well, but the article has Hutton's fault of seeing so very far into a millstone. No one has a stronger or more abiding sense than I have of the "daemonic" element, – as Goethe called it, – which underlies and encompasses our life; but I think, as Goethe thought, that the right thing is, while conscious of this element, and of all that there is inexplicable round one, to keep pushing on one's posts into the darkness, and to establish no post that is not perfectly in light and firm. One gains nothing on the darkness by being, like Shelley, as incoherent as the darkness itself.[31]

This does not contradict Hutton, who had said, not that Arnold had no sense of the "daemonic element," but that he preferred to ignore it, and

Arnold is clearly articulating exactly that preference to his mother. What to Hutton is the moral atmosphere in which a writer breathes is to Arnold the anarchy which lies beyond his culture, an uncultivated undergrowth through which he makes his way. What to Hutton is characteristic of Goethe, Arnold sees as lying all around himself, and it is this self-conscious playing of a role in literary history which Hutton identified as Arnold's "aesthetic melodrama."

The analogy drawn upon by Arnold in that letter is that of the explorer, and it is significant that Hutton (though not only he, since exploration, metaphorical and literal, was a Victorian preoccupation) often uses this analogy himself to represent the cultivated autonomy of the secular individual in the nineteenth century. As he writes in an essay on "The Influence upon Morality of a Decline in Religious Belief," the failure of the Christian teleology to provide content and purpose to life leaves a person "a mere pioneer amidst dangers and difficulties to which it may turn out that both he and his race are quite unequal."[32] Ironically, one of Hutton's own reviewers, S.D. Collet, described him as belonging to "an advanced guard of religious pioneers" who were establishing religious outposts in a new secular world.[33] Hutton's emphasis upon "integration" is of a piece with his concern to maintain Christian teleology which, in turn, is reflected in his interest in narrative and character, in the whole stories of whole lives.[34] Paradoxically, as Collet's remark suggests, Hutton's work is more "worldly" than Arnold's. Arnold imagines himself establishing isolated landmarks, "outposts" and "touchstones," in works taking the shape of prestigious lectures published between hard covers. Hutton's work is substantial but dispersed, inextricably tangled with the products of the culture to which it is a contingent response. He tries to give voice to the needs and perceptions of "common men" and, in contrast to secular moralities such as Arnoldian culture or Comtean humanism, to integrate contemporary politics, art and science with the desires and partial perceptions of people living in the world rather than surveying it. Arnold needs to preserve the purity of disinterestedness because he is trying to provide a secular equivalent for the disinterestedness of divine perception. Hutton is not constrained by such a project, and is able to pay attention to a number of human points of view.

The complaint that Hutton saw too much in texts not only defines his practice against Arnold's, it also helps us to trace the roots of his literary criticism back to his early training in biblical exegesis in England and Germany. It was a complaint with a history. James Martineau had written to him in 1849 sympathizing with Hutton's "mortification at being called too profound in [his] preaching" and counseling him to "bear up against this reproach, and speak faithfully what is given us to say, without much regard to that standard of usage which regulates 'intelligibilities'."[35]

Hutton was simply not understood by his old-fashioned Unitarian congregation, and, as he had just returned from his studies in Berlin, G.H. Lewes was quite right to associate with German idealism the criticism which looks for "meaning" behind the letter. This is certainly what German biblical criticism was doing, and though Hutton did not approve of its theological results he seems to have translated them into literary criticism, just as George Eliot translated them not only into English (in her versions of Strauss's *Das Leben Jesu* and Feuerbach's *Das Wesen des Christentums*) but further, into literary practice. Hutton probably knew more about the theories, practices and implications of current biblical hermeneutics than any other Victorian critic who was not a professional biblical scholar. Hermeneutical practice seems to have influenced his historicism and his textual interpretation — that close scrutiny which no other critic applied with such consistency and which was consequently perceived, as Leslie Stephen expressed it, as finding more in a text than "really exists" there (whatever that might mean). In looking "behind" a text, Hutton is carrying out his manifesto-claim that "criticism must have at least enough of the creative power it deals with to feel completely its power and fascination."

Such a hermeneutic is alluded to in Hutton's words on the poetry of Tennyson: "There is what theologians call 'recollection' in every line" (see below, "The Genius of Tennyson"). For such interpretation of the "body" of a writer's work is a re-collection of the scattered signs of that personality in the world, a body remembered by the interpreter.[36] Hutton's one exclusively religious tract, *The Incarnation and Principles of Evidence* (1862), might be taken as a metaphor for his literary work. Indeed, Hutton's religious development from the Unitarianism of Martineau to the Anglicanism of Maurice and on to the threshold of Newman's Catholicism, is a movement towards belief in the Incarnate autonomy of Christ (most Unitarians did not, and do not, call themselves "Christians" at all). Wilfrid Ward, writing in 1888, described Hutton's religion as "an individual and self-evolved creed of his own manufacture" and suggested that "a more individual and independent journey forward in religious truth has rarely been accomplished."[37] For Hutton the body of the text incarnates the word and the author.

It could be argued that Hutton, in trying to go to the individual roots of his subjects, is merely making a virtue of necessity; that he is trying to justify and elevate the weekly reviewer's limited frame of reference and his temptation to fill it with a portrait of the artist. However, the particular significance of these words to Hutton's own intellectual life will show that they have considerable importance beyond self-justification.

Hutton is, first, criticizing the inadequacy of certain kinds of critical language which take for granted the expectations and categories of a known readership. Second, he is attacking a judgement which puts "style" and "class," in society and in writing, before "personality." The first must be related to Hutton's ideas about the sort of language which truly represents the "heart" of a writer. The second must be related to his ideas of what constitutes "character," and a discussion of this relation will suggest the importance to Hutton of the literary form which depended on the development of "character": the realistic novel. It will also suggest some reason for Arnold's antipathy to that form.

On the question of language, Hutton writes frequently of writers whose language is "unreal," and of the necessity to employ "real words" in every kind of writing. In a review in the *Spectator* in 1886 he argued that "if any one idea has been common to the religious and to the sceptical thinkers...in this curious century of ours" then that common idea was "the duty of not using 'unreal words' " (July 24, pp. 982-84). He draws together under this common idea the work of Carlyle, Ruskin, James Stephen, James Martineau, Huxley, Spencer, Frederic Harrison, and Wilfrid Ward but refers to Newman as "the first to inculcate this, in one of the earliest and finest of his Oxford sermons" (p. 982). The sermon which he takes as his source and authority for the duty of using "real words" is entitled "Unreal Words" and was written in the 1840s but reprinted in 1868 in *Parochial and Plain Sermons*. His reference to the sermon and his appropriation of Newman's principles demonstrate the ultimately religious basis of his work as a literary critic. This notion of "real words" was his authority for a criticism which seemed to go "too far" into language in allowing him to question what a writer "meant" behind what he had "given."

Hutton discusses the sermon in his review, included in this volume, of the 1868 reprint of the sermons. Hutton, ironically employing Darwinian language but trying to fulfil the self-made law of his 1861 manifesto, begins, of the sermons: "it seems the right time to say something of their adaptation for the wants of the generation which only knows him as the greatest of the Roman Catholic converts." He goes on to give this account of "real words":

> Dr. Newman points out that words may be, so to say, *more* real than those who use them are aware of. They may be the indices of powers and forces far beyond what those who use them suspect, because those who use them have only got a superficial glimpse into the action and heart of those forces. Just as 'weight' meant a great deal more than Newton himself knew when he first began to suspect what the moon's weight really meant, and as the idea of which the word was the index carried him far beyond his own meaning when he first used it, so Dr. Newman points out that moral professions often mean far more than those who make

them know, and thus commit the soul to the larger meaning, not
the less, embarking those who use them on enterprizes far
beyond their immediate intention, nay, far beyond their
immediate strength.

The sermon is an early unmasking of the fallacy of intentionality, a
warning specifically against the unmindful or diluted use of sacred terms,
a warning which Hutton applies to those attempting to retain sacred
terms in secular morality. He also takes from the sermon a more generally
applicable stress on the responsibility of using words, especially those of
other people. This stress places a peculiar burden on those using
quotations, particularly as a kind of prayer, or pagan "touchstone,"
vaguely to refer to meanings which may not be fully comprehended.
Arnold's use of the "indices" of touchstones would thus have been
condemned by Newman as "unreal" in that Arnold did not attempt to
"mean the meaning" of, say, Dante's "In la sua voluntade e nostra pace."
Hutton similarly dismissed Arnold's attempts to construct what has
subsequently been called "process theology," to conceive of God as a verb
rather than a noun or person, as simply an "unreal" use of the religious
language (see below, "Arnold on God"). As Newman wrote in the
sermon:

> Words have a meaning, whether we mean that meaning or not,
> and are imputed to us in their real meaning, when our not
> meaning them is our own fault. He who takes God's name in
> vain, is not counted guiltless because he means nothing by it, — he
> cannot frame a language for himself; and they who make
> professions of whatever kind, are heard in the sense of those
> professions, and are not excused because they themselves attach
> no sense to them.[38]

The importance of the text to Hutton as a literary critic and weekly
reviewer, heavily reliant on quotations from texts which his readers will
not necessarily have yet read, can hardly be exaggerated. He took
Newman to suggest that language always means more than it says and that
its users are accountable to its full meaning, and that whatever his
intention a writer's words have tendencies which are not under his
control. To write in controlled language is to try to "mean the meaning"
of your words, and any disparity between the meaning of the words and
the intention of the writer threatens to work to his disadvantage by inviting
contrast or bathos. Hutton sees Wordsworth as particularly open to this
danger. Newman's account did not, for Hutton, free language of the
writer's intention, but it did invite him to measure the distance between
the writer's meaning and the autonomous movement of the language.

In his extensive writing on Newman, Hutton repeatedly refers to him as a "realist," meaning, it would seem, a realist in seeing human emotions, beliefs, and language as having deeper sources than the apparent vehicle of them. In the review he refers to Newman's "realism in the truest and most modern sense of that term, — in that sense in which modern science has taught us to understand the full depth of realism." Hutton is thinking of scientific laws which are, like realistic religious distinctions, not created by the human mind but immanent in nature: so Newton's word "gravity" was realistic in carrying him beyond a meaning he could comprehend to one which was in the world and not in him. Similarly, Hutton takes the meaning of literary texts to lie in the world and not in the inaccessible subjectivity of the writer.

This way of reading a text applies to Hutton's use of Newman's sermon in that he places it in the world rather than saying what he "personally" thinks of it. This personal side informs the reviews but is never made the subject of them. Hutton and Newman were, indeed, in regular correspondence for long periods of Hutton's *Spectator* editorship, though the reader of the reviews could not have suspected it. Hutton's letters express an emotional yearning for the sort of certainty offered by Roman Catholicism, combined with an intellectual severity which prevented his conversion. He knew that simply to follow Newman into the Church would be like merely repeating a quotation without understanding it: it would be an "unreal" belief.

The intellectual severity is the side seen by the public. So while stringently (if favourably) reviewing Newman's *Grammar of Assent* in 1870 as if he were fully in control of both the argument and his own beliefs, he ends a letter to Newman on the same book with the plea: "God give me some deeper knowledge of the truth before I die." A year later Hutton is reviewing *Middlemarch*, as it appeared in installments, and regretting George Eliot's disbelief in the divine source of the higher life she admires, while writing almost hysterically to Newman: "I sometimes almost despair of gaining in this life the light I crave."[39] This despair is the reverse side of the assurance his contemporaries saw in him — it expresses a despairing desire to believe as an intellectual, the desire addressed in Newman's *Grammar of Assent*. He wrote, apologizing to Newman for the conflicting tone of his letters: "The sight of your handwriting always unlooses something in me." Intellectual control over the emotional response is reasserted in the weekly review, where Roman Catholicism has to be unambiguously called a "false creed" even though he was as close as possible to conversion and known as a "champion" of Newman. Was this insincerity? He might have argued that his language in the *Spectator* is "real" (or "so just") in deriving from and containing the recognition that his words carry meanings of which he cannot personally be completely assured. "Real" writing does not refer to that sanctioned by the new, secular virtue of "sincerity," though it was precisely the failure to be sincere that Kingsley saw in Newman. Hutton, significantly, was Newman's most influential defender in the fight with Kingsley.

The notion that "real" writing expresses not only the intentions of the writer but also meanings which he could not "mean" produces in Hutton a way of reading which looks at moments like Practical Criticism, though it is more historically based. His position can again be seen clearly in contrast to that of Arnold. Reviewing one of Arnold's lay sermons, Hutton asks, "Has Mr. Arnold lately read Dr. Newman's great Oxford sermon on 'Unreal Words'?", and goes on to accuse him of "a great literary misdemeanour" in using sacred terms without a meaning adequate to them. He accuses Arnold of "a hardened indifference to the meaning of words and the principles of true literature" (*Spectator*, December 6, 1884, p. 1611). This general accusation is the most important. Just as Arnold translated "God" as "that stream of tendency not ourselves that makes for righteousness," so Hutton attacks him for seeing the intention and movement of any author's work as a mere "tendency" without historical roots, a tendency which can be categorized and imitated. In the case of Arnold's touchstone, "In la sua voluntade e nostra pace," Hutton suggests that Arnold had replaced by an ahistorical drift the volition, the "voluntade," both of God and of Dante.

Hutton's opposition to Arnold's notions of realism in both meaning and character brings us to the form of "true literature" which Hutton most valued. Hutton was a careful and regular reviewer of the novel for half a century, unusually unapologetic in treating this ephemeral form as the vehicle for the permanently valuable. This interest in permanence was a reflection both of the potentially ephemeral form in which he himself wrote and of a general obsession in the last decades of the century with the question of which emotions and beliefs will last. Hence the question in an 1892 review, "How Long Will Dickens Hold his Place in the Future?". But the principled interest in the novel has more complex motives. Like "real words" which are indices of the writer's powers and other forces beyond his control, the realistic novel depicts characters whose lives are within their control and have personal meaning and yet who are taken by others to be acting out complete narratives. As early as 1850 Hutton wrote that the unique interest in fiction lies in this combination of the objective and the subjective, resisting the division of ethics into the utilitarian and the intuitionist. Its interest, he wrote, "lies in the simultaneous exhibition of the internal and external history of a human life, in the display to a single glance of the inward forces and the external fate...the creation of a double life." Indeed, all Hutton's early reviews can be seen to look forward to George Eliot for the satisfaction of their aesthetic expectations. When he wrote, reviewing Elizabeth Sewell and Elizabeth Gaskell in 1855, that "a great artist must, in a certain sense, be the providence to the conceptions he has created," he could not have foreseen how literally he was later to see in George Eliot "the spectacle of a woman who was her own God."[40] She is, even before she had published a novel (*Adam Bede* appeared in 1859), the ideal novelist who would do more than simply depict either the manners of cultivated society (as Hutton sees in the work of Austen and Thackeray) or the merely accidental and eccentric (as he sees in Dickens and Collins). Hutton criticizes Dickens for being "much encumbered by life-choking detail that was not life." For Hutton, the novel struck a blow for freedom from the conditions of the quotidian. He wrote in an early essay that the function of the novelist is to "decipher latent and suppressed realities by *translating* them into other moral situations so as to make them speak for themselves."[41] The special function of the novel seems to be, then, to provide occasions for the "real" sources of human nature and action to emerge by giving them an autonomy they do not "really" possess. The novel provides special occasions for the expression of the latent and the unself-conscious. Despite his religious beliefs, Hutton had no time for "religious novels" precisely because they made autonomous just those parts of human life which were not independent. The novel was and was not, for Hutton, "like life." The novel was like life as Hutton saw it in providing the occasion for meaning and growth but not their cause. To look to experience as both the ground and verification of belief is pure materialism. Although he defends George Eliot's ethics as having "all the inwardness of Christian ethics," Hutton's reviews barely control a terrible disappointment that she did not actually believe in the convictions which she seems to sanction. Her novels are intended as causal agents in a moral process. His weekly reviews, by contrast, are occasional on principle and not merely as a result of commercial pressures. They refer to convictions which they cannot fully contain or explain, to an Author besides R.H. Hutton.

Hutton did not have a consciously articulated "theory" of the novel, but it is clear how and why characterization and narrative are vital to him. In the essay on Browning in Hutton's *Literary Essays* — an essay which, like most of his long collected essays, is a series of previously published reviews connected together in one narrative — Hutton remarks of the poet:

> He conceives men in their relation to each other, and in mental collision with each other; but, after all, he does not care which way the battle goes, except so far as that is involved in his interpretation. There is no *narrative* force in him at all. He hardly enters into the story, and even in his dramas...evades a

plot as far as he possibly can.... [W]e never lose sight of the critical eye of the poet himself....[42]

The italics in this passage are Hutton's, though the force of the word is not easy to explain. Narrative seems for Hutton to be associated with sympathy, with "entering into" a character and a situation while still "caring which way" the story goes. The 1863 review of "Mr. Browning's Poetry" in this volume predates all the pieces which made up the long essay, but shows signs of the formation of those ideas. Browning has, Hutton says, "a keen, cold, dramatic intellect which takes infinite pleasure in reflecting all sorts of life without giving us any impression of sympathy therewith.... There is none of that narrative interest in his dramas which is as essential to a good drama as the power of interpreting character itself." Hutton seems to foresee the preoccupations of late twentieth-century theorists with narrative as a form of ethics and of interpretation, as a means of constructing teleological accounts of human life and making them available for communication and evaluation. Narrative seems to be for Hutton the means of maintaining in a secular world a balance between understanding and evaluating the lives embodied in other individuals, a means of making sense of life.

In Hutton's own lifetime the progressive secularization of society provoked fears that individual lives would become meaningless, as John Stuart Mill perceived his own life, as he describes in his autobiography, as purposeless. Hutton was not alone in perceiving the importance played by narrative in the secular project of constructing meaning, in making sense of life. W.H. Mallock argues in his *Is Life Worth Living?* (London, 1879, reviewed by Hutton in the *Spectator*) that fears of meaninglessness were caused by the loss of an object in life, meaning both the loss of an object of veneration and the loss of a function in life which allowed lives to be seen as wholes, or metaphorically as journeys or quests toward known ends. For Hutton the history of ideas in the nineteenth century was a series of attempts to defend or replace objects of veneration or activity, to construct teleological, narrative schemes of life. Hutton constantly finds in these secular constructs expressions of a human nature which is "really" divine in origin. Mallock found in secular humanist ethics "a mere mutilated reproduction of the very thing it professes to be superseding."[43] Hutton, similarly, thought secular ethics "unreal" in its use of religious language, an attempt, like Arnold's co-option of Spinoza or Christ, to re-member the body of Christian teaching without the motivating force of its origin. "It is only Christianity," wrote Hutton, "which makes modern secularism look plausible. By long dwelling on the type of the Christian character men have learnt to imagine that that type of character could stand alone."[44] This is precisely the self-dependence which Hutton saw represented in the work of Arnold.

Mallock suggests the connection between the moral and aesthetic results of secularization in his review of George Eliot's last work, *The Impressions of Theophrastus Such*, which he develops into an essay on her whole work, arguing that both the narrative form of her novels and the human idealism behind them "assert the part to be more complete and greater than the whole...that those human hopes, loves and enthusiasms which Christianity has developed for us and bequeathed to us are in reality complete in themselves."[45] This relation between the part and the whole, simultaneously and interdependently an ethical and an aesthetic concern, was also vitally important to Hutton. Reviewing an early part of *Daniel Deronda* in 1876 (reprinted below), Hutton makes a tentative criticism, one he offers to withdraw if the novel evolves along different lines from the ones he foresees, of the tentativeness of Deronda's character. Daniel Deronda, he suggests, "runs the risk of appearing to the end as little more than a moral mist, – a mere tentative, or rather group of tentatives, in character-conceiving, which the author may find it exceedingly difficult to crystalize into distinct form." This failure to embody the character in distinct form Hutton blames directly on George Eliot's secular moral philosophy which separates the substance of religious ethics from the body of Christ and the form of Christian teaching: "Is not his," he continues of Deronda, "the result indeed of George Eliot's philosophy, which has parted with all the old lines of principle, except the keen sympathy with every noble sentiment which she always displays, and imported nothing new and definite in their places, except the vaguest hopes and aspirations?" Hutton was acutely aware that sympathy could become characterless and relativizing. "We admire, but we do not believe in, the states of mind which are attributed to him," Hutton skeptically says of Deronda. George Eliot would, Hutton knew, have said the same of the personal God.

Hutton's literary and religious instincts came together in his evaluation of the novel and his attention to the function of narrative, the distinct embodiment of character, and the employment of "real words." Though Hutton reviewed an enormous number of novels his reading did not sacrifice detailed observation to general categorization, nor did he wait until a novel was published complete. Trollope tells the story of how Hutton exposed his scheme to publish three anonymous novels while at the height of his success. The reviewer, always suspicious of anonymity in fiction, recognized a single phrase of *Nina Balatka* as characteristically Trollope's! The phrase was "he made his way," meaning, Hutton defined with his usual humorous solemnity, "walking where there is no physical difficulty or embarrassment, but only a certain moral hesitation as to the end and aim of the walking."[46] More importantly, on the matter of reviewing novels published in instalments, Hutton opens his review of the complete *Middlemarch* with a contemptuous reference to those who "say with a kind of virtuous assumption of artistic feeling" that they will not read novels until they appear as books. He welcomes the chance to study novels in parts because, as he says while reviewing *Middlemarch*, "that is the only way in which life itself can be studied" (*Spectator*, December 7, 1872, p. 1554). For Hutton, the novel was a secular form which none the less retained an interest in the relationship between the conceptions of ordinary people and the great generalizations of culture and science in which "life itself" is studied.[47] The novel was published in a new form, in eight long parts (a compromise between serialization and multi-volume book form) and Hutton read and reviewed the instalments with enthusiasm ("not a few of us calculate whether we shall get the August number before we go for our autumn holiday"), predicting what might happen, making mistakes, correcting his first impressions — revising, for example, his first views of the depiction of Rosamond Vincy. It was, for him, an exercise in developmental hermeneutics, and an opportunity to place parts in relation to an imagined whole, or members in relation to an ideal body. He was also acutely sensitive to George Eliot's own changes and second thoughts. As Rosemary Ashton has shown, George Eliot's tone of irony towards her heroine disappears as the novel progresses until, in the Finale, Dorothea's disappointed life is blamed on "the society which smiled on propositions of marriage from a sickly man to a girl less than half his own age."[48] Hutton was the first to point out the change of perspective (since, far from "smiling" on the marriage, Dorothea's friends utterly disapproved of it). Following his objection, George Eliot paid Hutton the ultimate compliment, one which she afforded no other critic before or after, of cutting the passage from the 1874 book version, the version on which all subsequent editions have been based.

In objecting to George Eliot's revisions Hutton is not only exhibiting his customary and attentive scrutiny of text and development. He is specifically objecting to George Eliot's "teaching" that human acts can be explained by reference to "society" or the material world: they provide the occasion, not the cause. As he says in a late essay on "The Atheistic View of Life," this is the narrowing effect of secularism itself: "Our moral life becomes, on this philosophy, a series of careful adjustments to the great object of rendering that part of the world within our influence, beginning with ourselves, capable of as much healthy and happy life as may be in our power."[49] The placing of a part before the whole is the focus of Hutton's criticism — whether the text be a novel or the world, whether the "character" be a mark on the page or a person in the world.

Indeed, just as Hutton blurs the distinction between literary and religious or ethical concerns, so he saw and represents the blurring of the distinction between the categories of "fact" and "fiction." The treatment of fiction as "fact" or as "real" is only possible as one half of a transaction by which what was once perceived as historical "fact" was now interpreted as fiction and with the interpretative models which Ricoeur has characterized as "the hermeneutics of suspicion." To put it in terms that make sense of Hutton's dual concerns and their transactional relation — the forces which produced fictional realism also produced, simultaneously and necessarily, the secularization of biblical hermeneutics. In an early essay on the novel Hutton gives a warning on this sort of reading. He writes in the first number of his and Bagehot's *National Review* in 1855: "Already a sceptical generation is springing up, which will question the author's omniscience, and take leave to doubt, here of a fact, and there of a feeling.... An unbelieving generation will probably some day question whether, in fact, Ivanhoe had the unfortunate taste to prefer Rowena, or Rebecca the still more unfortunate taste to prefer Ivanhoe. Where art ceases to be art, faith will not be persuaded to go its way, nothing doubting."[50] In other words, art must be real just as faith must be real, and vice versa: the novel, important as it is for Hutton, does not have a monopoly on realism.

Hutton was a representative of the sceptical generation of readers. He reported that the most popular response to the realistic novel was "It is all so true!," but suggested that the more serious question was "To what is it all true?"[51] His implicit criteria seem to be "truth to life," "truth to nature" and "truth to type." His review of Henry James in this volume is one long expression of doubt. Again, writing on *Middlemarch*, he doubts that Lydgate would have married Rosamond. Here his thinking is essentially taxonomical — he doubts that *a* Lydgate would have married *a* Rosamond. This is where the weekly review is for Hutton importantly close to life. His defence of the weekly reviewing of parts of novels suggests both that "life itself," life as it came to be seen during his lifetime, could be judged only in parts, and that these parts could be understood only when related as a narrative. His valuation of the novel seems to anticipate Barbara Hardy's conception of the importance of narrative structure in making sense of life, of being "real" because, like Newton's gravity, it revealed the way the world was.[52]

Hutton was George Eliot's only contemporary critic fully to appreciate the specific origins of her conceptions of character and narrative in her 1854 translation of Feuerbach's *Das Wesen des Christentums*. Her irony, like her sympathy, he attributes to her scepticism, and suggests that she came to use irony freely because "Feuerbach's is an essentially *ironic* explanation of the religions of the world...which makes the most momentous factor in the history of the world to consist in a grand procession of pure illusions."[53] He wrote to her of the heroine of her historical novel: "She struck me throughout as rather modern and as separating the doubtful form from the ethical germs of Savonarola's faith.... Romola seems to me not so much to take, as almost to *imply* a knowledge of, such distinctions, as she might have picked up by a study of L. Feuerbach."[54] This is a considerably more acute perception than Arnold's of the modern element in literature. Hutton had to admire her attempt to translate the essence of Christianity into aesthetic form. Indeed, in 1877 we find him defending George Eliot from an attack on her morals (for not marrying G.H. Lewes) in the *Church Quarterly*. While not regarding her ethics as Christian, he says, "we do hold them to have all the *inwardness* of Christian ethics, all the sincere desire to judge not by outward acts and conventional appearances, but by the quality of the interior motive and purpose...."[55] The *Church Quarterly*'s morality, says Hutton, "stands on too conventional a ground to enter into George Eliot's ethics." Hutton's whole attitude to George Eliot is probably the single most remarkable example of that "entering into" which he recommended in his manifesto. Furthermore, this is for him itself a demonstration of Christian ethics, of looking at the "inwardness" of the author, into the characteristic motive and purpose of the author.

The novel was clearly to Hutton both the focus and the vehicle for this sort of inwardness and characterization. It was more than just a "conventional form": the attack on the *Church Quarterly* writer is both ethical and aesthetic. Hutton was a realist in recognizing the lasting effects of secularization while believing it to be a transient phase. He seems to have valued the novel as a symptom and product of this phase but also as a means of resisting specific results of secularization. The novel seems to fulfil for him in England the more positive functions of sceptical theology in Europe, in expressing doubts about the stability of Christian virtues but retaining and idealizing human selfhood. For Hutton the novel kept alive a sense of "character" as something which could be objectively judged and which had internal meaning, and which kept alive in a secular reading public the biblical form of teaching by story-telling and by incarnating the creations of the author. It enabled Hutton to resist the notion that character was "only a development of nervous function" and to counter the identification of character with temperament which he saw as Arnold's error and which "must diminish incalculably the sacredness of the individual and personal to the advantage of the general and the impersonal."[56] The nearest Hutton could get to producing such a form was writing biographies, and it is significant that, apart from collections of his and others' essays, the only books Hutton published were critical biographies of Newman and Scott. Generally, though, the sacredness of the individual was to him preserved in the novel, and was precisely what Arnold found "provincial."[57]

The grounds on which Hutton and George Eliot both agree and disagree are on the function of narrative and its associated possibilities of constructing teleologies. Hutton's notion of the self that is allowed to emerge in the novel carries with it the idea that human nature is unchangeable, because its source is divine and the truth of this is unchangeable. To him a progressive teleology such as Eliot's is worldly and materialistic. Hardy's static teleology is in one sense close to Hutton's, since neither puts his trust in earthly progress or happiness. Nevertheless, the novel could to Hutton provide a teleology and a moral vocabulary against which the world could be meaningfully compared. Writing on the novel in 1855, before Marian Evans uses the novel and long before Frank Kermode uses the idea, Hutton writes of the writer's and reader's construction of and anxiety for "a sense of an ending" in fiction:

> The Germans teach of the "retarding nature" essential to a romance...a sense, throughout the tale, of an end, but a constantly increasing anxiety as to *what* end: a feeling of convergence of moral destinies to an unseen focus.... A great artist...must, in a certain sense, be the providence to the conceptions he has created...so as to give a unity of meaning to the whole, as well as individual life to the parts.[58]

This central and abiding interest in the relation of the parts to the whole is confirmed in George Eliot's famous reply to Hutton's letter about *Romola*, where she says: "I believe there is scarcely a phrase, an incident, an allusion, that did not gather its value to me from its supposed subservience to my main artistic objects."[59] Unfortunately, to Hutton, she was too literally the providence to the characters she created; there was no sense of the ending to which she appeared to direct the reader: *Middlemarch*, said Hutton, "conveys the same sort of shock with which, during the early days of eclipses, men must have seen the rays of light converging towards a centre of darkness...[for] one feels a positive sense of vacancy."[60]

In the work of both George Eliot and Arnold, Hutton perceives a raising of the human critical powers above the creative powers of the divine. F.D. Maurice, writing to Hutton, expresses what seems to be in Hutton's mind when he speaks of the need to "preserve men from substituting the intellectual discerner, the man of religious instincts, *the exalted critic*, for the living God," and again, in a letter published in the *Spectator*, he warns that "the literary critic must be the omnipotent, if there is not a real judge higher than he is."[61] The history of literary criticism after Hutton is the story of the exaltation of the critic and the adaptation of the religious instinct: the Arnoldian animal survived and evolved.

In a moving obituary of Hutton, Julia Wedgwood began by comparing her reluctance to write about him with the reluctance she felt to write about George Eliot who was also "a great genius dealing with the problems of the hour" and who wrote in a style as "involved" as were those problems.[62] The *Athenaeum* commented less generously that "his sentences are frequently of an exasperating length and of the most ungainly character; he gives the impression that his thoughts are running away with his pen and that he is ignorant of the virtues of revision."[63] Julia Wedgwood's comparison with George Eliot is, however, illuminating. Hutton's prose seems to indicate a mind which was not unlike George Eliot's in being not ignorant of revision but full of second thoughts, expressing doubts yet also containing assurance. Ruby Redinger's description of George Eliot's style is appropriate, and for good reason, to Hutton's prose also: "...the long and usually well-balanced sentence served her well, protectively enveloping the pith of the content...even if at times rendered almost incomprehensible by an excessive burden of meaning...[but] she paid a price for the style which emerged as her own, for as it was being shaped, it was also determining she would never be a true wit or a genuine poet."[64] In her obituary of Hutton in the *Contemporary Review*, his admirer Julia Wedgwood wrote: "I remember well the laugh...of a Saturday Reviewer, who confessed he found it difficult in the way of reading the *Spectator*, that it was 'so just.' He was the spokesman of the larger half of the newspaper-reading world. Nothing, indeed, is really less dull than justice."[65] Both Hutton and George Eliot developed a prose style which embodies a moral concern with justice, and both paid the price. In its obituary of Hutton the *Athenaeum*, reflecting the current Wildean taste for the memorable and self-contained witty thrust, regretted Hutton's "lack of excursions into brilliant paradox or exaggerated epigram."[66] This is, though, to ignore Hutton's talent for pastiche (as in his celebrated version of "Carlylese," exemplified in "Mr. Carlyle and his Constituency," reprinted in this volume), or his wonderful, if infrequent, use of satire illustrated in the superb "Get Geist" or his depiction of Forster's *Life of Dickens* as "like reading the biography of a literary race-horse" (see below, "The Tension in Dickens"). He is also capable of describing himself, with a mixture of whimsy and sincerity, as one "who is inclined to prefer *good* children's stories to almost any other species of literature" and argues, earnestly straight-faced but utterly tongue-in-cheek, that the age's "worship of children" is a much more characteristic feature of the nineteenth century than "railways and the electric telegraph and other such arts and inventions [which are] mere accidents" (see below "The Worship of Children"). In this Hutton, like all good humorists, tells an important truth. He also discriminates between various kinds of humour, their tones and intentions and finds George Eliot one of the great English humorists. But Hutton paid an even higher price for having become stylistically but not fashionably "involved": he was not merely dismissed as no "true wit" by the fin-de-siècle intelligentsia exhibiting their Wildean detachment or their Paterian disinterestedness, but also by having that exclusion from the line of wit and the canon of critics largely uncontroverted by subsequent criticism, bifurcated as it was immediately to become into the "impersonal" code of T.S. Eliot and the "personal" creed of, say, John Middleton Murry.

Notes and References

1. "The Modern Press IX. – 'The Spectator'," *Speaker*, March 4, 1893, pp. 242-43; William Watson, *Excursions in Criticism* (London, 1893), p. 113.

2. Hugh Walker, "Living Critics IV. – Mr. R.H. Hutton," *Bookman*, 9 (January 1896), 118-20; Owen Chadwick, *The Victorian Church*, 2 vols., Second Edition (London, 1972), II, 123.

3. *Memory and Writing from Wordsworth to Lawrence* (Liverpool, 1983), p. 492 n. 11.

4. See *Letters to a Victorian Editor, Henry Allon*, edited by Albert Peel (London, 1929), p. 171; *The Letters of George Eliot*, edited by G.S. Haight, 9 vols. (New Haven, 1954-78), IV, 97 (letter of August 8, 1863); *Anthony Trollope, An Autobiography*, edited by Frederick Page (London, 1950), p. 205.

5. See *George Eliot* (Oxford, 1983), p. 40; *Memory and Writing*, p. 40; *Mill's Essays on Literature and Society* (New York, 1965), pp. 413-14; *Major British Writers*, edited by G.B. Harrison, 2 vols. (New York, 1959), II, 380.

6. A.H. Clough, *Correspondence*, edited by F.L. Mulhauser, 2 vols. (London, 1957), II, 582.

7. See J.W. Sanders, *The Profession of English Letters* (London, 1964), p. 200. See also H.D. Jordan, "The Daily and Weekly Press of England in 1861," *South Atlantic Quarterly*, 28 (1929), 302-17.

8. See M. Woodfield, "Periodical Literature," *Essays in Criticism*, 33 (1983), 68-75 (pp. 68-69).

9. "The Modern Press: 'The Spectator'," *Speaker*, p. 242.

10. On Hutton's "preaching," see W. Robertson Nicoll, *The Day Book of Claudius Clear* (London, 1905), pp. 303-4. On the *Spectator* readership, see John Hogben, *Richard Holt Hutton of the "Spectator"* (London, 1899), p. 39; "Aspects of Religious and Scientific Thought," *Academy*, 56 (1899), p. 451; Marcus Dodds, "*Criticisms on Contemporary Thought and Thinkers*," *Bookman*, 6 (1894), 85-86.

11. Letter of May 22, 1886, W.E. Gladstone Papers, BL Add. MS 44215/332.

12. Review of *Criticisms on Contemporary Thought and Thinkers*, *Dial*, 17 (1894), 17-18.

13. See Alasdair MacIntyre and Paul Ricoeur, *The Religious Significance of Atheism* (New York, 1969), and Bernard Lightman, *The Origins of Agnosticism: Victorian Unbelief and the Limits of Knowledge* (Baltimore, 1987).

14. Chadwick, *The Victorian Church*, p. 124.

15. *Spectator*, June 29, 1861, p. 697. See, by contrast, the account in William Robbins, *The Arnoldian Principle of Flexibility*, University of Victoria English Literary Studies, 15 (Victoria, British Columbia, 1979).

16. *Academy*, 2 (1870), p. 1.

17. *Letters of Matthew Arnold*, edited by G.W.E. Russell, 2 vols. (New York, 1900), 1, 438; *Complete Prose Works*, edited by R.H. Super, 11 vols. (Ann Arbor, Michigan, 1960-77), III, 282-83.

18. See *Essays on Some of the Modern Guides of English Thought in Matters of Faith* (London, 1887), p. 127. This collection, despite its ponderous title, reprints excellent long essays on Carlyle, Newman, Arnold, George Eliot (two essays), and F.D. Maurice.

19. *Complete Prose Works*, ed. Super, VI, 293.

20. See "Newman and Arnold – II: Matthew Arnold," *Contemporary Review*, 49 (April 1886), 513-34 (p. 524).

21. *Literary Essays* (1896), pp. 314-15 (our italics).

22. For the theory of narrative in literature, theology and ethics, see Seymour Chatman, *Story and Discourse* (Cornell, 1978), Michael Goldberg, *Theology and Narrative: A Critical Introduction* (Nashville, Tenn., 1982) and Alasdair MacIntyre, "Epistemological Crises, Dramatic Narrative and the Philosophy of Science," *Monist*, 60 (1977), 453-72.

23. Arnold, Preface to *Poems* (1853), *Complete Prose Works*, ed. Super, I, 1.

24. *Literary Essays* (London, 1896), p. 351.

25. op. cit., p. 459.

26. *Sir Walter Scott*, Second Edition (London, 1902), p. 121. George Eliot was powerfully moved by Hutton's attempt thus to embody Scott. G.H. Lewes wrote to Alexander Macmillan: "Although Scott is to her an almost sacred name, she was so delighted with Hutton's largeness of

feeling and sympathetic insight that, as she told a lady yesterday, 'she was in a glow all the time she read it'," *Letters*, VII, 65 (letter of August 25, 1878).

27. Arnold, "The Study of Poetry," *Complete Prose Works*, ed. Super, IX, 170-71.

28. G.H. Lewes, *The Life and Works of Goethe*, 2 vols. (London, 1855), II, 202.

29. Leslie Stephen, "Hutton's Essays," *Saturday Review*, February 18, 1871, pp. 214-15; *Letters of Matthew Arnold, 1844-1888*, edited by G.W.E. Russell, 2 vols. (London, 1895), I, 248.

30. *Spectator*, February 25, 1865, p. 215.

31. *Letters*, ed. Russell, I, 249.

32. See *Nineteenth Century*, 1 (May 1877), 543-44.

33. S.D. Collet, "Mr. Hutton as Critic and Theologian," *Contemporary Review*, 16 (1871), 635.

34. See Stanley Hauerwas, *Character and the Christian Life* (San Antonio, Texas, 1975), Jeffrey Stout, *The Flight from Authority: Religion, Morality and the Quest for Autonomy* (Notre Dame, 1981), especially Chapter 12, "Explicating Historicism," and Alasdair MacIntyre, *After Virtue: A Study in Moral Theory* (London, 1981), Chapter 15, "The Virtues, the Unity of a Human Life and the Concept of a Tradition."

35. See *The Life and Letters of James Martineau*, edited by J. Drummond and C.B. Upton, 2 vols. (London, 1902), I, 337.

36. See Paul Ricoeur, *Time and Narrative*, translated by Kathleen McLaughlin and David Pellauer, 3 vols. (Chicago, 1983-87), I, 114-19.

37. Wilfrid Ward, "Mr. R.H. Hutton as a Religious Thinker," *Dublin Review*, Third Series, 20 (1888), 1-21 (pp. 18-19, 5).

38. J.H. Newman, *Parochial and Plain Sermons*, 8 vols. (London, 1868), V, 33-34.

39. See *Letters and Diaries of John Henry Newman*, 31 vols. (Oxford others, XXV (1973), 37; XXVII (1975), 39 (letter of March 1, 1872).

40. "Puseyite Novels," pp. 512-13; *Essays on Some of the Modern Guides of English Thought in Matters of Faith* (London, 1887), p. 264.

41. "The Author of *Heartsease* and Modern Schools of Fiction," *Prospective Review*, 10 (1854), 460-82 (pp. 472-73, Hutton's italics).

42. *Literary Essays*, Third Edition (London, 1888), p. 197.

43. *Is Life Worth Living?* (London, 1879), p. 138.

44. "Secularism," *Expositor*, New Series, I (1881), 1-12 (p. 11).

45. *Edinburgh Review*, 150 (October 1879), 557-86 (p. 564).

46. Anthony Trollope, *Autobiography*, Second Edition, 2 vols. (Edinburgh, 1883), II, 12.

47. See Gillian Beer, *Darwin's Plots* (London, 1983), and Richard Kerridge's review of Woodfield, *R.H. Hutton, Critic and Theologian, Swansea Review*, 3 (May 1987), 84-89 (p. 88).

48. Rosemary Ashton, *George Eliot* (Oxford, 1983), p. 70.

49. *Fraser's Magazine*, New Series, 21 (May 1880), 652-67 (p. 665).

50. "A Novel or Two," *National Review*, 1 (October 1855), 336-50 (pp. 340-41).

51. See "Ethical and Dogmatic Fiction: Miss Yonge," *National Review*, 12 (January 1861), 211-30 (p. 211).

52. See Barbara Hardy, "Towards a Poetics of Fiction: An Approach Through Narrative," *Novel*, 2 (1968), 5-14. See also Alasdair MacIntyre, *After Virtue: A Study in Moral Theory* (London, 1981), especially pp. 196-97.

53. *Modern Guides to English Thought in Matters of Faith*, pp. 275-76 (Hutton's italics).

54. Yale University Library Eliot MS (letter of August 6, 1863).

55. *Spectator*, November 3, 1877, p. 1363 (our italics).

56. R.H. Hutton, "Secularism," *Expositor*, New Series, I (1881), 1-12 (p. 9).

57. See also the comment by Thomas Hardy: "Arnold is wrong about provincialism, if he means anything more than a provincialism of manner and style in exposition. A certain provinciality of feeling is invaluable. It is of the essence of individuality, and is largely made up of that crude enthusiasm without which no great thoughts are thought, no great deeds done" (F.E. Hardy, *The Life of Thomas Hardy, 1840-1928* (London, 1962), pp. 146-47).

58. *National Review*, 1 (October 1855), 336-38.

59. See *Letters of George Eliot*, ed. Haight, IV, 97.

60. *Spectator*, December 7, 1872, p. 1556.

61. Frederick Maurice, *Life and Letters of F.D. Maurice*, 2 vols. (New York, 1884), II, 442 (my italics); *Spectator*, February 7, 1863, p. 1608.

62. "Richard Holt Hutton," *Contemporary Review*, 72 (1897), 457-69 (p. 460).

63. *Athenaeum*, July 2, 1894, p. 704.

64. Ruby Redinger, *George Eliot: The Emergent Self* (London, 1975), pp. 78-79.

65. op. cit., p. 458.

66. *Athenaeum*, July 18, 1897, pp. 389-90.

Mr. Grote on the Abuses of Newspaper Criticism

Mr. Grote, in a controversial criticism on an able contemporary with which we have nothing to do, takes occasion to make some admirable general remarks on the spirit and honesty of modern newspaper criticism, with which we and all other newspaper critics have a great deal to do.[1] "There is one thing," he says, "that this criticism never seems to have a notion of, and that is the possibility of criticism on itself." Mr. Grote encourages the common-sense reader not to be afraid of us. Such a reader is, he says, and very justly says, often a person of far better judgment than the anonymous critic whom he peruses, if it would but enter his head that he may use his own judgment and throw off the newspaper-yoke to which an Englishman so willingly submits. The readers should rally their strength against this imposing power of type. The historian of Greece himself[2] is willing to lead the forlorn hope, and has made a spirited onset in the pamphlet before us:

> "I think there is but little doubt that reviewing in our day is in one respect inferior to what it has been, namely, that there is less in it of the element of discussion, that each reviewer has pretty much the impression that with his own readers he has the last word, and that he need not fear anybody looking after *him*. If the reader would do a little criticism for himself, or care a little more to see criticism answered, some pretended critiques which he might otherwise believe in and be amused at would indeed lose their interest for him, or indeed, perhaps, excite indignation; but I do not think he would lose in pleasure. There wants a little fresh recollection with us that the end of criticism is to bring out and set in clearest light the *truth*, and that divorced from that purpose, it is almost the lowest kind of literature, a parasitical appendage to that which makes effort to be real literature, which like the ivy strangles what it feeds on, offering *itself* only as the wretched substitute, and really extinguishing in the readers everything that is intellectually valuable."

This is excellent advice, and nothing would improve newspaper criticism so much as the knowledge that it was to be read by men too hardy to acquiesce in the authoritative statement of the reviewer. Criticism, despite all that is urged in its favour, especially the short criticism of newspapers, is always tending to become positively injurious. "Newspaper old age seems to come speedily," says Mr. Grote. And no doubt there is a tendency in all professional critics, still more if they be successful writers, to put out less and less positive appreciative effort as they grow old; and, except in the rare cases where they are really fascinated themselves, to deliver their oracles from their own traditional point of view without any laborious attempt to see with their author's eyes what he really believes that he has achieved. For, all true criticism on worthy subjects does involve effort, and considerable effort. No one can fairly judge what another has done without genuine study of something which is generally in some degree alien to one's own thought. And it is so much easier to stay at one's own centre and rail at another man for not coming to us, than to migrate to his point of view, that criticism is always tending to degenerate into a list of excellent reasons why an author should have been other than he is in order that he might have written his book from a centre of conviction similar to our own, instead of the one which he has chosen.

In order to see what true criticism, and especially newspaper criticism, may and ought to be, the first step is to keep its *aim* within modest and moderate bounds. It is not the great judicial function that it affects to be; — that it is often said to be. If critics mistake their duty, it is, as Mr. Grote hints, very much because the public encourage them to do so; and not the public only, but thoughtful and far-sighted men. We are always hearing the relative importance of true criticism exaggerated (we do not mean its absolute importance, for that we do not esteem lightly), but its importance relatively to a higher and more creative task. It was only the other day that Mr. Matthew Arnold, a poet who can utter his own critical thoughts in sentences so lucid and harmonious that even when they seem most false they cling to the mind with a fascination far beyond that of the finest and most perfect criticism, did what he could to perpetuate this cant about the yearning of the age for criticism. He laid it down in his recent lectures, with the calm dogmatism which seems an essential part of his mind that, "of the literatures of France and Germany, as of the intellect of Europe in general, the main effort, for now many years, has been a critical effort; the endeavour, in all branches of knowledge — theology, philosophy, history, art, science — to see the object as in itself it really is." "But owing," he adds, "to the presence in English literature of this eccentric and arbitrary spirit, owing to the strong tendency of English writers to bring to the consideration of their object some individual fancy, almost the last thing for which one would come to English literature is just that very thing which now Europe most desires — criticism."[3] Surely Mr. Arnold, when he pronounces such a sentence as this, is guilty of the very sin he is condemning — that of boldly importing, namely, a very strong individual peculiarity of his own into the universal European mind. As far as our experience goes, Europe does not pant after criticism, nay, is rather weary of it, and would fain see something more spontaneous and more likely to draw men into closer social unity. In the mean time, such criticism as the age is condemned to elaborate will be most likely to lead us to something higher, if it knows its own place. It is good when it is a link in the passage to what is better, when it is so sensitively alive to every gleam of true genius and nobility in creative minds that it can translate and spread what it discerns so as to render this more widely apprehensible. But if it does not take this modest attitude towards the great living words and thoughts and realities that are above criticism, it abolishes its own function; nay, it does more, it intervenes to shut out the light; for no sooner does the critic cease to look up to the finer minds above his own than he begins to grudge the appearance of new power altogether, and to do much towards persuading those who are under his influence to share his own jealousy and scepticism.

It is obvious that what an ordinary critic can do for the society he addresses is not disposed of by Mr. Arnold's dictum, that he should teach people to see each of the various objects of the intellectual world "as in itself it really is." No doubt this is so; but how can he do this? Not certainly, as Mr. Arnold would have us believe, by simply striving to sweep his own mind clear of eccentricities and prejudices, and then coldly contemplating by the "dry light" of modern culture what he wishes to describe. No work of genius, no triumph of faith, was ever appreciated and translated into the language of less cultivated minds by such a process as this. Criticism at its highest — as Mr. Arnold's own writings show — must have at least enough of the creative power it deals with, to feel completely its spell and fascination. And this is not got by critical habits; it is got by a long apprenticeship to uncritical habits; by readiness of sympathy, flexibility of taste, and the modesty which is ever willing to abandon a lower standard of judgment for a higher, so soon as it is convinced that it is higher. What criticism can do, then, for works of a power or genius higher than its own, is this: Its first and by far its highest function is to apprehend that which lies really above its own sphere; to be accessible to thoughts, or aims, or beauties which it can appreciate but could not have created; and to delineate them for those who might not otherwise have time or culture to find them out. Its second and secondary task — too often made its first and primary — is to rectify the exclusiveness and frequent one-sidedness of genius by the broader sense of ordinary judgment. This is a very useful and, for the most part, an easy part of its work; but it is useful and easy only so far as the critic duly discharges the higher part of his task. If a critic can translate for others what the few teach or conceive, it is more than his right, it is his positive duty, to piece it out by insisting on the directions in which it will fail to satisfy the wants of the many. For instance, those who can teach us to see deeper than ever into the infinite beauty of Homer, or Chaucer, or Shakespeare, are bound to point out, if they can, what parts of the human mind these great poets wholly fail to express. But to insist on the latter without the former, is rather to blind the eyes of their readers than to open them – to give them the impression of more darkness instead of more light.

But what, it will be said, has newspaper criticism to do with such tasks as these? It is not once in a year that a really great work, measured even by the standard of a single generation, appears, and barely once in many years that a work of lasting genius is produced. This is perfectly true. But the only criticism which is really likely to be useful on the minor works of every-day literature is that which has been trained and disciplined in worthier studies. Here is the mistake of the cut-and-dried man of culture. He goes about with the secret of having learned to appreciate the "grand style."[4] He has lived in Homer till he can recall the roll of that many-sounding sea. He has pored over the lofty and pictorial thought of Plato till he begins to pique *himself* upon its grandeur. His fancy has been fed on the quaint old-world genius of Herodotus, his judgment on the melancholy wisdom of Tacitus and the complacent cynicism of Gibbon, – and of all this he is conscious and proud. When first fortune compels him to deal with the daily literary efforts of ordinary Englishmen, he chooses such as are more or less connected with his real admirations, and the slowly developed intellectual worship of his youth; and while this lasts his work is fresh and true criticism; it translates the higher thoughts that have entered into him, for those who have not yet learned to apprehend them, and supplements them by the common-sense wants of the class with which he is in daily intercourse. But when this period has passed by, and reputation as a critic has been fairly won, there is more and more temptation to cloak himself in the culture of which he is so proud, and rebuke the raw thoughts of an uncultivated world.

> "Mox sesse attollit in auras
> Ingrediturque solo, et caput inter nubila condit."[5]

This is in some measure, we take it, the secret of the premature old age which is apt to afflict, if not newspapers, at least newspaper critics.

And no doubt it is a trial to men steeped in the culture of the noblest literature of the world, to appreciate fairly the ephemeral productions of a busy generation. It seems beneath them, and the more they trample it beneath them, the less are they competent to detect its higher tendencies. But still the critic who allows this feeling to grow upon him abdicates his true office. Unless he can enter into the wants of his generation, he has no business to pretend to direct its thoughts. He becomes really a mischief instead of a benefit if he puts his heel scornfully on all that is less artistic than his own tastes. The passion for putting an extinguisher on incomplete or half-successful efforts is a very growing and a very fatal one. It is as injurious to the critic himself as to the public whom it defrauds. An extinguisher of real flames, however tiny, cannot help being soiled and blackened by the work. And no man can really ignore from intellectual pride any sign of just or timely thought without some injury of an analogous kind.

There is, however, a sphere for just severity in newspaper criticism. To some extent the public look to newspaper notices as guides to what they shall read or neglect. In an age of unscrupulous and shameless book-making, it is a duty to give notice of the rubbish that cumbers the ground. There is no credit, no real power required for this task. It is the work of an intellectual scavenger, and far from being specially honourable. Still, if done scrupulously, it is not dishonourable. If a man, after hunting for the true aim and purpose of a work, finds none such of any worthy kind, if he can detect no new store of information, no single gleam of well-directed purpose, no glimpse of any element that may serve anyone except the seller of the commodity in question, it is right to say so, though every critic should be sure that the irresponsibility of anonymous writing in no way sways his mind. But it is well to recollect that the sentence of condemnation is always easier to pass than any other; and, when unjust, reflects more seriously upon the critic than on the condemned. It is not only easier to destroy than to create, but far easier to imagine worthlessness than to appreciate worth.

Tom Brown at Oxford

It is not often that considerable literary power is found in connexion with the ethical instincts of a genuine wrestler — we do not mean, of course, with the spirit of irritable, nervous antagonism, for that is one of the commonest types of literary temperament — but with that which loves a struggle for its own sake, and is happier in it, and less likely to contract a deeper prejudice thereby than in a life of tranquil sympathy or observation. There is something usually of softness of nature inherent in literary power, and something also of a softening effect resulting from its exercise. Literary creativeness begins in flexible, and even feminine sympathies, and is apt to end in melting away the healthy firmness of moral convictions. Nowhere do we find more limpness of mind, or latitudinarianism in the weakest sense, than among the literary class. Partly, as we have said, this arises from the wide and genial tastes which render men literary; partly from the modes of thought to which those tastes lead. Literature necessarily softens the austerity of many a traditional moral judgment. Its motto is, *Emollit mores nec sinit esse feros*.[1] The habit of looking at human character as a study which it is pleasant to explore, rather than as a power for good or evil which it is necessary either to obey or to control, is apt to undermine the *personal* view of good or evil. It leads us to think of human acts, impulses, and affections as phenomena due to complex and hidden currents of the great world of Nature, with which it is as Quixotic to do battle as with the revolving sails of the windmill itself. Sympathy, from which springs so much of the knowledge of human character, melts away much both of the defensive and aggressive military spirit; and the habits which literature forms too often complete the dissolving process. This tendency of literary tastes robs our literature of a great part of its life and animation. Those who enter most fully into the secrets of human nature, seem to care nothing for its battles; to them it is enough to receive true pictorial impressions of the many contests in which they do not care to mingle; while, on the other hand, militant minds generally have their surface too much disturbed by the stir and emotion of the strife to be clear cameras for the scenes around them. Indeed, this is more or less true of Mr. Kingsley, who was the first of the wrestling novelists. None of his pictures are clearly drawn, though many are very finely conceived. There is a turbidness about the medium which always, more or less, confuses the outlines, and sometimes dims the purity, of the picture. But there is none of this haze about Mr. Hughes's mind. The images of the men whom he paints for us are often mere sketches, and generally reflect characters of a simple structure; but they are as clear and vivid as the hills in a bright autumn sunlight, when the mists have risen, and the landscape seems cut in crystal.

In fact, there is nothing turbid or passionate at all in the wrestling instinct which runs through the fascinating history of Tom Brown's school and college life. The great *vis* with which it is written is not, however, purely ethical. There is much in it of the mere expanding elasticity of vital force measuring itself cheerfully against the other forces of the world, delighting in the sense of honourable rivalry, and respecting those principles of natural aristocracy which result from such rivalry: there is still more of genuine reverence for intrinsic nobility of character, and of appreciation for the strange influence which the "weak things of the world" can exert in confounding the mighty[2] when the faintness of that influence arises from its divineness. The pleasure in hearty battle of all kinds which runs through these volumes, is not the pleasure belonging to the battle of hot blood, but rather arises in a genial faith that the truth of life is generally best tested by such battling. The author seems to have learned by conflicts, generally friendly and never blind, to recognize his own and others' strength and weakness; in short, to have found hearty strife the first condition of true order and true peace. Just as there are minds which gain their insight into truth chiefly by sympathy and reflection, so there are others which gain it principally by sympathy and wrestling — by a fair struggle with the influences, whether friendly or hostile, which conflict with their own previous impressions. Such a nature, apparently, has the author of these volumes; he settles the true relations of life by provisional struggles in which we may say either that moral nobility reckons more than force, or that it counts by its marvellous influence in subduing and developing force. Even in the Oxford boat races, which he describes with so vivid and brilliant a pen, he makes you see equanimity of character telling on the crew as much as physical force, — nobility almost as strong as strength. And if we look carefully at the sunny pictures which fill these tales of school and college life, the keen perceptive faculty which they imply is of that practical kind which consists quite as much in the vigilance of a wakeful will measuring itself against the obstacles of life, as in the acuteness of a wakeful eye. Even the characters are gauged in great measure by the tone given out in those slight mutual jars by which moral mettle is tested. And the humour pervading the book, which is thoroughly genial and enjoyable, springs mainly from the quick consciousness of broad contrasts between the purposes of different natures when they come into blind collision, needlessly and blindly knocking their heads together in the narrow eagerness of their various pursuits. In short, it is humour of Carlyle's genus.

Delightful as "Tom Brown's School Days" seemed to us, we have enjoyed yet more the Oxford life. One of Mr. Hughes's greatest literary merits is that he really can depict mental and moral growth. Tom Brown keeps the same type of character throughout, but he changes from year to year. In the school life, all the usual moral dangers of a strong, hearty, and healthily animal, but intrinsically noble and simple nature, are vigorously delineated. But in the Oxford life there was a far more difficult task — to draw the half morbid fermentation through which almost all men pass in early manhood, and yet to adapt it to the simple and healthy type of character chosen — to pick out the appropriate intellectual, moral, and sentimental phases of development — and to show Tom Brown working himself gradually clear again towards the mature form of the well-marked early type. All this Mr. Hughes has done with very remarkable success, and, without any wandering from his main purpose, has given us some of the most fresh and humorous English village pictures we have ever met with. We can only attempt in this review to indicate some of the leading thoughts and most vigorous pictures in the book.

All the figures by whom Tom Brown is surrounded at Oxford are skilfully chosen to bring out the broad common grain, and hearty, practical warmth of the central character. The high-minded, but not very amiable and rather atrabilious servitor, Mr. Hardy, who is Tom's main friend throughout the book, is in curiously well-marked contrast to him, because he also is of the athlete type. Yet the pictures are as different as they can be. We never thoroughly like Hardy, from beginning to end; while we never cease to like Tom for a moment. Both are of the broad grain of practical Englishmen; but the one is of a hard and stiff, the other of an open, flexible type; the one self-conscious, reserved, and almost jealous; the other unconscious, frank, and pliant. The jars between the two men are very skilfully drawn, and are made to illustrate the most sombre and the most genial influences of University life; its influence on a man who, wrapt up chiefly within himself, extorts the maximum of intellectual benefit and social induration from an uncongenial atmosphere and its influence on a man who answers readily to every social attraction of the place, and is not exposed to its harder discipline. The scene in which the austere Hardy takes Tom to task with schoolmasterish dictatorialness for his attentions to a pretty girl of poor station, — overshooting the mark by his curt, magisterial manner, — and the tumult of self-assertion which the quarrel and the blank exposure of his own passions arouses in Tom's heart, is one of the most powerful in the book:

"'I don't mind your sneers, Brown,' said Hardy, as he tramped up and down with his arms locked behind him; 'I have taken on myself to speak to you about this; I should be no true friend if I shirked it. I'm four years older than you, and have seen more of the world and of this place than you. You shan't go with this folly, this sin, for want of warning.' 'So it seems,' said Tom, doggedly. 'Now I think I've had warning enough; suppose we drop the subject.' Hardy stopped in his walk, and turned on Tom with a look of anger. 'Not yet,' he said firmly; 'you know best how and why you have done it, but you know that somehow or other you have made that girl like you.' 'Suppose I have, what then? whose business is that but mine and hers?' 'It's the business of every one who won't stand by and see the devil's game played under his nose if he can hinder it.' 'What right have you to talk about the devil's game to me?' said Tom. 'I'll tell you what, if you and I are to keep friends, we had better drop this subject.' 'If we are to keep friends we must go to the bottom of it. There are only two endings to this sort of business, and you know it as well as I.' 'A right and wrong one, eh? and because you call me your friend you assume that my end will be the wrong one.' 'I do call you my friend, and I say the end *must* be the wrong one here. There's no right end. Think of your family. You don't mean to say — you dare not tell me, that you will marry her.' 'I *dare* not tell you!' said Tom, starting up in his turn; 'I dare tell you or any man anything I please. But I won't tell you or any man anything on compulsion.' 'I repeat,' went on Hardy, 'you *dare* not say you mean to marry her. You don't mean it — and, as you don't, to kiss her as you did to-night —' 'So you were sneaking behind to watch me,' burst out Tom, chafing with rage, and glad to find any handle for a quarrel. The two men stood fronting one another, the younger writhing with a sense of shame and outraged pride, and longing for a fierce answer — a blow — anything to give vent to the furies which were tearing him. But at the end of a few seconds the elder answered, calmly and slowly: 'I will not take those words from any man; you had better leave my rooms.' 'If I do, I shall not come back till you have altered your opinions.' 'You need not come back till you have altered yours.' The next moment Tom was in the passage; the next, striding up and down the inner quadrangle in the pale moonlight. Poor fellow! it was no pleasant walking ground for him. Is it worth our while to follow him up and down in his tramp? We have most of us walked the like marches at one time or another of our lives. The memory of them is by no means one which we can dwell on with pleasure. Times they were of blinding and driving storm, and

howling winds, out of which voices as of evil spirits spoke close
in our ears — tauntingly, temptingly whispering to the mischievous wild beast which lurks in the bottom of all our hearts,
now, 'Rouse up; art thou a man and darest not do this thing?'
now, 'Rise, kill and eat — It is thine, wilt thou not take it? Shall
the flimsy scruples of this teacher, or the sanctified cant of that,
bar thy way, and balk thee of thine own? Thou hast strength to
brave them — to brave all things, in earth, or heaven, or hell; put
out thy strength, and be a man!' "[3]

It is certainly in keeping with the type of Tom Brown's character, but
it is somewhat unfortunate that it should be so, that none of the more
characteristic intellectual influences of Oxford take any powerful hold of
him. One of the best sketches, that of Grey, the shy, nervous, scrupulous
high-churchman, remains throughout a sketch, simply because the
substance of his character has no affinity with that of Tom Brown's, and
could not be brought in in detail except by main force. For the same
reason, the more purely intellectual type of Oxford man, Blake, who is
again admirably sketched, appears in outline only, and has no close
concern with the progress of the book. We regret this the more, as he is,
in some measure, the type of the modern Oriel school, though a cross
between that and the fast set. In a book on Oxford University Life, we
should have been glad of a careful study, illustrating the intellectual
characteristics of this school. They are skilfully outlined, but only
outlined in a letter from Hardy (who is "coaching" Blake) to his friend:

"I think I have told you, or you must have seen it for yourself,
that my father's principles are true blue, as becomes a sailor of
the time of the great war, while his instincts and practice are
liberal in the extreme. Our rector, on the contrary, is liberal in
principles, but an aristocrat of the aristocrats in instinct and
practice. They are always ready enough therefore to do battle,
and Blake delights in the war, and fans it and takes part in it as
a sort of free lance, laying little logical pitfalls for the combatants
alternately, with that deferential manner of his. He gets some
sort of intellectual pleasure, I suppose, out of seeing where they
ought to tumble in; for tumble in they don't, but clear his pitfalls
in their stride — at least my father does — quite innocent of having
neglected to distribute his middle term; and the rector, if he has
some inkling of these traps, brushes them aside, and disdains to
spend powder on any one but his old adversary and friend....
Besides putting some history and science into him (scholarship
he does not need), I shall be satisfied if I can make him give up
his use of the pronoun 'you' before he goes. In talking of the corn
laws, or foreign policy, or India, or any other political subject,
however interesting, he will never identify himself as an

Englishman; and 'you do this,' or 'you expect that' is for ever in his mouth, speaking of his own countrymen. I believe if the French were to land to-morrow on Portland, he would comment on our attempts to dislodge them as if he had no concern with the business except as a looker-on."[4]

The purely fast set belong more naturally to Tom's world, and are very graphically delineated in the persons of Drysdale and his gentlemen-commoner friends. Our only complaint of the college life is, that except Tom and Hardy, all the characters arc mere sketches — none of them finished pictures. Little as we hear of them, we long to know more. What became of Grey? Did he go to Rome, or was he too shy for that bold-faced Church? If so, Did he settle down finally into night schools or patristic theology — the beneficent or the scholarly type of "high and dry?" Why are we not told what degree Blake took in the end; and why have we none of the old Rugby figures again, except East's? We yearned after Digges and Martin; and should have preferred even the Slogger to Miller. It was almost a waste of power to introduce so many new figures, instead of deepening the lines in the old characters.

But we must not leave this delightful picture of University life without some specimen of the fresh rural scenes which diversify and yet properly belong to it. Tom Brown's early education and best nature, as well as the result of his greatest moral temptation at Oxford, naturally lead him into very close relation with the agricultural labourers in his native county, and nothing is more skilful and thoughtful in the book than the way in which his extra-academical life is woven in with the fruits of his social and mental culture at Oxford. Social temptations, rather than individual ones, beset him from the first; and, consequently, social problems rather than individual ones press on his intellect as it gradually ripens. His actual life has drawn him into close intercourse with that class that is so hardly used in the agricultural districts around his home, and it is his warm sympathy with that class which first shakes his faith in the aristocratic theory of English society. Hence the village scenes, which are interspersed throughout the book, are really as essential to the student's life at Oxford, as they are fresh and graphic. In one very powerful scene, but too long for extract, Tom, who has perplexed himself very much with the justice or injustice of game-laws, and at the same time pledged himself to watch a night for a suspected poacher, finds himself, after a hard struggle with this poacher, face to face with the humble village friend and companion of his childhood. The perplexity of thought and emotion to which this situation gives rise is described with fine humour and with great force, and this is the main link in the chain of circumstances which at length leads Tom into a thoroughly revolutionary theory of English society. This hint will be enough to show how truthfully the academical and the non-academical scenes are linked together, and to prevent any false impression that the following graphic sketch of village life, in the isolation in which we are compelled to give it, is in fact foreign to the proper development of the story. It is an interview between the old gardener in a rector's family, who has been injured by a fall from a ladder, and his young mistress, Tom Brown's cousin: he is explaining his doctor's and his own view of the injury:

" 'Zummut inside o' me like, as wur got out o' place,' explained Simon; 'and I thenks a must be near about the mark, for I feels mortal bad here when I tries to move;' and he put his hand on his side. 'Hows'm'ever, as there's no bwones bruk, I hopes to be about to-morrow mornin', please the Lord — ugh, ugh!' 'You mustn't think of it, Simon,' said Miss Winter. 'You must be quite quiet for a week, at least, till you get rid of this pain.' 'So I tells un, Miss Winter,' put in the wife. 'You hear what the young missus says, Simon?' 'And wut's to happen to Tiny?' said the contumacious Simon, scornfully. 'Her'll cast her calf, and me not by. Her's calving may be this minut. Tiny's time wur up, miss, two days back, and her's never no gurt while arter her time.' 'She will do very well I dare say,' said Miss Winter. 'One of the men can look after her.' The notion of any one else attending Tiny in her interesting situation seemed to excite Simon beyond bearing, for he raised himself on one elbow, and was about to make a demonstration with his other hand, when the pain seized him again, and he sank back groaning. 'Theere, you see, Simon, you can't move without pain. You must be quiet till you have seen the doctor again.' 'There's the red spider out along the south wall — ugh, ugh,' persisted Simon, without seeming to hear her; 'and your new g'raniums a most covered wi' blight. I wur a tacklin' one on 'em just afore you cum in.' Following the direction indicated by his nod, the girls became aware of a plant by his bedside, which he had been fumigating, for his pipe was leaning against the flower-pot in which it stood. 'He wouldn't lie still nohow, miss,' explained his wife, 'till I went and fetched un in a pipe and one o' thaay plants from the greenhouse.' 'It was very thoughtful of you, Simon,' said Miss Winter; 'you know how much I prize these new plants: but we will manage them; and you mustn't think of these things now. You have had a wonderful escape to-day for a man of your age. I hope we shall find that there is nothing much the matter with you after a few days, but you might have been killed, you know. You ought to be very thankful to God that you were not killed in that fall.' 'So I be, miss, werry thankful to un — ugh, ugh; and if it plaase the Lord to spare my life till to-morrow mornin', — ugh, ugh, — we'll smoke them cussed insects'."[5]

These extracts, good as they are, can give no adequate impression of the literary vividness and noble ethical atmosphere which pervade the whole book. Mr. Hughes describes in it the gradual steps by which a fine, warm, social nature, open to every human influence, and, through human influences, also to the divinely-human, passes through the fermenting years of youth and college life, and wins its way clear to the calmer practical world beyond. Were it not too sad for Tom Brown's hopeful nature and cheerful destiny, the motto to the book might almost have been those noble lines in which a modern poet denounces the passive theory of quietist Christianity; for it expresses perfectly the essence of the ethical side of Mr. Hughes's genius:

"Always in his nature
Eager antagonism, not passive spirits,
Oppose the dangerous devil's mastery,
But sworded and aggressive warriors,
Who, with swift charge, beat down the mustered ranks
And all day long maintain the weary war,
And die in faith of unseen victory."[6]

This is, as we said, too sad for the motto of Mr. Hughes's book. Tom Brown is not a martyr, but a successful soldier, and the tale is clear and bright almost throughout. Even when clouds hang in the air, that air is still pure and fresh. In fact, we know of no book half so sunny in which there is at once so much graphic painting and so strong a current of courageous faith. It is worthy of the truly great man to whom it is dedicated, and we can give it no better praise.[7]

Ineffectual Novels

There is a principle well known to the natural philosopher, called the "principle of the want of sufficient reason," which asserts, that where you know all the causes in operation, and can find none why an event should happen in one way rather than another, it will in fact not happen in either of those ways for which there is no reason.[1] For example, it is explained to the youthful student of mechanics, that if two towing-horses on opposite sides of a canal pull with exactly equal force and at exactly equal angles at a barge in the centre, there being no assignable reason why it should be deflected to one side which could not with equal plausibility be alleged for its going to the other side, there is in fact a "want of sufficient reason" why it should leave the middle of the stream, and that *therefore* it will not leave the middle of the stream—*facts* (as the Emperor of the French now frequently reminds us) having in themselves "an inexorable logic"[2] quite as absolute as Reason itself. We often wish that this useful and admirable principle had any certain application to literary works. On the other hand, we fear there is a certain class of them, certainly of novels, in which "want of sufficient reason" hangs like a fog, not over those imaginary alternatives which are ineffectual candidates for existence, but over the whole current of the narrative. *Baronscliffe* is an example, a wonderful example, of this class of books. Everything is ineffectual about the book; there is a "want of sufficient reason" for almost every dialogue and every incident mentioned. Nothing hangs together; nothing goes on. It is a species of intellectual treadmill to read it, with the incidental aggravation of knowing that there is no mill turned after all, and that you are exhausting your intellectual feet on the ostensible steps called chapters in vain. As soon as you get your foot on the chapter it sinks beneath you to the same level on which you were before. No new ledge of the plot is ever gained, no new development of character; you have but made a troublesome effort to find yourself just where you were.

The disappointment is greater in this case, because the story is a genuine old ghost story, containing a ghost of the proper kind, who is not explained away. Now we do expect ghosts of the *old* sort to do something to make their influence felt. They are there to disclose dark proceedings, and bring down vengeance upon the heads of living evil-doers. But this ghost, though orthodox, and of the good old sort, not given to rapping, using alphabets, and table-inspiring, but wailing on stormy nights as worthy ghosts with any self-respect always do, is as ineffectual as everything else about the book. He is only heard, not seen; he does nothing, produces no effects, and has no influence on the story, though the story appears to have, not unnaturally, a soporific influence on him, and induces him to breathe more tranquilly, and finally subside at the close. The refreshment, therefore, which we not unnaturally looked for from an orthodox old ghost, not scientifically resolved into nothingness, was denied us. Like everything else in the book, even the ghost rather fagged us before the end: he gives rise to so many discursive conversations between housekeepers and ladies'-maids, which have neither sufficient nor insufficient reason for occurring at all. When a ghost turns out an imbecile and inefficient agent, of course we can look for nothing better from the other and more human personages. There is a kind of Lancashire sybil of the Meg Merrilies[3] description, who rolls her eyes and wanders about the country with a terrible secret in her possession, which she confides to everybody she meets with, and yet makes as much of as before. She, of course, is entirely ineffectual, and except that she says "yo" instead of "you," and "nobbut" instead of "nothing but," or "nobody but," her individuality remains to the end entirely undefined. The purely human agents are just as bad. Whenever they are really likely to do anything, they die or abscond, to evade the uncomfortable necessity. The evil-minded attorney, and demon of the piece, who appears to have done some mischief forty years before the story begins, but certainly does none in its course, and who remains quietly at his post so long as he is in daily danger of being found out, runs away in a tumult of fear directly that danger is temporarily removed by his employer's loss of the papers which are supposed to establish his guilt. The cold-hearted and worldly sister-in-law of the heroine, who has an evil and malignant smile on her countenance when she looks at her, expends her evil energies in persuading her brother to take his wife (the heroine) to the south of France when she appears to be consumptive; and though the motive is *stated* to be interested and not affectionate, yet the evil character of the design is never explained, while its expediency is certainly justified by the heroine's early death of her disease in *this* climate. But the most ineffectual person is perhaps the wronged heir, whose exclusion from the property is the subject for the story. He appears but once, with a black veil over his face, rescues the papers which are to prove his title, and departs with them to his mother in Australia, where he carefully dies, lest he should have to do something. In short, the whole *provision* for great events of any sort is cancelled before we get to the end—the plot committing suicide, as it were, lest there should be any necessity for *dénouement* at the end, which is accordingly skilfully avoided.

The same amazing ineffectuality as exists in the plot is to be found also in the characters, though this is a fault much more common in other novels. To find characters which are always speaking and never expressing themselves, is unfortunately so ordinary as to excite no attention. But the weakest of feminine novels often show a very considerable command of incident, and weld events together with a good deal of skill. Indeed, they are far less often deficient in this mere narrative coherence than novels of masculine authorship, which frequently betray a certain discontinuity. But in this novel, a continuous story is even more "conspicuous by its absence"[4] than continuous concepts of character, and the only motive adequate to bring any reader through it, is the curiosity aroused as to the propelling power in the mind of the authoress. The production of a book would seem to be easy enough by the number which now appear, but still it is an effect which requires a cause; and not only a final cause, such as the hope of selling the book, but an efficient intellectual cause for the process itself. The coherent interest of a real story, however impossible, would be sufficient cause; development of character would be sufficient; descriptive talent or taste might be sufficient; but here the story, though *arranged for*, is omitted; the characters, though *named*, are scarcely even so much as vaguely conceived; and what is said by those who are *only* named is narrated with as much irrelevant detail and care as what is said by those who are intended to be something more than names; and the descriptions *are not*. We are compelled to suppose there must be a certain pleasure in writing chapters on chapters of mere talk, which bring out nothing whatever, either in relation to the so-called story, or the so-called characters; — which begin in nothing, end in nothing, and *are* nothing. Even when "secret drawers" are discovered, and we suppose that a new feature is occurring, we are mistaken — the secret drawer, like the ghost, and the sybil, and the villain, and the wronged rightful heir, all occur with the same view of agitating the mind with a disclosure which is immediately discerned to have nothing in it.

The only striking observation which this remarkable production, and the many ineffectual novels which resemble it, justifies, is this, that there must be in some minds a sort of disinterested delight in the *technical machinery* of novels quite apart from the human interests which that machinery used to subserve. Just as gold, which is valued first as a means, itself inspires in the end a far stronger passion than anything which it can procure; just as stealing will become a devouring passion, even when there is no object to be gained by it, — so the "properties" and forms of a novel appear to possess an intrinsic interest of their own to some, even though they involve none of the human interests by which they first gained their popularity. "See," they say, "a ghost — a walled-up tower — a secret cabinet — a beldame — a wronged heir — a villainous attorney, — here are all the great interests together;" and though the ghost does nothing, and the secret cabinet produces no secret, and the beldame does not intervene in perilous moments, and the wronged heir stays away, and the villainous attorney is harmless, and nothing comes of any of them, still they do in themselves constitute the objects of a disinterested passion wholly unconnected with consequences to human fortunes. Ineffectual novel-machinery, like ineffectual money, may, after all, inspire a deeper and more abstract and concentrated passion than their legitimate use has ever inspired. We warn the novel-producing and reading community of the danger of this artificial state of things. Whoever can read *Baronscliffe* with interest is already a victim to it.

Mr. Arnold's Last Words on Translating Homer

Mr. Arnold is the most lucid and delightful of living English critics. No one can deny that he has that great qualification of every true critic which he himself so well defines as consisting in a hearty wish as well as capacity "to press to the heart of the thing itself with which he is dealing – not to go off on some collateral issue about the thing."[1] Not only does he do this, but he does so with a fine and discriminating taste, with a distinctness of thought singularly bright, and an elegance that is at once classical and modern. Still, for a critic, he remains too much himself. "The critic of poetry," he says, "should have the finest tact, the nicest moderation, the most free, flexible, and elastic spirit imaginable; he should be the *ondoyant et divers*, the undulating and diverse being of Montaigne."[2] The definition is perfect, but Mr. Arnold is too intellectual to attain the flexibility – the undulating, elastic nature he describes. His head is too clearly lifted above his subject to permit him to enter into it with full sympathy. He is a purely intellectual critic. The grace of his mind, which is very marked, verges somewhat on the thin and stiff type of modern culture. There is a touch of the French *renaissance* school about his classical elegance. When he tells us about the "grand style,"[3] we cannot help noting this, for "grand" is half a French expression which seems to give a touch of pedantry to that inward *nobility* of which he makes it the outward expression. And this very slight flavour of something too intellectually *magnificent* in Mr. Arnold's standard which runs through all his criticisms is distinctly visible even in the style of his lectures. There is humour, no doubt, but what magnificence too, in the lectures which he reads to his critics! His motto to this rejoinder is characteristic: "*Multi qui persequuntur me et tribulant me; a testimoniis non declinavi,*"[4] he says, with a smile no doubt, but still a smile more at his defeated enemies than at his own loftiness. Again: "For those, then, who ask the question – What is the grand style? with sincerity, I will try to make some answer, inadequate as it must be. For those who ask it mockingly I have no answer, except to repeat to them with compassionate sorrow, the Gospel words, *Moriemini in peccatis vestris.* Ye shall die in your sins."[5] Mr. Arnold need not have gone further. The quotation from Milton is a superfluous illustration. His own words had given us a much more perfect one: *that*, surely, if such a style exist, is "the grand style."

We venture this personal criticism on this accomplished critic, because it will simplify the criticism we have to make on this delightful and lucid supplement to his former lectures on translating Homer. Mr. Arnold is evidently quite unaware of the true sting of his former criticism on Mr. Newman. It was not so much in anything he said as in the ineffable superiority of manner with which he said it; and this, though quite consistent with the genuine modesty of the present lecture in all that refers to scholarship or acquirement, is certainly a deeply-rooted characteristic of his fastidious intellectual taste. However, we have no concern with the personal aspects of his collision with Mr. Newman, and only refer to it to illustrate one important point in dispute concerning the proper ideal of a translation of Homer.

Mr. Newman had said, and we to some extent agreed with him, that many of Homer's modes of thought and speech must have seemed antiquated to the Athenians of the age of Pericles, however *familiar* Homer may have then been to them. Mr. Arnold now replies that familiarity or non-familiarity is the whole and sole point of issue; that if Homer's language were as familiar (for epic poetry) to the first Greek tragedians as the language of the Bible is to us for solemn and epic themes, the whole question is settled. In that case Homer was not in any sense "quaint" to the great Attic poets, and if we are to receive as faithful an impression of him in English as Pericles received in Greek, it must be in a style which never startles us by the quaint simplicity of its manner. Chaucer, Mr. Arnold says, is, to a great extent, really grotesque and unfamiliar to us. Homer never was to the Athenians. Therefore it must be into a style much more familiar and smooth to our ears than Chaucer's that he ought to be translated. Such a style is the style of the translation of the Bible—neither too modern for the genius of the poetry, nor so antique as to disguise it.

We confess this seems to us very imperfect reasoning and criticism, though leading to a perfectly sound practical rule. It is, of course, as impossible to translate into a dead language without mannerism, as to adopt an antiquated costume without self-consciousness, awkwardness, and affectation. Mr. Newman's translation appears to us a serious warning against so unnatural an attempt. But though it may be a most mistaken course to make this attempt, it by no means follows that had the translation been done, and done successfully, at an earlier period of English history, it would not have had a far better chance of faithfully rendering Homer in spirit and tone than it can ever have now. Mr. Arnold evades the true issue, which is *not*—was Mr. Newman right?—but, was not he aiming at something which, though unattainable now and not to be

aimed at, should yet be ever recognized by a translator of Homer as one
of the constant disturbing forces and difficulties in his way without vain
struggles to annihilate it?

We understand Mr. Arnold to express his deliberate belief that there
is *more* true harmony between the genius of a high intellectual civilization
and the genius of Homer than between the genius of a rudimentary and
germinal civilization and the genius of Homer — that the cast of Homer's
thought was more akin to that of Athenian literature in its meridian
splendour than to the ruder days and ruder tribes among whom he sang.
For he says boldly:

> "As a poet he belongs, — narrative as is his poetry, and early
> as is his date, — to an incomparably more developed spiritual and
> intellectual order than the balladists, or than Scott or Macaulay;
> he is here as much to be distinguished from them, and in the same
> way, as Milton is to be distinguished from them. He is, indeed,
> rather to be classed with Milton than with the balladists and
> Scott; for what he has in common with Milton, — the noble and
> profound application of ideas to life, — is the most essential part
> of poetic greatness. The most essentially grand and
> characteristic things of Homer are such things as

> ἔτλην δ' οἷ' οὔπω τις ἐπιχθόνιος βροτὸς ἄλλος,
> ἀνδρὸς παιδοφόνοιο ποτὶ στόμα χεῖρ' ὀρέγεσθαι...

> 'And I have endured, — the like whereof no soul upon the
> earth hath yet endured, — to carry to my lips the hand of him who
> slew my child.' — *Iliad,* xxiv. 505.

> or as

> καὶ σὲ, γέρον, τὸ πρὶν μὲν ἀκούομεν ὄλβιον εἶναι...

> 'Nay and thou too, old man, in times past wert, as we hear,
> happy.' — *Iliad,* xxiv. 543. [In the original this line, for mingled
> pathos and dignity, is perhaps without a rival even in Homer.]

> or as

> ὡς γὰρ ἐπεκλώσαντο θεοὶ δειλοῖσι βροτοῖσιν,
> ζώειν ἀχνυμένους· αὐτοὶ δέ τ' ἀκηδέες εἰσίν...

> 'For so have the gods spun our destiny to us wretched
> mortals, — that we should live in sorrow; but they themselves are
> without trouble.' — *Iliad,* xxiv. 525.

> and of these the tone is given, far better than by anything of the
> balladists, by such things as the

> > Io no piangeva: si dentro impietrai:
> >   Piangevan elli . . .

'*I* wept not: so of stone grew I within: — *they* wept.' — *Hell*,
xxxiii. 49 (Carlyle's Translation, slightly altered).

of Dante; or the

Fall'n Cherub! to be weak is miserable ...

of Milton."[6]

Mr. Arnold is surely overbold. It is, we think, less wide of the truth
than the extravagant description of Homer, which he quotes from Mr.
Newman, as the "savage with the lively eye," whose verse would affect us
if we could hear the living Homer "like an elegant and simple melody
from an African of the Gold Coast."[7] But the intellectual critic certainly
does not make good, and almost makes us smile at, his comparison
between Homer and Milton. No critic can, we think, *enter into* Homer,
though he may gaze down upon him with keen intellectual eye, who would
say this. That Homer's characteristic power is "the noble and profound
application of ideas to life," sounds to us a criticism either conspicuously
erroneous or needing an interpretation which relieves it of all its
originality. If Mr. Arnold means that Homer is greatest when he
generalizes on human fortunes and characters, when with sublime pathos
he brings out the dark side of human destiny, or distinguishes between
the type of different characters among statesmen and rulers, what he says
is most true; but it describes with equal truth the elementary stages of
intellectual power in many great nations. Chaucer, for instance, though
seldom sounding the deepest places of human emotion, generalizes and
depicts the outlines of character with Homeric simplicity and accuracy;
and where shall we find a deeper pathos, a truer power for this very same
"application of great ideas" to human life — if that is really the proper
term for the noble poetry of which Mr. Arnold has just given us such
magnificent specimens — than in the early Hebrew pastorals and history?[8]
Yet who would call the Hebrew pastorals poems of a "developed
intellectual order," or dream of comparing them in *this* respect with
Milton? It seems to us that Mr. Arnold has attributed to Homer the
processes of his own intellect when working upon Homer. He has not
appreciated the full difference between the Homeric thought and the
intellectual estimate of that thought. Homer's intellect was doubtless
infinitely wider than "Macaulay's or Scott's," but to say that the kind of
intellect running through the "Iliad" was equally "developed," seems to
us a confusion of terms. We measure the development of intellect by the
degree in which it seeks for causes and reasons, or innocently, so to speak,
assumes them; — by the elaborateness of its moral analysis — by the
richness and complexity of the converging experience of centuries in its
tests of practical wisdom. All this we see in Milton in the highest possible

degree, and in the least possible degree in Homer. In the poorest of Macaulay's rhetorical lays there is ample sign of the intellectual culture of centuries – of an intellect that has been unfolded under the pressure of a thousand intellectual atmospheres such as that which saw the unfolding of Homer's.[9] It seems to us unworthy of Mr. Arnold's insight to deny that there is a kind of simplicity which belongs expressly to the youth of the world, and of each nation which rises to greatness in that world – and that Homer's simplicity is of both kinds, and is open to a more effective rendering from a nation in the bud than from the same nation in the flower. The hopeful forward glance, the innocent assumption of agencies not only unproved but undoubted and undiscussed, the *kind* of importance given to the physical nature, the absence of shame, the childlike first-hand intellect – all these are striking characteristics of Homer which give him half his charm, and are about as abundant in Milton as dew under the burning noon of a tropical sun. To us Mr. Arnold's conception of Homer as, in the *modern* sense, a highly intellectual poet, is the one glaring deficiency in this series of exquisite critical lectures. It is the kind of magnificent error which the French classical school might have made.

Miss Mulock's Fairy Book

"This is meant," says Miss Mulock, "to be the best collection attainable of that delight of all children, and of many grown people who retain the child-heart still—the old-fashioned, time-honoured, classic fairy tale." Whether or not we retain the child-heart, we do not know, and perhaps, as Dr. Johnson said to Boswell about the wisdom of wearing nightcaps, "Perhaps no man shall ever know,"[1]—for we are not at all sure what that favourite term of the modern sentimentalism means,—but we do know that we feel very tenderly attached to the memory of the gracious and melancholy White Cat, that the Bean-stalk, though Jack cut it down, has never ceased to blossom perennially, and diffuse its more than bean-flower fragrance over our memories,—that little One Eye's and little Three Eyes' conspiracy against little Two Eyes, has still a profounder interest for us than any conspiracy of the Reds in Paris or Rome; and that the seven little (surely Eureka) shirts which retransformed the seven little white swans into the seven little princes (except the one wing where the shirt-sleeve had not been white-seamed into the shirt), have ever shed for us an air of romance round that admirable garment which has done something to transfigure the oppressive monotony of underclothes. If this is to have the child-heart, we are very glad to know and own it; but it is at least compatible with a very grave sense of the unremunerative elderly fag of ordinary life.

However, Miss Mulock has really redeemed her promise, so far as a single volume could redeem it, of presenting the "best collection attainable of the old-fashioned, time-honoured, classic fairy tale," in which we are happy to say, the "child-heart" does not reappear, nor, indeed, any vestige of sentimental ethics, unless, indeed, this sentence, at the close of the tale called "The Butterfly," betray Miss Mulock:—"We are informed that Papillette had at first some slight returns of her natural disposition; but in one year she became a mother, and from thenceforward never knew frivolity more." If any old fairy story contains that, it must be a French one, and seems to us to flavour not a little of "A Woman's Thoughts about Women."[2] But we hear no more of this state of feeling. The ogres are duly beheaded, the wicked fairies (magic permitting) burnt to ashes, the deceits by which the malicious are outwitted are all cheerfully related, and the Welsh giant falls a victim to his emulation of Jack the Giant-killer's "second stomach," as kindly as our modern theologians to their zeal for the second stomach of the hare.[3] Miss Mulock idealizes nothing, carefully abstains altogether from appending "morals," narrates every incident conscientiously, and, where an English version of a foreign fairy tale is required, gives it with great spirit, and in the style of the old-fashioned simplicity. We think she has not taken quite as much as she might have done from the incomparable collection of Grimm. There is no nation so great in fairy tales as the German, because there is none so genuinely child-like in its humour. We could well have exchanged the story of "The Prince with the Nose," for the much more humorous German story of the apple which had the curious specific effect of causing the nose to grow for miles and miles through a great forest, and the pear which caused its equally rapid "absorption." But it must be admitted that Miss Mulock's collection is much less monotonous than most collections of fairy tales, from the pains she has taken to get the best of each national collection, so that the national fancy of England, France, Germany, Scandinavia, and the East has each its representative elements. And though there are no large illustrations, the admirable drawing of the little initial letters to each tale, which are always in fact pictures belonging to the tale, partly supply the place of those marvellous illustrations of Cruikshank's to the old English translation of Grimm, which have almost identified themselves in children's imaginations with the tales themselves.[4] Why, by the way, has Miss Mulock been so hardhearted as to withhold that story of "The Golden Bird," wherein "the Prince rides on the fox's tail over stock and stone till his hair whistles in the wind," and which Cruikshank has immortalized for children by his unrivalled picture of that curious feat of foxmanship?[5]

Miss Mulock has evidently a true insight into the secret of a perfect fairy tale. First, it should be marvellous but not mysterious, exciting wonder but not awe. The more astonishing the magical laws which replace those of life, the more delightful they are; but they should not touch a great truth or even a dim faith, for then, instead of merely refreshing the mind and stimulating the fancy, they put it on the stretch again. The harmless deceits and tricks of the good princes are even a fresh excellence in a fairy tale, for they simply have the effect of releasing the child's imagination from the stress of any weight of reality, and matching the capricious marvels of the external world in which the scene is laid. Any approach to a genuine mystery in a fairy tale is a defect. The nearest approximation to it desirable is, for instance, the appearance of the twelve torch-bearing Hands in the story of the "White Cat," which usher the happy prince through the palace. That is just on the verge of the awful; and, perhaps, the spiritualists would claim it as a testimony to the spiritual hands now in vogue;[6] but it is saved from becoming so by the physical details of opulence by which they are surrounded, and the melancholy, ladylike, little white puss, with the miniature at her side, who receives him from the attendant Hands. Had the Hands been given to expressive gestures, to beckoning, or folding, or wringing, or "pointing upwards,"[7] they would be formidable, and not fairy hands; but as they only bring silver goblets and rich brocade dressing-gowns, wait obsequiously at table, and ignore the owners' minds altogether, they fill a child's fancy without tasking its imagination. The "White Cat" is, indeed, almost equal to some of the best of the German tales in everything but humour. The nut out of which the exquisite little dog jumps so cheerfully, – the still more marvellous walnut, which contains a filbert, which contains a cherry-stone, which contains a kernel, which contains a grain of wheat, which contains a millet seed, which contains 400 yards of the finest cambric, all woven by the attendants of the White Cat expressly to go through a needle's eye, and enveloped for delivery in this very elaborate form by something more than feline subtlety, – these are the sort of marvels which a child intensely appreciates. Then there is that fine touch of feline magic, when the prince's faith fails at the millet seed, and he reproaches the pussy in his heart, "upon which he felt his hand scratched by the claw of a cat," – a lesson after which the child feels it a kind of treason to suggest criticisms upon the possibility of the incidents related, though he well knows in the background of his mind, what he barely admits to himself, that they are all, of course, make-belief.

But besides being marvellous without mystery, it is a great excellence in a fairy tale to be exceedingly grotesque in its choice of means, and to insist a good deal upon them. For example, it would be (humanly) exceedingly difficult to understand how three needles could help a princess to climb a glass mountain, but it is just the charm of the thing to tame and subdue the imagination to these unexpected exigencies. If the needles were the thing which did help the princess over the glass mountain, why it is clear they were the right means to do so, which is all the more delightful to think of. An ordinary mind would not feel a plough-wheel a great assistance for rolling safely over three sharp-cutting swords, – but then the fact that the Princess did get over those obstacles by this remarkably unsuitable contrivance – (we do not think of asking whether she revolved with the wheel, or whether she sat on an axle which is not mentioned, for that, as the bishops say, is of the nature of neological speculation, and the child is not a neologist) – is far more gratifying than if she had walked round them, or avoided them, in a more common-place way.

Then, in a good fairy tale there should be always a clear discrimination between the good and evil agencies, and it is very gratifying when the evil agencies can also be made the confusing ones, and the good the discriminating ones, — only the discrimination should not be done by the intellect (which is a laborious human idea) but by a magic wand. The classificatory sciences are so far recognized in fairy tales, that the good magic has a very satisfactory power of classifying properly, and sorcery of causing chaos and error. Nothing is more pleasing in the old fairy tales than the instances, of which there are so many, of the good fairy unravelling the intricacies of a perplexed task with a mere stroke of her wand. How pleasant was it when the Duchess Grognon had set poor Princess Gracoisa to classify under their right head all the feathers in the basket belonging to nightingales, canaries, linnets, larks, doves, thrushes, peacocks, ostriches, pheasants, partridges, magpies, eagles, and all other kinds of birds, to have Percinct touching them with his hand, so that they all flew by millions out of the basket, and "arranged themselves in little heaps, each belonging to a different bird." That is much better than Professor Owen's art,[8] for the child's ideal of discriminating faculty is magical power and order, — not arrived at by the intellect, but by the wave of a wand. If only one could separate and combine at will! From the fairy wand to conchology and logarithms is such a great and degrading descent.

The only kind of fairy tales scarcely adequately represented here are the humorous German ones. The "Bremen Musicians" and the "Seven Goslings" are of this class, though scarcely the best, and Rumpelstilzchen is here, and is one of the very best. But nearly the best tale in Grimm's collection, "Death as a Godfather" (Der Gevatter Tod), the "Golden Goose," again the one called the "Goose Maid," and that of the six friends who travelled through the world together, aiding each other with their wonderful gifts, and many others of the same kind, whose beauty is rather in their childlike humour than in their fairy marvels, are inadequately represented here. *Fortunatus*, who is rather a dull hero, or "Clever Alice," who is not really amusing, might fairly have been sacrificed for some of these. But the book, on the whole, is a delightful selection, in a delightful external form; full of the physical splendour and vast opulence of proper fairy tales, where the hens not only freely lay golden eggs, but eggs, not golden, hatch gold and silver dresses; abounding, too, in the charming little rhyming spells which wring responses from magic mirrors, and weave a charm round the child's understanding, in the scrupulous matter-of-fact details which realize to children's minds the orbit of wonder in which the tale moves, and finally in the quaint transformations which touch springs of subtle association in every child's memory.

Mr. Kingsley's Water-Babies

Mr. Kingsley's genius is so remarkable for its sympathy with the irrational forms of animal life, and the rational element in it is so often merged in a sort of noble but furious bark at what he dislikes, that we seldom read his tales without a feeling that the ideas with which he begins, often subtle and fine enough, are sure to tail off into something half animal before the conclusion. In this fairy story, begun with a clear purpose enough, the water-dog in Mr. Kingsley has prevailed more than usually early in the book, and before the end of it we have almost literally nothing left but the swishing of his wet tail, his floundering in the water, and the deep bay of his liberal conservatism. He has prefixed a kind of warning to the critics which would appear to deprecate any remarks we may have to offer on this eccentric gambol of his genius: —

> "Hence, unbelieving Sadducees,
> And less believing Pharisees,
> With dull conventionalities;
> And leave a country Muse at ease
> To play at leap-frog, if she please,
> With children and realities."[1]

Well, we have no objection to Mr. Kingsley's freaks either with children or realities; but we rather wish that when he is playing at leap-frog with children he would suit the dimensions of his realities to his small play-fellows, and not insist on their taking such tremendously high metaphysical backs, at times, which are certainly quite beyond the little arms of his infantine friends. He dedicates the book to his youngest son, Grenville Arthur, with the motto —

> "Come, read me my riddle, my good little man;
> If you cannot read it, no grown-up folk can,"[2]

and we are quite content to abide by Grenville Arthur's judgment. If he understands the joke about the Gairfowl's objecting to marry his deceased wife's sister, about the whales "butting at each other with their ugly noses day and night from year's end to year's end," like "our American cousins," — about the "abolition of the Have-his-carcase Act," and the "Indignation Meetings," — or the Back-stairs way out of Hell, or

65

the Hippopotamus major in the brain,[3] — or a hundred others, we will pronounce Mr. Kingsley's tale a good fairy tale for children, — for we do not deny that it had an idea; — but if not, as we feel tolerably confident, why, then we arraign Mr. Kingsley of that half-animal impatience which cannot be satisfied with working out patiently a single distinct idea, — but must interpolate arrogant inarticulate barks at a hundred things which have no business at all in his tale, and tumble head over heels in scores of unfit places just because there and then his intellect feels inclined for a somerset of which neither men nor children will appreciate the fun.

The purpose of the tale, — and it was a fine one — seems to have been to adapt Mr. Darwin's theory of the natural selection of species to the understanding of children, by giving it an individual, moral, and religious, as well as a mere specific and scientific application. He took the watery world, principally because he knows it so well, and because the number of transformations which go on in it are so large, and so easily capable of a semi-moral significance, that it served best to illustrate his purpose. For example, the specific difference between salmon and trout Mr. Kingsley interprets as a difference between enterprise and industry on the one hand, and stupid greediness on the other, — as shown in this conversation between his water-baby and the salmon: —

> " 'Why do you dislike the trout so?' asked Tom. 'My dear, we do not even mention them, if we can help it; for I am sorry to say they are relations of ours who do us no credit. A great many years ago they were just like us: but they were so lazy, and cowardly, and greedy, that instead of going down to the sea every year to see the world and grow strong and fat, they chose to stay and poke about in the little streams and eat worms and grubs; and they are very properly punished for it; for they have grown ugly and brown and spotted and small; and are actually so degraded in their tastes, that they will eat our children'."[4]

The same general drift is intended to pervade the book, which contains numberless hints that wherever moral qualities, or the germs of moral qualities, begin, there, at least, is a turning point of natural development or degradation in the individual, and thence also in the species. Thus Mr. Kingsley hints that the specific difference between the Irish and Saxons may be originally rooted in moral, more than in physical distinctions, and might be ultimately traced to the love of giving "a pleasant answer," if we take into account the long accumulations of generations of dispositions of the same sort. Again the Gairfowls are meant to be the types of races who die out through mere traditional pride, from refusing to avail themselves of the alliance of fresh blood, and determining to stand all alone on the precedents and etiquettes of ancestral usage. The same moral Darwinism is the idea of the story of the idle Doasyoulikes, and also, of course, of the water-baby's own history. Indeed, all the various physiological transformations in the story are intended to illustrate some such notion as this. And the fairy whose watchwork-nature obliges her to punish everybody's mistakes by treating them exactly as they have treated others, "Mrs. Bedonebyasyoudid," is meant, we suppose, to represent the invariable and unalterable principle of God's universal Providence. She is, as we are taught at the close, after all but another form of divine Love, which is the motive, if not the principal agency in effecting these transformations. Yet surely it is not quite true to represent men's actions as generally returned upon them in kind, – the bleeding doctors and over-cramming schoolmasters being by no means uniformly bled and over-crammed in their turn. However, the fairy is commissioned, we suppose, to show generally that individuals, and therefore races, suffer degradation in consequence of the accumulations of their errors and sins; – in consequence of not keeping their eyes open to God's laws, and still more of not obeying them when they do know them.

Well, this conviction of Mr. Kingsley's, and its many lively (if often fanciful) illustrations, was worth a fairy story, and none could be more spirited or vigorous than this up to the point when he gets his transformed chimney-sweep (who, coarse and ignorant, but wishing to be clean, was by the law of fairy consequences transformed into a water-baby) to the mouth of the salmon river. Even this portion has been improved considerably since its first publication, and made a more coherent fairy story by the earlier introduction of the fairy.[5] The description of the storm, which fills the stream and enables all the living things in it if desiring to reach the sea, to sweep down upon its swollen waters, is one of Mr. Kingsley's finest descriptive efforts. We have room but for a short passage: –

> "But out of the water he dared not put his head; for the rain came down by bucketsful, and the hail hammered like shot on the stream, and churned it into foam; and soon the stream rose, and rushed down, higher and higher, and fouler and fouler, full of beetles, and sticks and straws, and worms, and addle-eggs and wood-lice, and leeches, and odds and ends, and omnium-gatherums, and this, that, and the other, enough to fill nine museums. Tom could hardly stand against the stream, and hid behind a rock. But the trout did not; for out they rushed from among the stones, and began gobbling the beetles and leeches in the most greedy and quarrelsome way, and swimming about with great worms hanging out of their mouths, tugging and kicking to get them away from each other. And now, by the flashes of the lightning, Tom saw a new sight – all the bottom of the stream alive with great eels, turning and twisting along, all down stream

and away. They had been hiding for weeks past in the cracks of
the rocks, and in burrows in the mud; and Tom had hardly ever
seen them, except now and then at night; now they were all out,
and went hurrying past him so fiercely and wildly that he was
quite frightened. And as they hurried past he could hear them
say to each other, 'We must run, we must run. What a jolly
thunderstorm! Down to the sea, down to the sea!' And then the
otter came by with all her brood, twining and sweeping along as
fast as the eels themselves; and she spied Tom as she came by,
and said: — 'Now is your time, eft, if you want to see the world.
Come along, children, never mind those nasty eels; we shall
breakfast on salmon to-morrow. Down to the sea, down to the
sea!' "[6]

But no sooner does Mr. Kingsley get out of the salmon stream, than
his pen begins to flag, his power to spend itself in the most eccentric
capers, and his proper theme to fade away at intervals from his
imagination. He begins chaffing the scientific men, — and his chaff is
neither subtle to men nor intelligible to children. He barks right and left
at everything he does not like, whether it has anything to do with his
leading idea or not. Professor Owen is chaffed for insisting on the
hippocampus minor as the specific distinction of man; the cram-systems
of education and examination are chaffed; the nescience of medical men
is chaffed; universal progress and Mr. Lincoln are chaffed; the orthodox
fanatics who believe in hearsay, and don't want to be set right, are chaffed;
the positive philosophy, collecting multifold experiences, but refusing to
learn their meaning, is chaffed, and all in a way very few men will be able
to laugh at, and no children at all (unless it be Grenville Arthur) to
understand. What is the use of *four whole* pages of this sort of thing?

"Now the doctors had it all their own way; and to work they
went in earnest, and they gave the poor Professor divers and
sundry medicines, as prescribed by the ancients and moderns,
from Hippocrates to Feuchtersleben, as below, viz.: — Hellebore, to wit — hellebore of Æta; hellebore of Galata; hellebore
of Sicily; and all other hellebores, after the method of the
helleborizing helleborists of the helleboric era. But that would
not do. Bumpsterhausen's blue follicles would not stir an inch
out of his encephalo-digital region. . . ." "And if he had but been
a convict lunatic, and had shot at the Queen, killed all his
creditors to avoid paying them, or indulged in any other little
amiable eccentricity of that kind, they would have given him in
addition — the healthiest situation in England, on Easthamp-
stead Plain, free run of Windsor Forest, the *Times* every
morning, a double-barrelled gun and pointers, and leave to shoot

three Wellington College boys a week (not more) in case black game were scarce."[7]

We may smile a grim smile at first, but it is impossible to smile when that sort of nonsense is prolonged beyond a certain point. And this kind of thing strays at large through the book, and is seldom very amusing. We may smile when we are first told that Professor Ptthmllnsprts, Professor of Necrobioneopalaeohydrochthonanthropopithekology would have called a water-baby by two long names, "of which the first would have said a little about Tom, and the second all about himself, for, of course, he would have called him Hydrotecnon Ptthmllnsprtsianum," but when the same species of fun goes on for a great many pages together, we feel as if we were hearing one of those insane extravaganzas at the minor theatres, which are meant apparently to cast a gloom over the very name of fun, and induce early idiocy in the actors. And this fault is repeated so systematically during the latter part of the tale, that it quite sickens the reader, even though he may have what Miss Mulock painfully denominates "the child-heart."[8] Indeed, the worst of it is, that when the child might possibly enjoy the caricature, the idea caricatured is quite beyond his grasp, — as, for example, in that ecstatic apostrophe to the Backstairs, — and when the man might, perhaps, enjoy the idea, the caricature is far too broad and its tone too screaming for his taste. For example, the following is said by the fairy to a water-baby to explain why she cannot let him know the back way out of the place of punishment, *i.e.*, the way which saves you from the *effect* of evil without saving you from the cause. People would importune him as follows, she says, to divulge the secret: —

> "For thousands of years we have been paying, and petting, and obeying, and worshipping quacks who told us they had the key of the backstairs, and could smuggle us up them; and in spite of all our disappointments, we will honour, and glorify, and adore, and beatify, and translate, and apotheotize you likewise, on the chance of your knowing something about the backstairs, that we may all go on pilgrimage to it; and, even if we cannot get up it, lie at the foot of it, and cry — 'Oh! backstairs, precious backstairs, invaluable backstairs, requisite backstairs, necessary backstairs, good-natured backstairs, cosmopolitan backstairs, comprehensive backstairs, accommodating backstairs, well-bred backstairs, comfortable backstairs, humane backstairs, reasonable backstairs, long-sought backstairs, coveted backstairs, aristocratic backstairs, respectable backstairs, gentlemanlike backstairs, ladylike backstairs, commercial backstairs, economical backstairs, practical backstairs, logical backstairs, deductive backstairs, orthodox backstairs, probable backstairs, credible backstairs, demonstrable backstairs,

irrefragable backstairs, potent backstairs, all-but-omnipotent backstairs, &c. Save us from the consequences of our own actions, and from the cruel fairy, Mrs. Bedonebyasyoudid!' "[9]

This sort of thing might clearly be expanded by the Binomial Theorem to any number of terms you pleased.[10]

Upon the whole, in spite of some passages of great beauty, a fine idea, and much knowledge to work with, Mr. Kingsley has, as he too often does, spoiled a good story by his undisciplined and ill-concentrated imagination, which induces him to interrupt one train of thought just to vent his disgust at a dozen follies or crimes which occur to him while he is at work. He is like a dog which constantly loses the scent by turning aside to worry cats, bark at ill-looking beggars, or simply to play with a bone with his four legs in the air. However noble the bay, or however graceful the frolics of such a creature, the fairy Mrs. Bedonebyasyoudid will be obliged to reward him with a very mutilated and unsatisfactory fame, – unworthy both of Mr. Kingsley's real genius and of his noble aims.

Mr. Browning's Poetry

This is a good and welcome edition of works that deserve to live. Mr. Browning is by far the most difficult to appreciate truly of our modern poets. In the first place he is *hard* reading, and his thread of meaning is as difficult to follow as the thread of a mountain watercourse that loses itself continually among rude blocks of granite. The intellect not unfrequently aches with false steps and bad falls, after following his brisk, careless, rough-paced motion over stony places and through dark places, till at last he disappears abruptly, you don't at all know where. Then Mr. Browning almost always begins in the middle and leaves you to find your bearings as you may, which starts us with the same kind of dizziness as one experiences in blind man's buff, when you are made to "turn round three times and catch whom you may." Then, again, there is no *minute* fascination in his poetry, no lines of rare power that fill the brain, no "beauty born of murmuring sound"[1] that lingers in the ear and in the heart, — very little indeed that feeds and satisfies the craving for pure loveliness at all. And yet there are unquestionably great powers and originality in his writings, — powers that strike the reader more the more they are studied. He has a keen, cold, dramatic intellect, which takes infinite pleasure in reflecting all sorts of life without giving us any impression of sympathy therewith. His poems, if you gaze into them long enough, show us men much as the magic crystal might do that there was such a fuss about the other day.[2] You see them in a cold crystal medium as it were, in all sorts of costumes and attitudes, thinking, loving, hoping, dreaming, believing, but always external to you, — a picture generally furnished with an intellectual key, if you search enough for it, — but never a scene with which you find yourself involuntarily identified, a drama that sucks you into its eddy of exciting interests. Mr. Browning has a wonderful dramatic intellect, but scarcely a dramatic imagination. He never makes your heart beat with the stir of the action, or hang poised on the turn of an event. It is a keen, careless, restless form of art, which scampers about with us at its own will, and never seems identified with the interest of its own themes.

Mr. Browning speaks of himself, in one of his least characteristic and far his most *beautiful* poem, as "blowing through bronze,"[3] which exactly expresses the effect of the form and no-form of his verse upon us; a cold, often harsh, always powerful volume of sound, that comes irregularly and in puffs, telling us nothing of its source, and often giving hoarseness to the tone where the thoughts themselves are gentle; enduing with a sort of monotonous ruggedness and abruptness all the voices it gives out, whether it be the mere whistle of the driving wind, or the polished chat of a man of the world soliloquizing through its brazen throat; whether it be speaking-trumpet to a woman's passion, a monk's hissing envy, or a mystic's shadowy dreams. The *form* of the poetry not only seldom adds to Mr. Browning's poems, but it often takes from them, like the trumpet which the Greek actors used in the amphitheatre. Not that there is anything loud or screaming in Mr. Browning's style; quite the reverse. It is careless, often to the doggerel point; but his style does not give any new organization to the thought; his expressive power is not flexible clay to his imaginative power; when he has a fine thing to say, which he very often has, it does not make for itself a fine way of saying it. His imaginations, instead of *embodying* themselves in his poetry, only divulge themselves in it. You feel they were better and completer in his mind than they are in his words, instead of feeling, as we do with many poets of less than half his power, that you could as soon separate flesh from spirit as separate the poetry from the words. Here, for instance, is a passage of more than common power of expression for Mr. Browning. He is painting a formalist Duke of some place in Moldavia, who lives to institute a sort of *renaissance* of all worn-out customs, of all the extinct forms of former ducal grandeur: —

> "So all that the Dukes had been without knowing it,
> This Duke would fain know he was without being it.
> 'Twas not for the joy's self, but the joy of his showing it,
> Nor for the pride's self, but the pride of our seeing it,
> He revived all usages thoroughly worn out,
> The souls of them passed forth, the hearts of them torn out;
> And chief in the chase his neck he perilled,
> On a lathy horse all legs and length,
> With blood for bone, all speed no strength;
> — They should have set him on red Berold,
> With the red eye slow consuming in fire,
> And the thin stiff ear, like an abbey spire!"[4]

One feels at once how strongly Mr. Browning imagines what he is painting, and also how little the language contributes to the aid of the thought. The expression is universally ordinary and colloquial, often even slipshod, not, indeed, with any affectation of false simplicity, such as the Lake School at one time introduced, but of that kind which seems to show that the heat of the creative intellectual effort has subsided before the words are chosen at all, so that the wording is the cold choice of ordinary fluency *after* the imaginative thought has crystallized, instead of part of the moulding power of the mind itself. The lines we have chosen are not, perhaps, as far as the theme is concerned, a fair specimen of the defect we speak of (though they are quite as cleverly *worded* as any we can find), for the theme is not a poetical one. But take the following description — which transmits far more of the glow of feeling than most of his verses — of a moment of passionate despair, and compare it, as to mere power of expression, with Tennyson: —

> "Hush! if you saw some Western cloud
> All billowy-bosomed, over-bowed
> By many benedictions — sun's,
> And moon's, and evening star's at once —
> And so you, looking and loving best,
> Conscious grew, your passion drew
> Cloud, sunset, moonrise, starshine, too,
> Down on you, near and yet more near,
> Till flesh must fade, for Heaven was here!
> Thus leant she and lingered, — joy and fear!
> Thus lay she a moment on my breast."[5]

That is passion powerfully conceived, but far from powerfully, almost harshly, expressed. What, for instance, can "over-bowed" mean? Hear Tennyson: —

> "For how hard it seemed to me,
> When eyes love-languid through half-tears would dwell
> One earnest — earnest moment upon mine,
> Then not to dare to see! When thy low voice,
> Faltering, would break its syllables, to keep
> My own full-tuned, — hold passion in a leash,
> And not leap forth and fall upon thy neck,
> And on thy bosom (deep desired relief!)
> *Rain out the heavy mist of tears*, that weighed
> Upon my brain, my senses, and my soul."[6]

This may seem, and perhaps is, too relaxed in feeling, too little self-contained, less masculine than Mr. Browning, — but if we contrast the rich power of expression it contains with Mr. Browning's almost crabbed and quite awkward style, we shall see at once that Tennyson's imagination moulds its thoughts and words simultaneously, while Browning conceives his poem apart in his intellect, and trusts to an ordinary fluency of language to render it into speech. In the form and *medium* of poetic expression Mr. Browning is barely a poet; he is clever, striking, often grotesque, very often picturesque, but there is never that absolute identity between vision and speech which is the characteristic charm of verse, — the melody which carries "far into your heart"[7] the thought struggling for utterance.

This is Mr. Browning's great defect. On the other hand, how rich and varied is his intellectual imagination, how vigorous and full of width, and insight, and dramatic turns! His dramas are tame only because his own interest in them ceases when he has exhausted the illustration of his conception. He does not seem to wish to follow his characters through the turning point of their fortunes, in order to see the result to *them*. Dramatic as he is, he cares only to make his "men and women" explain themselves, not to see how they acquit themselves in the battle. There is none of that narrative interest in his dramas which is as essential to a good drama as the power of interpreting character itself. And hence his dramatic sketches, — of which, indeed, almost all his poems consist, — are more complete and satisfying than his regular dramas. Nothing can be more perfectly imagined than the poem called "The Bishop orders his Tomb at Saint Praxed's Church," — a mediaeval study[8] of unmatched force and humour, in which the physical aspects of the Catholic faith of that era, the jealousy of ecclesiastical rivalry, the passion for a splendid monument, which run through the piece are all rendered so life-like that it seems to introduce us into a new world of realities. Again, no one has ever drawn the worldly Catholic theologian as Mr. Browning has drawn him more than once in different aspects, — Bishop Blougram is one, — the legate Ogniben in the "Soul's Tragedy" another, — characters that live in the intellect, even without the aid of any high poetical expression, as long as the finest turns of poetical thought. Again, what a picture has Mr. Browning given in the epistle detailing the "strange medical experience of Karshish, the Arab physician," who, while Titus is besieging Jerusalem, stumbles on Lazarus at Bethany, and tries to account for the peculiar delusion of the man concerning his own death and resurrection by speaking of it as the result of violent epilepsy suddenly cured by a powerful physician but, nevertheless, gropes about between his obscure sense of something strange and subduing in the man's faith, and his own medical lore, with stately Oriental simplicity. Indeed, there is something peculiarly powerful about most of Mr. Browning's treatment of theological or semi-theological subjects. His strong intellectual imagination in dealing with the attitude of the mind towards naked truth, impresses one with far less sense of incompleteness than in dealing with the attitudes of human sentiment. To us the finest poem he has ever published is "Saul." In it even the metre and language are more expressive and noble than in any other, and the thoughts, at once dramatic and full of grandeur, rise gradually to a climax. The thoughts which fill David after he has played away Saul's madness are, indeed, in some sense an anachronism, and yet they seem to delineate the mingled innocence and depth of the

young shepherd's heart with a power that only the rarest poetic
imagination could give. It is Mr. Browning's characteristic that there are
so few parts of any of his poems which will impress the reader at all
adequately if severed from the whole. But, perhaps, the final burst of
David's faith when he finds that he has charmed away the horror for the
moment but can do no more, much as it suffers by being torn from the
more childlike image of him in the earlier part of the poem, will present
the fullest idea of Mr. Browning's peculiar power which it is possible to
give in our limited space: —

> "See the King—I would help him but cannot, the wishes fall
>   through.
> Could I wrestle to raise him from sorrow, grow poor to enrich,
> To fill up his life, starve my own out, I would—knowing which,
> I know that my service is perfect. Oh, speak through me now!
> Would I suffer for him that I love? So wouldst Thou—so wilt
>   Thou!
> So shall crown Thee the topmost, ineffablest, uttermost crown—
> And Thy love fill infinitude wholly, nor leave up nor down
> One spot for the creature to stand in! It is by no breath,
> Turn of eye, wave of hand, that salvation joins issue with death!
> As Thy Love is discovered almighty, almighty be proved
> Thy power, that exists with and for it, of being Beloved!
> He who did most, shall bear most; the strongest shall stand the
>   most weak.
> 'Tis the weakness in strength, that I cry for! my flesh, that I seek
> In the Godhead! I seek and I find it. O Saul, it shall be
> A Face like my face that receives thee; a Man like to me,
> Thou shalt love and be loved by, for ever; a Hand like this hand
> Shall throw open the gates of new life to thee! See the Christ
>   stand!
>
> "I know not too well how I found my way home in the night.
> There were witnesses, cohorts about me, to left and to right,
> Angels, powers, the unuttered, unseen, the alive, the aware—
> I repressed, I got through them as hardly, as strugglingly there,
> As a runner beset by the populace famished for news—
> Life or death. The whole earth was awakened, hell loosed with
>   her crews;
> *And the stars of night beat with emotion, and tingled and shot*
> *Out in fire the strong pain of pent knowledge*; but I fainted not,
> For the Hand still impelled me at once and supported,
>   suppressed
> All the tumult, and quenched it with quiet, and holy behest,
> Till the rapture was shut in itself, and the earth sank to rest."[9]

The two lines we have italicized are lines of expressive beauty rare in Mr. Browning; but even in this fine passage we see a certain hardness and inadequacy in the expression, while no one can ignore for a moment the great imaginative intellect at work. A more dramatic *intellect* than Mr. Browning's it would not be easy to find, — though it is somewhat too masculine, and his men, we think, are more perfectly conceived than his women. The reason why his dramatic genius is so incomplete seems to us to be that while intellectually dramatic he is not practically so. His dramas seldom breathe the living excitement of risk and hope. They have all but the one element which carries us through a drama, — the eagerness of forward glancing calculation, the venturesome passion, the march and procession of events towards loss or gain. This, for instance, is the chief thing which makes the tragedy of "Strafford" a failure. The minor characters are, it is true, too thin and sketchy. But Mr. Browning's intellectual conception of Pym, Strafford, and Charles is quite powerful enough for a fine drama, if there were any *vis* and passion in the events to equal the still-life study of the characters. Mr. Browning understands men chiefly on their intellectual side, — he paints the *tendencies* of a character, but not its action, and hence the want of popular force. Then, too, he never sufficiently prepares his ground; he expects his reader to plunge with him into the heart of a mediaeval or Italian situation without any gradual guidance.

All these things prevent Mr. Browning from being as popular as his great intellectual strength and variety of mind would deserve. But there is no living poet who commands a wider circle of ideas, a larger insight into the fundamental modes of thought which influence the most opposite classes of men, or whose works involve a more vigorous exercise to the imagination and richer food for thought.

A Luckless Poet

The *Quarterly Review*, while still fresh from the stupid and cruel intellectual onslaught which is said to have hastened the death of Keats, published an article in the number for May, 1820, on "The Poems of John Clare, a Northamptonshire peasant,"[1] which reads like an attempt to atone for that offence by the generous and even lavish appreciation which it bestowed on a young poet of real, though infinitely fainter, genius, but also of far lower station and apparently far more dependent on the kindly appreciation of the world. Neither the unkindness nor the kindness of the *Quarterly* was destined to have a fortunate issue. The former wounded a sensitive nature to the quick, which the writer could not have wished, while it probably raised the fame of the poetry which the critic could not understand and injured that of the critic – a result he can be still less supposed to have desired; the latter answered its kindly purpose better at first, for it brought a sudden gust of popularity to the author, but it issued in a result still sadder, – broken ambition and disordered reason, a manhood of deepening gloom as the visions of youth sank slowly into melancholy distance, and a "dreary gift of years"[2] that only terminated on the 20th inst. in the wards of an asylum for the insane.

John Clare was born on the 13th July, 1793, at Helpstone, where the border of Northamptonshire touches the fens of Lincolnshire. He was the son of Parker Clare, an agricultural labourer, one of "the toiling millions of men sunk in labour and pain,"[3] who earned his ten shillings a week in prosperous times, but who, when rheumatism had made him a cripple long before young Clare grew up, was receiving five shillings a week from the parish to eke out the scanty wages of his weakly son. John Clare was the elder and the smaller of twins, but yet the only survivor, – the sister who died immediately after her birth being, according to the testimony of the mother, Ann Clare, "a bouncing girl, while John might have gone into a pint pot." John had very early a thirst for knowledge, and, delicate as he was, before his father broke down used to earn by the labour of eight weeks enough to pay for a month's rude schooling. As soon as he could lead the forehorse of the harvest team he was set to work, and the *Quarterly* reviewer tells us, on knowledge derived from his mother, that while thus occupied he had the misfortune to see

77

the loader fall from the waggon and break his neck, which threw him into a fit, from the liability to which he did not recover till after a considerable lapse of time, and which even in 1820 was liable to return. No doubt this planted the seeds of that madness which the abrupt changes of his future fortunes, the fitful petting and neglect of high society, and, still more, pecuniary care, developed. He used to tell of the horror which his imagination caused him in the dark winter walks home from Maxey, a neighbouring village, where he was sent to buy flour for the family. His mother's ghost stories would all recur to his mind, and to drive them out he formed the habit of walking with his eyes fixed immoveably on the ground, versifying to himself some adventure "without a ghost in it," an intellectual effort which so effectually exorcised the goblins that he often reached home before he was himself aware of his approach. The preface to his first volume, written for him by some more practised hand, tells us that his first passion for poetry was excited by a glimpse of Thompson's "Seasons," which a fellow-labourer showed him in a field. He was so much delighted that he never rested till he had earned a shilling to buy himself a copy, and then set off on his errand to Stamford for that purpose so early that he reached the town before any shop was open. He brooded over Thompson till his own thoughts took a similar shape; and his father and mother, who always feared for his mind, admitted that "the gear was not mended" in their estimation when they discovered his habit of writing, and of writing, moreover, in verse. "When he was fourteen or fifteen," says Dame Clare (we quote the *Quarterly* reviewer) "he would show me a piece of paper, printed sometimes on one side and scrawled all over on the other, and he would say, 'Mother, this is worth so much;' and I used to say to him, 'Aye, boy, it looks as if it warr!' But I thought it was wasting his time," — a view which, according to the preface to one of his volumes, the old woman illustrated practically by going to the hole where he kept his verses, when she wanted paper to light the fires. When his father broke down, it was a hard toil to him to supply his place with the feeble frame which nature had given him. All his poems betray a profound sensitiveness, not only to the beauty of nature, but to the physical pain of the drudgery he had to endure, and which he seems to have endured with a good courage, if not quite without repining. This was one of his complaints: —

> "Toiling in the naked fields
> Where no bush a shelter yields,
> Needy Labour dithering stands,
> Beats and blows his numbing hands,
> And upon the crumping snows
> Stamps in vain to warm his toes."[4]

A delicate poetic organization earning a maximum wage of nine shillings a week on condition of going honestly through all the exposure and toil of the coarsest labour must indeed have had much to suffer, and felt a passionate desire to escape as from a life of slavery. At length, in 1818, when he was already 25 years old, and in great poverty, he determined to make an effort for a hearing. A printer at Market Deeping introduced him to a bookseller in Stamford, who thought well of his poems, gave him a few pounds at once, and promised more if they should succeed. Messrs. Taylor (of the firm of Taylor and Hessey), of Fleet street, took them from the Stamford publisher, and in 1820 they appeared, and were almost immediately made famous by the favour of the *Quarterly Review.*

There is reality, the sincerest love of nature, the minutest observation of nature, in the first of Clare's volumes, which, under the favourable notice of the *Quarterly Review,* speedily reached a fourth edition, but there is far less of the real breath of poetry than in what he afterwards wrote in dejection, and even in the intervals of madness. It is difficult to account for the enthusiasm of the *Quarterly* reviewer on any but the expiatory theory. "Some of his ballad stanzas rival the native simplicity of Tickel or Mallett," says the Reviewer, quoting not unpleasing stanzas, which may perhaps deserve that not very impressive praise, but which certainly could never take hold of any one's imagination, while some of Clare's later efforts do, we think, approach, though only approach, in depth of pathos to the heart-breaking but most musical wail of Cowper's lines on the "Castaway."[5]

The world, however, was not more fastidious than the *Quarterly* reviewer, and was delighted with the promise of a new pet. It was a danger not entirely unforeseen by Clare's kind friend in the *Quarterly.* The article ends with saying, "We counsel, we entreat him, to continue something of his present occupations; to attach himself to a few in the sincerity of whose friendship he can confide, and to suffer no temptations of the idle and the dissolute to seduce him from the quiet scenes of his youth, — scenes so congenial to his taste, — to the hollow and heartless society of cities; to the haunts of men who would court and flatter him while his name was new, and who when they had contributed to distract his attention and impair his health would cast him off unceremoniously to seek some other novelty." The danger was indeed only too great. Clare was sent for to London, and became the darling and lion of a season or two, and for a time a favoured contributor to keepsakes, annuals, and literature of that sort. But his was not a head to gain by experience of this kind; for his simple daisy-like poetry was always born of solitude and fresh air, and he tells us in one of the best of his early couplets that even in the country he loved most to walk and brood at dawn,

"Ere smoking chimneys sicken the young light
And Feeling's fairy visions fade away."[6]

And clearly he did not gain as a poet by his shortlived social success.
The volume he published in 1827, called the "Shepherd's Calendar,"
seems to us much inferior to either his earlier or his later verses, and
apparently it had little popularity. Indeed, his popularity, never
grounded on anything that had much real *root* in the public estimation,
had now greatly declined. No doubt neglect and this comparative literary
failure did much to depress him in health and spirits. He speaks of
imperfect health in his preface, and mentions it again with a more
melancholy air in the few lines of preface to the last volume he published
in 1835, – and not without reason. In 1837 his mind gave way, and he was
placed under the care of a physician at Epping Forest, with whom he
continued with intervals of improvement for many years. In 1841 an
appeal was issued on his behalf stating that anxiety for his wife and family
chiefly retarded his recovery, that 393*l.* had been raised for him and
invested in 1820, which produced, however, less than 14*l.* a year, that the
Marquis of Exeter and Earl Spencer allowed him 25*l.* a year more
between them, and that if 20*l.* a year more could be raised, his mind might
be sufficiently at ease to give his health a fair chance. How the appeal
was responded to we do not know; – he never rejoined his family, and
resided for many years before his death, with wandering mind but quite
harmless, and able often both to read and write, in the Northampton
County Lunatic Asylum, where he died last week.

The best lines Clare ever wrote were written during the dejection
which preceded and followed the partial alienation of his reason. In his
earlier poems there is simplicity, deep love of nature, but a want of
pervading unity of either thought or feeling. There is a tendency to
vagrancy of mind, to almost child-like cataloguing of natural objects and
impressions, which makes his poetry scrappy, – often, too, a fault of
Cowper's, whose verses his sometimes resemble. Indeed he says of
himself with touching simplicity in the volume of 1835: –

"I dwell on trifles like a child,
    I feel as ill becomes a man,
And yet my thoughts, like weedlings wild,
    Grow up and blossom where they can."[7]

But when he was sinking into dejection, the key-note of melancholy which
runs through his lines alone suffices to give them a certain unity of feeling,
and to impress a definite aspect on the natural scenes he still loves to
depict, more touching and specific than if you could see a sun setting in
soft glooms behind them. Thus he sings of "the poet" (evidently himself)
in his last issued volume: –

"He feeds on Spring's precarious boon,
  A being of her race,
Where light, and shade, and shower, and sun,
  Are ever changing place.

"To-day he buds and glows to meet
  To-morrow's promised shower,
Then crushed by Care's intruding feet
  He fades a broken flower."[8]

And probably the verses he wrote at intervals after his loss of reason are more expressive of the poet's own nature than anything he had yet published. One who visited him a few months since, and who found him deep in a volume taken from the library of the asylum, has placed at our disposal verses of no ordinary pathos, though broken by incoherencies corresponding probably to the chasms in the poor poet's own thought: —

I AM.

"I am, yet what I am none cares or knows,
My friends forsake me like a memory lost,
I am the self-consumer of my woes,
They rise and vanish in oblivious host,
Like shades in Love's and Death's oblivion tossed,
And yet I am, and live with shadows lost.

"Into the nothingness of scorn and noise,
Into the living sea of waking dreams,
Where there is neither sense of life nor joys,
But the vast shipwreck of my life's esteems,
And e'en the dearest whom I loved the best
Are strange, nay, far more strangers than the rest.

"I long for scenes where man has never trod,
A place where woman never smiled or wept,
There to abide with my creator God,
And sleep as I in childhood sweetly slept,
Untroubling and untroubled where I lie,
The grass below, — above the vaulted sky."[9]

It is a sad picture this of the rescue of a poet's nature from mere mechanic toil and drudgery only at the cost of his understanding and judgment, — though it may be that the fanning of that vital spark of his nature which made him a poet could not but have involved, in this life, the withdrawal for a time of that never large stock of vitality which he threw into the more common duties and relations of life. When the vital powers are small the concentration of them at the true focus of the nature not unfrequently involves their failure in the outlying faculties. This was what Wordsworth feared when he drew with so much power the panic of his own soul in contemplating the possible future: —

"We poets in our youth begin in gladness,
But thereof come in the end despondency and madness."[10]

That was the fate of Clare. During his long insanity, from the age of forty-four to his death at seventy, he probably realized far more keenly the strength and weakness of a merely receptive nature than at any period of his life. The lines we have just quoted express the shrinking anguish of a spirit which is acted upon by the life around him, but cannot re-act upon it, with an exquisite intensity. Everything was strange to him *not* because it was new, but because there can be no familiarity, no warmth of feeling without reciprocal influence, and he felt that he could not return to the world around him any part of the influence it exerted over him. So he attempted it less and less, and that distortion of imagination and of intellectual conception which follows a real abdication of all natural influence over the world, not less surely though more indirectly than an original twist in the faculties which report to us what goes on outside us, followed. He was even more unfitted to bear solicitude than neglect; and his physician thought that the solicitude had more to do with his insanity. We can well believe it. His poems show a very simple, if any, kind of vanity; but the evidence of a nature apt to brood, and to brood over trivial themes till it almost lost the power to act, is very great.

Few souls seem to us to need more distinctly something of a *new creation* than delicately receptive natures like Coleridge's, and, in a much lower sphere, Clare's, which have half-merged their voluntary in their receptive life. It is a relief to think of him as he loved to think of himself, asleep "with God," and breathing in, during that slumber of an eternal childhood, some fresh supply of a spiritual fire of which in this world he had enough for *either* poetry or life, but not enough for both.

Mr. Bagehot on Tennyson

Mr. Walter Bagehot is one of the very best of our English literary critics, and his recent essay (to which we briefly referred last week) on "The Pure, Ornate, and Grotesque Schools of Poetry," is one of the ablest of his many masterly and easy criticisms.[1] It would be far beyond the limits of a newspaper article to follow him through the thread of his reasoning, but as he aims at modifying one very important literary estimate of the present generation, the esteem, we mean, in which our only great living poet, Tennyson, is generally held, and, as we think, at modifying it, in great measure at least, erroneously, it is worth while explaining and discussing his doctrine. Mr. Bagehot's teaching is, that poetry should delineate *types*, classes, objects of more or less universal interest, and not descend to *mere* individual life, that the individualizing touches should be such, and such only, as bring out the universal features with greater force, that Tennyson's bias, the bias to which at least he too frequently yields, is towards "ornate" art, which smothers these universal or typical characteristics in accidental beauties, and that the most perfect example of this fault is to be found in his recent poem of "Enoch Arden," as the most perfect example of his purest style is to be found in the poem on "The Northern Farmer."[2] We suspect the theory of its practical applications may be partially right; that the critic, able as he is, has given a false reason for a correct general taste; and that the tendency of that theory, if it be admitted, is to condemn many of the Poet Laureate's most characteristic poems, — not only "Enoch Arden," still less, such traces only of excessive luxuriance as may no doubt be detected in many of the poems of Tennyson. Mr. Bagehot's theory seems indeed almost to ignore that field of poetry in which Tennyson's power is most singular and most perfect.

In the first place, we cannot believe it to be, as Mr. Bagehot evidently considers it, the *characteristic* of either art or poetry to "explain" to us our own experience. *That*, we should say, was rather the characteristic of philosophy than of poetry; and though it may be an incidental charm which some fine art and some fine poetry has that it does so, it is in the expressive rather than the "explanatory" power that the essential worth of both art and poetry consists. The powerful expression of the most vital and therefore generally the most latent characteristics of either nature, or man, or what lies partially above man, – *that* we take to be of the essence of the various fine arts, not the exposition or explanation of typical qualities, to which, indeed, either art or poetry may contribute much, and not perhaps accidentally, but which is by no means its first aim. Mr. Bagehot says a true picture is that which catches most perfectly the *general* character of the scenery it delineates, so as to embody it in an individual scene. But this reference back to the number of particular experiences embodied and generalized, cannot surely be of the essence of a fine picture. It is quite conceivable that a scene such as had never been beheld would make the noblest of pictures. Mr. Bagehot may say, "Yes, because it would be itself a type, though it were the only individual of that type." Then how is it *known* to be a type? Surely he is substituting the philosophical idea for the artistic? That which tells us that a scene to which we have never beheld anything analogous is a great subject for a picture, is, not its explaining or interpreting power, but that deep sense of vital harmony in the artist's mind which measures almost instantaneously the quantity, if we may so call it, of concordant living expression which any particular scene contains. It is not because it is a typical scene, but because it is full of mutually enhancing effects, because it has a capacity for bringing out living features which are elsewhere latent, that the artist knows it to be a great subject for his art. It may no doubt also be typical, – but it is not its capacity as a type, it is not its universality, but its fulness of qualities which agree with and set off each other, that recommends it to the artist. Raphael's "Madonna di San Sisto" is probably the greatest picture of its kind in the world,[3] and yet does much less to interpret any man's past experience than to give him one wholly new. It expresses a combination of infantine innocence and divine depth of nature, – it gathers into a baby's eye the gleam of the eternal world, the novel wonder of life, the foreboding of victorious passion, and the perfect rest of love, which we should say it was simply idle for an artist to attempt if the artist had not first shown us that the attempt could succeed. Well, surely the characteristic of this picture is not that it represents a type of which it is the only specimen, but that it gathers together for the first time a combination of harmonious expressions which only the greatest of artists could conceive and realize to others. It is in the individualizing power that the artist shows himself. Of course the larger the number of harmonious effects which he brings to a focus, the wider is the field of intellectual memory to which he appeals, but it is not the characteristic test of his success that he clears and deepens your understanding of the past, but that he thrills you with a sense of living power and harmony, of latent life brought to the surface, of new creation such as nature in her highest and happiest moments produces.

Precisely the same remark seems to us to apply to Mr. Bagehot's theory of poetry. He objects to "ornate" poetry because it drowns "the type" in overgrowths of individualizing effect. We should object to ornate poetry simply because it does *not* individualize, because it fails to connect together the many touches into a living whole. If it does this, we should deny that it could be ornate, and should care nothing about the type. If it fails to do this, whether through exuberance in detail, or through any other cause, it fails in art, because all art aims at life-like unity, and poetry especially aims at expressing the deepest unity of life. So far we are agreed with Mr. Bagehot in objecting to ornate poetry, though for a different reason. But his "typical" theory misleads him, we think, in his estimate of Tennyson. Thinking of a type as the true object of poetic delineation, he asks himself if Enoch Arden is a typical sailor. He discovers that Enoch Arden is not a typical sailor, that his feelings are too fine for a sailor's, his perceptions too delicate, his appearance too clean, and his fish-basket too ornamental. By the way, we may just observe that Enoch Arden is not properly a sailor at all, but a *fisherman,* – a very different class of man indeed, one much more trained to self-denial, and even generous heroism, than sailors – and not liable to many of the influences which have a peculiar effect in making the sailors as a class coarse, loose, and untidy. But to criticize "Enoch Arden" fairly, we do not think we have any business with the question of type at all, but only with the poet's conception. We do not think Mr. Tennyson had the slightest intention of describing the class even of fishermen, – still less of describing this fisherman dramatically, and from his own point of view. The whole idea of the poem seems to us to be, to describe an act of heroism from the poet's own centre of thought, – to describe it in the unity of its effect on his own imagination. And it seems at least as irrelevant to say that Enoch Arden, being a poor fisherman, would never have noticed the beauties of the tropical scenery in his desert island as it was in Lord Jeffrey, for instance, to describe Wordsworth's poem on "The Thorn" by saying that a woman in a red cloak went up to the top of a hill, said "Oh misery!" and came down again.[4] The whole perspective of Wordsworth's poem is false if you do not recognize the meditative centre of it in the poet's own mind, and the whole perspective of Mr. Tennyson's poem is also false if you transfer yourself to Enoch Arden's own point of view, except so far as a poet fashioning for himself the details of the story and following his hero in imagination through every step of it, would identify himself with it. You must grant a poet his own point of view as much as you would a painter. Mr. Bagehot looks through the fisherman's eyes and says Mr. Tennyson's picture is false. But Mr. Tennyson did not attempt for a moment to look through the fisherman's eyes, but to look through his own at the story of the fisherman's heroism. And surely it is artistically as justifiable to reflect the impressions which a great action produces on a poetic imagination, as it confessedly is to paint a landscape, as Wordsworth almost always does, through the subjective impressions it awakens rather than to paint its mere external features. We admit that Mr. Tennyson throws few meditative touches into the picture, but still everything seen and everything suffered is, without disguise, described as it would appear to the poet's narrating imagination, not dramatically.

But further, to view Mr. Tennyson's luxuriance as due to the love of ornament is, we think, to ignore his greatest power as a poet. It seems to us that his special genius is shown in delineating the highly complex moods of mind, — half observation, half thought, half feeling, half humour, — so characteristic of modern reflection. His finest moods are all highly composite. We find in most of them a relaxation and a nervous strength, a strong fibre of thought and a languor of sentiment, a flash of faith, a vivid pictorial instinct, and then a dying away of impulse, which represents the strangely mixed elements of our modern life making its first effort to combine in earnest the material and spiritual worlds, and scarcely knowing how to weave its science and its faith, its melancholy and its earnestness together, without doing injustice to something else in which it earnestly believes, or believes that it believes. Look, for instance, at such a poem as "Will Waterproof's Lyrical Monologue," — the wonderful ease with which it passes through the various moods of slight vinous exaltation, tender memory, wistful hopes, humorous observation kindling the fancy, freaks of conception dying away into bantering melancholy half grave, half gay: —

"No vain libation to the Muse,
    But may she still be kind,
And whisper lovely words, and use
    Her influence on the mind,
To make me write my random rhymes,
    Ere they be half-forgotten;
Nor add and alter, many times,
    Till all be ripe and rotten.

"I pledge her, and she comes and dips
    Her laurel in the wine,
And lays it thrice upon my lips,
    These favour'd lips of mine;
Until the charm have power to make
    New lifeblood warm the bosom,
And barren commonplaces break
    In full and kindly blossom.

"I pledge her silent at the board;
     Her gradual fingers steal
And touch upon the master-chord
     Of all I felt and feel.
Old wishes, ghosts of broken plans,
     And phantom hopes assemble;
And that child's heart within the man's
     Begins to move and tremble.

"Thro' many an hour of summer suns,
     By many pleasant ways,
Against its fountain upward runs
     The current of my days:
I kiss the lips I once have kiss'd;
     The gas-light wavers dimmer;
And softly, thro' a vinous mist,
     My college friendships glimmer."[5]

If Mr. Tennyson sometimes falls into over luxuriance, it is not usually through any tendency to adorn, but through the press of complex moods, – observing, thoughtful, religious, scientific, humorous, imaginative, – which cry for delineation in the same reverie. Sometimes no doubt he may fail to give the perfect unity to this complexity, and then Mr. Bagehot would call him ornate. But it is not due to the love of studding a bright picture with brilliant ornaments, but to the number of flying threads of feeling, fancy, and faith which he feels to be really wanting to the unity of his own conception. It is not that he is trying to beautify a "type" with a crowd of harmonious associations, but that he has not truly individualized his own conception till he has introduced the complex delicacies of expression all of which are of its very essence. Mr. Bagehot may say that a poet should choose simpler subjects. But if he did, he would fail to express the most characteristic life of the day, – which is not simple, but full of flickering lights and flying shadows. With a simple subject like "The Northern Farmer (Old Style)" Mr. Tennyson can be simple and direct enough. But "The Northern Farmer" *is* of the "old style," nor would Mr. Tennyson be the great poet he is if he had limited himself to poems on subjects so simple and massive, while he can paint so powerfully an inward life by no means simple and massive, but on the contrary, various, fitful, involved, eager, speculative, – yet still the life of our time, the best life we have, – *our own.* Classical and typical poetry may be good in its way; but it is not in classical and typical poetry that you can delineate the involutions of modern thought and feeling.

Atalanta in Calydon

There can be no question but that Mr. Swinburne is a true poet, though there certainly is a question whether *Atalanta in Calydon* is a great poem. Its choral songs — the drama is in imitation of the Greek tragedies — literally bubble over with melody, in which, by the way, they are *not* Greek; for no Greek poems, either in the iambic or the more lyrical measures, and the tragedies least of all, indulge in these thick-coming fancies, these *rushes* of feeling, these clouds of blossom on a single stem. The difference between the Greek poetry and the modern is to a great extent the same as the difference between single and double flowers. Not that Greek poetry has anything of the *wild* flower in it, for it is impossible to conceive anything more stately, more solemn, more perfectly imbued with the discipline of true culture, than the Greek tragic poetry. But it has the *singleness* of the wild flower, as compared with the complexity of the garden flower.[1] Indeed, so true is this that "classical" beauty, which *means* Greek beauty, has come to be another term for simplicity in the elements of beauty, as distinguished from the manifoldness of the romantic art. Nothing can be more striking than the contrast between the workmanship of Mr. Swinburne and the workmanship of his great models. The attempt to imitate the Greek tragedians in English verse has once before been made in our time by Mr. Matthew Arnold in *Merope*. That poem was a great failure as a poem, for it was unluckily quite devoid of life and interest. Merope sighed out her melancholy like a languid Oxford gentleman rather than like Antigone or Electra. There was nothing of the keen and solemn irony of the Greek sadness in her. Still the drama had its merits, not as a poem, but as a lesson in the singleness of conception which belongs to the Greek school of imagination. Mr. Arnold succeeded in imitating the fine thin fibre of thought or feeling which winds through a Greek tragedy. *Merope* was dull, but it was in some respects classical. Mr. Swinburne is curiously unclassical in his workmanship. His fancies and illustrations throng upon us with the short, quick panting breath of Shelley rather than with the single, measured chaunt of the Greek imagination. Take for instance the following from one of his many beautiful but very unclassical choral songs — songs, which

try to be, and are to a great extent, classical in the drift of their thought,
but to no extent classical in the mode of their expression: —

> When the hounds of spring are on winter's traces,
>   The mother of months in meadow or plain
> Fills the shadows and windy places
>   With lisp of leaves and ripple of rain;
> And the brown bright nightingale amorous
> Is half assuaged for Itylus,
> For the Thracian ships and the foreign faces,
>   The tongueless vigil and all the pain.
>
> Come with bows bent and with emptying of quivers,
>   Maiden most perfect, lady of light,
> With a noise of winds and many rivers,
>   With a clamour of waters, and with might;
> Bind on thy sandals, O thou most fleet,
> Over the splendour and speed of thy feet;
> For the faint east quickens, the wan west shivers,
>   Round the feet of the day and the feet of the night.
>
> Where shall we find her, how shall we sing to her,
>   Fold our hands round her knees, and cling?
> O that man's heart were as fire and could spring to her,
>   Fire, or the strength of the streams that spring!
> For the stars and the winds are unto her
> As raiment, as songs of the harp-player;
> For the risen stars and the fallen cling to her,
>   And the southwest-wind and the west-wind sing.
>
> For winter's rains and ruins are over,
>   And all the season of snows and sins;
> The days dividing lover and lover,
>   The light that loses, the night that wins;
> And time remembered is grief forgotten,
> And frosts are slain and flowers begotten,
> And in green underwood and cover
>   Blossom by blossom the spring begins.
>
> The full streams feed on flower of rushes,
>   Ripe grasses trammel a travelling foot,
> The faint fresh flame of the young year flushes
>   From leaf to flower and flower to fruit;
> And fruit and leaf are as gold and fire,
> And the oat is heard above the lyre,
> And the hoofed heel of a satyr crushes
>   The chestnut-husk at the chestnut-root.

And Pan by noon and Bacchus by night,
    Fleeter of foot than the fleet-foot kid,
Follows with dancing and fills with delight
    The Maenad and the Bassarid;
And soft as lips that laugh and hide
The laughing leaves of the trees divide,
And screen from seeing and leave in sight
    The god pursuing, the maiden hid.

The ivy falls with the Bacchanal's hair
    Over her eyebrows hiding her eyes;
The wild vine slipping down leaves bare
    Her bright breast shortening into sighs;
The wild vine slips with the weight of its leaves,
But the berried ivy catches and cleaves
To the limbs that glitter, the feet that scare
    The wolf that follows, the fawn that flies.[2]

Now take only the very first four lines; any one of the many metaphors crowded into them might, perhaps, be found in a stanza of equal length of Greek tragic poetry, but that would be as much as would happen, and assuredly it would not be followed up so closely, so crushed by the fertility of a prolific fancy into a space almost too narrow to leave a distinct impression on the mind. The exquisitely fine metaphor, "lisp of leaves," just reminds us of Aeschylus's beautiful expression of the sea's "unnumbered laughter" (ἀνήριθμον γέλασμα),[3] but Aeschylus would certainly never have introduced it in a position where it is in so much danger of being caught by the "hounds of spring," or entangled in "winter's traces," or given birth to by the "mother of months," or drowned in the "ripple of rain." Then, again, as poetry of nature, Mr. Swinburne's is much fuller of a certain sort of *sentiment* than the Greek. The Greek impersonations of nature are often bright and joyous, but seldom have even a touch of human sadness in them. Nature was beautiful to the Greeks, and not what we should call *heartless*, for they do not seem to have felt any anticipation of that keen modern feeling of desolation when the sun shines and the landscape sparkles around a new grave without betraying any shadow of sympathy with the mourners; but Greek nature was without a heart. It would be difficult to find many expressions such as those of which Shelley is so full, and which are common enough in Mr. Swinburne, representing Nature as sharing the sense of human exhaustion, sickness, faintness, and so forth. Such a line as —

    For the *faint* East quivers, the *wan* West shivers,

in which the eastern and western horizons are made to suggest two young ladies in different stages of hysteria, is to our ear entirely unlike the old

Greek nature-poetry. Nature was personified by them, no doubt, but it was personified by soulless beings, in whom the physical expressions were much more prominent than those half-suggested by "faint" and "wan," which introduce etherealized passions – the latter, "wan," especially, which is almost always applied to the sort of exhaustion in which the soul shines through the transparency of the physical system.

It may be thought that we are criticizing only the pseudo-antique form of Mr. Swinburne's poetry, and that the drama need not be the less effective for being full of the modern complexity and modern subjectivity (we apologize for the word, but know no better) of feeling. But this seems to us precisely the mistake of the poem. Mr. Swinburne, whose own imagination is in its forms in the highest degree romantic, or at least complex, has tried to bind it by a mould not at all adapted to it, and the resulting effect is, we think, less a poem than a number of different poems interspersed through a rather uninteresting framework of story. We do not mean to deny that the struggle in Althaea's mind between putting an end to her son's life and being guilty of the impiety of letting her brothers die unavenged and her mother's shade go unappeased, is drawn with wonderful force and passion. The physical *instincts* of a mother have never been more finely painted than in one of her speeches; but this is the sole beauty of the drama. There is no interest at all in the hero Meleager and his passion for Atalanta, no interest at all in Atalanta herself, no interest at all in the boastful brothers of Althaea, none in the King Oeneus, none in anyone but Althaea. Moreover, there is nothing of that awful solicitude concerning the divine *destiny* of the characters, which was of the very essence of the Greek tragedy. Mr. Swinburne does not feel, and consequently could not depict, that awe of the exploring intellect with which the higher Greek minds tried to pierce the gloom of mortal destiny, almost shrinking back from the task as profane, yet no sooner shrinking back than again forced forward by the very law of their nature to reach again into the cloud. If he had done so, his tragedy would have had a unity in it of which it is quite destitute. The curtain which gradually draws up before the eye in all the greater tragedies of Sophocles and Aeschylus showing us the shattered hopes behind it, with yet some dim bright point in the background from which consolation and strength may be derived, is not to be found here. The stimulus which carries us through the poem is the stimulus of very luxuriant poetic powers, not the stimulus derived from any movement in the plot. Till the final conflict in Althaea's mind begins, we may fairly say there is no interest in it as a drama at all. Then for a time no doubt the mind is fixed on a very powerful picture of human passion. Still, even then Mr. Swinburne has not succeeded in realizing for us the strength of the motive which induces Althaea to terminate her son's (and her own) life. The *resisting* force, maternal love and instinct, are very finely drawn; and from the resisting force we can infer, of course, the strength of the impelling force which finally conquers.[4] Still the Greek idea of impiety, of something due to the shades of Althaea's mother and brothers, is but feebly given; we can see what the poet means to delineate, but not realize its force.

The play will scarcely be more popular than Shelley's attempts in a similar direction, which are all now remembered for exquisite songs interspersed through them, but never cared for as wholes. Yet Mr. Swinburne's powers are very different in kind from Shelley's, though his mistake reminds us, especially in the choral songs, of Shelley's similar mistakes. For Mr. Swinburne is often difficult, but never mystic; confused, but not shadowy; he depicts desire, too, in a less etherealized and pallid form than Shelley, and, consequently, without that chief characteristic of Shelley's feverish poetry, the wonderful genius for expressing the cry of an eager and yet unsatisfied, insatiable passion. The bitter wail of Shelley's vivid yet forlorn desires really constitutes him a poet. Mr. Swinburne is much more concrete and bright with the actual colours of life, but then, as far as we can see, he expresses no *one* mood or attitude of mind with anything like Shelley's wonderful and yet hectic genius.

The Reporter in Mr. Dickens

At the dinner of the Newspaper Press Fund on Saturday last Mr. Dickens gave a very amusing reminiscence of his life as a reporter for *The Morning Chronicle* during the six or seven years – the years, we conclude, from 1829 to 1836, or thereabouts[1] – previous to the success of his *Sketches by Boz* and the consequent recognition of his original genius by the English public. The brief autobiographic sketch had more, we think, than the *ad captandum* interest of recommending to the generosity of the public a profession which had been distinguished by once numbering a man of genius in its ranks; it throws some light on the merits and defects of his own great powers as an author. He speaks of his old profession as inspiring him (then a boy) with a sort of passion, by its adventurous character in those years and the call it made on his energy and skill. "Returning home," he says, "from excited public meetings to the waiting press in London, I do verily believe that I have been upset in almost every description of vehicle known in this country.... I have often transcribed for the printer from my shorthand notes important public speeches in which the strictest accuracy was required, and a mistake in which would have been to a young man severely compromising, writing on the palm of my hand by the light of a dark lanthorn in a postchaise and four, galloping through a wild country through the dead of the night at the then surprising rate of fifteen miles an hour. The very last time I was at Exeter I strolled into the castle yard there, to identify for the amusement of a friend the spot on which I once 'took,' as we used to say, an election speech of my noble friend Lord Russell, in the midst of a very lively fight, maintained by all the vagabonds in that division of the county, and under such pelting rain that I remember two good-natured colleagues who chanced to be at leisure held a pocket handkerchief over my note-book, after the manner of a State canopy in an ecclesiastical procession. I have worn my knees by writing on them on the old back row of the old gallery of the old House of Commons, and I have worn my feet by standing to write in a preposterous pen in the old House of Lords, where we used to be huddled like so many sheep kept in waiting till the woolsack might want re-stuffing." No wonder Mr. Dickens adds that he never has forgotten the fascination of that old pursuit, that "the pleasure I used to feel in the rapidity and dexterity of its exercise has never faded from my heart, — whatever little cunning of hand or head I took to it or acquired in it I have so retained that I fully believe I could renew it to-morrow," — for in some important intellectual, if not mechanical respects, Mr. Dickens has never intermitted "the cunning taken to or acquired in" that pursuit, and did not cease to be a reporter even after he became an author. In listening to a dull speech his fingers still, he says, will frequently trace automatically on the table-cloth the characters that would be requisite to record it; and even when this is not the case, we have little doubt that his observation follows the various events he witnesses with that vigilant reporting *sense* — that habit of business-like mental notation — which absorbs itself in engraving their outward form and connection as indelibly as may be on the surface of the memory, using such notes and signs for that purpose as will make it most easy to recall their essential features. In short, even if, as is most likely, it were Mr. Dickens's original genius for observation which made him so good a reporter, it seems pretty certain that his habit of reporting re-acted on his genius for observation and moulded it in a particular direction; for the greatest characteristic in all his works after their humour (which of course reporting could neither give nor strengthen) is deeply marked by the influence of this profession in that more exciting and eager form which in those days of few conveniences it assumed.

There is probably no other novelist in English literature who can catalogue all the minutiae of every scene he wishes to describe with anything like the accuracy and effect of Mr. Dickens. It has been said that if he goes down a street he will note involuntarily every piece of orange-peel or loose paper which he passes in that street,[2] but he uses this power with nothing of the tediousness of literal observation, and also with nothing of that kind of not infrequent art which uses outward associations as the mere paints with which to externalize an inward mood. What Mr. Dickens does in painting is, to let the impression of a scene fill his mental retina, and then selecting any distinguishing feature, whether fog, or drizzle, or rapid motion, or squalor, or cold, or what you will — which gives a character and unity of effect to the whole — to throw all the emphasis of his description on that, and make all the subsidiary touches centre in that and return into that. He is in this only an ideal reporter, whose business it is to keep strictly to what he sees, and yet introduce if he can sufficient perspective into his picture to prevent his sketch from falling into an auctioneer's catalogue. In general Mr. Dickens is wonderfully effective in this sort of work. No one who has ever read the description of a London Christmas Eve in his *Christmas Carol* will be likely to forget his picture of the gaslit streets and their plethora of preparation for high feeding; and still better is the picture of the utter dismalness of Snow Hill and the neighbourhood of the Saracen's Head on a wet Sunday.[3] In fact the examples of admirable realistic reporting of this kind in his works are almost innumerable. But there are not a few cases in which the reporter's instinct for getting a point of sight, a centre, for his picture, has not been corrected by any artistic instinct, and the consequence is a vulgar sort of emphasis on some one external string, caught at in a hurry, as it were, and twanged at with a triumphant sort of pertinacity till, as he makes Mrs. Gamp say, "fiddle-strings is weakness to expredge my nerves this night."[4] For example, there is the famous drive in *Martin Chuzzlewit*, when Tom Pinch goes up to town outside the coach, and Mr. Dickens considering that fast motion and high spirits were the true leading features to dominate the variety of that changing picture, insisted upon putting 'Yoho!' before every sentence for a matter of three close pages of description, after this fashion: — "Yoho past hedges, gates, and trees, past cottages and barns, and people going home from work. Yoho past donkey-chaises drawn aside into the ditch, and empty carts with rampant horses whipped up at a bound upon the little watercourses and held by struggling carters close to the five-barred gate until the coach had passed the narrow turning in the road. Yoho by churches dropped down by themselves in quiet nooks," and so on, and so on, yoho *ad infinitum*.[5] Now, if any one will try to read this passage aloud he will feel so heartily abashed and humiliated at about the third or fourth yoho that he will, we venture to say, break down long before he gets through the thirty or forty to which the author condemns him for the sake of this artificial effect. The same fault may be remembered in the passage where "the Temple fountain sparkles" with such damned iteration "in the sun" to keep time to Ruth Pinch's love-making.[6] If Mr. Dickens throws far more than the art of the reporter into most of his scenery, he throws far more than his artificial trickery into a few scenes, where his genius is merged in the mere glaring trade-effects of the catchword style of description. There is a very marked predominance of this worst feature of his external descriptiveness, in his most recent work, — the one still in course of publication. Here is the description of a dinner-party as reflected in a big mirror in the dining-room, — the central feature being no really characteristic effect at all, only that very remarkable physical property of the human body, liability to reflection in looking-glasses: —

> "The great looking-glass above the sideboard, reflects the table and the company. Reflects the new Veneering crest, in gold and eke in silver, frosted and also thawed, a camel of all work. The Heralds' College found out a Crusading ancestor for Veneering who bore a camel on his shield (or might have done it if he had thought of it), and a caravan of camels take charge of the fruits and flowers and candles, and kneel down to be loaded

with the salt. Reflects Veneering; forty, wavy-haired, dark, tending to corpulence, sly, mysterious, filmy — a kind of sufficiently well-looking veiled-prophet, not prophesying. Reflects Mrs. Veneering; fair, aquiline-nosed and fingered, not so much light hair as she might have, gorgeous in raiment and jewels, enthusiastic, propitiatory, conscious that a corner of her husband's veil is over herself. Reflects Podsnap; prosperously feeding, two little light-coloured wiry wings, one on either side of his else bald head, looking as like his hairbrushes as his hair, dissolving view of red beads on his forehead, large allowance for crumpled shirt-collar up behind. Reflects Mrs. Podsnap; fine woman for Professor Owen, quantity of bone, neck and nostrils like a rocking-horse, hard features, majestic head-dress in which Podsnap has hung golden offerings. Reflects Twemlow; grey, dry, polite, susceptible to east wind, First-Gentleman-in-Europe collar and cravat, cheeks drawn in as if he had made a great effort to retire into himself some years ago, and had got so far and had never got any farther. Reflects mature young lady; raven locks, and complexion that lights up well when well powdered — as it is — carrying on considerably in the captivation of mature young gentleman; with too much nose in his face, too much ginger in his whiskers, too much torso in his waistcoat, too much sparkle in his studs, his eyes, his buttons, his talk, and his teeth. Reflects charming old Lady Tippins on Veneering's right; with an immense obtuse drab oblong face, like a face in a tablespoon; and a dyed Long Walk up the top of her head, as a convenient public approach to the bunch of false hair behind, pleased to patronize Mrs. Veneering opposite, who is pleased to be patronized. Reflects a certain 'Mortimer,' another of Veneering's oldest friends; who never was in the house before, and appears not to want to come again, who sits disconsolate on Mrs. Veneering's left, and who was inveigled by Lady Tippins (a friend of his boyhood) to come to these people's and talk, and who won't talk. Reflects Eugene, friend of Mortimer; buried alive in the back of his chair, behind a shoulder — with a powdered epaulette on it — of the mature young lady, and gloomily resorting to the champagne chalice whenever proffered by the Analytical Chemist. Lastly, the looking-glass reflects Boots and Brewer, and two other stuffed Buffers interposed between the rest of the company and possible accidents."[7]

This is no doubt clever reporters' art, very artificial, and woven together by a trick of mechanical perspective both fatiguing and disagreeable.

In higher matters, too, than mere external description you see both the good and bad influence of Mr. Dickens's old profession upon his genius; though probably its good predominates. In sketching a personal character, wherever the sketch is worth anything the key-note is uniformly some mere external mark or peculiarity by which a reporter would label a passing figure and again recognize it. The examples are so numerous that it is scarcely worth while even to recall any instances beyond those of the above extract. In all Mr. Dickens's novels there is the same trick of labelling characters either by wry legs which carry them in unexpected directions, or by a habit of biting the thumb, or by malicious dwarfishness, or a pokerish stiffness of bearing, or by peculiar cotton umbrellas, or by the loss of an eye, or by some other of the thousand trade-marks Mr. Dickens stamps on his *dramatis personae*.[8] With an ordinary novelist this practice would be a pure evil. With Mr. Dickens (though often abused by him) it proves the secret of a great power. For he is not in any sense a painter of human nature, – he is a great humourist in human affairs, and it is round this personal label which he fixes on his figures that he accumulates all possible or conceivable illustrations and variations of the same characteristic till it becomes magnified to the most ludicrous dimensions. Hence the reporter's habit of affixing a sort of graphic personal note to each principal figure in any scene he is describing becomes in Mr. Dickens's hands the medium of most happy and humorous caricature, as well as of a little dull and over-emphatic exaggeration. Nothing would be more tedious than the harping on an obvious personal peculiarity if Mr. Dickens had not so large a power of humour, but *with* this, he makes it the centre of a world of grotesque similarities and contrasts. The hurried reporter's *note* becomes a mere hint for the accumulation of a host of novel situations, all gathered from real life, but all related to the particular pattern suggested by the initial trait. Yet there is always that total absence of judgment and reflecting power which one would expect from the hasty superficial survey of life requisite to get graphic effects out of hurried and pre-occupied observation. Whenever Mr. Dickens puts an *idea* into his novels, it is a crude, broad, hasty, claptrap idea, such as his crusade against Chancery in *Bleak House.* His eye catches traits far more quickly than his imagination deciphers their real meaning *as* traits of character, but then that does not matter; for, the basis of a picture once given him, the superstructure is all fiction supplied by his own deep sense of humour and his enormous scrap-book of illustrations, not fact at all. There is a certain flavour of humour, too, in the mere idea which Mr. Dickens carries with him more or less into all his stories, that he is a sort of invisible reporter, taking graphic notes for the world of the actions of his own fictitious figures. From this cause he never seems *inside* even his own creations, but always watching them and their peculiarities from outside, like one engaged to look after them. He even writes at times as if he had all the associations of a public meeting around him, he being in the reporters' gallery, — as when he says of some poor woman chastising her child in the primitive manner, that she inflicted "a rapid succession of sharp sounds *resembling applause*, and then left him on the coolest paving-stone in the court weeping bitterly and loudly lamenting."[9] A keen-eyed reporter of the universe, who sees hastily and then fetches illustrations from all quarters of the horizon with the utmost fertility of humour, to create a conception in conformity with the figure that just flashed for a moment across his field of view — such is Mr. Dickens.

Clarissa

It is almost as much a change of air to turn from the lively rattle of our railway novels to the solemn coach-and-six of Richardson's full-dress genius, as to exchange London for the old towns of Germany, where the outside dress of the middle ages still abides, even within hearing of the express trains. What a gulf, for example, between Richardson and Mr. Trollope![1] And the difference is not exactly in the rate of their own movement as authors, for Mr. Trollope is tranquil and minute enough, and on proper occasion Richardson can be as lively and effervescent as any novelist of any day. The difference is in the movement of the world which they describe. A hundred modern interests ripple the mind of to-day for every one that swept across that of Richardson's day, and hence he studied the breaking of a single wave with as much care and art as a modern artist would give to a whole storm at sea. Richardson made men and angels lay aside their proper concerns, – almost brought the whole world to a standstill, – to gaze on the trial of one woman's virtue. Every one whom he introduces, he introduces only with relation to this one purpose. Clarissa's own family have their meaning only in Clarissa. They live but to persecute her into dangers from which she cannot escape, and to mourn over their own life as a wreck when their stupidity and obstinacy have borne their natural fruits. Lovelace, superior as he is as a dramatic creation to Clarissa and every other character, exists only to tempt and betray her; Miss Howe only to receive her confidences and sustain her by her sympathy; Belford but to show what was her persuasive power over a dissolute heart. Enormous as are the proportions of the narrative, one centred more completely in one figure, and almost in one attitude of that figure, is nowhere else to be found. The long eight volumes in which it was formerly published are wholly occupied with an account, the *full* size of life, of every incident which contributed to or impeded and delayed the *dénouement*. While Mr. Trollope travels rapidly and lightly over hundreds of little incidents which are almost independent of each other, and related only as illustrating the various characters he has brought together in his tales, Richardson accompanies slowly in his state coach the slow march of the single temptation with which he occupies his story. No doubt there are very few even of modern writers who travel over so much ground of miscellaneous incident as Mr. Trollope, but even those who adhere most closely to the development of a single story, take care to give a constantly changing attitude to the principal actors in relation to it; they do not magnify a single moral attitude with Richardson's magnificent pertinacity and microscopic minuteness till they have exhausted its significance and sculptured it, as it were, in solid marble; rather do they give a series of successive sketches of the same characters in different aspects. As we have implied, much of this fixity of manner may be due to the time. In that less busy age, the leisurely classes made a great deal more of one purpose than we do of many, and hence the characters themselves were less mobile than now, fell into stiffer moulds, brooded more over a few subjects, and made more solemn and elaborate preparations for given effects. But still if a Richardson would be more surprising than ever in the present age, he was a curious literary phenomenon even then, almost as strong a contrast to Fielding as to our modern writers. His imagination was microscopic, and required as definite a focus to its object-glass as a microscope. If any family nowadays could by any chance devote the *time* to breaking in a refractory girl to a disagreeable alliance which the Harlowes devoted to attempting to force Mr. Solmes on Clarissa, certainly no other artist could reproduce those tedious months with the patient exactitude of Richardson. Precisely three months given up to family councils, voluminous letters, interviews, negotiation, diplomacy, protests, protocols, threats of war, and this only the introduction to the real story! The first two volumes of the old edition are exactly like the Schleswig-Holstein blue-books, only that Mr. James Harlowe, junior, was much more peremptory than Lord Russell.[2] And this is all prelude. Clarissa does not take up the attitude in which Richardson really designs to sculpture her till after her flight from home, till after the rash step when, as she pathetically wails in her letter to Miss Howe, "your Clarissa is gone off with a man."[3] Then, the delicate but respectful inflexibility with which she has resisted the mixed prayers and bullyings of the family league, is changed into an equally keen but more proud and suspicious resistance to Lovelace's gay frauds and deep scheming passion. Yet even in the introduction she is thrown into the attitude which Richardson thought the most characteristic of feminine purity, — one of perpetual guard against masculine encroachments; but while the earlier struggle is a mere test of pertinacity under almost brutal pressure, the engagement with Lovelace is one which calls for subtlety, skill, vigilance, and the courage of despair.

It is easy to criticize Richardson's conception of a paragon of feminine excellence in Clarissa. Her notion of purity is clearly legal, her humility is far from genuine; she is evidently as conscious as her biographer that she is a spectacle for angels and for men, and her demure saintship, when she devotes herself with almost the relish of an epicure to dying in the way that may heap the most glowing coals of fire on her persecutors' heads, though never without a certain transparent beauty and sweetness, is still full of didactic triumph. Then, in spite of the real sweetness, there is a drop of feminine venom, of which Richardson himself is scarcely aware, at the bottom of Clarissa's character from beginning to end. In her very first letter, before her sister Arabella has begun her malignities, Clarissa dissects the vanities and radical vulgarity of her sister's mind to her friend Miss Howe with the most unflinching hand. And at the very last, though she professes to have forgiven all her enemies, she launches little poisoned arrows at them in her pious will and farewell letters which render the title so often applied to her of "divine lady" not a little amusing. This, for instance, is the red-hot coal she bequeaths to her sister's maid, Betty, who harassed her much through the preliminary home persecution: — "To my sister's maid, Betty Barnes, I bequeath ten pounds, to show that I resent not former disobligations, which I believe were owing more to the insolence of office and to natural pertness than to personal ill-will."[1] That is a pretty effectual retaliation for a saint to launch at a waiting-maid from the tomb. Towards her betrayer, Lovelace, of course something of natural horror might fairly be mingled with her Christian forgiveness, but the actual state of her mind seems to us to have in it more of lingering spite and less of Christian forgiveness or profound pity than the author wished to delineate. The nice little dramatic scene in which she intends her own corpse shall play the most impressive part, looks to us rather more like feminine revenge than it seemed to Clarissa's admirers: — "I could wish, if it might be avoided without making ill-will between Mr. Lovelace and my executor, that the former might not be permitted to see my corpse. But if, as he is a man very uncontrollable, and I am nobody's, he insist upon viewing *her dead* whom he once before saw in a manner dead, let his gay curiosity be gratified. Let him behold, and triumph over the wretched remains of one who has been made a victim to his barbarous perfidy, but let some good person, as by my desire, give him a paper while he is viewing the ghastly spectacle, containing these few words only, — 'Gay, cruel heart! Behold here the remains of the once ruined yet now happy Clarissa Harlowe! See what thou thyself must quickly be, and REPENT!' Yet to show that I die in perfect charity with *all the world,* I do most sincerely forgive Mr. Lovelace the wrongs he has done me."[5] That is, she forgives him in the sense of reserving to herself the complete monopoly of wounding him by verbal taunts and stings, posthumous or otherwise. That privilege, even though it require little theatric arrangements over her coffin, she cannot give up. But all this is only criticism on Richardson's conception of feminine perfection, not on the picture of Clarissa, which is studied with absolute consistency and wonderful nicety throughout. She is brought up to think herself the centre of the universe, — grandfather, father, mother, uncles, brother and sister, servants, every one bowing down before her, even as a child, as the sheaves of Joseph's brethren bowed in his dream towards his own sheaf.[6] Her "friends and favourers," as in the time of her adversity she writes to Dr. Lewin, one of her principal "favourers," have a sort of right, she thinks, to know the history of her trials and of her glorious justification. She is fully aware of all her gifts. "Did I not," she writes to Miss Howe, "did I not *think* more and deeper than most young creatures think; did I not *weigh*; did I not *reflect*; I might perhaps have been less obstinate. Delicacy (may I presume to call it?) *thinking, weighing, reflection* are not blessings, — (I have not found them such), — in the degree I have them. I wish I had been able in some very nice cases to have known what indifference was; yet not to have my *ignorance* imputable to me as a fault. Oh my dear! the finer sensibilities, if I may suppose mine to be such, make not happy."[7] Yet in spite of all this didactic egotism in Clarissa, not unmingled with a resentment to those who do not recognize her merit which has often a touch of spite, there runs a delicacy of fibre — (*purity* meant something quite different in Richardson's day and in our own), — a sweet persuasiveness, and a high-bred feminine *mettle,* which fascinates us almost against our will. In letter after letter, volume after volume, she is represented almost in the same attitude of half-affrighted, half-resentful feminine pride, longing to trust and finding no one near her to trust, thinking "deeper than most young creatures think," half detecting falsehood by the slightest and most uncertain signs, waging dangerous war with the most prolific and unscrupulous schemer ever represented in English fiction, and overwhelmed at last only to rise with keener and more statuesque pride out of the struggle. The moral perfection Richardson attributes to Clarissa few modern readers will concede. Her family early took the right way to make her self-sufficient and pragmatic, and therein, in spite of her natural sweetness, they fully succeeded. But no one can deny the rare delicacy of conception and finish in the execution of the figure, though few will subscribe to the sculptor's standard of moral beauty.

But if the central figure is striking, the secondary one is infinitely more so. Richardson is said to have borrowed the notion of Lovelace from Lothario in Rowe's *Fair Penitent,* and Dr. Johnson asserted that the superiority of the great novelist lay in the more effectual rendering of Lovelace's evil qualities, so that the reader loses his wonder at the man's irrepressible elasticity and gaiety in indignation and hatred.[8] But this is a very false criticism — the reverse of the real truth. Rowe's 'Lothario' is a less guilty but also a much less distinguished profligate than Lovelace. He is almost a common-place rake, with little more than a hint of the wonderful *diablerie* and shining qualities of Richardson's greatest dramatic creation. The wonderful element in that creation is that though so treacherous, hard-hearted, selfish, cruel, fertile in plots, Richardson never does make Lovelace hateful, although he never gives the slightest false colour of attractiveness to his vices. There is a strange buoyancy about him, which makes his various attempts to subdue his "dearest creature," as he calls Clarissa, to his will, seem almost more like the onset of a leaping wave than the wickedness of a perverted conscience. His worst crimes are more like a gay demon's wanton tricks than a devil's delight in guilt. His plotting nature overflows involuntarily; there is the permanent exaltation of high spirits about him, — the temper of a man who sees only *mischief* in ruining women, and has never had a glimpse of the meaning of sin; — then there is an absolute candour in his treatment of himself to his friend; though he will contrive any lie, however elaborate, to effect his purpose, he palliates nothing in confessing himself, though he confesses with the levity and *verve* of a mind unable to realize the monstrous nature of his own guilt. His own purposes, once taken, are so completely a law to him that they obliterate all moral objections; but then where candour does not stand in the way of his ends, his candour is perfect. Altogether a more extraordinary conception of crimes and sins almost beyond the possibility of pardon springing out of a self-willed and mischief-making, rather than a diabolic *spirit*, was never realized. The man's brilliant nature seems to dance in the buoyancy of its tormenting inventiveness, and yet his truthfulness concerning himself to himself never fails him, and his eye for moral beauty is never clouded. He seems driven by the mere swelling of his irresistible impulse to dishonour Clarissa, because he feels her so worthy of all honour; his complete horror of a constraining law and absolute repulsion to anything like legal restraint is vexed within him by her conspicuous legality. The *diablerie* within him leaves him no rest till he breaks down the barrier. His evil is all wantonness. Richardson assuredly did not and could not hate this villain, and even throws out a vague hope of his final penitence. The wit, spring, and vivacity of the character, — contrasting strikingly as it does with Richardson's formal and ceremonial style, — evidently endeared it to him, for the favourite child is frequently the one most unlike the parents. Yet nowhere is there the faintest approach to embellishing his vices. It is the enormous surface-vitality, not the licence, that Richardson is proud of. He makes Miss Howe, in one of her lively letters draw this happy conjectural sketch of Lovelace as a child, which sufficiently shows what Richardson intended to be the *root* of his levity and licence: — "I have supposed Lovelace a curl-pated villain, full of fire, fancy, and mischief; an orchard robber, a wall climber, a horse rider, without saddle or bridle, neck or nothing; a sturdy rogue, in short, who would kick and cuff, and do no right, and take no wrong of anybody; would get his head broke, then a plaster for it, or let it heal of itself; while he went on to do more mischief, and if not to get, to deserve broken bones."[9] It is the want of any purely evil *motive*, though with a complete absence of any good motive, — the intrinsic wilfulness of Lovelace's purposes, which cannot give up their own tyrannous desire to prevail, and are not sufficiently impressionable by the wishes of others to be moved by pity or sympathy, — which a little palliates Lovelace's iniquities to Richardson and his readers. His evil is due to a sort of physical levity, to the playing of a gay fountain of pure self-will, that sparkles away in the sun, like a natural spring that has no responsibility for its own course.

Nor are any of the minor figures in this wonderful book less completely finished. Though they all have their centre and unity in the paragon Clarissa in a manner highly improbable and irritating, nothing can be more minute than the characteristic finish given to each; — the obstinate, selfish, imperious brother, whose intelligence is so inferior to his pertinacity; the vain, spiteful sister, who almost enjoys her sister's dishonour, but is overwhelmed with grief at her death; the weak, fond mother, who dare not assert her own will to save her daughter; the gouty, querulous father, who is persuaded he is doing it all himself when he is the mere instrument of his son; the uncles, equally weak, but after so different a fashion, — one with all the tenderness of a soft nature, the other with all the bustle of a vulgar "plump soul," as Miss Howe calls the retired naval officer; Miss Howe, again, the piquant auburn beauty, with her lively wit and knowledge of character, and her ingrained impertinence to all who attempt any control over her except Clarissa; then, her mother, who in spite of her own vulgar vanity and stinginess is really wrapt up in the daughter, whose more free and generous nature she so profoundly admires, — even Mr. Brand, the pompous curate, with his string of classical quotations, and Joseph Leman, the semi-hypocritical man-servant who delights to call himself a "plain man," — all are chiselled out with wonderful fidelity and often with a humour which ought to have gained Richardson a place with Fielding and Smollett in Thackeray's *English Humourists*.

Clarissa is a book in which the lines are cut so much deeper than any novelist cares to cut them now, the whole treatment is so completely the size of life, without being (after the first two volumes) in any degree dull, that though no one character except that of Lovelace reaches to the highest standard of originality, they together form a group impressed with the manners of the seventeenth century,[10] which takes its place amongst those most vivid of all memories which we retain some vague impression of having derived from personal experience. It is a strange and somewhat quaint result of Richardson's didactic design that he succeeded in making for ever memorable a wanton being without any very distinct trace of a conscience, and gave the *artistic* triumph at least to his villain, instead of to the paragon of excellence whose character he had so painfully and minutely laboured.

Mr. Carlyle and his Constituency

The Edinburgh students have conferred their highest honour – 'what honour their votes could confer,' as Mr. Carlyle might say, – on Mr. Carlyle, and elected him their new Rector by a majority of more than two to one over the "Phantasm Captain" of her Majesty's Opposition, Mr. Disraeli.[1] The *Saturday Review*, in its able scorn for their not very important proceedings, and its desire to see the youngsters of the University falling into the regular intellectual drill of the session a day or two sooner, instead of wasting, as it thinks, the time intended for lessons in a semi-political mock fight with no consequences, perhaps forgets that, after all, one of the most important parts of a University education is the opportunity for frequent and eager intellectual collision between young minds in nearly the same stage of growth concerning the literary interests which come home most closely to them. The *Saturday Review* evidently prefers the stricter discipline of the *"Hinterschlag Gymnasium"* – "Hindersmite Academy" – at which Professor Teufelsdröckh studied in his youth, to University freedom for men of this age.[2] But though doubtless a good deal of nonsense would be talked in public by very young men on all such occasions, as happens indeed in every college and university debating society, the occasion for such nonsense is probably the occasion also for far the most *spontaneous* intellectual efforts which men under University training ever put forth; and we very much question whether any days of the University session are really more fruitful of those awakening efforts due to eager private reading and discussion on hotly contested points which first teach the student something of the nature and limits of his own powers, than those spent in canvassing the literary claims of such a man as Mr. Carlyle against those of such a man as Mr. Disraeli.[3] As for the intrinsic utility of the proceeding, what is the intrinsic utility of a blundering Greek exercise beyond a lesson in accuracy? And is a lesson in intellectual accuracy always more important than a lesson in intellectual activity? Anything to awaken the intellectual society of a University into real vitality cannot well be a superfluous part of its routine. Young men teach each other in college life at least as much as they are taught by superior knowledge and wisdom. And on the whole, the Edinburgh students have in their instance done credit to their usage.

They have practically declared that Mr. Carlyle's writings have stirred them much more than Mr. Disraeli's, which is a very proper state of mind for University men. Perhaps indeed the Scotch clannishness had as much to do with the votes of the great majority as literary qualities or political principle. But without reference to politics we think an English university would have pronounced the same verdict. For Mr. Carlyle's genius is far better suited to tell with full effect upon the young than that of any other great man of the day. Even his greatest faults have strong fascinations for men just beginning to think of what life means. He makes old truths loom gigantic, vague, and fresh upon the eye, and stimulates the dreamy germinating conceptions of early thought. To a few this may be a dangerous excitement, but to the many, even of the young (since the chief danger of regular education is the danger of mere humdrum acquisition of classified scraps of information), Mr. Carlyle's writings are certainly likely to do infinitely more good than harm. What has the new Rector of Edinburgh University effected on the whole for past generations of young men?

One of the most brilliant preachers of the day commenced a certain sermon — preached, if we remember rightly, on the text, "And their foolish heart was darkened" — by the remark that "Any one who looked at a familiar landscape *with his head inverted*" would be struck by the extraordinary softness, beauty, and brilliance of a scene which under its ordinary aspect has ceased to fascinate or strike the attention at all.[4] The preacher explained this effect by the deadening power of custom on all human faculties of perception, not only visual, but moral, — the eye being darkened by habit to natural loveliness or deformity, and the heart by the same narcotic power to moral loveliness or deformity. If we could but break through the moral customs as we can through the physical by applying a topsyturvy retina to the same scenery, he argued that we should see the 'wonder and bloom' of the world,[5] and also its hideous evils and distortions, as we seldom see them now. This is true philosophy, and it hits better than any other illustration the exact value of Mr. Carlyle to the world he lives in. He has been created, as it seems to us, on purpose to look at the English world "with his head inverted," and no wonder therefore that he turns the heads of those who read him for the first time, for that is his legitimate function. His writings have all the vividness and all the faults of a man who, for the purpose of morally couching the eyes of the present generation, has been sent into the universe with a commission to report upon it for us with his head between his legs. Of course it is not a report on which men with their heads not between their legs can wisely act, but it is one which, once thoroughly studied, sweeps away the all-enveloping mist of custom from the mind's eye, restores meaning and colour and light to human phenomena, and re-awakens that wholesome wonder in the mind of the observer which monotony so rapidly paralyzes. Such a picture as the following, for instance, could only be seen by such a seer as Mr. Carlyle, and whether it is in the narrower sense practically instructive or not, in the wider sense it certainly is, for the painter has the art to brush away the *mental* films, that is, the worst kind of films, from the mind of his spectators. Teufelsdröckh is talking in his attic at *Weissnichtwo*: — "Ach mein lieber!" — said he, "it is a true sublimity to dwell here. Those fringes of lamplight struggling up through smoke and thousandfold exhalations, some fathoms into the ancient reign of Night, what thinks Boötes of them, as he leads his hunting dogs over the zenith in their leash of sidereal fire?.... Upwards of five hundred thousand two-legged animals without feathers lie around us in horizontal positions, their heads all in night-caps and full of the foolishest dreams. Riot cries aloud, and staggers and swaggers in his rank dens of shame, and the mother, with streaming hair, kneels over her pallid, dying infant, whose cracked lips only her tears now moisten. All these heaped and huddled together, with nothing but a little carpentry and masonry between them, crammed in, like salted fish in their barrels, or weltering (shall I say?) like an Egyptian pitcher of tamed vipers, each struggling to get its head above the others; — such work goes on under the smoke counterpane! But I, *mein werther*, sit above it all; I am alone with the stars."[6] The pictorial character of the physical universe in all its wonder, Mr. Carlyle certainly does restore by his odd inverted glance.

But the inconvenience of the method, as well as its value, is better tested when we come to something beyond the pictorial character of the universe. Mr. Carlyle's sacrifices for the good of his younger fellow-creatures are scarcely appreciated till we get to his topsy-turvy view of human society; — not, we must remember, by any means a view which turns society topsy-turvy, for the inverted eye sees everything in the same posture as before, — the only change being that as it has dispensed with the numbing influence of habitual experience, it has necessarily dispensed also with the aid of that mass of time-honoured rules and influences which experience gradually works into the very act of perception, — just as the sense of *distance* (in itself originally a mere result of intellectual inference) becomes embodied by the power of habit in the very act of vision itself. And so it is with Mr. Carlyle. He sees the moral universe with a wonderful freshness that seems to show you the life tingling through it as you had never seen it before. But then all the truth which the slow experience of time has gradually embodied with our moral and mental perceptions is cast away in order to obtain this freshness. We see things as nearly as may be as one of Mr. Carlyle's rugged inarticulate chiefs of men might have seen them — "a *könig* or canning man"[7] without any "book on his premises, whose signature was a true sign-*manual*, the stamp of his iron hand duly inlaid and clapt upon the parchment, and whose speech in Parliament, like the growl of lions, did indeed convey his meaning, but would have torn Lindley Murray's nerves to pieces." By thus blotting out the inferences of experience now become ingrained in our moral perceptions, of course Mr. Carlyle's *fresh* impression of the moral universe becomes tolerably false as well as fresh, – might standing out, as it did to the old buccaneers, before right, – slavery and "Beneficent Whip" acquitted of all wrong, – despotic strength glorified, – the "sciences called pure" decried, – a few imperious personalities, often by no means either called or thought pure, exalted, – "M'Crowdy and his dismal science" of economy trampled under foot, – parliaments or human babblements condemned, – all prison-humanities vehemently denounced, – tolerance to Jesuits and jibbering phantasms generally, repealed, – and "beaverish" commerce discouraged.[8] Such is Mr. Carlyle's interpretation of the "Eternal Verities," and doubtless it has all the merit of *obliging* us to reconsider how much of that gradually accumulated experience of the ages which is embodied with the ordinary moral vision of ordinary men is defensible or not, – how much of it is mere dull imitative or fashionable opinion, which has nothing to say for itself to any one who has the courage to challenge it boldly, and how much of it will force us to take it back again even after we have attempted to dispense with it. But this latter part of the question Mr. Carlyle gives no aid at all in deciding. Indeed it is a part of his usefulness to young men that he wipes clean out all customary ethics and philosophy, treats the false and the true elements in them with much the same complete scorn, and obliges his readers to sift for themselves what he has rejected, and to resume what he has rejected on weak grounds. In this way he is, no doubt, one of the most useful teachers of young men, if they have any head to discriminate those rejections of modern habits of thought which are wise, or even sometimes wise, from those which are an attempt to cast away all the surest results of patient experience.

If the new Rector addresses his young constituents as he has thought, or wished to think, for many years past, he will give them a capital exercise in this sort of discrimination. Perhaps he may say something of this kind: – "I am credibly informed, my young brothers and fellow-learners, that a worthy friend of mine, with discernments quite beyond the common, has in these present times undertaken to teach you of this University something (among others) that men call rhetoric and letters, – utterances of great men in this common tongue of ours, and the power resulting thence to all true learners among you, with leave of favouring nature, of distinctly articulating such word of God as may be in you: – if such word be already there. If such word be already there! here is the grand condition of all true utterance, without which Rhetoric

Professors, with huge midwife apparatus of various discernments, can do nothing for you but deliver you of dark, extensive mooncalves, metaphysic abortions, wide-coiled monstrosities of ineffable foolishness, such as it were better for the world not hitherto to have seen. Rhetoric professors, my young brothers, of howsoever various discernments, can at most help you to articulate such true word as may be in each of you, and if, in your chaotic, yeasty flounderings of blind desire you cannot yet find such word, may instead thereof surely help you to lose such word, beyond hope of ultimate finding, in froth-oceans of logical jargon, dismal science formulas, and sciences 'called pure.' In which too possible case, not I, but the solemn fact of the universe, must warn you, at peril of drowning for ever in said froth-oceans of logical jargon, to desist from long-eared hallelujahs and laudatory psalmody to middle-class education, sciences 'called pure,' University extension, and the like, and retire into the silences, till you can catch some audible whisper of an everlasting yea announcing, as with clap of thunder, what sort of body-pilgrimage nature and fact have enjoined upon you, under peril of your soul, in this distracted universe, to pursue." Even if this be exaggerated, which we doubt, there is a little too much of this sort of humorous and windy dilation on a few favourite and partially true ideas of Mr. Carlyle's to be found in his writings. Nevertheless, he may do, perhaps has already done, a good deal for the young men of Edinburgh, — such of them at least as are able to winnow the chaff of this sort, — much nearer 'chaff' in the slang sense of the term than Mr. Carlyle has any idea, — and the latent falsehood with it, out of his discourses.

An Intellectual Angel

An essay by Mr. Matthew Arnold on the narrow and dimsighted views of the English middle class is like the visit of an intellectual angel, not unconscious of angelic graces, to the dull and earthly sphere of our political literature. In the new number of the *Cornhill Magazine* there is another, and perhaps the most perfect specimen yet published of Mr. Arnold's exquisitely polished English, his keen and delicate irony, his dogmatic mock humility, his airy scorn, his luminous exposition, and his entire indifference to any but aesthetic principles.[1] We dull laborious critics cannot but think of him as he, having delivered his message, disappears again into upper air, with much the same kind of envy as the spectators of the pain and anguish of Prometheus in Shelley's poem thought of Mercury, the message-bearer of Jupiter, lightly coming and lightly going between the painless heavens and the painful Caucasus, —

"See where the child of Heaven, with winged feet,
Runs down the slanted sunlight of the dawn."[2]

Mercury certainly did not manage any of his little diplomatic missions to earth with more graceful ease than Mr. Arnold, who brings to the English nation, "the weary Titan, with deaf ears and labour-dimmed eyes," as he finely terms it,[3] useless but beautiful messages, pointing out with the most exquisite precision and delicacy of insight the miseries of its actual position, and the beauty of the supernal world to which it has no access, — messages the peculiar value and merit of which in the exalted messenger's own eyes is, that they do not even affect to suggest any mode of winning the heights from which he descends upon us. Mr. Arnold engaged in the delivery of one of these messages is really a subject for artistic study. The unquestionable truth of the matter, the condescending grace of the manner, the serene indifference to practical results, the dogmatism without faith, the didacticism without earnestness, the irony without pain, the beauty without love which mark the message, are all equally remarkable.

Mr. Arnold has accused us as a nation, and our middle class especially, — most justly, as we believe, — of a wide-spread and profound Philistinism, by which he means, we suppose, that disposition to measure all the world by the standard of our own narrow and often accidental usages and habits of life, which renders it impossible to us to appreciate the great ideas which influence other nations, or the customs, — even when not founded on ideas, founded on tastes and preferences quite as good as our own, — by which the life of Continental civilization is moulded. For this very just accusation, enforced with his own refined and light-flying banter, and perhaps, too, in no small measure for the Olympian superiority to our English narrowness of thought which Mr. Arnold displayed in his manner of criticism, Mr. Arnold has been beset by a host of bitter critics, — by a *Saturday* reviewer who maintained that England is the most logical of nations, and by a number of other censors who esteem the English middle class the best educated class in the world, and the most able to "penetrate through sophisms, ignore common-places, and give to conventional illusions their true value."[4] Mr. Arnold had even once ventured to recommend Government inspection and a few great State schools as a remedy for what he thought the very defective middle-class schools, and to insist generally on some of the advantages accruing to French literature from the French Academy. He now repents himself bitterly for this very faint infraction of his rule never to recommend any practical measure whatever, and avows that in breaking this rule he has fairly laid himself open to the censure he has incurred: —

> "After a long and painful self-examination, I saw that I had been making a great mistake. I had been breaking one of my own cardinal rules: the rule to keep aloof from practice, and to confine myself to the slow and obscure work of trying to understand things, to see them as they are. So I was suffering deservedly in being taunted with hawking about my nostrums of State schools for a class much too wise to want them, and of an academy for people who have an inimitable style already. To be sure, I had said that schools ought to be things of local, not State, institution and management, and that we ought not to have an academy; but that makes no difference. I have been meddling with practice, proposing this and that, saying how it might be if we had established this or that. I saw what danger I had been running in thus intruding into a sphere where I have no business, and I resolved to offend in this way no more. Henceforward let Mr. Kinglake belabour the French as he will, let him describe as many tight merciless lips as he likes; henceforward let Educational Homes stretch themselves out in the *Times* to the crack of doom, let Lord Fortescue bewitch the middle class with ever new blandishments, let any number of Mansion House meetings propound any number of patchwork schemes to avoid facing the real difficulty; I am dumb. I let reforming and instituting alone; I meddle with my neighbour's practice no

more. *He that is unjust, let him be unjust still, and he which is filthy, let him be filthy still, and he that is righteous, let him be righteous still, and he that is holy, let him be holy still.*"[5]

After this act of mock retractation, he runs on through many pages in a very skilful defence of his former position, that the English, especially the middle class, are blinded by ignorance and narrow prejudices to the great ideas of their time; that they have lost intellectual and political weight on the Continent by this narrowness; that they do not care for any but industrial culture, ignoring intellectual culture, and love of beauty; that "your middle-class man thinks it the highest pitch of development and civilization when his letters are carried twelve times a day from Islington to Camberwell and from Camberwell to Islington, and if railway trains run to and fro between them every quarter of an hour," thinking it "nothing that the trains only carry him from an illiberal dismal life at Islington to an illiberal dismal life at Camberwell, and that the letters only tell him that such is the life there." Then Mr. Arnold again reiterates with new emphasis and deeper satire than ever his resolve not to be mixed up with practical life and its details: —

"The old recipe, to think a little more and bustle a little less, seemed to me still the best recipe to follow. So I take comfort when I find the *Guardian* reproaching me with having no influence; for I know what influence means, — a party, practical proposals, action; and I say to myself: 'Even suppose I could get some followers, and assemble them, brimming with affectionate enthusiasm, in a committee-room at some inn; what on earth should I say to them? what resolutions could I propose? I could only propose the old Socratic common-place, *Know thyself*; and how blank they would all look at that!' No; to inquire, perhaps too curiously, what that present state of English development and civilization is, which according to Mr. Lowe is so perfect that to give votes to the working class is stark madness; and, on the other hand, to be less sanguine about the divine and saving effect of a vote on its possessor than my friends in the committee-room at the 'Spotted Dog,' — that is my inevitable portion. To bring things under the light of one's intelligence, to see how they look there, to accustom oneself simply to regard the Marylebone Vestry, or the Educational Home, or the Irish Church Establishment, or our railway management, or our Divorce Court, or our gin-palaces open on Sunday and the Crystal Palace shut, as absurdities — that is, I am sure, invaluable exercise for us just at present. Let all persist in it who can, and steadily set their desires on introducing, with time, a little more soul and spirit into the too, too solid flesh of English society."[6]

So writes the angelic doctor of our own time, and while it is impossible for any one to admire the delicate thrusts of his satire at our limited English institutions and almost vulgar English belief in the infinite value of those limited institutions, more than we do, we cannot extend our admiration either to the godlike messenger himself, or to the means which he uses, or to his ostentatious abstinence from other means which he repudiates, for our further enlightenment. As for him, our instructor, there is far too much of the Epicurean gods about him to inspire any sympathy. The dogmatism which is natural to the temperament of the earnest practical zealot is in him perverted into alliance with the temperament of the calm, purely contemplative thinker. No doubt there is a sincere desire to see things as they are about Mr. Arnold, and as a consequence his discriminations are so delicate, and his thoughts, many of them, so true. But then he regards the power of seeing things as they are as the monopoly of a class; and indeed, arrived at as he arrived at it, it must always be the monopoly of a class. There are two ways of getting at almost all true discriminations, — the mode of calm and leisurely intellectual survey, and the mode of upward-labouring faith, — by the clue of pure thought, and by the clue of moral sympathy, — by the practice of an intellectual gymnastic, and by tracking home the higher instincts of the spirit. All the recent political blunders of which Mr. Arnold convicts the great English middle class, such as the vulgar policy of threatening Italy with the letter of the treaty of Vienna before her war of emancipation, and vindicating what she had done directly our alarm at the aggressive attitude of France was removed, or railing against the Northern States while their success seemed impossible and wishing to fraternize with them directly it was certain, — of all these blunders he convicts them from his serene station above the clouds of their dull atmosphere. But others have convicted them of the same blunders from a far less elevated and yet far more hopeful position in the very midst of that zone of prejudice and custom-blinded intelligence, by the mere force of that genuine sympathy with freedom which overpowers, even without dispelling, the cautious fears of selfish conservatism. Mr. Arnold in his refined intellectual culture only cares to point out the *blunders* of the great middle class. But we venture to say that those blunders will never be removed by revelations such as his, — which, while they charm the purely literary taste of all true culture, fall like melting snow flakes, leaving absolutely no impression, on the minds of the Philistines he is criticizing. Does Mr. Arnold suppose that "the young man from the country," to whom with exquisite raillery he likens this dense class of money-getters, in the following passage, would feel in the very least degree disturbed by his criticism, or even understand its drift? Of course he does not. But he pours in his running fire of intellectual grapeshot without the slightest desire to show anything except the enormous chasm which separates his intelligence from that of the class he is criticizing: —

> "I wonder if there can be anything offensive in calling one's countryman a young man from the country. I hope not; and if not, I should say, for the benefit of those who have seen Mr. John Parry's amusing entertainment, that England and Englishmen, holding forth on some great crisis in a foreign country, — Poland, say, or Italy, — are apt to have on foreigners very much the effect of the young man from the country who talks to the housemaid after she has upset the perambulator. There is a terrible crisis, and the discourse of the young man from the country, excellent in itself, is felt not to touch the crisis vitally. Nevertheless on he goes; the perambulator lies a wreck, the child screams, the nursemaid wrings her hands, the old gentleman storms, the policeman gesticulates, the crowd thickens; still that astonishing young man talks on, serenely unconscious that he is not at the centre of the situation."[7]

Nothing can be more exquisite in satire than that. And nothing can be less calculated to awaken the British "young man from the country" to the vital element in the crisis which he so obtusely ignores. What might be felt, however, by far blunter minds than this angelic critic's, is the vulgar selfishness of the young man's absorption in his own irrelevant remarks, — remarks indeed which can usually be only satirically spoken of as "excellent in themselves," quite apart from their "not touching the crisis vitally." Mr. Arnold had probably just as little sympathy with those who wished to rouse the middle class, through their moral feeling, to some true intelligence of the issue in America, as he had with the selfish middle-class insulation of feeling itself. All he saw was the *idea* at work in the Northern States, and the stupid vacancy of the English mind with respect to that idea. But in the true means by which that might have been remedied, and perhaps was partially remedied, — the stirring up of English moral feeling against a gigantic moral iniquity, — he felt as little interest as the torpid class he denounces.[8] If you look for it, you may always find a way by which men with torpid minds may be stirred, *through* their conscience, into true moral and therefore also intellectual discriminations. But Mr. Arnold does not care for such a process. He prefers contemplating blankly the gulf between him and the uncultured people he pities. He exults in the intellectual paces which he displays before them, and to the beauty and delicately graduated variety of which they are simply blind. He is almost supercilious in his disdain for their clumsy and heavy tread. "Let them that be filthy be filthy still," is too accurate an expression of his grand unconcern. If we, the "dim common populations," get a blessing from Mr. Arnold at all, it will only be as Jacob obtained it from the angel who wrestled with him "till the breaking of the day." He has no spontaneous blessing to bestow on the class whose culture he despises; and as that culture begins to light up their sky he would only find a reason in it for leaving them, — "let me go, for the day breaketh."[9] Yet they might wring a blessing from him which it is not in his angelic intellect to offer. But if they do, it will be through their own earnestness, and not through his compassion.

"Get Geist"

While the outer mind of London has been fermenting all the week with the turmoil of the Hyde-Park Riot, the inner mind of London has been travailing still more painfully with the birth of a new intellectual obligation – "to get Geist" – cast upon it by our greatest intellectual seer, in the last number of last week's *Pall Mall Gazette*, and which may perhaps have worked even more powerfully on our spirits in consequence of a dim perception that the teaching of Saturday received a certain amount of practical commentary in the explosion of Monday.[1] The *Pall Mall Gazette* is itself edited by *Geist*, – *esprit*, mind, intelligence, or whatever may be the true equivalent of Mr. Matthew Arnold's German word; but then even of *Geist* there is a more and less, and probably *Geist* has never taken an English shape so pure and doubly refined as the late Professor of Poetry at Oxford, the seer all whose woes are reserved for the gross and carnal mind of English middle-class prejudice. When, then, we poor learners, who pick up so greedily every grain of golden wisdom that the only pure intellect in England deigns to cast for us on the periodical press, went home last Saturday night with this great duty laid upon us by the command of Mr. Matthew Arnold's rather shadowy Prussian guest,[2] – the Prussian-ized form of Mr. Arnold's own genius, – it was not easy to keep the mind from working almost too powerfully under the new burden of duty, and when a day or two afterwards there came the great practical explosion of *Ungeist*, – Philistinism, stupidity, *bêtise*, Unintelligence, Mental Carnality, or whatever Mr. Arnold regards as the equivalent of that expressive word, in the thick-headed determination of one-idead politicians to talk seven-poundism[3] in one particular spot, and the equally thick-headed determination of authorities, destitute of mental resource or adaptability, to prevent it without sufficient means, – the words of the great master fell on his disciples with even too startling and exciting an emphasis. There were many and many a poor soul, like the present writer for instance, scarcely yet purged even of the first film of *Ungeist*, – only just beginning to apply feebly that elementary common-place of philosophy which Mr. Arnold found himself obliged to address to his political supporters at the "Spotted Dog," *Know thyself*,[4] in whom the new leaven of the teaching "Get Geist" began to work even too powerfully, till

117

their minds were almost overwhelmed in the sense of confusion at the prevalent Ungeist. The search after Geist haunted them painfully in railway carriages, and possessed their reins in the night watches. They had most of them learned indeed in their youth that comparatively uninstructive lesson, "Wisdom is the principal thing, therefore get wisdom, and with all thy getting get understanding."[5] But then that is by no means the equivalent of "Get Geist." When we learn, as Mr. Arnold's Prussian tells us, that "what unites and separates people now is Geist;" that "France has Geist in her democracy, and Prussia in her education;" while England has Geist nowhere — since her "common people are barbarous, in her middle class Ungeist is rampant, and as for our aristocracy, Geist is forbidden by nature to flourish in our aristocracy;" that we too often suffer ourselves to be deceived "by parallels drawn *from the times before Geist*;" that "what has won the battle for Prussia is Geist; Geist has used the King, and Bismark, and the Junkers, and Ungeist in uniform, all for its own ends; and Geist will continue so to use them till it has triumphed,"[6] — and finally that Geist is especially opposed to any fanatical belief in "railways, banks, finance-companies," and most of all to that manufacture of bottles which was so great a rock of offence to the Prussian manifestation of Geist delineated by Mr. Arnold, — when we learn all these attributes of Geist, it is clear that "getting Geist" means a great deal more or a great deal less than "getting Understanding" in the old proverb; for it is pretty clear at all events that Mr. Arnold's "parallels drawn from times before Geist" are parallels drawn from times a score of centuries later than Understanding.

Well, as all true learning is born of tears and travail, the little difficulties about Geist are probably only notes of a new truth, and it is but by way of calling fresh attention to the new spiritual teaching, not of throwing any doubt upon it, that we set down some of the first efforts of eager minds to push their way through the low brushwood in the foreground of Mr. Arnold's teaching. Exhausted last Tuesday in a railway train by fruitless travail of the soul, and dreamily wondering why Geist had not condescended to use Mr. Walpole, and Mr. Beales, and the Reformers, and Ungeist in fustian, as readily as it seems to have condescended to use "the King of Prussia, and Bismark, and the Junkers, and Ungeist in uniform," feebly speculating whether English bottle manufactories had anything special to do with it, — for Mr. Arnold half hints that Geist has a special repulsion for the special limitation of things so easily seen through as bottles — sleep fell upon the present writer, and the much conned Saturday's *Pall Mall* fell from his hands, in the midst of a confusion of images wherein England appeared as bottleholder in a struggle between Geist and Ungeist, which gradually dissolved into a grotesque appeal by Professor Arnold to Ungeist to make some small allowance per dozen for the return of the bottles. When the drowsiness went off, the first words audible, proceeding from a thoughtful, elderly gentleman, with a pale face and white moustache, who had picked up the well conned journal, and was reading aloud from it eagerly, were "What unites and separates people now is Geist." They were the very words which had exercised many willing minds most powerfully for the last seventy-two hours, and they seemed to be bearing fruit even in the very headquarters of Ungeist, — a railway carriage full of season-ticketholders, most of them probably living in semi-detached villas within twenty miles of the City. "Oh, that's Mat Arnold pommelling away again at his English Philistine, or his 'young man from the country,' I suppose," said a florid and able-bodied youth in the corner, who looked as if he might be going to row somewhere on the river: "He told us all that, you know in the *Cornhill* in February, and I think the man who is 'something in the bottle line' is the only new thing in that article; but after all what does he mean by Geist, I should like to know?" "Geist," said the pale-faced gentleman, with a superior smile, "is what we call the higher intelligence, creative intelligence, that knows how to select and mould instruments of a lower order to its more refined purposes." "That's all very well, you know," said the muscular sceptic, "and I see he calls the Emperor of the French[7] the representative of Geist because he said boldly that he detested the treaties of 1815, and that it is only among the working class of France that he finds the true genius of the people and breathes freely, — but what are 'the times before Geist?' Has Geist or your 'higher intelligence' been brought into exertion since 1815, expressly to 'detest the treaties of 1815,' and to 'breathe freely' among the working people of France? or is it possible that Geist can show itself by detesting the class compromise of 1832, and breathing freely among the working class of England? If the Emperor of the French is Geist, why not Mr. Beales? Mr. Beales detests the actual treaty by which English politics are now limited, and he seems to breathe freely enough, by Jove! among those London roughs, which is more than I should or Arnold himself, for that matter." "You mistake our great teacher," replied the pale gentleman loftily, with something approaching to a mild sniff, "when you confuse the spirit of English democracy, which with characteristic genius Mr. Arnold has painted, you know, as

    ' "The weary Titan with deaf
    Ears and labour-dimmed eyes," '[8]

with the genius of French democracy expressed by the Emperor of the French. Geist is chiefly shown by truly discerning *ends* of living, Ungeist by confounding ends with means. Our Beales and his Reformers concentrate all their laborious energies on obtaining permission for our

working people to vote for men who never think of any sort of higher end
beyond the vote. 'Drugged with business,'—I use the master's own
words,—they think it a great matter to have cheap letters, and cheap
trains, 'when the trains only carry them from a dismal illiberal life at
Camberwell to a dismal illiberal life at Islington, and the letters only tell
them that such is the life there;' and their friends of the working class are
no better than themselves, than Beales and their organ the *Morning Star*,
witness the Ungeist shown in pulling up the railings of the Park meant for
their enjoyment, in order that they may contest a figment of abstract right,
which, if they possess it, would only injure them. No, Geist could never
breathe freely among our English Reformers. And if Geist detests the
compromise of 1832, it is only because it was that compromise which
made our middle class idolize itself, and mistake means for ends, till at
last it dotes upon the liberty which permits 'Cole's Truss Manufactory to
stand where it ought not, a glorious monument of British individualism
and industrialism.' Geist, my dear Sir, is shown less in political formulae,
than in recognizing what is worth living for and in never confounding the
end with the means. It can approve an Emperor and detest Beales and
ballot, if the Emperor understands his age, and Beales and ballot look
more to what British citizens shall have a right to do—which they ought
to leave undone—including building Truss manufactories on conspicuous spots suitable for public buildings, than to what the spirit of the
age requires them to do or leave undone." "Ah! Geist concerns itself with
ends chiefly, does it?" said the other; "and claptrap, which I see is the
English form of Ungeist, is always making a clatter about means, and
ignoring ends. But then, why should Geist care about democracy, you
know?—and it stands expressly written that it does. Why is democracy
'the triumph of reason and intelligence over blind custom and prejudice?'
Is not democracy a means, and a frightfully vulgar, windy, flatulent,
dismal, illiberal sort of means too, if we may judge by American
Congresses and State Legislatures? That fellow Arnold has one word for
democracy when it is out of this country, and another when it is in it. For
my part I do not see what the French blouses in Auxerre have about them
to make you breathe more freely than our bottle manufacturers. The
bottle man read his *Punch*, and enjoyed his little joke, and saw probably
just as far into Continental politics, if not a little farther, than the Auxerre
operative would see into English. Your oracle speaks double. If
democracy is good for its own sake, why not praise Beales and the
Hyde-Park Riots? Democracy is their ultimate end. If it is not good for
its own sake, but only when the people know what they want, and don't
mistake a dismal, illiberal life for a liberal and refined one, then where is
the democracy that does know this? The rule of Geist should seem to
mean the rule of the educated, and not the rule of the masses;—of such

fellows as Arnold, you know, who have 'the Idea' in them, and can tell where to forbid the Truss manufactories and where to permit them. I don't see much democracy, for my part — except that mere giving of votes he despises so much — in France. If there *were* a democracy there, I am not at all sure the Emperor would breathe freely, or breathe at all. If Geist means Napoleonism, Geist means enlightened absolutism to my mind, — anything but democracy. This is the sort of thing that puzzles a poor fellow so about your 'great teacher' and his Geist. I am not sure Geist means anything in the world except what a poetical sort of fellow, with a good deal of French culture, and a high-trotting intellectual pace, chooses to smile upon. Is it government *for* the masses by the light of a better taste than theirs like Arnold's, — or government *by* the masses by the light of their own vulgar tastes, which Geist approves? Why does he say that the Geist which used Bismark has an alliance with democracy, when Bismark did nothing but thwart the educated Prussian Liberals?[9] It seems to me not that 'Geist used Bismark,' but on the other hand that Bismark used Geist, and made a very vulgar, physical sort of use of it, too, as mere *materiel* for supplying that single little deficiency in breech-loaders, — their unfortunate need for a partially rational being near the breech. If Geist discriminates the proper ends for Ungeist to follow, — that is not democracy, but enlightened despotism. Democracy means to my mind the creed that Ungeist should grope blindly and stupidly its own way to Geist, *without* imperial assistance." As our muscular friend proceeded in this harangue, the pale, elderly philosopher's face turned gradually upwards in an illuminated kind of gaze upon his own hat, which was swinging at the top of the carriage, and without turning his face to the other speaker he said, in a sort of ecstasy, "It hath not been given to the carnal mind to judge the operations of Geist. Geist is at once imperial and democratic. Geist is her own interpreter. Geist is justified of her children." But here a porter's voice shrieking, "All change here for Wraysbury, Datchet, and Windsor,"[10] brought the "gentlemanly soul," as the American paper says, of our pale illuminatus, back in a hurry to his face; he caught at his hat, returned the sacred *Pall Mall* to its owner with a start and a half-reverential bow over the paper, and rushed from the carriage, followed by the other party to the dialogue, who muttered audibly between his teeth, as he got out, "Damn Geist!"

Mr. Arnold on the Enemies of Culture

Mr. Matthew Arnold has given, in his farewell lecture at Oxford, reproduced in the July *Cornhill Magazine*, not only a broader definition, but broader practical illustrations, of what he really means by the religion of "culture" which he preaches than in any of his former essays. His adieu to his Professorship at Oxford is conceived in a higher spirit, and expressed with a less supercilious and compassionate intellectual air, than any of his former addresses to "his countrymen." Indeed, with but one important exception, it is a lecture in which we can wholly concur, and which scarcely any one who has any defects can read without sincere admiration and sympathy. Mr. Arnold strenuously denies that culture implies mere training to *see* things truly. That is, no doubt, he says, one important end of the training which culture demands. But 'curiosity,' in the purely intellectual sense, is not the true motive of culture. "There is of culture another view in which not solely the scientific passion, the sheer desire to see things as they are, natural and proper in an intelligent being, appears as the ground of it; a view in which all the love of our neighbour, the impulses towards action, help, and beneficence, the desire for stopping human error, clearing human confusion, and diminishing the sum of human misery, the noble aspiration to leave the world better and happier than we found it — motives evidently such as are called social — come in as part of the grounds of culture, and as the main and primary part. Culture is then properly described, not as having its origin in curiosity, but as having its origin in the love of perfection; it is a study of perfection. It moves by the force, not merely or primarily, of the scientific passion for pure knowledge, but also of the moral and social passion for doing good. As in the first view of it, we took for its worthy motto, Montesquieu's words, 'To render an intelligent being yet more intelligent,' — so in the second view of it there is no better motto it can take than these words of Bishop Wilson, 'To make reason and the will of God prevail.' Only, whereas the passion for doing good is apt to be over-hasty in determining what reason and the will of God say, because its turn is for acting rather than thinking, and it wants to be beginning to act, and whereas it is apt to take its own conceptions, proceeding from its own state of development, and sharing in all the imperfections and immaturities of this, for a basis of action, what distinguishes culture is that it is possessed by the scientific passion as well as by the passion of doing good; that it has worthy notions of reason and the will of God, and does not readily suffer its own crude conceptions to substitute themselves for them; and that knowing that no action or institution can be salutary and stable which are not based upon reason and the will of God, it is not so bent on acting and instituting, even with the great aim of diminishing human error and misery ever before its thoughts, but that it can remember that acting and instituting are of little use, unless we know how and what we ought to act and institute." That is finely enough conceived and expressed, and, so far, the religion of culture has nothing unduly intellectual or superciliously critical about it. Nothing can be more complete than Mr. Arnold's demonstration of its superiority to the worship of mere machinery which is so common with both the middle-class enemies and the democratic enemies of culture, both those who denounce it with Mr. Bright because it expresses a little contempt for the excessive value set on the mere machinery of politics, the mere voting power, the policy of local self-government and the rest, and those who denounce it with Mr. Frederic Harrison because it does not come with an abstract creed and with fire, burning up everything that is apparently opposed to the immediate interest of the proletariat class and to the political gospel of M. Comte. To both these enemies of culture Mr. Arnold says that they set means, — perhaps very useful means, — above ends, and talk of freedom, and popular power, and enthusiasm itself, as if they were the final ends of life, instead of the mere instruments for securing good or bad final ends, according as the freedom is nobly used, the popular power is wisely wielded, and the enthusiasm is controlled by a harmonious and balanced nature. Freedom is no doubt the condition of all good, but then it is equally the condition of much that is evil, and unless used for good is not good. Popular power without at least something of wisdom is a sheer danger, and enthusiasm without truth of nature is a blind destructive force. Mr. Arnold cries in the wilderness that while battling for freedom, we must train the mind of the people to understand the true use of freedom; while demanding popular power, we must seek to make it altogether subordinate to popular wisdom; while cherishing enthusiasm, we must keep it strictly checked by wide and harmonious sympathies. These mere *instruments* of progress, says Mr. Arnold, must be controlled by culture, in the sense of a true love of "sweetness and light" — the 'sweetness' or love of beauty and harmony, with which culture corrects the hideous and grotesque rawness of our limited English conceptions of moral good, the 'light' with which culture insists upon inundating our narrow and meagre prepossessions concerning intellectual good. Oxford has, in the past, says Mr. Arnold, insisted much more successfully on the claims of sweetness than it has on the claims of light. Oxford has always felt the rawness and hideousness in what many English sects regard as sacred, much more deeply than it has felt the narrowness and ignorance of what many English sects regard as true. The Oxford movement, headed by Dr. Newman, did much to expose the baldness, rawness, and vulgarity of orthodoxy as conceived by our Protestant sects, and to sow the seeds of a more harmonious and catholic taste; but it did very little to expose the ill-founded and irrational assumptions of much which that Protestant orthodoxy regarded as sound reason and convincing evidence, or to sow the seeds of scientific candour in relation to critical investigation.[1] Oxford has insisted on a deeper and wider moral harmony much more successfully than on a more abundant flood of light. True culture asks for both, – a richer appreciation of the harmony of the various moral and spiritual motives, and also a more consistent and unswerving love for every attainable ray of intellectual light. "Sweetness and light," that is what the gospel of culture demands over and above that moral "resistance of the Devil," that "overcoming of the Wicked One," which Mr. Arnold admits that English religion has already preached with sufficient force.

Now, with most of this so far as it is merely a criticism on the shortcomings of our various forms of popular faith, we cordially agree. Nothing, as Mr. Arnold says, can be more sterile and disheartening than the professed object of many of our miserable little sectarian organizations, such as that which he quotes as the motto of an exceedingly honest and vigorous paper, – the *Nonconformist*, – "the dissidence of Dissent, and the Protestantism of the Protestant religion."[2] To ask men to make great sacrifices for, and attach a high moral and religious value to, the objects held up to admiration in such a standard as that, is as Mr. Arnold truly says, to show how far short religious organizations often fall of even any *attempt* to aim at "a counsel of perfection." We do not quarrel with Mr. Arnold's criticism on those who aim at something less than a moral and spiritual perfection, we only object to the *form* of the substitute which he proposes, for we do not believe that a conscious aim at *beauty* of character will ever result in attaining beauty of character. We have no belief in the result of cultivating a harmonious development of motives and feelings as a conscious end. A "study of perfection" such as Mr. Arnold proposes to us – that is, a study of mental and moral grace – may result in a great enfeeblement of the whole character, must result in a certain growth of moral affectation, but will never result in real beauty. Our answer to Mr. Arnold is, that his poetic standard of culture is a very good standard for testing by, for wise criticism, but no starting-point at all for real improvement. Show an ungainly mind how ungainly it is, and it will only become more ungainly in its "study of perfection." The aesthetic aims which Mr. Arnold insists on holding up before us are, we contend, not moral means of regeneration at all. When he praises Dean Stanley's wisdom and sweetness, and Mr. Jowett's moral unction, and Spinoza's "beatific vision," as a critic, he does well. But any one attempting to subdue his own ruggednesses from an aesthetic perception of the beauty of Dean Stanley's sweeter wisdom, or to attain unction because he sees that Mr. Jowett's unction is a real beauty of his character, or to reach a "beatific vision" of his own because it added something to the richness and serenity of the great Pantheist's philosophic calm, would only fall into conscious affectations. We deny that the aesthetic culture which Mr. Arnold holds up before us as one of the highest conscious ends of existence can be attained by conscious pursuit at all. What irritates wise men with Mr. Arnold's teaching is not its drift, but its implied method. We believe that the sweetness and beauty of which he justly makes so much, is, whenever it is genuine sweetness and beauty, the growth, not of conscious yearning after sweetness and beauty, but of the moral and religious submission of our will to the inspiration of a divine love. Beauty is the incidental glory of a moral and spiritual perfection attained, whenever it is not inborn and natural, by direct converse with, and love of, a higher nature. Sentimentalism is the only result of a direct effort after beauty or harmony of character. We differ from Mr. Arnold wholly in thinking that the love of perfection goes beyond religion. "Perfection," he says, "as culture, from a thorough disinterested study of human nature and human experience, learns to conceive it, is an harmonious expansion of *all* the powers which make the beauty and worth of human nature, and is not consistent with the over-development of any one power at the expense of the rest. *Here it goes beyond religion, as religion is generally conceived by us.*" Does it go beyond the religion of "Be ye therefore perfect, even as your Father in heaven is perfect?"[3] Does it go beyond the religion which loves "sweetness and light," not because they present our nature with a more attractive glow upon it, but because the Light of the world was full of sweetness, and makes us all feel the *moral* authority of His saying, "By this shall all men know that ye are my disciples, if ye have love one to another?" What we maintain is that the moral restraint or moral impulse given by the touch of a higher nature on our own, impels us to actions by which we grow in "sweetness and light," without aiming at them, while aiming only to obey the higher Will within us. Attained thus under the moral and religious sanction as a mere matter of conscience and duty, they bring with them none of the affectations and conscious intellectual posture-making of the direct aim at beauty of character. Why it is so, it is, of course, impossible to say; but we believe it is true that no one ever aimed directly at greater beauty of nature without a spoiled simplicity, and therefore a growth in ugliness. The weakness of the gospel of culture is that it gives us no impulse, no natural motives, — that to follow its mandates you have to go through a mental attitudinizing which destroys all strength and earnestness. It is by simply opening the conscience to the teaching and inspiration of the perfect Will, by acts of duty, not by acts of sentimental aspiration, that men absorb the real sweetness and light of Him who was all sweetness and all light. Mr. Arnold's doctrine of culture is a good school of criticism, but a wretched school of progress. It is better to grope your way almost blindly to what seems morally better and better, till the submission to duty begins, as it always does at last, to widen the apprehension for divine perfections, than to begin aiming at a quality which really has no direct moral authority over us, — mere harmony or mental grace, — and which inevitably lands those who cultivate it in the most ugly of all ugly qualities — constant self-consciousness, moral affectation, aesthetic melodrama.

Mr. Arnold's New Poems

Any one who, like ourselves, has always procured and read Mr. Arnold's poems with eagerness, from the first series of *Poems by A.*[1] to this volume, will now be possessed of nearly every one of his poems in a double form, and of two or three of them in a triple form, – a result which, though it does not diminish their merit, is rather vexatious to the possessor of books. Mr. Arnold says that "Empedocles on Etna" cannot be said to be republished in this volume, because it was withdrawn from circulation before fifty copies of it were sold, but as the present writer, at all events, was amongst the fifty buyers, he now finds himself in possession of the whole poem, as well as of most of the others belonging to the same volume, in a double shape, and of part of "Empedocles on Etna" – the exquisite verses called "The Harp Player upon Etna" – in a treble shape, which is a vexation that Mr. Arnold might perhaps have spared his readers. Nothing is less pleasant to the true lover of a poem than to have it in two or three different forms, – generally with minute differences in phrase in each, – and always associated with a different page, and different print, and different memories as regards the external shape of the volume in which it is contained. It dissipates to a certain extent the individuality of a poem to have it issued by its author in two or three distinct volumes, embedded in different company in each, and clipped or modified to suit its various settings. We feel now towards some of Mr. Arnold's poems as we might towards friends who had two or three different bodies, and who were fond of trying the permutations and combinations of bodies in which they could appear to us. If they came with an entirely new gait, or with different-coloured eyebrows, or a different voice and accent, we should feel inclined to beg them to keep as much the same in future as might be consistent with the law of growth and change in personal characteristics, and should be a little troubled to which form of friend to refer our own private feelings. So it is with Mr. Arnold's various editions of his poems. We always feel a certain amount of embarrassment, whether it is the form in *Poems by A.*, or in the first or second series of Mr. Arnold's acknowledged poems, or in the "new" poems that we are thinking of.[2] It is a small matter to cavil at, but an injury of this kind thrice repeated vexes the best disciple. We should scarcely have expressed our chagrin had not

Mr. Arnold quoted two or three lines as motto to one of his pieces from *Lucretius, an Unpublished Tragedy*, and so refused us deliberately what we want, while giving us duplicates and triplicates of what we have. However, much as there is, — near half the volume, — which is not only known to the students of Mr. Arnold, but already in their possession in volumes of his poems, we are not really ungrateful for anything new which he gives us stamped with the peculiar mark of his genius, and there are several new and fine poems here, though from one of the finest (on Heine's grave) Mr. Arnold had quoted the finest passage, likening England to Atlas, "the weary Titan with deaf ears and labour-dimmed eyes," in that memorable address of his, a year and a half ago, to his "countrymen."[3]

There is something, we take it, really characteristic in this pleasure which Mr. Arnold takes in falling back, as it were, on himself, or anticipating himself, — in quoting bits of his published, or disclosing bits of his still unpublished poems, just as thinkers like Mr. Mill quote from late or early essays little bits of philosophical exposition which they think they could not improve by rewriting. For the fundamental essence of Mr. Arnold's poetry, crystalline as it often is in the clearness and beauty of its pictures, is after all dogmatic. He has a "vision of his own,"[4] and very clearly he paints it in the purest water-colours of poetic language, but the vision is almost always the illustration of a dogma, and not itself the primary fact to Mr. Arnold's imagination. There is a thread of theory at the centre of all his delineations. Hence, we think, his pleasure in quoting himself and restoring himself — the didactic pleasure of a teacher. Most poets have a different mood for every poem. Mr. Arnold has scarcely two moods in the whole range of his poems. Everywhere there is the same poetic movement, the same underlying rhythm of feeling, — a desire for the rapture of contemplative insight first, and next, the love of all such undertones of emotion as are not incompatible with this conscious superiority to the mere ripple of feeling, as tend indeed to heighten the glow of the insight without confusing or disturbing it. Where Shelley pants with quick short breath for the full intensity of any momentary emotion, where Tennyson seeks to enrich his picture with as rich a mass of living touches as he can crowd into it without destroying its unity of effect, where Wordsworth gives the reins to the rapture of his own solitary imagination, Mr. Arnold, unlike them all, never loses himself in either emotion, or delineation, or meditation, but uniformly studies to take the intellectual measure of the subjects he deals with, to temper the throb of individual grief or joy with some reference to the movement of the ages, to make his figures or his landscapes stand out visibly against the great horizon of human life, and so to focus his meditative rapture as to bring within its field of view some general drift of human affairs rather than any merely arbitrary reveries of his own soul. All his poems are the same in tone, — calm, thoughtful, and almost philosophic in essence; and if they are steeped in a glow of rich pictorial feeling or tender personal emotion, still so steeped as to make the reader see that the pictorial touches or the personal emotions are secondary to the thought, and valued chiefly as heightening its effects and giving vividness to its teachings. Take the fine, though thoroughly pantheistic, lines in the poem called "Obermann Again,"[5] in which Mr. Arnold compares the Roman world and its wants with our own modern world and its wants, and you will see in it the great fundamental principle of Mr. Arnold's art, — a philosophy of history illustrated by a clear, sweet and mellow picture, drawn in conformity with his theory: —

> "Well nigh two thousand years have brought
>   Their load, and gone away,
> Since last on earth there lived and wrought
>   A world like ours to-day.
>
> "Like ours it look'd in outward air!
>   Its head was clear and true,
> Sumptuous its clothing, rich its fare,
>   No pause its action knew;
>
> "Stout was its arm, each pulse and bone
>   Seemed puissant and alive —
> But, ah, its heart, its heart was stone,
>   And so it could not thrive!
>
> "On that hard Pagan world disgust
>   And secret loathing fell.
> Deep weariness and sated lust
>   Made human life a hell.
>
> "In his cool hall, with haggard eyes,
>   The Roman noble lay;
> He drove abroad, in furious guise,
>   Along the Appian way;
>
> "He made a feast, drank fierce and fast,
>   And crown'd his hair with flowers —
> No easier nor no quicker pass'd
>   The impracticable hours.
>
> "The brooding East with awe beheld
>   Her impious younger world;
> The Roman tempest swell'd and swell'd,
>   And on her head was hurl'd.

"The East bow'd low before the blast,
    In patient, deep disdain.
She let the legions thunder past,
    And plunged in thought again.

"So well she mused, a morning broke
    Across her spirit grey.
A conquering, new-born joy awoke,
    And fill'd her life with day.

" 'Poor world,' she cried, 'so deep accurst
    That runn'st from pole to pole
To seek a draught to slake thy thirst —
    Go, seek it in thy soul!'

"She heard it, the victorious West!
    In crown and sword array'd.
She felt the void which mined her breast,
    She shiver'd and obeyed.

"She veil'd her eagles, snapp'd her sword
    And laid her sceptre down;
Her stately purple she abhorr'd
    And her imperial crown;

"She broke her flutes, she stopp'd her sports,
    Her artists could not please;
She tore her books, she shut her courts,
    She fled her palaces;

"Lust of her eye and pride of life
    She left it all behind
And hurried, torn with inward strife,
    The wilderness to find."[6]

That is beautiful poetry, but it is thought, criticism, embodied in vision, — not vision first and criticism afterwards. The power of Christ, Mr. Arnold teaches, was not in Him, but in those who needed some such vision to satisfy their own restless yearnings. The Roman world was too external. The East, conquered physically, overcame its victor by asserting the superiority of the inner vision, of the soul. Christ was the occasion, not the cause, of this great reaction. And Mr. Arnold applies his historical theory, after he has developed it, to the wants of modern thought.

"And centuries came, and ran their course,
    And unspent all that time,
Still, still went forth that Child's dear force,
    And still was at its prime.

"Ay, ages long endured His span
    Of life, 'tis true received,
That gracious Child, that thorn-crown'd Man!
    He lived while we believed.

"While we believed, on earth He went,
    And open stood his grave.
Men call'd from chamber, church, and tent,
    And Christ was by to save.

"Now He is dead. Far hence he lies
    In the lorn Syrian town,
And on His grave, with shining eyes,
    The Syrian stars look down.

"In vain men still, with hoping new,
    Regard His death-place dumb,
And say the stone is not yet to,
    And wait for words to come.

"Ah, from that silent sacred land,
    Of sun, and arid stone,
And crumbling wall, and sultry sand,
    Comes now one word alone!

"From David's lips this word did roll,
    'Tis true and living yet:
No man can save his brother's soul,
    Nor pay his brother's debt.

"Alone, self-poised, henceforward man
    Must labour; must resign
His all too human creeds, and scan
    Simply the way divine."[7]

And he adds that the great want of our time is, —

"One mighty wave of thought and joy,
    Lifting mankind amain,"[8]

— a mighty wave of joy, which he evidently thinks, quite consistently with his philosophy of Christianity, needs no ground or justification in fact. Just as the power of Christ was not wielded by Him, but, muses Mr. Arnold, "received" from the human race, who were in want of some such vision, so the "mighty wave of thought and joy," of which we now stand in need, needs no justification, no actual cause but itself. It might swell up any day, either taking an excuse, like the Christian "wave of thought and joy," from what Mr. Arnold holds to be an imaginary fact, or probably even without taking the trouble to justify itself by any external excuse at all, — like a high tide without a lunar or solar attraction. We need not say

that Mr. Arnold's theory seems to us utterly false and his poem therefore
philosophically faulty. For we have not quoted it on this account, but
because it is the most perfect illustration of Mr. Arnold's poetic
method, — and shows in the most perfect combination that cool, calm light
of thought, steeped only in the mild, violet tints of personal feeling, which
is of the essence of Mr. Arnold's poetry, — poetry often not the worse *as
poetry*, for the illusory theory which is its essence.[9]

Following the same method, but truer in tone, is the exquisite poem
on Heine's grave, which includes the criticism on England to which we
have already referred. The lines we speak of are perfect in their kind,
and even grand as an imaginative effort: —

> What so harsh and malign,
> Heine! distils from thy life,
> Poisons the peace of thy grave?
>   I chide with thee not, that thy sharp
> Upbraidings often assail'd
> England, my country; for we,
> Fearful and sad, for her sons,
> Long since, deep in our hearts,
> Echo the blame of her foes.
> We, too, sigh that she flags;
> We, too, say that she now,
> Scarce comprehending the voice
> Of her greatest, golden-mouth'd sons
> Of a former age any more,
> Stupidly travels her round
> Of mechanic business, and lets
> Slow die out of her life
> Glory, and genius, and joy.
> So thou arraign'st her, her foe;
> So we arraign her, her sons.
> Yes we arraign her! but she,
> The weary Titan! with deaf
> Ears, and labour-dimm'd eyes,
> Regarding neither to right
> Nor left, goes passively by
> Staggering on to her goal;
> Bearing on shoulders immense,
> Atlantean, the load,
> Well nigh not to be borne,
> Of the too vast orb of her fate.[10]

But the intellectual thread at the basis of every one of Mr. Arnold's
poems, sometimes gives a curious hardness and even prosiness to
fragments — chips of thought — here and there which Mr. Arnold has not

taken pains thoroughly to saturate with any glow of feeling or visionary brightness. How *can* the lines we have italicized in the following passages be even read, so as to be in the smallest harmony with the general rhythm of the poem? —

> But was it thou — I think
> Surely it was — that bard
> Unnamed, who, Goethe said,
> *Had every other gift, but wanted love, —*
> Love, without which the tongue
> Even of angels sounds amiss?
>
> . . . . .
>
> Ah! as of old, from the pomp
> Of Italian Milan, the fair
> Flower of marble of white
> Southern palaces — steps
> Border'd by statues, and walks
> Terraced, and orange bowers
> Heavy with fragrance — the blond
> German Kaiser full oft
> Long'd himself back to the fields,
> Rivers, and high-roof'd towns
> Of his native Germany; so,
> So, how often! from hot
> *Paris drawing-rooms, and lamps*
> Blazing, and brilliant crowds,
> Starr'd and jewell'd, of men
> Famous, of women the queens
> Of dazzling converse, and fumes
> Of praise — hot, heady fumes, to the poor brain,
> That mount, that madden! — how oft
> Heine's spirit outworn
> Long'd itself out of the din
> Back to the tranquil, the cool
> Far German home of his youth!
>
> . . . . .
>
> The spirit of the world
> *Beholding the absurdity of men —*
> Their vaunts, their feats — let a sardonic smile
> For one short moment wander o'er his lips.
> That smile was Heine! for its earthly hour
> The strange guest sparkled; now 'tis pass'd away.[11]

Perhaps it may be said of the last passage that it is meant to be an ordinary blank verse with a defective line at the commencement; but even if so, what a flaw in the workmanship to interpose a passage in blank verse, in the midst of a poem written in the peculiar, and in its way peculiarly effective metre, which Mr. Arnold has invented, and of which he is so fond. Even if one did not break one's knees over the rhythm, the ideas are here expressed in mere stony prose.

One of the most beautiful poems in the volume is that on the "Grande Chartreuse," which expresses the melancholy of a mind preferring contemplation to action, and yet radically dissatisfied with the results of its own contemplation, with a tenderness, a music, and a spiritual beauty which are scarcely equalled in any other poem of Mr. Arnold's. It is scarcely dogma which pervades this poem so much as hopeless and passionate desire for dogma, but then that is just the sort of mental state which Mr. Arnold's art can express with the most perfect success, with a soft twilight mystery, which is wanting in his more didactic poems. The lines, too, on "A Southern Night" are wonderful in their melancholy serenity. On the whole, the volume is one of singular beauty, with many curiously prosaic flaws like knots in the grain; and to those who are not, like ourselves, already familiar with the greater half of it, will be a rich accession to their stores of contemplative delineation.

Mr. Emerson's Poems

Mr. Emerson fails as a poet. This book is very interesting reading considered as Mr. Emerson's philosophy chaunted with an emphasis that gives it a vitality it would not otherwise have, but the full depth and warmth of life, the "lyrical cry," as Mr. Arnold calls it,[1] is never here. It is at best intellectual conviction spread downwards till it touches the *surface* of feeling, – generally not so much as that, – intellectual conviction joined with a certain insight into beauty, and nothing more. What appears to us to persuade Mr. Emerson that he is a poet, is a certain fanatical belief in Nature which is more than even his pantheistical philosophy can fully justify. He has a true eye for external Nature, and a fanatical feeling about the wisdom and virtue she gives. But fanaticism of conviction is not by any means always, – nor often, – poetical. On the contrary, it may be safely laid down that only those emotions, however powerful, are poetical which, instead of pressing directly *outwards*, tend to press inwards on the other elements of our life, to saturate the whole character with their influence, and to borrow from these other elements of life all the harmony and analogy they are able to lend. Thus the same eager belief in Nature which, in Mr. Emerson, remains little but an intellectual fanaticism, has in other poets, – Wordsworth, for example, – sunk into the whole character, and borrowed life from the whole range of his character, till it has been transmuted into poetry. Where Wordsworth tells us of the daffodils, –

> "For oft when on my couch I lie
> In vacant or in pensive mood,
> They flash upon that inward eye
> That is the bliss of solitude,
> And then my heart with pleasure fills,
> And dances with the daffodils,"[2]

– you feel at once not only that the love of nature is blended with his whole being, – so it is, we have no doubt, with Mr. Emerson's, – but that the expression of that love enlists and harmonizes every faculty of his nature, so that the joy of freedom, and the delight of luminous thought, and the rapture of solitude, all flow at once into that glory of the eye and freshness of the senses, with which he is possessed as the breeze that blows upon his own cheek tosses the yellow daffodils and the lake's tiny waves. This is what we always want to feel in lyrical poetry, not only that it expresses keen and strong feeling, but feeling that enlists the whole character in its tones, feeling that has kindled the whole nature, and spread a light through it such as sunset spreads over the most leaden clouds and the coldest rocks. Now, this is what we never really feel with Mr. Emerson, — and even when we are half doubtfully beginning to feel it, the illusion vanishes in a moment. The chief part of his nature stands outside his verse, watching, lynx-eyed, the failure of his philosophy to account fully for the strength of his own belief. You are never for a moment able to forget the keen transcendentalist toiling away at the impossible task of getting his philosophy to explain fully his delight in external nature, — his preference of nature to man; — for in his philosophy nature's highest life is in man, and yet man only half interests him. The critic, standing outside his own feeling, lurks behind every line, peeps out in almost every phrase. For instance, by far the most musical and least intellectually interrupted lines we have been able to find in this little volume are the following, in *May Day*, on the music of the Æolian harp: —

> "Æolian harp,
> How strangely wise thy strain!
> Gay for youth, gay for youth,
> (Sweet is art, but sweeter truth,)
> In the hall at summer eve
> Fate and Beauty skilled to weave.
> From the eager opening strings
> Rung loud and bold the song.
> Who but loved the wind-harp's note?
> How should not the poet doat
> On its mystic tongue,
> With its primeval memory,
> Reporting what old minstrels said
> Of Merlin locked the harp within, —
> Merlin paying the pain of sin,
> Pent in a dungeon made of air, —
> And some attain his voice to hear,
> Words of pain and cries of fear,
> But pillowed all on melody,
> As fits the griefs of bards to be.
> And what if that all-echoing shell,
> Which thus the buried Past can tell,
> Should rive the Future, and reveal
> What his dread folds would fain conceal?
> It shares the secret of the earth,
> And of the kinds that owe her birth.

Speaks not of self that mystic tone,
But of the Overgods alone:
It trembles to the cosmic breath, —
As it heareth, so it saith;
Obeying meek the primal Cause,
It is the tongue of mundane laws.
And this, at least, I dare affirm,
Since genius too has bound and term,
There is no bard in all the choir,
Not Homer's self, the poet sire,
Wise Milton's odes of pensive pleasure,
Or Shakespeare, whom no mind can measure,
Nor Collins' verse of tender pain,
Nor Byron's clarion of disdain,
Scott, the delight of generous boys,
Or Wordsworth, Pan's recording voice, —
Not one of all can put in verse,
Or to this presence could rehearse,
The sights and voices ravishing
The boy knew on the hills in Spring,
When pacing through the oaks he heard
Sharp queries of the sentry-bird,
The heavy grouse's sudden whirr,
The rattle of the kingfisher;
Saw bonfires of the harlot flies
In the lowland, when day dies;
Or marked, benighted, and forlorn,
The first far signal-fire of morn.
These syllables that Nature spoke,
And the thoughts that in him woke,
Can adequately utter none
Save to his ear the wind-harp lone.
And best can teach its Delphian chord
How Nature to the soul is moored,
If once again that silent string,
As erst it wont, would thrill and ring."[3]

Some of that is musical and pleasant, especially the lines describing

"The sights and voices ravishing
The boy knew on the hills in Spring,"[3]

but in almost all the lines you see the intellectual struggle going on, the thinker bending his cold intellectual eye upon the emotion which the Æolian harp gives him, and trying to believe that it has more of "cosmic breath" in it, though it only expresses the harmony of physical laws, than those poets who, according to the Emersonian philosophy, are nothing but far higher steps in the organization of laws of the same kind and the same immutability. He feels that such poets do *not* tell "how nature to the soul is moored," as he awkwardly phrases it, as well as natural sounds; but there is a secret puzzle in him on this score which keeps the greater part of his nature outside the feeling he expresses. His real philosophy is given elsewhere in still colder verses. He has half forgotten and half remembers it here, when he praises the Æolian harp thus: —

> "One musician is sure,
>   His wisdom will not fail:
> He has not tasted wine impure,
>   Or bent to passion frail.
> Age cannot cloud his memory,
> Nor grief untune his voice,
> Ranging down the ruled scale,
> From tone of joy to inward wail,
> Tempering the pitch of all
> In his inward cave."[4]

You can almost see, at all events, think you see, in the very hesitating sway of the rhythm that Mr. Emerson is discontented with his own poetical reasons for preferring the Æolian harp, and is questioning himself from outside himself, as he pours out drop by drop this temperate expression of his secretly intemperate feeling. The warm emotion passing through the mould of a cold intellect is repelled, as it were, and kept at a distance by something analogous to a capillary repulsion, and the reader feels a separating space between the intellectual mould and the feeling poured into it.[5]

By far the greater part of the book has not even as much of a struggle between feeling and intellect as this, but is pure intellectual opinion metrically — and not always very rhythmically — expressed. Take the following expression of his true theory about the share Nature has in man's highest works: —

> "NATURE.
> "She is gamesome and good,
> But of mutable mood, —
> No dreary repeater now and again,
> She will be all things to all men.
> She who is old, but nowise feeble,
> Pours her power into the people,
> Merry and manifold without bar,
> Makes and moulds them what they are,
> And what they call their city way
> Is not their way, but hers,
> And what they say they made to-day,
> They learned of the oaks and firs.

She spawneth men as mallows fresh,
Hero and maiden, flesh of her flesh;
She drugs her water and her wheat
With the flavours she finds meet,
And gives them what to drink and eat;
And having thus their bread and growth,
They do her bidding, nothing loath.
What's most theirs is not their own,
But borrowed in atoms from iron and stone,
And in their vaunted works of Art
The master-stroke is still her part."[6]

No one can call that poetry. It is a cold version of Mr. Emerson's old doctrine in *Representative Men* that "incarnate chlorine discovers chlorine."[7]

It is very curious to learn that Mr. Emerson's semi-political odes have been sung in Boston and Concord *by public meetings*. Nothing less popular and more doctrinal was surely ever sung, even out of the old Presbyterian hymn-books.[8] Take the following, not exactly indeed in the spirit of Artemus Ward's saying that "the earth revolves upon its axis subject to the Constitution of the United States,"[9] but still embodying the same profound emotion of ever fresh wonder at that great achievement: —

"Ode Sung in the Town Hall, Concord, July 4, 1857.

"O tenderly the haughty day
    Fills his blue urn with fire;
One morn is in the mighty heaven,
    And one in our desire.

"The cannon boom from town to town,
    Our pulses are not less,
The joy-bells chime their tidings down,
    Which children's voices bless.

"For He that flung the broad blue fold
    O'er-mantling land and sea,
One third part of the sky unrolled
    For the banner of the free.

"The men are ripe of Saxon kind
    To build an equal State, —
To take the statute from the mind,
    And make of duty fate.

"United States! the ages plead, —
    Present and Past in under-song, —

Go, put your creed into your deed,
    Nor speak with double tongue.

"For sea and land don't understand,
    Nor skies without a frown
See rights for which the one hand fights
    By the other cloven down.

"Be just at home; then write your scroll
    Of honour o'er the sea,
And bid the broad Atlantic roll
    A ferry of the free.

"And, henceforth, there shall be no chain,
    Save underneath the sea,
The wires shall murmur through the main
    Sweet songs of LIBERTY.

"The conscious stars accord above,
    The waters wild below,
And under, through the Cable wove,
    His fiery errands go.

"For He that worketh high and wise,
    Nor pauses in His plan,
Will take the sun out of the skies
    Ere freedom out of man."[10]

The only verse here of real life is the last. The "ferry of the free" is a new form of the "herring-pond" metaphor, and the wires murmuring liberty is mere "buncombe."

"To take the statute from the mind
    And make of duty fate,

is really fine, but it is less poetry than a sententious apophthegm of ethical wisdom.

On the whole, we do not doubt that this book will be read with pleasure as an expression of Mr. Emerson's remarkable character, at once grave and dreamy, playful and transcendental, shrewd and ecstatic, humorous and yet liable to the special Philistinism of Yankee provincialism, teeming with intellectual culture, and yet with a basis of distrust for intellectual culture at the bottom; in a word, delicate in critical insight, and yet disposed to grasp almost as a duty at the grandiloquent and gigantesque fancies of what we may call the Prairie school of metaphor. But, as poetry, this volume will not be read long. It touches the confines of poetry here and there, but even then only just takes from it a faint and evanescent glow.

Professor Huxley's Hidden Chess-Player

Professor Huxley has told the working-men of South London, in a very fine passage of his most masculine English, what seems to him the highest meaning of education. It is such a mastery of the laws of the great game which is always being played between the individual man or woman and an unseen player who plays the phenomena of the universe on fixed and more or less accessible rules, as will enable the human players to carry on the longest game with the most brilliant success. But we must not spoil by summarizing a passage which deserves to live in English literature, both for its vigour of style and the admirable, almost grand expression it gives to a particular creed which is gaining rapidly upon us, in spite of the desolation of its summit, – in spite of the stern, almost solemn, neglect with which it passes by our highest life: –

> "Suppose it were perfectly certain that the life and fortune of every one of us would one day or other depend upon his winning or losing a game of chess. Don't you think that we should all consider it to be a primary duty to learn at least the names and the moves of the pieces; to have a notion of a gambit and a keen eye for all the means of giving and getting out of check? Do you not think that we should look with a disapprobation amounting to scorn upon the father who allowed his son, or the State which allowed its members, to grow up without knowing a pawn from a knight? Now, it is a very plain and elementary truth that the life, the fortune, and the happiness of every one of us, and, more or less, of those who are connected with us, do depend upon our knowing something of the rules of a game infinitely more difficult and complicated than chess. It is a game which has been played for untold ages, every man and woman of us being one of the two players in a game of his or her own. The chess board is the world, the pieces the phenomena of the universe, the rules of the game are what we call the laws of nature. The player on the other side is hidden from us. All we know is that his play is always fair, just, and patient. But, also, that he never overlooks a mistake or makes the smallest allowance for ignorance. To the man who plays well the highest stakes are paid with that sort of overflowing generosity with which the strong shows delight in strength. And one who plays

ill is checkmated without haste, but without remorse. My metaphor will remind some of you of the famous picture in which Retzsch has depicted Satan playing at chess with man for his soul. Substitute for the mocking fiend in that picture a calm, strong angel who is playing for love as we say, and would rather lose than win, and I should accept it as an image of human life. Well, now what I mean by education is learning the rules of this mighty game. In other words, education is the instruction of the intellect in the laws of nature; and the fashioning of the affections, and of the will, into harmony with those laws."[1]

Surely Professor Huxley should have said "substitute for this mocking fiend," — *not* "a calm strong angel," but the celebrated Automaton chess-player which at one time went about the world defeating every antagonist who ventured to cope with him.[2] We do not mean that Professor Huxley denies in the least a large intelligence to his hidden player, but that he does mean expressly to affirm that his moves are not free, but automatic, in the sense of being divested of all personal reference to the individual character pitted against him in the contest. If the simile be accurate, indeed, there is no provision for a double bearing of every move, no analogy for the pity which manifests itself most when a piece is taken, for the flash of recognition between the earthly and the eternal player which so often begins with disaster, for the visionary joy which now and again illumines the face of the defeated player as he acknowledges the last awful announcement of checkmate. Mr. Huxley ignores, in his definition of education, all but the visible issues of the contest between the soul of the universe and the soul of man. It is true that at a late stage of his lecture he speaks of education as including "passions trained to come to heel, by a vigorous will — the servant of a tender conscience," — and the noble training which teaches "to love all beauty, whether of nature or of art, to hate all vileness, and to respect others as himself." And difficult as it seems to understand how such love as this could be learned out of the study of the game Professor Huxley had previously described, it seems clear that he so intends us to understand him. For he insists that moral law should be understood to be of the same self-executing kind as physical law; that "there lies in the nature of things a reason for every moral law as cogent and well defined as that which underlies every physical law; that stealing and lying are just as certain to be followed by evil consequences as putting your hand in the fire or jumping out of a garret window." If this be indeed so, then of course the moral laws of the universe are as much elementary rules of the great game which Mr. Huxley has so finely described as the physical laws; and the player who has the subtlest knowledge of the former and follows them with the truest fidelity, will gain thereby as much advantage in the conflict for existence[3] as he who has the subtlest knowledge of the physical laws, and conforms to them with the truest fidelity. But we very much doubt if the thinking men among Mr. Huxley's audience will admit it to be so. If they want the maximum of tangible success in the great tussle with the mysterious Automaton who moves so silently and inexorably those pieces which Professor Huxley calls the phenomena of nature, they will soon find that the only account they should take of moral laws, other than enlightened self-interest is comprehended under the best *average* morality of their day. While a man who has pierced a new secret of physical nature will probably reap the greatest reward both in power and fame from his anticipation of other discoverers, the man who has entered into a new secret of moral or spiritual life, will in all probability reap little but neglect and embarrassment from his keen vision and his faithful application of his new principle. It is true enough, no doubt, that if Mr. Huxley includes in his "laws of the game" those highest of invisible phenomena which relate the spirit of the visible and earthly player to that of the invisible and eternal, there may turn out to be, to him who does not calculate upon it as part of his wages, infinitely more than adequate reward, as well for the vision of new moral truth as for the practical confession of it. But then the difficulty of this higher view of "the game" is that it destroys the meaning of the metaphor altogether, since, in this sense, *he* may win the most who is soonest checkmated to mortal eyes; while he who carries on the struggle longest and with the most brilliant success, may wish, when the long evaded checkmate is pronounced at last, that it had preceded instead of following his most brilliant moves. In fact, the very essence of Professor Huxley's simile consists in the unknown character of the being within the Automaton, and the immutable character of the visible laws which determine his moves. Once admit a double bearing of each move, — a bearing on the free spiritual relation between the players, which may be (and often is), almost the converse of its bearing on the visible course of the game, — and the whole force of the illustration is gone. For then the greatest move of which the earthly player is capable may be one which leads directly to the checkmate; or it may be that a move which secures him the most brilliant position and protracts the inevitable defeat to the utmost verge of possibility, is, from that higher point of view, the most miserable of human blunders. If, then, the "laws of the game" are those the observance of which lead to visible and acknowledged success, or even which invariably preclude a visible and apparent failure, we think that any education which is satisfied with such a study may prove to have been of the poorest; while if, on the other hand, the "laws of the game" include all the moral and spiritual, no less than the visible and tangible issues of the struggle, we should utterly deny Mr. Huxley's principle that the invisible player "never overlooks a mistake or makes the smallest allowance for ignorance," and that the man who plays ill is "checkmated without haste, but without remorse." It is obvious, we think, that Mr. Huxley is here carefully excluding the higher moral and spiritual issues of the various moves, and describing a game in which error is never beneficent except so far as it teaches the danger of error in future, in which suffering cannot be the minister of joy, nor failure the seed of triumph. If all the moral laws, the highest as well as the lowest, those not yet discerned and accepted by society, as well as those which are embodied in our existing system of things, were self-executing in the same sense as the physical laws, — if a man who was incapable (say) of the higher refinements, of scrupulous honour, or of glad self-sacrifice, were *ipso facto* the loser in this great game with the soul of nature by his want of knowledge, then Mr. Huxley's metaphor would be perfect. But the truth is that the loss in these cases is not a loss of success in the game (nay, often the reverse), but only a loss of mutual intelligence and love between the players; and of this Professor Huxley, by virtue of his assertion that the other player is unknown, can take no cognizance.

No account of education, — we do not mean here the education of schools and colleges, for, as we have often asserted, the highest education is barely ever attainable in schools and colleges at all, — but in that much larger sense in which Professor Huxley uses the term when he speaks of the education of life, — which does not take cognizance of the free spiritual relations between God and man, as well as the fixed physical relations between nature and man, is so much as half the truth. Mr. MacLeod Campbell, in the preface to his new edition of one of the deepest and noblest of modern contributions to theological study, says most profoundly: — "That place which the fixedness of law, as that which we may always assume, has in our practical relation to the reign of law, — the character of God as the hearer and answerer of prayer has in our practical relation to the kingdom of God. And as Science, in the largest sense of the word, is our practical light, under the reign of law, so is Christ the light of the kingdom of God."[4] And if he were to adopt Professor Huxley's metaphor, Mr. Campbell would doubtless say that in order to prevent our regarding a thorough mastery of "the laws of the game" as the final aim of human existence, the unseen Will within the automatic system called Nature, has from time to time sent amongst us earthly players who cared for "the laws of the game" mainly as a discipline leading up to a knowledge of Him who constructed them, — and has sent One especially, who came but to show that an early and crushing defeat might well be consistent with a perfect knowledge of the Spirit of Him who inflicted that defeat, and so to reduce the petty successes and failures of future games to their true spiritual value, measuring them not by their apparent results, but by the sympathy engendered between the infinite and the finite player. We suspect that Mr. Huxley himself, little as he would assent to such a statement, would not be satisfied without laying down some conditions under which he himself would choose to regard defeat as virtual victory. When he tells us that the passions of an educated man must be trained, "by a firm will, under the guidance of a sensitive conscience, to come to heel" whenever required to do so by their owner, does he imagine that this result can ever be attained through mere study of "the rules of the game?" As we have said before, a "sensitive conscience" is no part of the apparatus for a successful playing of the game, though an average conscience might be. A "sensitive conscience" is a condition of obedience not to the laws of the game, but to the spirit of the hidden player, and not the only condition either. For a sensitive conscience will do little except to hamper both the game and the player, unless it be accompanied by a faith which can look beyond defeat, and a love which can transform defeat itself into triumph.

We do not believe that Professor Huxley, if pressed, would accept his own illustration of the significance of the highest education, without some assumption of spiritual conditions far higher than those "of the game," and which should often override them. Were there not indeed such conditions, and were there not also an indestructible faith that they will be fulfilled even more perfectly when the game is over and the board is cleared, than even while it is playing, — we do not doubt that the noblest of all our players would themselves court the checkmate by which all this, in that case, unmeaning craft, and toil, and skill would at length be ended.

The Darwinian Jeremiad[1]

A letter from the able critic in the September *Fraser,* which we print in another column, attempts some reply to our notice this day fortnight of his curious jeremiad over the failure, in the case of Man, of the Darwinian principle of "natural selection through the struggle for existence."[2] The critic's candour, however, induces him to concede so much to us, and to shift so widely the field of discussion, that we should be quite content to leave the matter where he does, but that one side of our belief as to the different "law" which comes into action in the case of man, and that, as it seems to us, the most important, seems neither to have been adequately brought out by us nor apprehended by him. Our correspondent has, we think, partly forgotten that the question, as he originally raised it, was not directly one of practical duty or social policy, but one of pure scientific fact. His case was this: — In the lower races of animals the better organized displace the worse organized, as Mr. Darwin has shown, partly by securing the best portions of the common food for which they compete, partly by conquering them if it comes to direct battle, partly by being better adapted in general to the circumstances in which they are placed. Our correspondent lamented that this law fails when we come to the competitions of classes and individuals in human societies. Instead of finding, he said, that the men and women of the best physique, the best intelligence, and the best morale edge out of existence those of poorer physique, lower intelligence, and a worse morale, almost the opposite tendency may be noted. Our elaborate modern medicine patches up the worn-out constitutions of the luxurious and dissipated; our property-worshipping institutions secure the greatest hereditary wealth, the largest material advantages, for men far too degenerate to have won any place for themselves, had they been born anywhere but on the vantage-ground of inherited wealth; and our charitable institutions give to the ignorant, the brutal, the coarse multitudes of the semi-pauper classes just sufficient assistance to keep up their rate of multiplication. Under these circumstances the section of society which is most fit for the parentage of the people of the future is least likely to claim the people of the future for its posterity. It is the section which has too little means to marry early with prudence, and too much prudence to marry early without means.

Hence, while the indolent and worn-out upper classes, and the ignorant and careless multitude multiply rapidly, – those who have no wealth to begin with, and have the virtue and wisdom to wait for it, multiply slowly. In other words, the best specimens of humanity do not edge the worst specimens off the face of the earth, but rather do the worst increase with a higher *proportional* rapidity than the best.

To this our reply was in effect as follows, – would you really wish the Darwinian law to extend in its full force to the case of man, even if you could have it so? What would that really *mean*? It would mean the strong snatching their food from the weak, the able clearing the field so effectually as to leave nothing for the less competent, the happy casting no glance either to the right or the left that might bring home to them the sufferings of the unhappy. The true Darwinian law is a law of unalloyed competition, – of "struggle for existence." If we could have it working with all its force, if we were to get rid of the "failure" which the reviewer has noticed, it could only be by expunging those elements in our nature which are the cause of this failure. But what are those elements? What is it which makes it impossible for *men* to clear away the ailing members of the human family as healthy buffaloes would gore to death their sick, and to leave paupers to be famished or plague-stricken by the results of their own imprudence or self-indulgence, as locusts leave locusts to rot on the plains they have devoured? Clearly that which *prevents* the true Darwinian consummation in the case of man, is the new principle of disinterestedness, of self-denial, of pity for the weak, of love for the miserable, of compassion for the poor, which is rooted in the highest part of our nature – in our religion, – and which distinguishes us from the animal tribes to which the Darwinian law absolutely applies. In historical fact the different Churches, Jewish, Christian, Mohammedan, and others, have done more than any other influences in history to counteract the influence of the Darwinian principle still working in our animal and, as St. Paul says, "carnal" nature. We were not discussing with the critic in *Fraser* a question of practical duty, but a question of historical philosophy. What we say is, – sigh for the perfect action of the competitive Darwinian principle as long as you please in relation to man, all history shows that you will not attain it, and, moreover, that that which prevents you attaining it is just that part of human nature which is best worth having and perpetuating. If there were no "failure" in the operation of the Darwinian principle of selection, there would be a failure in human nature. If there be no such failure in human nature, there must be this failure, which you so much regret, in the operation of the Darwinian principle. It is a mistake to imagine that we were either apologizing for or advocating any particular policy in relation to the physically, intellectually, and morally halt and blind; we were merely stating a visible fact of immensely broad proportions, which ought to arrest the attention of those who complain that "natural selection" does not do its perfect work for man, — namely, that if it did, or could, man would not be man, but something much below what he is. We did not attempt to explain away the evils enumerated by the essayist; we admitted them; but what we did object to, was the notion that any manipulation of the Darwinian principle could possibly be the cure. It would cure too much, we said, — extinguish all that is noble in humanity, as well as the evils arising out of that nobility. We ventured to suggest that with regard to man, the true providential method is different in kind from that which is used in developing the lower orders of creation; and that it may consist more in directly increasing and multiplying a higher order of positive qualities, than in merely eliminating imperfections. At all events, in fact, we do see a whole host of *new* evils springing into existence in the human race which do not affect the lower animals at all, and in all probability these new evils are to be contended with and extinguished, if at all, by conscious moral agency, at least as much as by that process of hereditary elimination which applies chiefly in the lower regions of creation.

Now, as far as we understand our correspondent, we have convinced him entirely of all this. He sings the praises of the law of "natural selection" no longer. He contends for a higher principle of moral selection which is not "natural," — which we call distinctly supernatural, — which, at all events, is not strictly competitive at all, — which is not due to a "struggle for existence", — which includes the idea of self-denial, — which, in a word, only differs from the ordinary moral criticisms on human nature in this, that it would aim as much as possible at the impossible task of restraining by every means in human power — (and practically there are none) — the *multiplication* of stocks tainted either by hereditary disease, or by hereditary poverty and incompetence. Now on this simply useless and impractical aspiration of the *Fraser* critic's, we passed no opinion, because it never occurred to us to discuss aspirations after the impossible. We only offered a suggestion as to the true moral makeweight which may probably, as a matter of historical fact, be found to supply in the case of man an *equivalent* for the useful influence of the Darwinian principle of purely 'natural selection' in the case of the lower orders of creatures. We said that it might be found that what is *lost* by the less speedy extinction of feeble physical types of constitution, and the more rapid multiplication of the lowest and least refined moral types, may be much more than regained by the new moral life which springs out of the demands of the weak and the miserable on the self-denial and benevolence of the strong and the happy. Our correspondent seems to concede as much. "I fully recognize," he writes, "that the existence of misery to be relieved, of sufferings to be sympathized with, of weakness to be borne with, of poverty to be assisted, of diseases to be treated, of degradation to be raised, is a most efficient, nay, perhaps an absolutely necessary instrument for the education and development of the best portions of our nature, and for bringing man up to the highest level he is capable of attaining." Well, then, he admits almost all we ask: — only he would *eradicate*, he says, all these evils rather than merely alleviate and propagate them. So, of course, would we, — if we could. That would indeed be sham benevolence, which, having it in its power to eradicate any evil, — be it disease, or pauperism, or anything else, — only alleviates it in order to leave a sufficient number of patients for the benevolence of the next generation. If we came to speak of concrete duties, we should be the last to deny that a man with hereditary insanity or scrofula, or any other hopeless and yet inevitably transmitted disease, in his family, would be performing a very high kind of duty in refusing to perpetuate it by marrying. But it never occurred to us that the *Fraser* critic had entered on a discussion of the limits of practical interference with the transmission of inherited constitutions, physical or mental; we thought he was drawing an unfavourable augury for the destiny of man from the fact that there is no fully adequate *physical* provision for eliminating any constitutional mischief, moral or physical, from the stock. We admit that there is none such.

Indeed, we are *comparatively* indifferent whether, as our correspondent asserts, the best classes are or are not the parents of the next generation, because we believe that the hereditary provisions for eliminating mischief, so essential in the lower races, are replaced by vastly larger *moral* provisions, independent of the hereditary principle, existing in the case of man. The organic arrangements for draining off imperfections are less, just because the spiritual machinery for doing so is much greater. And this is our answer, as far as one is conceivable, to our correspondent's last paragraph. He accuses us, very oddly and erroneously, of wishing to multiply and perpetuate moral whetstones, the race of *patients*, for the sake of the moral razors which are to be sharpened on them, *i.e.*, the consciences and feelings which are to be trained and disciplined by dealings with the sufferers. That is not our view at all. All we say is this: — As a matter of fact unquestionably, hereditary diseases will not be exterminated; as a matter of fact, pauperism, strive as we may, will always make head against our efforts; as a matter of fact, a great number of infirmities which would, under the law of "natural selection," disappear by the mere disadvantage they entail in the "struggle for existence" will not disappear so rapidly, if at all, and this because a *higher* law, not a *lower*, is at work. But what is the compensation? We believe it to be this, — not merely that the highest class of virtues are called out by the existence of such miseries and infirmities, in those who give their lives to eradicate or alleviate them, — but also that the existence of these infirmities and miseries becomes the condition of a great variety of higher types of character, even amongst those who *suffer from them*. Ill-health in animals is the condition of no higher class of moral qualities, and, therefore, ill-health in animals is soon eradicated by the law of "struggle for existence." Poverty for animals is the condition of no moral qualities at all, and therefore poverty for animals, if it can be said to exist at all, only means famishing and death. So, again, of deformity in animals, or defects of breed of other sorts such as indicate inferiority of capacity, — none of these are capable of leading, in creatures that are not free, to any variety of higher qualities. But with men it is not so. Ill-health, as everybody knows, is the condition of the growth of a great number of the finest qualities of the spirit; poverty is a condition of the discipline of another great group of virtues, so conspicuous, that "religious poverty" has been mistakenly erected into a merit by some of the most popular religions of the earth; — and humility, which so far as it is a true virtue, means a readiness to recognize fully all your own shortcomings and all the superior excellences of others, is a virtue which is rarely bred in the midst of perfect prosperity and wealth. We do not, then, in the least wish to pretend that our correspondent's difficulties are not difficulties. All we assert is that the Darwinian law, if it could be really efficient in the case of man, would kill a vast deal more than it would cure; and also that the very inherited mischiefs which our correspondent complains of are, to a large extent, the *conditions* of the growth of so much good, that we may fairly believe that the true remedy for these evils is not, for the most part, one which would extinguish them by extinguishing the physical stock to which they belong, — but rather the liberal administration, and the free and willing adoption, of large spiritual remedies calculated first to attenuate them, and finally to nourish and discipline a variety of the highest moral types.

Dr. Newman's Oxford Sermons

As this reissue of Dr. Newman's "parochial and plain" sermons preached at Oxford is now nearly completed, only one of the eight volumes remaining to appear, it seems the right time to say something of their adaptation for the wants of the generation which only knows him as the greatest of the Roman Catholic converts. We do not pretend to have read as yet all or nearly all the sermons in these seven volumes. With some we were familiar long ago.[1] With many we have made acquaintance fo.· the first time in this reissue; but each of them is a separate work in itself, and in all there are a set of common assumptions and common features which reappear so frequently that, for the purpose of estimating their general character, tendency, and influence, it is impossible to regard them as if they were chapters in a continuous treatise. The Rector of Farnham (Essex) who has republished them, has we think, done well. Certainly no sermons representing so vividly the real inner scenery of the preacher's mind have been preached in our generation. With the most perfect and unaffected simplicity of style, they combine every other trace of coming from a mind filled to overflowing with the faith and thoughts they express. There is none of the "made" eloquence of Church dignitaries, nor of the dry monotone of priests officially rehearsing a lesson. It is a life, and an intense life, and not merely a creed, which speaks in these volumes. That it is, however, not only a life, but also a creed, and in many respects, as we hold, a false creed, – false chiefly by its misinterpretation of and comparative contempt for the new intellectual forces of our own day, – is the chief, though a great, deduction from their value. Let us make some attempt at separating those elements of thought in Dr. Newman's sermons which have given him so singular a power over his own day, from those elements of thought which have separated him from it and driven him out of sympathy with, we do not mean merely the noisy, but the most sincere and earnest of those of his countrymen who have most cared not only to know truth, but to live for it.

On the first side of the account we must note that Dr. Newman has never treated revelation as a mere expression of the arbitrary or even purely inscrutable will of God, but always as expressing the deepest and most immutable distinctions in moral fact and nature, distinctions which *could* not be excluded from operating their inevitable consequences, whether a particular decree of revelation had been proclaimed or not. He is a realist in the sense of believing that all religious distinctions are distinctions not created either *by* our minds or even *for* our minds, but deeply rooted in the moral constitution of all moral beings. He is so far thoroughly scientific in his conceptions of theology. He regards the moral constitution of the universe not as a sic-volo, sic-jubeo of the Almighty's,[2] but as a chain of causes all in the closest connection, of which one could not be separated from another without a general overthrow of the moral foundations of human life. Thus in the very first sermon of this long series, Dr. Newman aims at showing that there is nothing arbitrary in the law which makes holiness here the necessary condition of happiness hereafter, – that it is not a law of the divine Will, so to say, so much as a law of the divine Nature. Dr. Newman, with his usual force, impresses on us how miserable an unrighteous and unholy man would be if he *could* be admitted into closer communion with God without any change in his inner nature; how he would find in the divine world "no pursuits but those which he had disliked or despised, nothing which bound him to aught else in the universe, and made him feel at home, nothing which he could enter into and rest upon." "A careless, a sensual, an unbelieving mind, a mind destitute of the love and fear of God, with narrow views and earthly aims, a low standard of duty, and a benighted conscience, a mind contented with itself and unresigned to God's will, *would feel as little pleasure at the last day at the words 'Enter into the joy of thy Lord' as it does now at the words 'Let us pray'.*"[3] Nothing could more forcibly illustrate than that, the joylessness of divine life to those unprepared for divine life, – the divergence of moral desires, of hopes and fears, and longings, between the mind which seeks God and the mind which does not. It is not a mere decree of God's that the latter must suffer; it is of the essence of its own nature, no less than of His. Dr. Newman says in another page of the same sermon, that, as it is part of the physical constitution of nature that straw ignites and burns away at a heat which leaves iron unaltered in form and substance, so it is of the moral constitution of nature that certain orders of minds must be simply inflamed and thrown into suffering by the very influences which are perfectly in harmony with the nature of others.

Nor is Dr. Newman only a realist in treating religious truth as the outcome of distinctions so deep in nature that no mere decree even of the Divine Will could change them. He is also a realist in treating human faith, and human thought and language on religious subjects, as worthless, unless they mark out and point to spiritual causes and tendencies infinitely deeper and more full of meaning than any mere acts and thoughts of ours. Just as the scientific man trusts not to the signs by which he reasons, but to the forces of which those signs are the mere calculus,

Dr. Newman constantly teaches that faith is the act of trusting yourself to great and permanent spiritual forces, the tidal power of which, and not the power of your acts of faith, is commissioned by God to carry you into the clearer light. He uniformly speaks of faith as a "venture," an act of the soul by which it throws itself on what is beyond its own power, by which it gives itself up without either the power or the right to know the full consequences, gives itself up to some power higher than itself and beyond itself, as a man trusts himself to the sea, or to a railway, or to any natural power beyond his own control. He speaks uniformly, just as a writer of a very different school spoke in a very remarkable parable in the *Pall Mall Gazette* of Thursday week, of faith as action, not feeling, but action which is taken in light "neither clear nor dark," as a venture of which we cannot count the consequences, and yet a venture for the highest end of life.[4] To use his own words, it consists in risking "what we have for what we have not; and doing so in a noble, generous way, not indeed rashly or lightly, still knowing accurately what we are doing, not knowing either what we give up, nor, again, what we shall gain; uncertain about our reward, uncertain about the extent of sacrifice, in all respects leaning, waiting upon Him, trusting in Him to fulfil his promise, trusting in Him to enable us to fulfil our own vows, and so in all respects proceeding without carefulness or anxiety about the future."[5] And as Dr. Newman is a true realist in speaking of acts of faith as ventures made in the dark, at least as to *results*, for the highest end possible to us, and in reliance upon forces which are not our own and to which we implicitly trust ourselves by our acts of faith, so again he is a true realist in speaking of human language. In the very fine sermon on "Unreal Words," he points out almost in the same strain as does the author of the fine parable above alluded to, how much unreal language men use, and how specially unreal it is on religious subjects, and how worse than worthless, mischievous, so far as it is unreal, *i.e*, without resting on a basis of facts.[6] But Dr. Newman goes further in his realism than this. He recognizes that no words on the subject of religion can be wholly real, any more than words on the subject of half-discovered forces in physical nature. They are as real as they can be, if they rest on fact, though they quite fail to express the full force and bearing of those facts. Dr. Newman points out that words may be, so to say, *more* real than those who use them are aware of. They may be the indices of powers and forces far beyond what those who use them suspect, because those who use them have only got a superficial glimpse into the action and heart of those forces. Just as 'weight' meant a great deal more than Newton himself knew when he first began to suspect what the moon's weight really meant, and as the idea of which the word was the index carried him far beyond his own meaning when he first used it, so Dr. Newman points out that moral professions often mean far more than those who make them know, and thus commit the soul to the larger meaning, not to the less, embarking those who use them on enterprizes far beyond their immediate intention, nay, far beyond their immediate strength. In this way words express powers outside the speaker, powers which have, when he speaks, only just taken hold of him superficially, but which, being divine powers, strengthen and tighten their grasp, till they carry those who half carelessly used them whither they had no intention of going. "We ever promise things greater than we master, and we wait on God to enable us to perform them. Our promising involves a prayer for light and strength."[7] In all these respects Dr. Newman's teaching in these sermons seems to us realist in the truest and most modern sense of the term, — in that sense in which modern science has taught us to understand the full depth of realism. And it is by virtue of this intellectual sympathy with the sincerest teaching of modern times, that Dr. Newman, applying the same spirit to moral and religious subjects, has exerted so great and so wholesome an influence on English theology.

There is, however, as a matter of course, in one who has become a Roman Catholic, another side to Dr. Newman's teaching, by virtue of which he has separated himself from all which is sincerest and best in the intellectual teaching of the day. And the root of all his errors seems to us to be this, that he practically applies his theory that faith, — the act, — is a *'venture,'* i.e., that we are morally bound to do much of the consequences of which we are necessarily kept in the dark, to the *intellectual* side of faith, not simply to the act of trust, but to the *belief* of creeds. Now here, as it seems to us, is the beginning of all sorts of insincerities. In action you may and must trust yourself to the highest motive which God puts into your heart, at a risk. But in intellectual belief there is no such thing legitimately as silencing a doubt. If you risk pain to do right, you do not play any tricks with yourself; you know that you are incurring a risk of suffering, and prefer to do it for the sake of the motive. But to risk error, in order to believe right, is a contradiction in terms. You cannot believe right unless you open your mind fully to all the risks of error, and look your uncertainties, your insoluble difficulties, in the face as fully as your certainties. Dr. Newman seems to us to make *obedience* the root, not only of moral and religious action, but of moral and religious thought. But in order to do so, he has to assume that we all have an intellectual authority over us as clear and articulate as the moral authority which speaks to our conscience. He speaks of dissent as necessarily sin, though not always conscious sin. He speaks of the right to differ from the Church as very much the same as the right "to damn yourself";[8] he identifies the submission to Church authority with the submission to God's voice, and even makes the reliance on the sacrament of ordination a duty of the same order, and resting upon the same sort of foundation, as the duty of prayer.

In other words, he sets out with a complicated Church organization as set over the conscience in the same sense as God's moral law, and assumes that a churchman may verify for himself the moral validity of apostolical succession just as truly as an ordinary soul may verify for itself the value of prayer, or as a chemist may verify for himself the significance and value of the laws of chemical affinity.[9] All this network of assumptions strikes us as having its root in the notion that obedience is *even more* the root of our intellectual than of our moral life, — since Dr. Newman would not ask us to obey any moral command which does not appeal to our conscience, whereas he imposes on our intellects a ready-made ecclesiastical system of the most complex kind, which it is quite impossible for any rational being to accept as a whole without knowing that he is going on a mere probability or possibility, — and, as it seems to us, on a strong improbability. And in thus rooting the intellectual act of belief in obedience, he has done what his great intellect could never have done if it had once been imbued with any sympathy with the science of the day. No wonder that in the striking sermon on "The Religion of the Age" (Vol. 1.), he tells us at once that man can find out nothing about himself by studying the outward universe, and that he himself would think the religion of the age much better than it is, if it were less merely amiable, and had more of the zeal and fear which, in excess, give rise to bigotry and superstition than it has.[10] The truth is that Dr. Newman has no sympathy at all with that latitudinarianism which arises from a genuinely scientific spirit of doubt carried into the region of ecclesiastical authority. He may be quite right in saying that the study of the material universe can never teach man his duty, but it *can* teach man his ignorance and the mistakes of intellectual theory to which his intellect is liable. It is the spirit of science much more than the spirit of selfishness and self-will that has made it impossible to the present age to accept the intellectual authority of any church organization. We *know* that in point of fact the principle of "obedience" to such authorities has led the intellect into all sorts of pitfalls. We know that we are on the track of physical laws which are inconsistent not only with the physical assumptions of Churches, but with the physical assumptions of many of the writers of revelation. We ought not to accept a mere intellectual guess out of obedience to anybody. Obedience is no duty except in relation to a moral claim. An intellectual conviction may come through obedience to a moral claim, but it cannot come from any act of intellectual obedience, for the words have no meaning. You may feel confident that a special authority on intellectual subjects is right, through having usually found him right, but you cannot *obey* him intellectually, you can only be convinced and persuaded by him. This assumption of Dr. Newman's that obedience is at the root of our intellectual faith, seems to us what vitiates a wide vein of reasoning in his sermons, and what has led him into the Roman Church, where there is at least an authority with *some* intellectual prestige to obey.

We have said nothing of the exquisite *manner* of these sermons, the manner of a mind at once tender and holy, at once loving and austere, at once real and dramatic, at once full of insight into human nature and full of the humility which springs from a higher source; but the following touching and musical passage will say more for Dr. Newman's manner than any words of ours. It is from a sermon called "Christ Manifested in Remembrance": —

> "Let a person who trusts he is on the whole serving God acceptably look back upon his past life, and he will find how critical were moments and acts which at the time seemed the most indifferent: as, for instance, the school he was sent to as a child, the occasion of his falling in with those persons who have most benefited him, the accidents which determined his calling or prospects, whatever they were. God's hand is ever over His own, and He leads them forward by a way they know not of. The utmost they can do is to believe, what they cannot see now, what they shall see hereafter; and as believing, to act together with God towards it. And hence perchance it is, that years that are past bear in retrospect so much of fragrance with them, though at the time perhaps we saw little in them to take pleasure in; or rather we did not, could not realize that we *were* receiving pleasure, though we received it. We received pleasure, because we were in the presence of God, but we knew it not; we knew not what we received; we did not bring home to ourselves or reflect upon the pleasure we were receiving; but afterwards, when enjoyment is past, reflection comes in. We feel at the time; we recognize and reason afterwards. Such, I say, is the sweetness and softness with which days long passed away fall upon the memory, and strike us. The most ordinary years, when we seemed to be living for nothing, these shine forth to us in their very regularity and orderly course. What was sameness at the time, is now stability; what was dullness, is now a soothing calm; what seemed unprofitable has now its treasure in itself; what was but monotony, is now harmony; all is pleasing and comfortable, and we regard it all with affection."[11]

Mr. Matthew Arnold on the Modern Element in Literature

Mr. Matthew Arnold has published in *Macmillan's Magazine* for February a demonstration that Athenian literature, in the age of Pericles, was much more *modern* than English literature in the age of Elizabeth, and we think we may add also, without endangering the least deviation from the accomplished author's real meaning and principle, than English literature in the present day. We need not say, therefore, that Mr. Arnold does not use the word "modern," as applied to literature, in the sense of advanced in the order of time. He uses 'modern' in a peculiar sense. "A significant, a highly-developed, a culminating epoch, on the one hand, — a comprehensive, a commensurate, an adequate literature, on the other, — these will naturally be the objects of deepest interest to our modern age. Such a literature and such an epoch are in fact *modern* in the same sense in which our own age and literature are modern; they are founded upon a rich past, and upon an instructive fullness of experience."[1] But it is not the fullness of experience on which Mr. Arnold chiefly relies in his definition of the *modern* element in literature; if we take him rightly, he thinks the thoroughly clear apprehension of a moderately rich experience contributes much more to what is properly the 'modern' element in literature, than a half-clear apprehension of a very much richer experience. He holds, for instance, that the great period of Rome was "the fullest, the most significant on record," that it was "a greater, a fuller period than the age of Pericles." "It is an infinitely larger school for the men reared in it; the relations of life are immeasurably multiplied, the events which happen are on a grander scale. The fact, the spectacle of this Roman world, are immense," — *but* its literature is not so modern as the literature of Athens in the age of Pericles, for it interprets that immense spectacle, that rich life, far less clearly.[2] The observing intellect was inadequate to the spectacle observed; the form of its expression, therefore, was less 'modern.' Hence, just as Mr. Arnold declares Virgil and Lucretius and Tacitus less 'modern' than Sophocles and Pindar and Thucydides, so also he declares Sir Walter Raleigh, as an historian, far less modern than Thucydides, — not far, perhaps, from the level of

Herodotus, — and probably considers Shakespeare himself far less modern than Sophocles. To Mr. Arnold the 'modern' element in literature depends upon "that harmonious acquiescence of mind which we feel in contemplating a grand spectacle that is intelligible to us, — when we have lost that impatient irritation of mind which we feel in presence of an immense, moving, confused spectacle, which, while it perpetually excites our curiosity, perpetually baffles our comprehension,"[3] — when, in a word, literature interprets and reflects the spectacle of a rich human life as calmly and clearly as astronomical science interprets and reflects the spectacle of a rich star-sown heaven. It is because Sophocles did this, that Mr. Arnold thinks him the most modern of poets, though he lived near 2,400 years ago. "The peculiar characteristic of the poetry of Sophocles," he says, "is its consummate, its unrivalled *adequacy*, that it represents the highly developed human nature of that age, — human nature developed in a number of directions, politically, socially, religiously, morally developed, — in its completest and most harmonious development in all these directions; while there is shed over his poetry the charm of that noble serenity which always accompanies true insight.... And, therefore, I have ventured to say of Sophocles that he 'saw life steadily and saw it whole'."[4] The 'modern element' in literature then depends, according to Mr. Arnold, on the complete translucency of the poet's insight into a rich life, even more than on the richness of that life, — on the *wholeness* and the lustre of the imaginative representation of the world around, even more than on the variety and fullness of the scene to be represented. If the literature of any day breaks into a hundred separate and partial pictures of the life of that day, then, however rich and complex that life is in reality, the literature is 'inadequate,' and so far not truly 'modern.' An age that is on the eve of disentangling great problems, that is struggling with its difficulties, that is rich in intellectual suggestion, but not tranquil in intellectual survey, that is awaiting new discoveries, not looking back on old achievements, is not in Mr. Arnold's sense a modern age, and its literature must be inadequate. Goethe, who said, —

> "The end is everywhere,
> Art still has truth,
> Take refuge there,"[5]

was a true 'modern.' Mr. Arnold himself, whose mood is almost always to proclaim the past 'out of date' and 'the future not yet born,' who writes the epitaphs of departed faiths with a sadness and transparent grace that are full of 'serenity,' who sees all, at least, that he *does* see, 'steadily' and 'whole,' is, again, a true modern. But Tennyson, who throws the mystic cloud of hope round all his finest thoughts, filling them with "that far-off divine event to which the whole creation moves;"[6] — Browning, who moulds his materials with the half-recklessness of buoyant trust and genius; — Buchanan, who fills the most piteous and miserable of his poetical children with vague snatches of triumph derived from a number of chords which vibrate with anything but serenity, and derived from all sorts of mysterious sources, — a mystic faith in the people, — a mystic faith in the future, — a mystic faith in God,[7] — all these are not, in Mr. Arnold's sense, the true poets of a modern age at all. They may all of them be critics indeed, but the note of criticism is drowned in the note of mystery. 'Serenity,' — the sense of clearly apprehending and commanding the well-discerned movements of a complex humanity, — the cessation of that pain and trouble of spirit which springs from the sense of a clouded vision, — belong to none of these poets. Half the spring of their poetry is a mystic spiritual instinct of which they can give little account. They all feel keenly the divergence between the tendencies of the modern science and the tendencies of the modern faith. None of them can reconcile these divergencies; none of them can ignore them. In a certain sense, Shakespeare, who *assumed* the reconciliation of these tendencies, then barely known to be even apparently divergent, was more serene, more able to "see life steadily, and see it whole," than the higher imaginative writers of our own day, — or, in Mr. Arnold's sense, was more 'modern' than the higher imaginative writers of our own day. Does not, indeed, Mr. Arnold's theory come to this, — that that literature can only be in his sense truly 'adequate' which is the fruit of a period of perfect intellectual calm, and at the same time of practical and political vitality; a period which is not one of decay, — for that brings with it restlessness, and cynicism, and despondent self-depreciation, — but which is also not a period of intellectual debate and spiritual enthusiasm, for that again brings with it perturbation to the calm of speculative vision.

What Mr. Arnold seems to us to demand as the condition of a truly modern or adequate literature, is the very unusual combination of a satisfied and resting imagination with a hopeful and energetic practical life. That is what he conceives to have been represented by the poetry of Sophocles at least, — hardly, we should have thought, by that of Æschylus: that is what he denies to the English literature of the age of Elizabeth; that is what we think he might with almost greater force deny to the English literature of the reign of Victoria. It is perfectly true that the historians of our own day do know how to separate their knowledge from their ignorance, do not confuse and mix the regions of legend and historical evidence, as Sir Walter Raleigh, for instance, confused them, and are, in this respect, much more like Thucydides than like historians of the age of Shakespeare. But the critical faculty is only one root of the modern spirit according to Mr. Arnold. The 'power to see life steadily, and see it whole,' is not stimulated, but probably weakened, by the critical spirit. Had Sophocles had the critical spirit as fully as Thucydides, he might have seen life "steadily," but he would *not* have seen it "whole." Mr. Arnold himself only sees life steadily at the cost of seeing it whole. He sees little bits of it with very perfect vision indeed, but his power of *integrating* life by his imagination, — we apologize for a pedantic and detestable word,[8] — is not large, not nearly so large as that of those who have less of the critical faculty than he, and more of the instinctive. It was in the spirit of a faith, not, indeed, very forward-looking, somewhat antique and melancholy with all its serenity, touched more with awe than with trust, but still of a *faith*, which the critical gaze of the subsequent philosophy of Greece began to dissipate, that Sophocles found a framework for his visions. Without that faith, — such as it was, — the poetry of Sophocles would not have been what Mr. Arnold calls 'adequate.' It was precisely its absence which prevented the poetry of Virgil and Lucretius from being 'adequate.' It is precisely its absence which prevents Mr. Arnold's own poetry from being 'adequate,' and which stamped a certain inadequacy on Goethe, who had to revive a sort of Hellenism, — which to him was false, though beautiful, — before he could get even an artistic unity for his finest compositions. Great masses of Goethe's writings fall asunder, into loose grains of sand, for want of this real ground of unity;[9] and, as a rule, we suspect that the exact condition which Mr. Arnold demands for a truly adequate and modern literature, — faith enough to give wholeness and steadiness to the general imaginative scene, — *not* enough to overpower or subdue, or even set up a conflict with the critical faculty, — is a rare accident of any age, and by no means a characteristic of our own modern age. We are disposed to think that the *only* 'modern' literature, — judged by Mr. Arnold's standard, — is the Athenian; that the only perfectly modern author is Sophocles, — surely rather a *reductio ad absurdum*. Shakespeare assuredly was not half as modern in this sense as Sophocles. His energy, his buoyancy, his abundant emotion and sympathy are far deeper, richer, and more diversified; but his lucidity of definition, his clearness of outline, are far less, because the world he reproduced was infinitely richer, denser, and more complex. Moreover, Shakespeare had not the critical faculty in Mr. Arnold's sense. Had he had it, it would have gone far to decompose the wholeness of his poetry. Shakespeare's faith is assumed, not reasoned, not even deeply meditated, much less analyzed.

Indeed, we are strongly disposed to think that what Mr. Arnold is so much in love with as the 'modern element in literature,' is either not properly modern at all, or else not properly literary. He confuses, we think, the simplifying tendency of the modern critical *intellect*, with the severe simplicity of classical art and taste. The art of Sophocles was sculpturesque, was severe, was simple, in great measure *because* the life he knew had so much unity and so little complexity in it; because it was, as compared with what we know now, or what even the Romans knew, all in one intellectual plane; because the civilization he understood, compared with that of later ages, was like a wild flower compared with a rich garden flower; because there had been no great convergence of different races and different nations and different wants in Athens, as there was in Rome and has been in Europe; because Athens knew so little of Hebrew prophecy, or African passion, or Teutonic affection. Mr. Arnold seems to us to confuse simplicity of this kind, arising from the absence of any high complexity of element, with the simplicity of modern criticism, of modern analysis which arises from the tendency to abstraction, to resolve back the complexity of life into distinct phases of law, – into distinct phases of speculation. But this last tendency, so far from being one that tends to make us see life "whole," tends to make us see life in parts and in very superficial phases. The true poetic "adequacy" is derived from the power to recombine the richness and complexity of life in imagination; but this is, we believe, inconsistent with the critical faculty, the mere explanatory faculty, the ordering and scientific faculty, with which Mr. Arnold seems to confound it. The modern critic and the modern poet, especially if he be a *great* poet, take more and more divergent paths. Mr. Arnold himself, it is true, is both a fine critic and a fine poet, but then he contrives to be both, only by confining his poetry to the most delicate films of life, – by utterly abandoning any pretence at "wholeness," substituting for it mere completeness in the finest and most fragile phases of human nature. But we are fully persuaded that the simplicity of classical art, and the simplicity of the modern spirit, are simplicities wholly different in origin. The one is artistic simplicity arising from simplicity of type; the other is an analytic simplicity arising from scientific analysis. The latter kind of simplicity can *never* produce an 'adequate' literature' – and the former could not, where the life to be represented is not simple in type, but like our modern life, the rich conglomerate of a hundred types. The poet who can 'adequately' see our modern life at once 'steadily' and 'whole' would necessarily rest upon a much deeper and more mysterious faith than that of Sophocles; his 'adequacy' could not very well be described as 'harmonious acquiescence of mind in a grand spectacle that is intelligible' to him; – for that would be scientific apprehension, not imaginative grasp. The true 'modern' spirit in literature can never be, we are convinced, classical in its type.

Weighing Tennyson

Have we any sure clue by which to measure the true greatness of the Poets of our own age, — any artifice by which we can relieve ourselves from the pressure of the present, and judge the greatest products of our literature by a standard wider than that of our immediate sympathies and slowly engendered tastes? There is a double difficulty in the matter, — not merely to set ourselves free from the exclusive domination of temporary influences, but also, *when* we have done so, to estimate fairly the charm which those temporary influences may rightly exercise over future ages, ages not subjected to them in anything like equal degree. There can be no doubt, for instance, that there is something in the age of Chaucer and the age of Shakespeare, and the age even of Pope and of Goldsmith, which now gives a special flavour to the writings of those various authors, but which did not half so much attract their contemporaries, because it was to them an imperceptible atmosphere, part of their very lives; while it is, to us, perceptible, unique, and attractive, just because it is *not* the echo of our own every-day thoughts, because it is so different from them, because it calls into life parts of our nature which are generally too little active, because it transports us into a new world. The exquisite charm of such lines as Shakespeare's,

> "Violets dim,
> But sweeter than the lids of Juno's eyes,
> Or Cytherea's breath,"[1]

is in some measure, no doubt, one which Shakespeare's contemporaries felt as deeply as we can, but in some measure also we do not doubt it is due to the refreshment of a mode of metaphor that would be strained, unnatural, and entirely out of date now, yet which bears on it the impress of ease, nature, and timeliness as it runs from Shakespeare's lips. Thus, in standing on tip-toe, as it were, to try and steal a march on the judgment of posterity as to the poets of our own day, we are, as it seems to us, almost, if not quite, as likely to depreciate them unduly through a too low estimate of the special qualifications of the time for grasping some aspect of life with force and beauty, as to over-estimate them through undue sympathy with temporary currents of thought. We are told that "the serious critic can put himself outside folks' various likings and preferences; he is not bound by the average tastes of his time; all literature is open to him, and he approaches the measure of any new poetical claimant with the standard left by the productions of bygone centuries."[2] No doubt he does, but this is almost as much his difficulty as his privilege. The "serious critic" comes to such a task saturated with the literature of his own age, and rather weary of it. He soaks himself in other literatures, and is like a man travelling in a new country. Every new feature delights him; the absence of any old feature is a stimulus to his imagination. He depreciates that with which he is familiar. He feasts himself on that which is fresh and full of intellectual surprises. Of course the danger is that he will run down the true greatness which has made the mind and imagination of his age what it is, and extol those other secrets of true greatness for which he has been hungering without any full satisfaction.

There is a curious instance of this sort of error in two articles which have appeared in separate quarters during the last week or two, both more or less leading a sort of reaction against the high modern estimate of Tennyson. The new number of the *Quarterly Review*, in an article of a good deal of literary ability, and not in any way intended as an assault upon Tennyson, still curiously enough denies him originality of intellect and comprehensiveness of grasp; while a paper in the May number of the *Temple Bar Magazine*, written with much force and knowledge, but with rather a hackneyed bumptiousness, — an Old Bailey Chaffenbrass style of aggressiveness[3] — (as if the writer had previously bound himself by an oath to "do for" the idolatry of Tennyson), goes so far as to cheapen Tennyson down to the standard of a mere minor poet. He tells us that Tennyson "is not a great poet, unquestionably not a poet of the first rank, all but unquestionably not a poet of the second rank, and probably, though no contemporary can settle that, — not even at the head of poets of the third rank, among whom he must ultimately take his place."[4] This might be true, for it is so very vague that we scarcely know its meaning. First-rate might be one of three or four poets of universal fame, second-rate one of ten or a dozen, and probably in such a sense Tennyson would be neither. But we know what the writer means when we come to detail. He appears to condemn "the universally jabbered opinion" (why this vulgar anger? it does not add to the strength of the paper) that Tennyson is *greater than Scott*. To us he seems a great poet, and Scott hardly more than a spirited and stirring versifier. But, in this writer's view, Tennyson is only a garden poet, not a poet of nature in the larger sense at all. He has, we learn, a "dainty and delicious" muse, and "a Pegasus with very decent legs, small elegant head, right well groomed and an uncommonly good mane and tail, but a Pegasus without wings."[5] The critic goes on to say of Tennyson, "Alas, he is no eagle! as we have said, he never soars! He twitters under our roof, sweeps and skims round and round our ponds, is musical on the branches of our trees, plumes himself on the edges of our fountains, builds himself a warm nest under our gables and even in our hearts, 'cheeps,' to use his own words, twenty million loves, feeds out of our hands, eyes us askance, struts along our lawns, and flutters in and out our flowery pastures, does all in fact that welcome, semi-domesticated, swallows, linnets, and musical bullfinches do, but there it ends."[6] Such is the curiously false estimate which this confident, conceited, somewhat coarse, though often eloquent and vigorous writer gives us of Tennyson, through a rash use of that comparative method of which we have spoken of the difficulties already. To a certain extent the *Quarterly* reviewer, to a much greater extent this slashing critic in *Temple Bar*, in whom we seem to recognize a writer of some name, seems to us vastly to underrate his genius, and to do so mainly because that genius is so near his mind's eye, and has affected the whole life of the day so powerfully, that he cannot even take in its outline. To our ears, the description of a dainty cabinet-picture maker, of a tame singing bird haunting trim gardens, has about as much true application to Tennyson as it would have to Goethe, perhaps rather less.

The great blunder which the critic of whom we speak makes in his estimate of Tennyson, and in a less degree the much juster critic in the *Quarterly*, seems to us to be this, — that in that abstract way which has so little of real instinctiveness in it, each of them compares him with other poets of quite different and more rapid or passionate genius, — and building on an implicit assumption, not fairly realized, much less examined and sustained, that rapidity, or passion, is the great criterion of great poets, classes him hastily with the smaller poets because he is found to be wanting in these qualities. But not only are there very great poetical faculties indeed which do not need rapidity and what is here meant by passion, but there are some which are hardly *consistent* with them. And one of the greatest of these qualities seems to us Tennyson's distinguishing, mastering, pervading characteristic, — we mean the imaginative faculty which corresponds to the microscope, rather than the telescope, in its treatment of human feeling, and instead of sweeping a wide horizon, and compressing much into little by the swiftness of its glance, keeps the object-glass fixed on one point, and compresses much into little by the fullness and variety and minuteness of its accumulations.[7] This seems to us not merely Tennyson's tendency, but the tendency in an even higher degree of the younger contemporaries of Tennyson, — of Matthew Arnold and of Clough. It is to our minds simply silly to say that because a great poet does not fly like Shelley in the thin air between earth and sky, or thunder like Byron in his passion, or muse like Wordsworth in his solitary rapture, he is destitute of the higher poetic gifts, nay, is even a sort of effeminate *petit-maitre* in poetry, which is almost what the *Temple Bar* critic implies. What can be more masculine, severely defined, strongly grasped, more directly built on the solid rock of human nature, than Tennyson's *Northern Farmer*, — which this presumptuous critic wholly ignores, venturing even to assert that since 1842 "he has added no fresh laurels, *in kind*, to his brow?"[8] The *Northern Farmer* was not only new in kind, but a picture that may well be held to outshine almost all Chaucer's grand portraits of his Canterbury pilgrims; and we will say with confidence that it is an absolute and final answer to that attempt which has been so elaborately made to paint Mr. Tennyson as a dainty and all but conventional poet. The poet who could draw as he has drawn the Northern Farmer cannot but be at bottom a poet of bold, hardy, and masculine genius, however tropical and luxuriant the overgrowth which often half conceals it. And that this is his true essence, we do not need even the *Northern Farmer* to prove beyond question. Would not that daring, original, and powerful, if painful poem, *The Death of Lucretius* alone have proved it? — a poem of a harder fibre, and far more thoughtful and full of genuine study than anything which Byron ever attempted, not to say produced. Indeed, the same might be said of either *Tithonus* or *Ulysses*, poems both of them unequalled in any other poet for the clear dominion of a ruling idea, and the sharp perfection of its execution (free altogether from the excess of detail by which Tennyson so often hides, only too successfully, the masculine, strongly marked type beneath). The truth seems to be that the writer in the *Temple Bar* has no power to enter into Tennyson's highest work. When he speaks of the *Gardener's Daughter*, — perfect as in its way it is, — as marking the high-tide line of his genius, the "smashing" critic smashes not Tennyson, but himself. Even the *Quarterly* reviewer seems to us to show a remarkable want of insight when he speaks of Tennyson's genius as almost feminine, and as showing the power of compression without the power of comprehension. If any woman had written any one of the four poems we have just named, what would have been the criticism upon her? — simply that she had absolutely overleaped all the imagined (and possibly imaginary) bounds of feminine genius; that she had produced a bold, massive, terse, absolutely perfect piece of poetic sculpture. Ulysses has, we admit, a dash of the modern in him. He is not absolutely Greek, — he speaks of all experience as

> "An arch wherethro'
> Gleams that untravelled world, whose margin fades
> For ever and for ever when I move."

But no figure was ever hewn out by a sculptor, in expression so perfect and form so stately. Byron, Shelley, Wordsworth, Goethe have nothing to equal it. That

"Grey spirit yearning in desire
To follow knowledge like a sinking star
Beyond the utmost bound of human thought,"

and cherishing an irrepressible scorn for his tame, domestic-minded son, the blameless Telemachus

"Centred in the sphere
Of common duties, decent not to fail
In offices of tenderness, and pay
Meet admiration to my household gods
When I am gone; — he works his work, I mine,"[9]

— that 'Ulysses' is a figure that will live in literature as long as literature is, and which it argues sheer dullness in the eye of any critic not to have recognized, with its various compeers, as marking the highest point literature has yet reached in severe and stately intellectual delineation.

Tennyson's greatness will, as we believe, be in many respects estimated by future generations as we are never likely to recognize it, though much of the popularity of his *Gardener's Daughter*, his *May Queen*, his *Locksley Hall*, and so forth, will undoubtedly pass away with the generation in whose tone of sentiment these are somewhat minute studies, — even perhaps overloaded with small ornament. He is the first and greatest of the true student poets, as the *Quarterly Review* justly observes, though Clough at least has written some things which even Tennyson will never equal. And by the true student poets we do not mean purely introspective poets, — on the contrary, no poet ever lived who can paint external landscape with the sure and rapid hand of Tennyson, — but those poets who have studied the limits of human knowledge, and know how to discriminate with subtle and accurate touch the false from the true, the showy from the substantial, in their own hearts and minds, and in the human world as well. Byron did not know this. Half his poetry at least is spurious stuff, with all its magnificent force. His Giaours and his Childe Harolds are buckram heroes. It was not till he got into his cynical vein and wrote *Don Juan* that he rose clear of the rubbish, the false stuff, in himself. Shelley never even tried for a moment to disentangle the mystical falsetto element in himself from the pure ethereal poetry. He is wild, sweet, eerie, supernatural, but he is never real. Wordsworth is meditative, but has no discriminating self-knowlege. Of all poets that ever lived, Tennyson is the greatest in painting human moods with a richness and subtlety of insight that a hair's-breadth of deviation would have spoiled. There is no human regret and yearning in our language equal to this: —

"Break, break, break,
On thy cold grey stones, O sea!

And I would that my tongue could utter
The thoughts that arise in me!

Oh, well for the fisherman's boy
That he shouts with his sister at play!
Oh, well for the sailor lad
That he sings in his boat on the bay!

And the stately ships go on
To their haven under the hill;
But oh, for the touch of a vanished hand
And the sound of a voice that is still!

Break, break, break,
At the foot of thy crags, O sea!
But the tender grace of a day that is dead
Will never come back to me."[10]

Shelley's: —

"When the lamp is shattered the light in the dust lies dead,
When the cloud is scattered the rainbow's glory is fled,"[11]

expresses a far wilder and more desolate mood, as of one shivering in the dark wilderness; but it is not so yearning and so human a mood as Tennyson's, whose greatness it is to be always self-possessed, even when most possessed by waves of emotion which he can neither sound nor measure. With what a firm and self-possessed sculptor's hand he carves out the vagrant longings and breaking threads of thought in that variable elation and depression of mood due to wine, in his marvellously fine poem, *Will Waterproof's Lyrical Monologue!*[12] Beneath that apparently wandering hand, there is as firm and sure and over-mastering a conception as runs through his *Tithonus*, or his *Ulysses*, or his *Lucretius*, or his *Two Voices*, or his *In Memoriam*, or his *Northern Farmer*. For the painting and sculpture of moods which require the fullest insight into a rich and complex nature, no poet, to our knowledge, has ever lived to rival Tennyson. No doubt to an ordinary eye the field of view is small, but it is not small under Tennyson's treatment. It is so full, fetches so real and true an illustration from an hundred sources, and follows so unflinchingly the true lines of nature even beneath all this tangle of detail, that you might as well call the Laocoon a small subject of art, as give that name to Tennyson's greatest themes. Where precisely he stands in the hierarchy of poets we do not feel either the power or the inclination to determine, — certainly we should say below Wordsworth; perhaps below Byron and Shelley; certainly above Keats. But of one thing we are very sure, that the critics of future times will not even try him by the tests of the somewhat rash and pretentious critic in the *Temple Bar*; and will see in him some far greater qualities than any that are indicated even in the criticism of the *Quarterly Review*.

The Worship of Children

When it is said that this is the age of railways and the electric telegraph and other such arts and inventions, it is described by mere accidents. Socially it has much more characteristic features. Consider, for instance, the excessive elaboration of the toys, books, pictures, and literature, produced specially for children. Here is a man of genius, Mr. George Macdonald, for instance, giving a great portion of his time to write and edit *Good Words for the Young*, and for years there has been produced by Mrs. Alfred Gatty a magazine for children, called *Aunt Judy's Magazine*, which is better of its kind than almost if not quite every magazine intended for grown-up people. And these are mere *specimens* of the abundant literature now dedicated to children. The Christmas books for children are just beginning to pour out of the press with that steady and incessant flow which never relaxes for the last two months of the year and the first of the new year. Rhymes, pictures, fairy tales, books of games, books of adventures, boys' magazines, girls' magazines, science made easy, poetry made childlike, the grotesque old ballads revived with humorous caricatures, translations from the German elaborately illustrated by German artists, translations from the French elaborately illustrated by French artists, everything that the highest and subtlest refinement of the most practised and diligent ingenuity can invent are prepared at the demand of elderly relatives anxious and ready to purchase all these inventions in large quantities at lavish expense, and pour them into the laps of the children whom they most do propitiate. The children of the present day are infinitely more thought of and better served not only than the children of any previous generation, but than anybody who has been unfortunate enough to pass the age of childhood. True it is that any one of us, — and the present writer is certainly one, — who is inclined to prefer *good* children's stories to almost any other species of literature, comes in for waifs and strays of good fortune in consequence of this fanatical cultus of children, and has now and then the grim satisfaction of growling to himself (as, for instance, while reading the admirable inquest held by Dr. Earwig over the dead moth in *Aunt Judy* of this month) — 'Ah, the little wretches won't understand *that*; I have that to myself, as it were.' But this is a mere accidental bonus for those grown-up people who are afflicted by the malformation of mind which delights in children's stories after they have ceased to have children's minds. We are not grateful for that sort of accident, for it was due to no intention of gratifying us. The horrible and profligate profusion of energy and invention on children's amusements and instruction is none the less, that sometimes the uncles and aunts may eat of the crumbs which fall from the nieces' tables. We were delighted to hear a critic who has taken some pains to get at the statistics of children's suffrages on such subjects say, with a sepulchral warning in his voice, of Mr. Macdonald's first number of *Good Words for the Young*, 'If Mr. Macdonald does not take care, he will injure the sale of that work by a redundancy of fairy stories.' Nothing could be more pleasant to hear, for the middle-aged auditor happened to be very greedy of fairy stories himself; and to know *both* that his own private taste was being consulted, *and* that the young people's taste had not been satisfactorily gratified, seemed almost too good to be true.

The truth is, that the worship of children has increased, is increasing, and ought to be diminished. It is the growing evil of the day. We know very well all about 'the fresh young soul' and the 'child-heart,'[1] and that sort of thing. It is that sort of thing which has seriously injured the children of this generation. When artlessness gets to know its power, it is very near to art. Children are too much consulted in our generation. Their pleasures are far too numerous and elaborate. A stern and healthy frugality, not to say asceticism, in relation to providing children with the means of enjoyment, and in administering their amusements, is the truest kindness to children. They are as incapable of valuing the high development and elaborate, Asiatic luxury of their modern play-rooms and play-things, as a labouring man would be of appreciating the luxury of French cookery. Simplicity, and we may almost say monotony, are of the essence of a true child's amusements. The same stories and the same rude toys amuse more the twentieth time than they did the first, and more the two-hundredth time than they did the twentieth. We have known a wooden doll with one arm give a vast deal more pleasure than a winking wax creature who runs on wheels and emits a sort of squeaking apology for the word 'mamma.' Among the bricks of the present writer's own childhood, – not the metaphorical 'bricks' among his playmates, but the play-bricks with which he built houses and round-towers, – there was one accidentally burnt and blackened by the smoke. That brick represented to his childish imagination an ecclesiastical personage closely related to himself, far more vividly than any formal imitation of the human form ever could have done, and he seriously believes that if that blackened brick had come to any untimely end, he would have felt that some great calamity impended over 'Papa' with an intensity of grief that could have been inspired by no accident to any of his toys.[2] We don't believe a bit in the voluptuous era for children. A few nursery rhymes, a few good old fairy tales, a wooden donkey with paniers to take to bed—(this apparatus, being so specially unsuitable to bed, has a special charm for that purpose)—a box of bricks, a whip, and, in good time, a ball of string and a knife, are all the playthings a child needs, and quite enough if his invention is to have the least play. Load him with elaborate ingenuities, with pictures so good that you feel bound to explain their finer touches, with tales of character where all the fitnesses of nature and circumstance are carefully attended to, with ballads of humour a hundred times as fine and elaborate as he can take in, and you only overload him and leave no room for the elastic power of invention and imagination, which is the best of all amusements for him.

The best thing benevolent uncles and aunts can do, if they have been so injudicious as to buy much of the admirable children's literature of the present day for their nephews and nieces is to *keep* it *themselves* and try to enjoy it. If they can do so, they may be sure that, in the fitness of things, it is more suitable for them than for the little ones. If they can't, it is a sign their minds need refreshing, and they should keep it till they can. *Good Words for the Young* and *Aunt Judy* are really capital magazines for the old; but for the young they are too luxurious, elaborate, and refined. The brown bread of literature is, after all, more nourishing for children than all these fine fancies and all this delicate humour. For instance, there is a little play about "Touching the Moon," by the author of "Lilliput Levee," in *Good Words for the Young*,[3] the drift of which is really far beyond them; it might, indeed, fairly be called a refined spiritual parable for the old, —a poetic adaptation of the theology of St. Paul.[4] If it did not bewilder children, it would only be because they would miss its meaning as completely as if it had had no meaning to miss. A bare, rugged, and almost grotesque simplicity of material is, we are disposed to maintain, the best possible food for ninety-nine children out of a hundred. If you tell them a fairy story, tell them one genuinely marvellous, capricious in its details, and wholly devoid of allegory. If you tell them a moral tale, put the moral in the nakedest possible form before them; —make your good boy very good, your naughty boy very naughty; your reward very plain, your punishment very clear, —and above all, avoid the *finesse* and complexity of real life. They will come to all that in time. Let them see the outlines and the opposites, before they begin to understand the shading and the mixture of colours. For our own parts, besides the grudge we openly profess to the children of this generation for monopolizing so many more of the good things of this world than they are able to enjoy, we sincerely believe that they would be happier on the plain food and limited enjoyments which alone were at the command of the last generation. Will the children of to-day ever feel towards the elaborate and, we admit, admirable, work produced for their amusement, half the yearnings of tender remembrance which we lavish on the wooden moral tales, grotesque as gargoyles, which we so eagerly consumed in our childish days? What child will ever turn to Mr. Kingsley's "Water Babies," or even Mr. Ruskin's delightful little tale of "The Black Brothers," or to any of the many masterpieces of modern art intended for children's amusement, with the sigh of mingled merriment and reverence with which the mediaevals of to-day turn to the little plays and stories in "Evenings at Home;" for example, the magniloquent patriotism of "Alfred, a Drama," or the irritating antithesis between "Eyes" and "No Eyes" (where every decent child heartily sympathizes with "No Eyes" and hates "Eyes"), or the awful and ghastly warning against instructive persons which used to be furnished by the conversations between "Tutor, George, and Harry" on "leguminous plants" and other sticky or earthy subjects?[5] We have often been gravely inclined to attribute the falling-off in patriotism and public interest in the young people of this generation to the absence from their modern literature of such very plain and didactic lessons as King Alfred's eloquent though arbitrarily timed resolve, after he has embraced his "brave Ella," "never to sheathe my sword against these robbers,"

> "Till dove-like peace return to England's shore,
> And war and slaughter vex the land no more."

Nowadays that sort of thing is left out of children's books as unsuitable to their age, which of course it is, — but it was exactly the old-fashioned things in the old children's books which sowed the seeds of manlier thoughts. When will literature of pure and artistic taste ever produce a book to which the childish reader will look back in maturer years with as much odd enjoyment and gratitude as the present writer does to that great work, in three minute volumes, illustrated by Blake, called "Elements of Morality," which was translated from a priggish German author in order to teach English parents how to educate their children into priggishness, — an object in which it gloriously failed, serving, indeed, to *un*teach priggishness by the splendid grotesqueness of the warning it held forth?[6] We are convinced that children learned more by the old, plain didacticism, both when they sympathized with it and when they could not refrain from ridiculing it, than they do by the higher art of modern times. Who has ever had so good a lesson against the Paleyan moral system in later life as he had in reading as a child such a dialogue as this in "Elements of Morality": — "*Curate*: What is the matter with my little guest? *Charles*: Nothing at all. *Curate*: Something must ail you, or you would not cry. *Charles*: Ah, if I were with my dear father and mother! *Curate*: You now feel, my child, sorrow, or a violent and uneasy desire to see some absent person whom you love. I do not blame you for it; no one ought to be so dear to a good child as his parents, and he should feel a little uneasy when he is parted from them. But, my dear child, if you will live contented, you must learn to moderate this as well as fear and joy, *or you will miss many pleasures*. Do you think you can bring them here by your longing and crying? Certainly not; you know it is impossible. Of what use, then, is this violent desire which makes you so very uncomfortable?"[7] That sort of naked teaching makes a far more educating impression on children — though it educates them in a direction often precisely opposite to that intended — than the high art of modern days, in which both the bitters and the sweets are too finely mixed to be easily discriminated and apprehended by children. We suspect there is a great deal to be said for the naked and grotesque absolutism of the didactic morality in the old-world children's tales. It did at least produce a definite impression either of attraction or repulsion. Life in its complex, unanalyzed form is too rich a thing to educate children as clearly.

On the whole, we think our grudge against the excessive culture of modern children is really justifiable on rational grounds as well as on that of private pique. A hardier and austerer fare, as regards pleasure, would keep up a healthier appetite for pleasure. A solider and plainer teaching as regards morality, even if it were grotesquely false at times, would keep up the independent action of children's consciences and affections. The era of elaborate sugar-plums and high art for children is certainly not one that produces the most vigorous and eager minds. The worship of children is throwing us all into the shade. Let us put them down for the future. It will do both us and them good.

The Memoir of Miss Austen

This little volume will be eagerly read by the now, we hope, very numerous admirers of Miss Austen's exquisitely finished novels, and not without real pleasure, though also with considerable regret to find how very little biographical material for any complete picture of her, remains in her family. Mr. Austen-Leigh has done all in his power; he has prefixed a very attractive and expressive portrait of his aunt; a great deal of pleasant gossip about the manners and times in which she was brought up; a very sensible and amusing letter by her great-great-grandmother, written from Constantinople (where her husband was ambassador) in 1666 to her daughter (Miss Austen's great-grandmother), proving that the excellent sense and sobriety of the novelist had been handed down to her through four generations at least; a few amusing anecdotes about Miss Austen's great-uncle, the Master of Balliol, Dr. Theophilus Leigh, showing that real wit as well as sound sense was indigenous in the elder branches of the family; a few lively family letters of Miss Austen's own, showing how dear to her her own creations were, and how well she estimated her own real powers; a few delightful reminiscences of her by nephews and nieces; and one piece of very good literary banter, a sketch by Miss Austen of the novel she should be compelled to write if she followed the suggestions of her many counsellors; and, finally, one or two treasured family traditions of Miss Austen's private explanations of matters referred to in the novels, but not there completely elucidated. The only thing that we could have well spared in Mr. Austen-Leigh's little book is his chapter of "testimonies" to Miss Austen's originality and power as a novelist, which is, to our minds, out of place and out of taste. No one with a grain of literary sense doubts her wonderful originality and artistic power. To dispute it now is simply to prove that the disputant does not know what he is talking about. Hence the chapter in question is a little too like a publisher's list of testimonies from the press to the worth of some bran-new writer's book. Who would not smile to see a biographer of Sir Walter Scott place at the end of his memoir testimonies by critics however respectable, — unless, indeed, they were artists as great as Goethe, for example, — to Sir Walter's eminence as a writer of romance? We do not, of course, object to hear the testimony of so great a master of the craft as Sir Walter Scott to Miss Austen's skill, especially when he speaks of his infinite inferiority to her in all the subtleties of discrimination between the finer shades of human character. But when a biographer of Miss Austen cites the approbation even of Archbishop Whately, or Robert Southey, or Dr. Whewell, for his heroine's works, and still more when he quotes the praise of persons of so very slight a literary weight as the late Marquis of Lansdowne or the late Lord Carlisle, we feel jarred by a certain deficiency in his perception of the true dignity of his subject. It *is* of some interest to know how stupid was the audience to whose ears Miss Austen made her first appeal, – how little they could understand the delicate truth and humour of her pictures. But to tell us that many worthy persons have since enjoyed her writings thoroughly, is like telling us that many have felt the warmth of summer. Specific testimony of that kind implies that the fact attested needs attestation, – that it is not matter of common notoriety and universal recognition, which, as regards Miss Austen's merits, we are happy to say that it is. But with this only exception, it seems to us that Mr. Austen-Leigh had made out of his very slender materials a very welcome and pleasant little volume, which all admirers of Miss Austen will eagerly read.

We learn from it that Miss Austen lived, like most of the upper-middle class of that age, in a world which was not one of by any means high pressure, in spite of the great political events brewing and bursting on the Continent of Europe. It could not certainly be said of *her*, in spite of the date of her birth (1775), and that she was just old enough to understand how vast and fearful was the French Revolution when it burst upon the world, –

> "But we, brought forth and reared in hours
>   Of change, alarm, surprise, –
> What shelter to grow ripe is ours?
>   What leisure to grow wise?"[1]

For Miss Austen's novels and her life, – so far as we learn its tenor from this volume – was one of perfect calm, and it was to this calm that we owe that fine, sedate humour and gentle irony which imply a settled standard of life, and an estimate of human follies quite unmixed with bitterness of motive or scepticism of inference. There was no mockery in Miss Austen's irony. However heartily we laugh at her pictures of human imbecility, we are never tempted to think that contempt or disgust for human nature suggested the satire.

Mr. Austen-Leigh evidently holds that his aunt derived a good deal of her liveliness and power of banter from her mother's family, – the Leighs. Her mother both wrote and conversed, he tells us, with much epigrammatic force and point, and her great-uncle, Dr. Theophilus

Leigh, the Master of Balliol above referred to, evidently had very much of that acidulated humour in him which constitutes the very essence of Miss Austen's literary style, and took form and substance in *Pride and Prejudice* in Mr. Bennet. A story is told here of Dr. Leigh's being visited at Balliol by a young cousin, then a freshman, who, unaccustomed to the fashions of the place, was about to take off his undergraduate's gown as if it had been a great-coat, when the old Master said with a grim smile — "young man, you need not strip, we are not going to fight."[2] Miss Austen herself quizzed her young relations more tenderly, as became an aunt and a woman of very gentle nature; but with her tenderness and gentleness, she showed a sense of amusement at their little blunders and weaknesses which no doubt greatly enhanced their affection for her. Children, directly they *feel* that they are loved, recognize the compliment of being so far analyzed as to be gently laughed at by elders for whom they feel real love. What Miss Austen's way with her nephews and nieces was, the following description of her manner to them as children, taken together with one or two of the letters to nieces and nephews, among others a Winchester schoolboy, which are here preserved, will sufficiently show: — "As a very little girl," writes one of her nieces, "I was always creeping up to aunt Jane, and following her whenever I could, in the house and out of it. I might not have remembered this but for the recollection of my mother's telling me privately, that I must not be troublesome to my aunt. Her first charm to children was great sweetness of manner. She seemed to love you, and you loved her in return. This, as well as I can now recollect, was what I felt in my early days, before I was old enough to be amused by her cleverness. But soon came the delight of her playful talk. She could make everything amusing to a child. Then, as I got older, when cousins came to share the entertainment, she would tell us the most delightful stories, chiefly of fairyland, and her fairies had all characters of their own. The tale was invented, I am sure, at the moment and was continued for two or three days, if occasion served."[3] This, taken with the pleasant quizzing in her letter to her schoolboy nephew on his inventiveness in filling up a letter to her by elaborately stating the fact that he had got home from school after previously dating from home, and with the bantering of the niece (who was trying her hand on a novel) on the great propriety of the conception of making her hero's previous love for the aunt a preliminary to his passion for the niece, shows the very heart not only of the woman, but the novelist. A real enjoyment (which had no malice in it) of the futilities and false hits of what is called human intelligence, and an apt power of just so far generalizing, and putting sufficient emphasis upon, its mistakes, as to sharpen the outline and bring it out clear against sober reason, was in her not only not extinguished by her love for those whom she laughed at, but probably somewhat sharpened by it. What can be better than this, in that letter to the novel-attempting niece to which we have just alluded: — "Julian's history was quite a surprise to me. You had not very long known it yourself, I suspect; but I have no objection to make to the circumstance; it is very well told, and his having been in love with the aunt gives Cecilia an additional interest with him. I like the idea. A very proper compliment to an aunt! I rather imagine, indeed, that nieces are seldom chosen but in compliment to some aunt or other. I dare say your husband was in love with me once, and would never have thought of you, if he had not supposed me dead of a scarlet fever."[4]

It is a great comfort to us to have so complete a verification of the theory we have always cherished, — that Miss Austen's personal character was a sort of medium between the heroine of *Pride and Prejudice*, Elizabeth Bennet, and the heroine of *Persuasion*, Anne Elliot, — that she had all the vivacity of the one and all the gentleness and sweetness of the other. Her own great favourite, it appears, among her heroines, was the former; but she was quite aware that there is in Elizabeth Bennet just the very slightest touch of that want of refinement which we may fairly attribute to the influence of such a mother, — and, indeed, in some sense of such a father as hers, for Mr. Bennet, dry and keen as is his humour, is too indifferent to the feelings of the persons he meets to have the manners of a perfect gentleman, — and to the general effect of the society of Meryton. Anne Elliot, though without the bright and mischievous playfulness of Elizabeth Bennet, is a far more perfect lady, has far more of the grace and refinement which we find from this short biography were the most distinguishing characteristics of the writer. The portrait prefixed to the volume, — a very remarkable one, — entirely bears out this double likeness to Anne Elliot and Elizabeth Bennet. It is a small head, with very sweet lively eyes, and a fullness about the face which seems to speak of health and spirit, but the air of high breeding and gentleness of nature is deeply impressed upon it. It is refinement, playfulness, and alertness, rather than depth of intellect, which the face seems to express. The little head is carried with great spirit, with a certain consciousness of seeing rapidly beneath the surface of life, and with an air of enjoying its own rapidity of vision, that speaks of the *ease* of power, and of power well appreciated by its owner. That Miss Austen did fully appreciate her own power, — appreciate, we mean, in the sense of truly estimating it, both what it could do and what it could not, — and did also appreciate the stupidity of those who did not understand her at all, and yet pretended to give her advice, this book gives ample proof. Take this, after the publication of *Pride and Prejudice*. "Upon the whole, however, I am quite vain enough and well satisfied enough. The work is rather too light, and bright, and sparkling; it wants shade; it wants to be stretched out here and there with a long chapter of sense, if it could be had; if not, of solemn specious nonsense, about something unconnected with the story; an essay on writing, a critique on Walter Scott, or the history of Buonaparte, or something that would form a contrast, and bring the reader with increased delight to the playfulness and epigrammatism of the general style."[5] And of Miss Austen's sense of superiority to her literary advisers and critics, there can be no more amusing proof than the following extract from her sketch of the novel she would have written if she had followed the advice of her many literary counsellors: —

> "Book to open with father and daughter conversing in long speeches, elegant language, and a tone of high serious sentiment. The father induced, at his daughter's earnest request, to relate to her the past events of his life. Narrative to reach through the greater part of the first volume; as besides all the circumstances of his attachment to her mother, and their marriage, it will comprehend his going to sea as chaplain to a distinguished naval character about the Court; and his going afterwards to Court himself, which involved him in many interesting situations, concluding with his opinion of the benefits of tithes being done away with.... From this outset the story will proceed and contain a striking variety of adventures. Father an exemplary parish priest, and devoted to literature; but heroine and father never above a fortnight in one place: he being driven from his curacy by the vile arts of some totally unprincipled and heartless young man, desperately in love with the heroine, and pursuing her with unrelenting passion. No sooner settled in one country of Europe, than they are compelled to quit it, and retire to another, always making new acquaintance, and always obliged to leave them. This will of course exhibit a wide variety of character. The scene will be for ever shifting from one set of people to another, but there will be no mixture, all the good will be unexceptionable in every respect. There will be no foibles or weaknesses but with the wicked, who will be completely depraved and infamous, hardly a resemblance of humanity left in them. Early in her career, the heroine must meet with the hero; all perfection, of course, and only prevented from paying his addresses to her by some excess of refinement. Wherever she goes, somebody falls in love with her, and she receives repeated offers of marriage, which she refers wholly to her father, exceedingly angry that *he* should not be the first applied to. Often carried away by the anti-hero, but rescued either by her father or the hero. Often reduced to support herself and her father by her talents, and work for her bread; continually cheated, and defrauded of her hire; worn down to a skeleton, and now and then starved to death. At last, hunted out of civilized society, denied the poor

shelter of the humblest cottage, they are compelled to retreat into Kamskatcha, where the poor father quite worn down, finding his end approaching, throws himself on the ground, and after four or five hours of tender advice and parental admonition to his miserable child, expires in a fine burst of literary enthusiasm, intermingled with invectives against the holders of tithes."[6]

Slight as the memoir is, then, we are heartily grateful for it. It is always a pleasure to know that any popular writer *was* what he or she "must have been," — so much easier is it to construct for ourselves a "must have been," than to draw a really sound inference as to the "was." But the inference is easier and more likely to be true when an author's works give us so strong a sense at once of the depth and the *limits* of the genius which created them, as Miss Austen's. It is impossible to suppose that the deeper problems of life weighed very oppressively on a mind which touches them so lightly and so gently as Miss Austen's. It is clear she did not at any time *arraign* either human nature or human society for their shortcomings and positive sins, as our modern novelists, George Eliot, or Thackeray, or even Mrs. Gaskell, either do, or try to do. She was content to take human society and human folly as they were, and to like while she laughed, instead of arraigning because she loved. And thus the limited work she had to do, she achieved with greater perfection and fineness and delicacy of touch than almost any other English writer with whom we are acquainted. Never was a definite literary field so clearly marked out and so perfectly mastered as by Miss Austen.

Pope Huxley

We have so hearty an admiration for Professor Huxley, and so genuine an enjoyment of his great literary as well as scientific powers, that we need hardly apologize for protesting against any assumption of his which tends to diminish his legitimate influence.[1] We believe we are not mistaken in supposing that amongst all our modern men of science there is not one who is so utterly opposed to the assumption of a tone of premature certainty; that Professor Huxley has been foremost, for instance, in declining to recognize the principles called "the conservation of matter" and "the conservation of force" as anything more than good working hypotheses, — that he has even reproached astronomers with having been in too great a hurry to assume the Copernican theory as absolutely certain, — that, in a word, he has set his face strongly against all possible attempts to ignore intellectual alternatives still so much as *possible*. In theory he is a great and even severe Agnostic,[2] — who goes about exhorting all men to know how little they know, on pain of loss of all intellectual sincerity if they once consciously confound a conjecture with a certainty. Now, we heartily admire Professor Huxley for preaching this doctrine, which many of us must find at times a most bracing and strengthening teaching. But we want to ask what the *temper* of mind of the man who prophesies thus ought to be, and whether Professor Huxley teaches us practically by example precisely what he teaches us theoretically by precept. Should not, then, the man who prophesies as Professor Huxley prophesies, be very careful indeed to recognize in himself the same vast liability to error and tendency to anticipate the evidence of facts, which he recognizes in all men? That, of course, he will strenuously assert. But if so, may we not further ask whether his tone in controversy should not be one of a certain diffidence and of respect for the opinions and judgments of others, even when they are least in accordance with his own? Should not the habit of mind of such a teacher be suspense of judgment, — and suspense of judgment not only on the evidence of facts, but on the apparent indications of motive, — suspense of judgment not only on scientific, but on moral phenomena? — and, if so, then also habitual caution in the use of that slashing rapier of his, by which he pinks or tries to pink his literary adversaries, with results which, if they are not the fruits of an all but infallible judgment, must be very often indeed both injurious and unjust?

Quite recently, Professor Huxley delivered a very able and interesting lecture on Basques, Celts, and Saxons,[3] the drift of which was to show that Celts and Saxons are, properly speaking, very much alike in all physical and moral qualities; that the conventional distinction between the tall, light-haired, blue-eyed Teuton and the short, black-haired, dark-eyed Celt is a blunder; – that the dark hair and dark eyes and low stature probably belong to the old Basque race of whose language there is no longer any trace except just on the Spanish border, and that the Basques have transmitted their physical peculiarities to very considerable numbers of persons speaking both Saxon and Celtic, without, however, thereby transmitting any very distinguishable moral characteristics which are more the result of circumstances and government than of race. Professor Huxley's thesis was, in short, that the Basque race had been pushed by invasion into the west of France, the west of England, and the west of Ireland, and had impressed its physical characteristics on the western races of all these countries; that the East of all of them still retains the tall, fair, light-haired physique of the old Saxon and Celt, and that the race is mixed in the central districts of these countries. He summed up by asserting that a "native of Tipperary is just as much or as little an Anglo-Saxon as a native of Devonshire." The lecture was full of Professor Huxley's characteristic ingenuity and power, – perhaps not quite so full as it should have been of his Agnosticism. Its language no doubt confounded at times a respectable but questionable "working hypothesis" with a probability so strong as to be not far from a scientific truth. Undoubtedly the working-men whom Professor Huxley was instructing must have gone away with the notion that one of the most learned ethnologists of the age *believed* that there was no material constitutional difference between the Celt and the Saxon, and without any solemn warning as to the precariousness of the grounds of that belief. Soon after the publication of the lecture, "A Devonshire Man" criticized it in the *Pall Mall*, with a view to prove that there is a great difference between Saxon and Celt, and that Devonshire, at least, is chiefly Saxon. He did not sign his name, but his letter was not marked, as far as we can see, by any positive acerbity of manner, though there was a taunt directed at the great range of Professor Huxley's dogmatic controversies, – a taunt which ran thus: – "Even Professor Huxley's enemies, if he has any, must admit that he is a very able man, and that his energy is, to say the least, quite equal to his judgment. If he has a fault, it is that, like Caesar, he is ambitious. We all know what Sydney Smith said of Dr. Whewell, – 'Science is his forte, but omniscience is his foible;' perhaps his playful wit would have passed the same kind of judgment, and with the same justice, on our ubiquitous Professor. He might have said, perhaps, that cutting up monkeys was his forte, and cutting up men was his foible. A little while ago he ran amuck at the Comtists, then he attacked the mathematicians; now he has undertaken to prove against all comers that there is no difference whatever, except in language, between the Teuton and the Celt." Perhaps the taunt was a little sharper than it need have been, considering that the attack on the Comtists was grounded chiefly on Comte's classification of the sciences, and especially his treatment of Professor Huxley's own science, physiology. Nor can we imagine a subject on which Professor Huxley has more right to offer an opinion than on the physiological side, at all events, of ethnology. But no one, we think, will say that the taunt contained in the above letter was very bitter or one unjustifiable in a man who did not sign his name. Indeed, we have no scruple in saying, in spite of our anonymousness, — which will be no veil to Professor Huxley, — that we know no judgments so unfair and intolerant, and indicating so little suspense of judgment, as those passed by literary men who sign their names on the motives of literary men who don't. We do not know who "A Devonshire Man" may be. We can hardly conceive any personal reason for the anonymousness of his first letter, except probably literary habit, and the natural aversion some men feel to the sight of their own names in print. Certainly, it covered no scurrilousness, and no trembling ignorance. The letter contained, no doubt, some vague and doubtful generalities, and some indefiniteness of phrase where definition was needed and has since been in part supplied. But it was full of relevant suggestions, and really advanced much tending to show that Devonshire, at least, though not Cornwall, is far more Saxon than Celtic, and perhaps more Saxon than Tipperary, at least as tried by the test of language, — though we must admit that while "A Devonshire Man" is strong on the philological features of his own county, he is very weak on those of Tipperary, where he would find, we suspect, a stronger Saxon element than he expects. He also advanced arguments which are far from contemptible, to show that in Caesar's time there was a marked moral distinction between Celt and Saxon, and that it is very like that which is still recognized. Had Professor Huxley been true to his own theories of intellectual modesty, he would have said in reply that this letter had done something towards inducing him to regard Devonshire as more Anglo-Saxon than Celtic, — that he himself would perhaps have been more correct if he had compared Cornwall with Tipperary instead of Devonshire — that there were respectable reasons for supposing that a Celtic race existed in Caesar's time with many of the moral characteristics of the Irish, but that it remains very doubtful if these characteristics are so much connected with physical organization as with political causes; probably that careful ethnologists would suspend their judgment.

But how *does* Professor Huxley reply? Very much in the tone of a
Papal bull, — containing violent censures — almost excommunications
latae sententiae,[4] — as well as dogmatic decrees. "Your correspondent, 'A
Devonshire Man'," he begins, "is good enough to say of me that 'cutting
up monkeys is his forte, and cutting up men his foible.' With your
permission I propose to cut up 'A Devonshire Man,' *but I leave it to the
public to judge* whether, when so employed, my occupation is to be
referred to the former or to the latter category," — *i.e.*, whether he is
cutting up a monkey or a man. This is witty, but it is wit passing beyond
all decent limits of personality. The Pope would never dream of hinting
that Father Hyacinthe himself, and still less that Monseigneur Dupanloup, may be a monkey, simply for entertaining doubts as to the Pope's
personal infallibility.[5] And yet we submit that the difference between Mr.
Huxley and "A Devonshire Man" practically turns much more on the
degree of Mr. Huxley's ethnological fallibility than even on the amount
of difference between Celt and Saxon; and also that the   scientific
difference between him and his opponent resembles much more nearly
in its degree the difference between the Pope and the Gallican party, than
it does the difference between the Church and an open rebel like Père
Hyacinthe. But this is not all. In the conclusion of his letter Professor
Huxley charges "A Devonshire Man" with having twitted him with the
mathematical controversy in which he is engaged, "with no other object,
that I can discover, except that of offence," — and while declaring his
perfect readiness to surrender to an open and loyal opponent who beats
him in fair argument, concludes thus: — "I confess my feeling is other
towards an adversary who hides himself behind the hedge of a
pseudonym, to fire off his blunderbuss of platitudes and personalities at
a man who has made a grave and public statement on a matter concerning
which he is entitled to be heard. And while fresh from 'tumbling' his man
of science, 'A Devonshire Man' seems to me to be inconsistent in so
haughtily repudiating all kinship with a 'Tipperary Boy'." Now, we
seriously put it to Professor Huxley whether this tone of bitterness and
even virulence is worthy of the very strongest man amongst us who is
labouring to preach to us all the gospel of suspense of judgment on all
questions, intellectual and moral, on which we have not adequate data
for a positive opinion? Does it not rather seem to presume the
infallibility of which he is the honest and frank assailant? The intention
to give offence which Professor Huxley assumes is to us quite invisible.
And what right has any man to take for granted that anonymousness is a
mere hedge behind which an adversary skulks from cowardice, — unless,
indeed, his charges be so grave and personal as to demand the assumption
of full personal responsibility, which, in this case, they certainly were not?
Ought not the evangelist of human fallibility to impose strictly on his own

judgment in every concern of life the law which he wishes us all to recognize, — and to admit that his assailant might, for instance, have had a dozen motives that would not be ignoble for not signing his name, — nay, even that his playful criticism on the number of Professor Huxley's controversies might fairly be due not to ill-nature and the wish to give pain, but to a sincere belief (we think, for our own parts, a mistaken one) that even so superlatively able a man as Professor Huxley could not be a first-rate authority in so many different fields. If we are to learn the suspended judgement and intellectual humility of true science, it will hardly be from the example of one who does not shrink from hinting that a thinker may well be more monkey than man if he can regard Professor Huxley as a greater authority for the anatomy of either men or monkeys than for the ethnology of men, or of one who suggests a parallel between a temperate anonymous criticism on an ethnological speculation and the act of a Tipperary Boy in "tumbling" his landlord.

We submit to Professor Huxley that his anonymous opponent, — of whom, as we have said, we know nothing, — sets him a good example in the exceeding good-temper of his last rejoinder, and that the Professor is gravely injuring the effect of his own sincerest teaching by the more than Papal arrogance of his recent tone in rebuke. In his great genius, of which his usually grand good-humour is the most conspicuous feature, we, like almost all the literary men of our country feel a cordial pride. But we must warn him that if once the students of positive science whom he usually represents not only so worthily, but so nobly, begin to unite the attitude of moral infallibility with the intellectual attitude of agnostic suspense, they will soon, and very justly, lose half their influence with the English people. Men will begin to say that confidence in the methods of physical investigation, too exclusively pursued, intoxicates the brain of even the wisest men, and makes them *fulminate* opinions, conjectures, and prepossessions, as if they were laws of nature or of thought, — and that a grain of spiritual faith may have more effect in producing charity and humility than even such lucid and marvellous mastery of vast fields of science, and such noble and untiring benevolence in utilizing his knowledge for the benefit of his fellow-men, as have already earned for Professor Huxley a distinguished and even illustrious name.

Mr. Arnold on God

Few writers of the day can rival Mr. Arnold's skill in the Socratic art of introducing the deepest questions in an informal and almost incidental way, – of insinuating an original criticism which involves a creed, a philosophy, a principle of literary interpretation, under the pretext of defending Literature against the scorn in which it is held, as an instrument of culture, alike by the aristocratic society, the physical science, and the dogmatic theology of the day. No one would dream that an essay beginning in this easy informal fashion was intended to launch us into the discussion of the very essence of religion, and to propound a view as bold and novel, as it is we imagine untenable, of what the writers of the Jewish and Christian Scriptures invariably assumed under the name of 'God.' Yet that is the real drift of Mr. Arnold's beautifully written and delicately dogmatic assault upon Dogma in the paper entitled "Literature and Dogma" in the July number of the *Cornhill*. It takes us down to the deepest of spiritual questions, and pours into our ears a continuous stream of solvent and reconstructive criticism, full of fine irony, of persuasive earnestness, of imposing illustration, all in the easiest way, and under the slight disguise of an apology for the special tact and good sense which literary culture teaches, and which aristocratic arrogance, scientific absoluteness, and theological dogmatism uniformly neglect. Any one who wishes to know how to slide in after the fashion of Plato's Socrates, by an apparently familiar criticism on modern tendencies, the exposition of a new, momentous, and subversive doctrine, without giving his readers previous notice of his drift, cannot do better than study some of Mr. Arnold's recent essays, but above all, this last on "Literature and Dogma."

For the real drift of Mr. Arnold's paper is no less than this, – to defend his own recent definition of the scientific substratum of the word 'God' as that "stream of tendency by which all things fulfil the law of their being," – a definition on which we commented at the time he first published it in his remarkable essays on St. Paul,[1] – and not only to defend it, but to maintain that it comprehends all that is essential even in the use made of the name of God in the Jewish and Christian Scriptures. The definition itself is startling enough, if only on this account, that 'the stream of tendency by which all things fulfil the law of their being' is not to be distinctly discriminated from the stream of tendency by which so many things seem displaced, diverted, distorted from the law of their being, on any view except that which gives such a wholeness, such an individuality, such an integrity, such a unity to the former stream of tendency as to warrant the use of a word attributing to it life and knowledge and love. But the definition itself, to those who know what philosophy has formerly done in this way, is ordinary compared with the critical thesis which follows. Mr. Arnold holds that the Hebrew and Christian teachers never grasped fully what they meant by "God" and "the Eternal" over and above "the enduring power, not ourselves, which makes for righteousness." And especially the freedom, life, and love which they attributed to God, — and which they had no better than a poetic right, according to Mr. Arnold, to attribute to him, since all such titles spring out of a tentative and hitherto unverified effort of the anthropomorphic imagination, — were apparently mere metaphors.[2] This, we say, is startling criticism, for never before was it, as far as we know, even so much as suggested that the Hebrew prophets and Christian apostles and evangelists grasped less fully the idea of the care, and mercy, and love by which they were surrounded, than they did the idea of "an enduring power, not ourselves, which makes for righteousness;" and such assertion from the pen of an accomplished critic like Mr. Arnold, who always endeavours to see things truly, fills us less with surprise than with sheer bewilderment. It is, of course, open to any critic to maintain that the spiritual assumptions of Israel and of the disciples of Christ were made on insufficient data, but to question for a moment the fact that the very centre and root of those spiritual assumptions was the existence of life, thought, judgment, love in that "enduring power, not ourselves, which makes for righteousness," to assert that they were even able to apprehend any such "stream of tendency," except as the self-manifestation of a living Being whose thoughts and ways are as much higher than our thoughts and ways, as "the Heavens are higher than the Earth," seems to us one of the mere eccentricities of self-willed criticism, and almost as different from the dry light of Mr. Arnold's usually impartial insight, as Dr. Cumming's readings of the Apocalypse would be from those of De Wette or Schenkel.[3] Still it is a view which Mr. Arnold seems seriously to have embraced, and which he has tasked all the resources of his delicate literary skill to make to a certain extent plausible and natural.

Let us explain how Mr. Arnold gets at his certainly eccentric view. He says: —

> When we have once satisfied ourselves both as to the tentative poetic way in which the Bible personages used language, and also as to their having no pretentions to metaphysics at all, let us, therefore, when there is this question

raised as to the scientific account of what they had before their minds, be content with a very unpretending answer. And in this way such a phrase as that which we have formerly used concerning God, and have been much blamed for using, — the phrase, namely, 'that, for science, God is simply *the stream of tendency by which all things fulfil the law of their being,*' — may be allowed, and even prove useful. Certainly it is inadequate; certainly it is a less proper phrase than, for instance, 'Clouds and darkness are round about him, righteousness and judgment are the habitation of his seat.' But then it is, in however humble a degree and with however narrow a reach, a *scientific* definition, which the other is not. The phrase, 'A personal first cause, the moral and intelligent governor of the universe, has also, when applied to God, the character, no doubt, of a scientific definition; but then it goes far beyond what is admittedly certain and verifiable, which is what we mean by scientific. It attempts far too much; if we want here, as we do want, to have what is admittedly certain and verifiable we must content ourselves with very little. No one will say that it is admittedly certain and verifiable that there is a personal first cause, the moral and intelligent governor of the universe, whom we may call God if we will. But that all things seem to us to have what we call a law of their being, and to tend to fulfil it, is certain and admitted; though whether we will call this *God* or not is a matter of choice. Suppose, however, we call it *God*, we then give the name of *God* to a certain and admitted reality; this, at least, is an advantage. And the notion does, in fact, enter into the term *God*, in men's common use of it. To please God, to serve God, to obey God's will, does mean to follow a law of things which is found in conscience, and which is an indication, irrespective of our arbitrary wish and fancy, of what we ought to do."[4]

Now we cannot help regarding this passage as containing very much less than Mr. Arnold's usual lucidity of thought. What induces the belief in "an enduring power, not ourselves, which makes for Righteousness"? Can any one even conceive a real separation between the drift of tendency outside ourselves which "makes for Righteousness," and the drift and tendency outside ourselves which makes for what is other than Righteousness, except on condition that the former drift of tendency is directed by a living aim and love? The truth is that Mr. Arnold's expression appears to assume that what "makes for Righteousness" has a distinct coherence, unity, and life of its own, and if so, what better name can we give to such coherence, unity, and life, than a name which implies purpose and love? Or if he does not assume this, if he means to leave it an open question whether or not the tendencies external to ourselves which "make for Righteousness" and those which make for unrighteousness are all inextricably mixed up together, then, those which "make for Righteousness" have no more title to a separate name, and to be the object of distinct emotions, than the resolved elements which analysis substitutes for a single pulling or pushing force have any title to a separate name, or than the various inconsistent manifestations of the same human character have a right to be completely disentangled in our emotions, as if they were not bound together by any concrete tie. Mr. Arnold is simply hiding his own difficulties from himself, like the ostrich hiding its head in the sand, when he attempts to justify our entertaining a distinct class of emotions towards an "enduring power, not ourselves, which makes for Righteousness," and yet to waive the question whether that power has any life, love, and unity of its own. If that power be isolated only by our own effort of abstraction, if it be nothing but what we discern in thought as contained within the Universal whole around us as the sculptor discerns in thought the future statue within the block of marble from which it is to be carved, it is sheer self-delusion, almost self-trickery, to speak of it as "making for Righteousness" in any sense that deserves emotion at all. Do we when swimming for our lives feel grateful to the flowing tide because it "makes for land," when we know that at any moment, by a law with which our destiny is in no way connected, it may "make for sea," and carry us to our destruction? Should we think it rational to discriminate in emotion between that part of our daily bread which 'makes for' health and that which 'makes for' disease, and cherish grateful emotions toward the one, emotions of detestation to the other? Unless the "enduring power, not ourselves, that makes for Righteousness," does so from love of righteousness, it is worthy of no emotion at all, and if it does so from love of righteousness, then it is, so far, precisely what we mean by personal.

Mr. Arnold defines religion as 'morality touched with emotion.'[5] That is a question of words, though we believe that, as a question of words, it is a mistake to exclude from Religion what it contains in nine hundred and ninety-nine cases out of every thousand in which it is employed, namely, the *particular* emotion created by faith in a living and guiding will, and that there is no reason at all for saying, as Mr. Arnold does, that such a maxim as "he that resisteth pleasures crowneth his life," contains more than morality, only because there is a certain vividness of feeling in the expression. He might as well say that this is religion, — it is certainly morality touched with emotion: —

> "I said my heart is all too soft,
> He who would climb and soar aloft
> Must needs keep ever at his side
> The tonic of a wholesome pride."[6]

Do we provide a separate name for political insight when touched with emotion? for scientific insight when touched with emotion? If not, why provide one for morality when touched with emotion, unless that emotion introduces an entirely distinct element, the relation of the moral agent to an invisible love and will which provides the *explanation* of the enhancement of moral feeling into religious feeling? Now, let us take some of Mr. Arnold's illustrations from the Bible, and ask wherein lies the real distinction which he recognizes between the purely moral and the religious sayings: —

> "First: 'It is *joy* to the just to do judgment.' Then: 'It becometh well the just to be *thankful*.' Finally: 'A *pleasant* thing it is to be thankful.' What can be simpler than this, and at the same time more solid? But again: 'There is nothing *sweeter* than to take heed unto *the commandments of the Eternal*.' 'I will *thank the Eternal* for giving me warning.' 'How *precious* are thy thoughts unto me, O *God*!' Why, these are the very same propositions as the others, only with a power and depth of emotion added! Emotion has been applied to morality. *God* is here really, at bottom, a deeply moved way of saying, *conduct* or *righteousness*. Trust in God is trust in the law of conduct; *delight in the Lord* is, in a deeply moved way of expression, the happiness we all feel to spring from *conduct*."[7]

Is it not obvious to the simplest critical intelligence not preoccupied with a theory, that one who speaks of "the sweetness of heeding the *commandments* of the Eternal," of "*thanking* the Eternal" for giving him "*warning*," who commemorates the preciousness of the "*thoughts* of God," is speaking of a being who commands, who warns, who thinks, who loves, and that if this assumption were excluded from his mind, all the power and depth of the emotion would go with it? Let us try the most deeply-moved way of substituting "conduct" or "righteousness" for "God" we can, and see if by any artifice, be it what we will, we can exclude the idea of life and love, and yet speak with emotion of the sweetness of the commandments of "an enduring power, not ourselves, which makes for Righteousness," or of thanking "an enduring power, not ourselves, which makes for Righteousness," for giving us warning, or of the preciousness of the thoughts of "an enduring power, not ourselves, which makes for Righteousness." The effort is simply impossible. Just so far as we slide back the thought and life and love into Mr. Arnold's non-committal phrase and only so far, can we use without absurdity the emotional language which the Psalmist uses. Sedulously exclude that thought and life and love from your meaning, and you find that you are betrayed into a language of ridiculously paradoxical and unmeaning emotion towards something about as capable of kindling it as that "pure being" of Hegel's, which his system begins by assuring us is "pure nothing."[8] In one word, Mr. Arnold's "enduring power, not ourselves which makes for righteousness," is incapable of generating emotion unless we attribute to it thought and will and love; and if we attribute that to it, there is no pretence for excluding even the idea of personality, whatever modifications in it we may admit to be needful in rising from the finite to the infinite. It is not an emotion in the abstract which turns morality into religion, it is the particular kind of emotion due to the faith we entertain in a being of thought and love and will. If we have no justification for that faith, we have no justification for the emotion, and the emotion will disappear. It is with unaffected wonder that we find Mr. Arnold seriously asserting that that which gives substance and solidity to the Jewish and Christian religious feeling is not the belief in personal justice, pity, and love, but simply the belief in a law of conduct the origin of which in personal or impersonal sources is a matter of indifference. The Jews, he says, and says truly, were not metaphysicians. No doubt. If they had discovered what personality means ever so much, they would have felt the personality of God no more than they did. But it is precisely because they were not metaphysicians that it never even occurred to them to think of "an enduring power, not ourselves, which makes for righteousness," as worth any emotion at all, unless there were thought and knowledge and justice and love inherent in that power.

Mr. Arnold says that his own definition of God is less "adequate" than the the language of the Psalmist: "Clouds and darkness are round about him, righteousness and judgment are the habitation of his seat;" — *why* less adequate, unless these poetical words, which go beyond science in Mr. Arnold's opinion, go beyond it in the direction of filling up with more truth than error the suggestions and implications of science? Yet if this be so, the suggestions and implications which lead the mind to use personal analogies are truer than those which lead it away from those analogies, and in that case the question which Mr. Arnold is so anxious to reserve is really prejudged already. An impartial critic reading such language as the Bible habitually uses of God has only three alternatives before him, — to declare that that language, being utterly rooted as it is in the faith that God rules freely, justly, piteously, lovingly, is true, or is false, or is grounded on an assumption not yet known to be either true or false. In either of the latter cases it ought to be utterly rejected by science; — if false because it is false, — if premature because it tends to prejudge a most momentous and unsettled question. To assert that this language is the most *adequate* that can be employed, and yet that our decision as to the existence of a free, just, pitying, loving ruler of the universe ought to be suspended, is a paradox quite unworthy of any fine critic. "Thy mercy, O Lord, reacheth unto the Heavens: and thy faithfulness unto the clouds.

Thy righteousness standeth like the strong mountains: thy judgments are like the great deep.... How excellent is thy mercy, O God: and the children of men shall put their trust under the shadow of thy wings.... For with thee is the well of life: and in thy light shall we see light." "Now is my soul troubled, and what shall I say? Father, save me from this hour? Yet for this cause came I unto this hour. Father, glorify thy name!"[9] If these are some of the most "adequate" expressions of religious feeling in the Old and New Testament, they are adequate not primarily through the depth of their emotion, but through the adequacy of the Object which is assigned for the emotion so expressed, and without that Object the emotion would be not only impossible, but, if possible, unmanly and unworthy. That Mr. Arnold should justify such emotion without justifying the faith which is its very principle and substance, seems to us to render questionable what Mr. Arnold is concerned to affirm, that the school of literature is a school of lucidity and common-sense. The Bible may have a true meaning, or it may have none as yet ascertained, but if it *has* a true meaning at all, it cannot possibly be going beyond what is "certain and verifiable" in the assumption which runs from its first page to its last, — that God *thinks*, though his thoughts are as much higher than our thoughts as the heavens are higher than the earth, and that God *loves*, though "as far as the east is from the west" so much greater is his love than our own.

The Tension in Charles Dickens

A great sculptor, commenting to the present writer on the physical features of the bust of Dickens, drew attention especially to "the whip-cord," — "the race-horse tension," — in all the muscles: — all the softer and vaguer tissues in the face and bust were pruned away, and only the keen, strenuous, driving, purpose-pursuing elements in it left.[1] The second volume of Mr. Forster's life of Charles Dickens brings out that criticism with extraordinary force. It is like reading the biography of a literary race-horse. The tension and strain go on through the whole ten years, 1842-52, which the book covers. There is no rest in the man's nature, even when he is professedly resting. He once proposed to himself to write a book like "The Vicar of Wakefield." He could just as easily have written a play like "Hamlet" or the Odes of Horace. He had not a touch of Goldsmith's ease and leisurely literary air. His nerves were never relaxed. A great element in the force of his genius, and a very great element in its principal limitations, is due to their constant strain, which spoils almost all the sentiment, makes it theatrical and always on the stretch, and not unfrequently lends a forced ring to the greatest of all his faculties, his humour. The biography is, of course, most amusing reading. Whether the moral tension is justified or in excess, it is always there, and therefore even if we are annoyed and repelled, our attention never flags. But Mr. Forster is not as fastidious as he might have been in inserting the would-be comic letters of his friend, and perhaps on that very account, he gives a picture that is the more complete, — complete in its unconscious as well as in its conscious contribution to our knowledge of the great humourist. Dickens is always on the double-quick march. If he hits the exact mark and his humour is at its best, it is still humour marching sharply on to the particular end in view. You can see its steady, swift current, none the less easily for the enormous wealth of detail which he snatches from all sides wherewith to enrich it. If he fails to hit the mark, and talks excited nonsense, as in the silly letter about his passion for the Queen in the first volume, and many a little note in this, it is nevertheless all in the same vein, jocosity stretching eagerly towards a given aim, though the aim is falsely taken. Consider, for instance, this answer to an invitation to dinner sent by Maclise, Stanfield, and Mr. Forster: —

"Devonshire Lodge, January 17th, 1844. Fellow Countrymen! – The appeal with which you have honoured me, awakens within my breast emotions that are more easily to be imagined than described. Heaven bless you. I shall indeed be proud, my friends, to respond to such a requisition. I had withdrawn from Public Life – I fondly thought for ever – to pass the evening of my days in hydropathical pursuits, and the contemplation of virtue. For which latter purpose, I had bought a looking-glass. But, my friends, private feeling must ever yield to a stern sense of public duty. The man is lost in the invited guest, and I comply. Nurses, wet and dry; apothecaries; mothers-in-law; babbies; with all the sweet (and chaste) delights of private life; these, my countrymen, are hard to leave. But you have called me forth, and I will come. – Fellow countrymen, your friend and faithful servant, CHARLES DICKENS."[2]

The idea is forced and the gaiety is unnatural, but the whole letter is written up to the idea, and you see the straining whipcord even in that bit of laborious comedy. The proclamation about the piratical republication of his works, put forth on the eve of the appearance of "Nickleby" (pp. 76-7 of this volume), is another bit of laboured pleasantry of the same kind, a violent straining after a pseudo-comic idea. But his true and most marvellous efforts of humour have all the same swift-running current in them, though of course, when the tide is triumphant, and sweeps all sort of rich spoils upon its surface, there is not the same sense of *effort*, – by which we usually mean force not quite adequate to its purpose. The exquisite illustrations which he gathers from all quarters of the sick and monthly nurse's world to enrich the technical vocabulary, and fill up to overflowing the strictly professional mould, of Mrs. Gamp's conversation and life, abundant and amazing in their abundance and in the variety and subtlety of their shades as they are, are all collected to convey the same drift, and all suggest to us a keen eye on the stretch, ranging over its various stores of mouldy associations, to pile up monthly-nurseisms of every kind. Mr. Forster quotes, for instance, in this volume one of the very best and also the very first of Mrs. Gamp's speeches: – " 'Mrs. Harris,' I says, at the very last case as ever I acted in, which it was but a young person, 'Mrs. Harris,' I says, 'leave the bottle on the the chimley-piece, and don't ask me to take none, but let me put my lips to it when I am so dispoged.' – 'Mrs. Gamp,' she says to me, 'if ever there was a sober cretur to be got at eighteen-pence a day for working-people, and three-and-six for gentlefolks' – 'night-watching,' said Mrs. Gamp, with emphasis, 'being a extra charge,' – 'you are that inwallable person.' – 'Mrs. Harris,' I says to her, 'don't name the charge, for if I could afford to lay all my fellow-creeturs out for nothink, I would gladly do it, sich is the love I bears 'em.' "[3] Now, anyone can see that the wonderful humour here is mainly due to the delightful intensity and extravagance with which Dickens could abandon his imagination to the train of associations proper to a thoroughly selfish and mouldy person of this class, who takes a positive professional pride in laying out her fellow-creatures. It is the singleness of his eager and strenuous search, as he follows up every cross-thread of association that his enormous power of observation had given him, never deviating for a moment from the two leading ideas, — selfish greediness with a cant of benevolence, and professional detail of all kinds, — that helps him to pile up the character into so wonderful an embodiment and illustration of these two notions. We are not in the least degree endeavouring to explain away his genius, but only to show that one feature of it, — the *constructive* power of his mind, — his accurate and omnivorous observing faculty being taken for granted, — depended on the extraordinary tension he could put on one or two leading threads of association, by the help of which he drew from his resources what they, and they alone, demanded. No man was ever able to stretch one or two lines of conception so tightly, and to exclude so completely all disturbing influences from the field of his vision. It was the source of his power and the source of the limitations on his power. It produced his great successes, — Pecksniff, Mrs. Gamp, Moddle, Micawber, Toots, and a hundred others. It produced also, when applied to types of character that would not bear so keen a tension of one or two strings, all the failures due to overstraining like Little Nell, Carker, Mrs. Dombey, Dombey, and a hundred others. You see the strain of the race-horse in all he did; and in creations which, with his wonderful wealth of observation, could be produced under sharp tension of the one or two humorous conceptions devoted to each creation, he succeeded triumphantly; while wherever the creation wanted a leisurely, reflective, many-sided mood of mind he failed. In sentimental passages, the string is almost always strained until it cracks. Mr. Forster is, of course, compelled to admire Little Nell, the pathetic elements in the Christmas Stories, and so on. But these are the repelling things to all true lovers of Dickens, rather than the attractions. Even in the death of little Paul Dombey, perhaps his closest approach to true pathos, you feel painfully the undue stretch of the sentiment, and turn away a little sickened. It is much worse in the case of most other of his efforts of the same kind; and Mr. Forster's "Life" shows that it must have been so, from the ostentation of Dickens' own feelings in speaking of these efforts. He tells you how much he weeps over them, how cut up he is with his own pathos, till you are quite sick of the glare and effort. When he is speaking of his really great efforts of humour he is altogether natural. You have no feeling then that he is whipping himself up to the point, and proud of being able to reach it.

But it is on the practical side of Dickens' life that this nervous tension comes out most curiously. What a fume he falls into when the sale of "Chuzzlewit" does not come up to his expectations, and his publishers hint at putting in force the clause empowering them to retain £50 out of the £200 allowed for the expenses of authorship on each number: – "I am so irritated," he wrote to Mr. Forster, "so rubbed in the tenderest part of my eyelids with baysalt, by what I told you yesterday, that a wrong kind of fire is burning in my head, and I don't think I *can* write. Nevertheless, I am trying. In case I should succeed, and should not come down to you this morning, shall you be at the club or elsewhere after dinner? I am bent on paying the money."[4] In his disappointment and fear of failure, he determines at once to go abroad, and these sort of resolves with him always hardened rapidly into fixity which no dissuasion would affect. When the "Christmas Carol" does not yield as he had hoped, we have the same sort of outburst again: – " 'Such a night as I have passed!' he wrote to me on Saturday morning, the 10th of February. 'I really believed I should never get up again, until I had passed through all the horrors of a fever. I found the 'Carol' accounts awaiting me, and they were the cause of it. The first six thousand copies show a profit of £230! And the last four will yield as much more. I had set my heart and soul upon a Thousand, clear. What a wonderful thing it is, that such a great success should occasion me such intolerable anxiety and disappointment! My year's bills, unpaid, are so terrific, that all the energy and determination I can possibly exert will be required to clear me before I go abroad; which, if next June come and find me alive, I shall do!'"[5] When the pirates are defeated at law, but being men of straw cannot pay the costs, so that Dickens has to pay his own costs, we have the same excessive tension of imperious disappointment: –

> "My feeling about the———is the feeling common, I suppose, to three-fourths of the reflecting part of the community in our happiest of all possible countries; and that is, that it is better to suffer a great wrong than to have recourse to the much greater wrong of the law. I shall not easily forget the expense, and anxiety, and horrible injustice of the 'Carol' case, wherein, in asserting the plainest right on earth, I was really treated as if I were the robber instead of the robbed.... It is useless to affect that I don't know I have a morbid susceptibility of exasperation, to which the meanness and the badness of the law in such a matter will be stinging to the last degree."[6]

His very idleness, as Mr. Forster well says, was "strenuous," like his work. He walked eighteen miles in four hours and half in the full heat of a glowing summer's day simply as a sort of relief for the strain of his nerves. On another occasion, Mr. Forster says: – "But he did even his nothings in a strenuous way, and on occasion could make gallant fight against the elements themselves. He reported himself, to my horror, thrice wet through on a single day, 'dressed four times,' and finding all sorts of great things, brought out by the rains, among the rocks on the sea-beach." When he is living in Genoa, in the middle of winter, he dashes over to London just to try the effect of reading "The Chimes" to his intimate friends. Between Milan and Strasburg he was in bed only once for two or three hours at Fribourg, and had sledged over the Simplon through deep snow and prodigious cold. His dash into the Editorship of the *Daily News* and out of it within three weeks was highly characteristic of the high pressure of his nervous decision. *A propos* of this matter, Mr. Forster says very truly that "in all intellectual labours his will prevailed so strongly when he fixed it on any object of desire, that what else its attainment might exact was never duly measured, and this led to frequent strain and uncommon waste of what no man could less afford to spare."[7] Everything he did, he did with this imperious resolve to let his volition take its own way, and it led him no doubt into some of the greatest mistakes of his life. He liked to have everything just as he has imagined it. His mind strained intensely towards the particular ideal he had summoned up in his fancy; nothing else would satisfy him for a moment.

Mr. Forster has a very fair laugh at M. Taine for his wonderful blunder in thinking that the maudlin youth whom Miss Charity Pecksniff captured, and whom she lost at the very altar, was meant for "a gloomy maniac," and one so powerfully drawn as to make us "shudder."[8] But there is something quite just in M. Taine's general criticism that Dickens does draw the madness of "fixed ideas" with extraordinary power. It is the secret of his marvellous descriptions of murderous feeling, — of Jonas Chuzzlewit's, for example, also of Sykes' wanderings after the murder of Nancy, and, again, of the murderous schoolmaster in "Our Mutual Friend." And it was precisely the extraordinary capacity of his own mind for the tension of fixed ideas which enabled him to do this so powerfully. Intellectually, indeed, he hardly understood anything else, — though some of the fixed ideas on to which he tacked his pictures were so delightfully limp, — as in poor Mr. Moddle's and Dick Swiveller's case, and many others, — that the fixity of the leading thought escapes the reader. As was the author, so was the man. Mr. Forster's admirable book will certainly carry one trait of Dickens right home to every devourer of his biography, — that all the veins and muscles in Dickens's nature were always on the stretch towards some eager end. A mind with less rest and less easy play in it, in spite of all its real fun and laughter, is hardly conceivable.

The Humour of Middlemarch

In one of the many at once fascinating and irritating sarcasms which it was impossible not to look forward to and backward at, while *Middlemarch* was still incomplete, and life had still a literary object, George Eliot says, "Some gentlemen have made an amazing figure in literature by general discontent with the universe, as a trap of dullness into which their great souls have fallen by mistake; but the sense of a stupendous self and an insignificant world may have its consolations,"[1] – a sharp saying and a sample of many another with which every chapter in *Middlemarch* is plentifully strewn. But it is not to sarcasms such as these that we should appeal as illustrative of the humour of *Middlemarch*. They gave a poignant flavour to the book, and made the reader feel a little afraid of his author, as well as wide awake to the general drift of her remarks; but painfully as the barbs of her psychological criticisms make themselves felt, these criticisms have not half the humour or zest of her manipulations of the ludicrous where her attitude is not critical, as it is here, but directly creative. What picture in English literature has ever had more of true humour in it than that of the slipshod good-nature of Mr. Brooke, with his inchoate aphorisms struggling into the purely suggestive existence of a cloudy hint for sharper-minded people; his embryonic "documents" which never get even as far as that; his shuffling, irresolute ambition; his immense satisfaction in dwelling on the mere names of eminent persons or interesting places he had known, – as a species of shorthand memories the real significance of which to himself he never took the trouble to decypher; – his fear of going too far, especially in the direction of expense; and his habit of introducing unpleasant information "in the midst of a number of disjointed particulars," "as if it were a medicine that would get a milder flavour by mixing"?[2] And how the humour of the picture is enhanced by the admirable contrast with Mrs. Cadwallader, whose mind may be said to live only in the sharpness and detail of particulars, who never attempts an aphorism, and says precisely what she means with somewhat startling abruptness and trenchant wit. A miscellaneous desultory mind like Mr. Brooke's, of would-be enterprise well down at heels, that harks back before it has well committed itself to anything, is a true enough and a humorous enough conception in itself, but when brought on to the stage in close contrast with one like Mrs. Cadwallader's, which, without a trace of this uncertain haze of aspiration, is full of the sharp settled self-confidence, mingled of high birth and wit, that hits its mark with precision for every helpless shuffle of Mr. Brooke's, the humour of the picture is doubled. That good-natured fog of drifting purpose and incoherent thought called Mr. Brooke, makes his first appearance at his own dinner-table, introducing the conversation with his usual good-humoured vague shuffling of desultory subjects: — " 'Sir Humphry Davy?' said Mr. Brooke, over the soup, in his easy, smiling way, taking up Sir James Chettam's remark that he was studying Davy's *Agricultural Chemistry.* 'Well, now, Sir Humphry Davy; I dined with him some years ago at Cartwright's, and Wordsworth was there too, — the poet Wordsworth, you know. Now there was something singular. I was at Cambridge when Wordsworth was there, and I never met him, — and I dined with him twenty years afterwards at Cartwright's. There's an oddity in things now'." Compare that with Mrs. Cadwallader, dark-eyed, high-coloured, driving simultaneously into Mr. Brooke's gates and the scene of the story, in her pony-phaeton, dressed in a shabby bonnet and very old Indian shawl, and doing her smart little stroke of business at the lodge-keeper's as she drives in, by asking Mrs. Fitchett how her fowls are laying, and on hearing that they eat their eggs, saying, "Oh the cannibals! better sell them cheap at once. What will you sell them a couple? *One can't eat fowls of a bad character at a high price.*"[3] This contrast between Mr. Brooke's mind, good-naturedly "going to be created," as it were, — so it was that some old German play introduced Adam to its audience,[4] — and Mrs. Cadwallader's keenly crystallised wit, runs through the whole story. One of Mr. Brooke's unhatched aphorisms is, as we have seen, that "there are oddities in things, — life isn't cast in a mould, — not cut by rule and line, that sort of thing." Mr. Brooke dwells on this "oddity in things" repeatedly, once, in the instance we have quoted, at his own dinner-table, — once in trying to make his niece see that life with Mr. Casaubon won't be exactly what she had fancied it, — and again in a feeble attempt to soothe down by anticipation the irritation of Dorothea's friends on the occasion of her second marriage, — which he does by opening to their vexed souls a prospective refuge in a species of philosophical predestination. "You see, Chettam, you have not been able to hinder it any more than I have; there's something singular in things; they come round, you know."[5] But Mrs. Cadwallader has no sympathy with that sort of generalisation of helplessness. She doesn't think there's anything "singular in things." They wouldn't "have come round," as Mr. Brooke calls it, if people hadn't acted like idiots. As for Dorothea's second marriage, "the only wonder to me is that any of you are surprised. You did nothing to hinder it. If you would have had Lord Triton down here to woo her with his philanthropy, he might have carried her off before the year was over. There was no safety in anything but that. Mr. Casaubon had prepared the way as beautifully as possible. He made himself disagreeable, – or it pleased God to make him so, – and then he dared her to contradict him. It's the way to make any trumpery tempting, to ticket it at a high price in that way."[6] The collisions between Mr. Brooke and Mrs. Cadwallader are triumphs of humour, as when she attacks him for his electioneering propensities on the Radical side, and says to him, "Now *do* not let them lure you to the hustings, my dear Mr. Brooke. A man always makes a fool of himself speechifying. *There's no excuse but being on the right side, so that you can ask a blessing on your humming and hawing;*" or when she advises his friends to play upon his dislike of spending money by making him feel sharply the expense of electioneering. "It's no use plying him with wide words like 'expenditure,' – I wouldn't talk of phlebotomy, I would empty a pot of leeches upon him. What we good, stingy people don't like is having our sixpences sucked away from us;" or when deprecating Mr. Brooke's ill-judged parsimony on his own estate, she says, "Oh, stinginess may be abused like other virtues; it will not do to keep one's own pigs lean."[7] The humour of the running contrast between the needle-point of Mrs. Cadwallader's criticism and the fermenting yeast of Mr. Brooke's helpless mixture of ambition, indolence, and good sense, is all the more telling because of the parsimony common to both, which, when joined with precision of purpose and wit, somehow becomes a new talent in Mrs. Cadwallader, or at least a new field of success and distinction, but joined with Mr. Brooke's hesitation of thought and intention becomes in him a new incapacity. After all, Mr. Brooke is the more humorous figure of the two; the election speech at Middlemarch is one of the most humorous passages in English literature;[8] but the peculiar blur of thought and purpose in his mind would never have been adequately appreciated without the keen foil of the companion picture.

There is nothing in which George Eliot's humour shows itself with more power than the fine shades with which she discriminates the different kinds of mental and moral haze. Mr. Brooke's haze is haze of purpose, chiefly due to indolence. He is not by any means without the yolk of sagacity, only it never gets developed into active life, in consequence of the native desultoriness of his character. But George Eliot paints haze of prejudice at least as well as she paints haze of purpose, and she paints it where there is no haze of purpose at all, but the clearest possible purpose looming red through a fog of dull notions, mixed up of creed and cunning, like the red-hot surface of Jupiter through his great belts of cloud.[9] What, for instance, can be fuller of grim humour than the picture of Mrs. Waule, Peter Featherstone's sister, who inveighs against the Vincys "not at all with a defiant air, but in a low, muffled, neutral tone, as of a voice heard through cotton wool," and who asks, in case Fred Vincy is to get her brother's, Peter Featherstone's, property, "what did God Almighty make families for?" and this though she quite agrees with her dying brother, who dismisses her curtly in the words, "Mrs. Waule, you'd better go," — that "entire freedom from the necessity of behaving agreeably was included in the Almighty's intention about families."[10] Of course, the evidence of humour here consists not in the accurate copying of the trait just as it would have been seen in a real Mrs. Waule, but in the indications that the conception of Mrs. Waule's family feelings and creed was even more due to the author's humour than to her mere power of observation, — that it was due at least to a power of observation inspired and guided by humour. The merely faithful painter would have given Mrs. Waule's remark, and might even have added that Mrs. Waule was not specially annoyed by her abrupt dismissal, but he would not have brought the two together as helping to interpret her view of the Providential purpose of a family. That could be only the work of a great humorist, just as the contrast between Mrs. Cadwallader and Mr. Brooke could only be the work of a great humorist. And in the same way the train of thought which is described as passing through the mind of the Middlemarch innkeeper, Mrs. Dollop, in relation to the asserted poisoning of Raffles, could only be the picture of a great humorist. Not that this train of thought is in any way, as far as we can tell, deflected from the truth of real life by the humour of the novelist, but that it required her strongly humorous imagination for incongruities to *supply the place* of the manifold confusions of association which would stand for thought and knowledge with Mrs. Dollop. Mrs. Dollop is the person who leads opinion in Middlemarch against post-mortem examinations at the hospital. She said that "Doctor Lydgate meant to let the people die in the Hospital, if not to poison them, for the sake of cutting them up, without saying by your leave or with your leave; for it was a known 'fac' that he had wanted to cut up Mrs. Goby, as respectable a woman as any in Parley Street, who had money in trust before her marriage — a poor tale for a doctor who, if he was good for anything, should know what was the matter with you before you died, and not want to pry into your inside after you were gone." This irrefragable argument for Mr. Lydgate's murderous intentions — that he had wanted to cut up a woman who had money in trust before her marriage, — would never have reproduced itself in a mind in which the humour involved in the anarchy of ideas had not replaced, like a second nature, the ignorance which rendered such an anarchy possible. And the humour is still more delightful in the picture of Mrs. Dollop's second great attack on Lydgate, — the attack founded on his supposed complicity in the poisoning of Raffles: —

" 'Why shouldn't they dig the man up, and have the Crowner?' said the dyer. 'It's been done many and many's the time. If there's been foul play they might find it out.' – 'Not they, Mr. Jonas!' said Mrs. Dollop, emphatically. 'I know what doctors are. They're a deal too cunning to be found out. And this Doctor Lydgate that's been for cutting up everybody before the breath was well out o' their body – it's plain enough what use he wanted to make o' looking into respectable people's insides. He knows drugs, you may be sure, as you can neither smell nor see, neither before they're swallowed nor after. Why, I've seen drops myself ordered by Doctor Gambit as is our club doctor and a good charikter, and has brought more live children into the world nor ever another i' Middlemarch – I said I've seen drops myself as made no difference whether they was in the glass or out, and yet have griped you the next day. So I'll leave your own sense to judge. Don't tell me! All I say is, it's a mercy they didn't take this Doctor Lydgate on to our club. There's many a mother's child might ha' rued it'."[11]

Mrs. Dollop's abject veneration for the latent power of drugs which "made no difference whether they was in the glass or not, and yet griped you the next day," is just such a touch of humour as Shakespeare delighted in. Indeed, perhaps the only other writer in fiction besides Shakespeare who could have created Juliet's nurse is George Eliot.

And even now we have but touched on the chief centres of the wealth of humour of *Middlemarch*. From little Benjamin Garth, who, when informed, while at his lessons, that his father is sent for again by employers who had previously abruptly dispensed with his services, cries out, "Hooray! just like Cincinnatus,"[12] *with a sense of discipline being relaxed*, to Bulstrode, the Evangelical banker who could not admit that Joshua Rigg's destiny was the concern of Providence, holding that "it belonged to the unmapped regions not taken under the Providential government, *except in an imperfect, colonial way*," there is hardly a character in the book which is not described from the humorous, as well as the merely pictorial point of view. From Mr. Bambridge, the horse-dealer, who says that Raffles was the kind of man who bragged so much that "he'd brag of a spavin as if it 'ud fetch money," to Mrs. Toft, the knitter, who was always catching up misleading fragments of conversation in the intervals of counting her stitches, every one of the slightest sketches is put in with a touch of humour that makes it bright and vivid.[13] Without counting George Eliot's bitterer sarcasms, – which are only too numerous, though hardly so numerous, we think, as in former books, and sometimes not altogether pleasant, – the wealth of genuine humour in *Middlemarch* is astonishing. And it is, so far as this, of the Shakespearian kind, – that it proceeds out of a fullness of insight into the commonest modes of thought and feeling which brings them before us to the very life; only it does not usually proceed from any considerable measure of *sympathy* with that mode of thought and feeling, as it does in Shakespeare even where, in an intellectual point of view, the popular way of looking at things is most indefensible. On the contrary, George Eliot laughs *at* the common modes of thought and feeling much more than with them, and it is only astonishing that, this being so, it seldom or never leads her to exaggerate common people's sayings into pure farce, or to starve them into pure inanity. She has always moderation enough to give to the absurdities and incongruities which she exposes the tone of absolute fidelity to life.

Mr. John Stuart Mill

Probably very few authors who have exerted so powerful an influence over the course of English thought as Mr. John Stuart Mill have ever been so wanting in superficially marked personal characteristics of style. He has recast our political economy, converted almost a whole generation of teachers to his own opinions on Logic and Ethics, and materially modified the view taken even by democratic thinkers of the machinery of political life; moreover, he has been for three eventful years a distinguished Member of the House of Commons, where he delivered probably the most thoughtful speeches of that Parliament,[1] and yet few of us would find it as easy to individualise our impression of him as we should our impression of many thinkers we have never seen or heard, — his own father, Mr. James Mill, for instance, or Jeremy Bentham, or Adam Smith, or Hume, or Locke, or Bishop Butler. There is a singularly polished uniformity, a want of light and shade in his style. It is always the style of flowing disquisition, without any relieving glimpses of either humour, or fancy, or moral inequalities of any kind. Locke's style is uniform and dry in its own shrewd, investigating way; but there is always the vigilant air of keen inquiry about it, and now and then, though very rarely, he breaks out into passages of a more personal character, like that on the fading of memory: — "Thus the ideas as well as children of our youth often die before us; and our minds represent to us those tombs to which we are approaching, where, though the brass and marble remain, yet the inscriptions are effaced by time, and the imagery moulders away."[2] In Mr. J.S. Mill's words we cannot at present recall one break of this peculiar kind, except, perhaps, the celebrated passage in his examination of Sir William Hamilton's philosophy, in which he declares, "I will call no being good who is not what I mean when I apply that epithet to my fellow-creatures, and if such a being can sentence me to hell for not so calling him, to hell I will go;"[3] and even that fine passage is not like the one we have cited from Locke, one of marked variety in style, a sort of shaft sunk into the inner character, but though deeper in conception, seems to be of one piece in rhythm and structure with the whole texture of Mr. Mill's writings, a part of the disquisition, not a light through it. No doubt there is a fine pale enthusiasm in the passage, but the same sort of pallid enthusiasm is visible on lower subjects, in the discussion of remedies for over-population, of safeguards against the dangers of democracy, of speculations as to the potentialities of education. What we miss in Mr. J.S. Mill are personal characteristics beneath and beyond the permanent characteristics of his rational disquisition. There is a monotony in the calm, evenly flowing, impartial, didactic pertinacity of disquisition, which is almost appalling, when we consider the number of volumes into which it has flowed with steady and uniform current, without a single important variety of doctrine or manner. Doubtless this is one of the causes of Mr. Mill's great doctrinal success. His books diffuse a fine all-interpenetrating intellectual atmosphere, more even than a body of individual conviction, and the less closely they are associated with his name and personality, the more do they seem to partake of the impersonal intelligence of his age, and the more readily do they pass into the very essence of what is called the Time-Spirit, and win their way without the necessity for a battle and a conquest. Still undoubtedly this great uniformity of style and want of individual touches, — read, for instance, through the three thick volumes of "Dissertations and Discussions,"[4] and hardly anywhere will you stop and say, 'There is the very man,' — make it more difficult to appreciate Mr. Mill's individual genius than it usually is in the case of men who have so powerfully influenced the thought of their day.

Yet after all, there is something characteristic of Mr. John Stuart Mill's genius in this uniform and colourless, but incessant stream of penetrating doctrine, in which an experience philosophy, a nominalist logic, a utilitarian ethics, a large-minded social economy, and a democratic political philosophy, are all taught in their most attractive and catholic sense, — no safeguard omitted which would help to make them more palatable to minds in doubt, and no difficulty ignored which is at all within the scope of Mr. Mill's wide intellectual horizon. His is the kind of style which is great in *method* and not great in dealing with first principles; for first principles require a close study of the roots of human character, while method occupies the middle-ground between those ultimate roots and the definite results of philosophical knowledge. Mr. Mill's strength lay in systematising, and especially in so systematising as to comprehend as much as possible within the limits of the same principle. This was what made his systematic books so much greater than his single papers. The "Dissertations and Discussions" are, except for their considerable range of knowledge and interests, almost common-place. There are but one or two of the essays in which you are compelled to recognise the great author of the "Political Economy" and the "New System of Logic."[5] It is in stretching an elastic method so as to cover a great subject that Mr. Mill's peculiar power comes out. In criticising

Grote, or Coleridge, or Alfred de Vigny he hardly gives one a conception of his own capacity at all.[6] But when in his "Logic" he has to connect together his nominalist doctrine and experience philosophy so as to cover the whole of deductive and inductive reasoning, and when in his "Political Economy" he has to apply the historical method so as to correct the narrow rules of a very provincial school, he shows at once the great grasp of his mind, which was unrivalled in its power of eking out a principle so as to make it cover as far as possible all the facts within his reach, but was by no means, at least in our view, of the first order in the discussion of ultimate speculative truths. We believe that for this reason his "Principles of Political Economy," as it is the less ambitious, is also by far the better of his two great works, and that his intellectual deficiencies come out most in the criticism on Sir William Hamilton, and his book on Utilitarianism, where he grapples most closely with the ultimate principles of psychology and ethics.[7]

We may illustrate what seem to us Mr. Mill's radical deficiencies as a philosopher, by his virtual evasion of four ultimate difficulties in the theories of perception, of reasoning, of moral obligation, and of volition. In the theory of perception, nothing can be more unintelligible and inconsistent than his leap from consciousness, – the only thing of which he admits any direct knowledge, – to the belief in an external world as the cause of certain states of our own consciousness. He has various very ingenious devices for getting more hay out of the field than there is grass in it, – for showing how, though we know nothing but states of our own minds, we are certain to come to believe in external objects as "guaranteed possibilities of sensation" outside our own minds; but the moment you look into his *rationale* of the process of inference, you discover at once that all he has any right to infer is a specific *order* of sensations, and that the notion of externality as the cause of that specific order could not possibly have entered into the inference, if it had not been put there by apprehensions quite different from any of which he will grant the reality. Again, in his theory of reasoning, Mr. Mill, true to the tenor of his system, maintains that all true inference is from particulars to particulars; that you argue from the death of certain men, A, B, and C, to the mortality of another man, D, and not from the death of A, B, and C to the mortality of all men, and then to the mortality of D. But he ignores the truth, as it seems to us, that unless the death of A, B, and C be regarded as enough to suggest the mortality of *all* beings resembling them as D resembles them, it will not establish the mortality of D, and that in point of fact, the mind does infer first a *general* cause for the death of A, B, and C, which also applies to D, and that it is through that general cause, – which is represented by the major premiss of the syllogism, – that we get our inference, which we could not get without it. Again, in relation to his utilitarian ethics, Mr. Mill never was able to explain how, without the help of a principle of obligation lying outside the utilitarian system, it could be obligatory on us to regard the happiness of others as claiming as much consideration from us as our own. He leaps the chasm from the claims of our own pleasures to the claims of the pleasures of other sentient creatures, without admitting any aid from a moral faculty endowed with an authority wholly underived from the selfish system, and yet nothing is more obvious than that Mr. Mill is really an intuitive moralist, if he assumes, as he does, that I am bound to sacrifice a certain amount of my own happiness for a grain more than the same amount of another's happiness, though it is clearly to my own disadvantage to do so. Lastly, the way in which he endeavours to get rid of the controversy as to necessity or free-will by simply throwing doubt on the meaning we attach to the terms, has always seemed to us the very acme of philosophical evasion. His solution is undoubtedly necessarian in spirit, but he tries to soften its real meaning by making much of verbal distinctions. On all these four fundamental points of psychology, Mr. Mill simply evades the stress of the argument against him.

We should be very sorry to seem to underrate the largeness and catholicity of Mr. Mill's intellect, — quite the largest and most catholic intellect that was ever well kept within the limits of a somewhat narrow system, of which, however, he knew well how to stretch the bounds, sometimes beyond, but more often only up to the full limits, that it would bear. He enlarged Utilitarianism in this sense till it was hardly recognisable as Utilitarianism; and he made Political Economy from a "dismal" and hardly credible science into a wide and historical study.[8] His genius for thus giving breadth and elasticity to an apparently inelastic and rigid set of notions was exceedingly marked, and was more or less connected, no doubt, with that fine susceptibility of his mind to all intellectual impressions which made it intolerable to him not to find room in his system for the recognition of so great a thinker, for example, as Coleridge. His essay upon Coleridge marked indeed a new era in the history of the philosophical Radicals, the era when their teaching may be said to have emancipated itself from the formula of a clique and to have become the doctrine of a great school of thought. Mr. Mill, who, like all great expositors of philosophical method, had a fine sense of what was local and provincial, and, on the other hand, of what was likely to be recognised by all ages as a factor in human speculation, was incapable of leading any school characterised by a harsh and jarring tone towards other wide schools of human thought. Keen as he was in controversy, — as, for instance, in defending Utilitarianism against the hasty and not very scientific criticisms of the late Professor Sedgwick,[9] — controversy had little charm for him. He greatly preferred so to interpret a great philosophical tenet as to bring it within his own philosophy, to any attempt to confute it. His essays show no very great critical power in relation to poetical subjects, and no very great pleasure in such criticism. His mind was more intellectual and didactic than artistic, in spite of his passion for music; and in the one essay in which he does criticise Wordsworth and Shelley, he seems to us to have missed their most striking poetic characteristics.[10] But on philosophical subjects, he loved to appreciate fully and to expound with power the view of his opponent.

As a practical politician, Mr. Mill might have risen to the first rank, had he entered Parliament earlier, and had more physical power of voice. He showed considerable skill in repartee, and with greater strength would have made a great debater. As it was, he held his own against Mr. Lowe in the discussions on the cattle plague; and we must remember that for the debates of Committee, the debates of short sharp dialogue, Mr. Lowe is probably as formidable an antagonist as it would be possible to find.[11] Perhaps the chief hindrance to Mr. Mill's political career was his high place in the hierarchy of philosophers. Having been so long looked up to as the head of a school, he could not quite divest himself of the didactic feelings of a philosophical bishop, and gave letters of recommendation to Mr. Chadwick, – and we believe to another candidate, – for the election of 1868 which materially injured his own chances at Westminster.[12] But these are errors which are of the minutest kind, and only worth mention at all as accounting for the arrest of a political career which was fairly successful, and might have been of the first order. His enthusiasm for all causes that he thought just was intense, though mild in its character, and more than once he administered a telling rebuke to the vulgar non-intervention doctrines of the commercial Radicals. We do not know that his Parliamentary life added greatly to his fame, but at least it showed that a thinker and a scholar is not disqualified by his studies for taking a very weighty part in the practical affairs of life. Whatever, indeed, were Mr. Mill's philosophical and political errors, we believe it may be truly said of him that no recluse was ever before so honestly devoted as he to the cause of the people, and that no popular reformer was ever before so honestly devoted as he to the cause of abstract truth.

Johnsonese Poetry

One of the Universities having chosen Dr. Johnson's Satires as their English subject for the local examination, those brilliant recasts of Juvenal's Third and Tenth Satires, — in the form partly of free translations, more frequently of original verse moulded in the moulds of Juvenal's thought, on the vices of the London Johnson loved so well, and on "the vanity of human wishes," — have received more general attention during the last few months than probably during any year since their first appearance, in 1738 and 1749.[1] And certainly they deserve this attention. It is but seldom in the present day that one hears any hearty appreciation of Dr. Johnson's poetry. The modern school of poetry runs in a completely different groove, — so different, that theories of poetry are constructed, not perhaps intentionally, but still, by the very materials from which they are generalised, necessarily, to exclude the sonorous and often grandiose verse of the eighteenth century's omnivorous student and knock-down wit. And yet it seems clear to us that no theory of poetry can be good at all which does not keep room for Dr. Johnson's best efforts. We take it that there are but two absolute essentials of poetry, — first, the resonance of feeling which finds its natural expression in the cadences of verse and in the subtle sweetnesses of rhyme; and next, enough, at least, of special genius for the selection of words, to give the power either of charming by their felicity or of riveting us by their pent-up force. Of course, these two gifts may range over a very wide or be confined to a very narrow surface. In Dr. Johnson's case there was assuredly but a very limited region within which his mind seemed to need the help of rhythm and rhyme, in order to convey perfectly what was in it; nor was the empire which he wielded over words either a very varied or uniformly a very happy one. But within the limits of his special range, we doubt whether either Pope or Dryden ever entirely equalled, or whether any English writer ever surpassed his verse. He was, no doubt, often pompous, and always a little ponderous. His manner is sometimes stately beyond the level of his feeling, and reminds us of stage thunder. There is little flexibility and no variety of movement in his verse. As Goldsmith said, he makes his little fishes talk like whales;[2] and even his whales are sometimes clumsy in their wrath, as well as always clumsy in their sport. Still,

Johnson had bigger thoughts and feelings of a kind which invited to stately
verse, than most literary men of any age, and at least as great a faculty for
choosing words with a certain spell of power in them, as many who have
written a great deal more, — probably only because they have had more
leisure to gratify their taste. Take, for instance, the well-known lines on
Shakespeare, written for Garrick to repeat on the re-opening of Drury
Lane Theatre: —

> "Each change of many-coloured life he drew,
> Exhausted worlds and then imagined new;
> Existence saw him spurn her bounded reign,
> And panting Time toiled after him in vain."[3]

We doubt if any English poet ever expressed so powerfully or so
pithily the inexhaustible force of creative genius, or the flight of
imagination into regions where it was always possible that nature might
yet follow with slower step, as Johnson expressed it in those four grand
as well as grandiose lines. It is true, we think, that Johnson can hardly be
called a great satirist, in the sense in which we apply that term either to
Juvenal, after whom he moulded his satires, or to Thackeray, for example,
to whose lighter shafts of scorn the present age is better accustomed.
Johnson was not light enough for satire, — of which a certain negligence,
whether real or skilfully simulated, is the very essence. For such
negligence he was too much in earnest. Juvenal himself, indeed, is often
too earnest for the genius of satire, but where he is earnest, his earnestness
is the earnestness of disgust; while Johnson is apt to throw in a drop of
genuine compassion. Thus Juvenal describes old age with a sort of
loathing; here, for instance, is the least scornful part of his sickening
picture: —

> "Da spatium vitae, multos da, Jupiter, annos
> Hoc recto vultu, solum hoc et pallidus optas.
> Sed quam continuis et quantis longa senectus
> Plena malis! deformem et tetrum ante omnia vultum,
> Dissimilemque sui deformem pro cute pellem,
> Pendentesque genas, et tales aspice rugas,
> Quales, umbriferos ubi pandit Thabraca saltus,
> In vetula scalpit jam mater simia bucca."[4]

But Johnson is touched with pity: —

> " 'Enlarge my life with multitude of days!'
> In health, in sickness, thus the suppliant prays;
> Hides from himself his state, and shuns to know
> That life protracted is protracted woe.
> Time hovers o'er, impatient to destroy,
> And shuts up all the passages of joy.

In vain their gifts the bounteous seasons pour,
The fruit autumnal and the vernal flower;
With listless eyes the dotard views the store,
He views and wonders that they please no more;
Now pall the tasteless meats and joyless wines,
And luxury with sighs her slave resigns."[5]

That is not bad verse of its sort, but it must be admitted that it does not paint the vanity of the wish for long life with anything approaching to the deadly scorn of Juvenal; there is far too much pity in it. But admit that Johnson does not write true satire, and then observe that wherever a vein of moral indignation, of generous contempt, can be brought into his theme, Johnson rises at once above his model. There is hardly any passage in Juvenal's terrible satire to compare in poetical fire with that in which Johnson depicts the pains of the severe literary life, as he himself, with his own deep vein of constitutional melancholy, had known them, of its high instincts, its ascetic impulses, its weariness, its poverty, its insolent patrons, and its glory reaped too late: —

"Yet should thy soul indulge the gen'rous heat
Till captive Science yields her last retreat;
Should Reason guide thee with her brightest ray,
And pour on misty Doubt resistless day;
Should no false kindness lure to loose delight,
Nor praise relax, nor difficulty fright;
Should tempting Novelty thy cell refrain,
And Sloth effuse her opiate fumes in vain;
Should Beauty blunt on fops her fatal dart,
Nor claim the triumph of a letter'd heart;
Should no disease thy torpid veins invade,
Nor Melancholy's phantoms haunt thy shade;
Yet hope not life from grief or danger free,
Nor think the doom of man revers'd for thee:
Deign on the passing world to turn thine eyes,
And pause awhile from letters to be wise;
There mark what ills the scholar's life assail,
Toil, envy, want, the patron, and the jail.
See nations, slowly wise, and meanly just,
To buried merit raise the tardy bust.
If dreams yet flatter, once again attend,
Hear Lydiat's life, and Galileo's end."[6]

This brief inclusion of "the patron" in the list of the almost unendurable evils of the literary struggle, — "Toil, envy, want, the patron, and the jail," — is a touch of scorn which only true genius could have conceived. And at least an equal power of concentrating a whole world of lofty feeling in a touch is illustrated in by far the best-quoted of all

Johnson's lines, the close of his picture of the career of Charles XII, — the lines in which he observes, with a half-smile, on the paradox that the best purpose left to which to turn so terrible a name should be the purpose of the moralist or the romance-writer: —

> "The vanquish'd hero leaves his broken bands,
> And shows his miseries in distant lands;
> Condemn'd a needy supplicant to wait,
> While ladies interpose, and slaves debate.
> But did not Chance at length her error mend?
> Did no subverted empire mark his end?
> Did rival monarchs give the fatal wound?
> Or hostile millions press him to the ground?
> His fall was destin'd to a barren strand,
> A petty fortress, and a dubious hand;
> He left the name, at which the world grew pale,
> To point a moral, or adorn a tale."[7]

But after all, Johnson's poetry was at its best when employed in giving expression to the vigorous piety of his ardent, though somewhat elephantine mind. No one ever realised more deeply than he, that life is disappointment; no one ever realised more deeply, that disappointment itself may be life, and a noble life, too. The verses in which he turns Juvenal's rather dry and languid admonitions to pray for a healthy mind in a healthy body, into a passionate protest against the 'agnostic' theory that because we never really know what will be for our benefit, we should not pray at all, are full of the concentrated lightning as well as the thunder of his noblest work. No doubt one is always a little sensible, in reading Johnson's poetry, that it appears to assume for human nature more mass and dignity in general than is quite consistent with our knowledge either of ourselves or of our fellow-creatures; and sometimes we are just a little ashamed of having so sonorous a voice given even to our deepest and most passionate feelings. There is in his noblest verse a sound which seems to be borrowed from the trumpet through which the Athenian actors conveyed their voice to the utmost limits of their great open-air theatre. But then, if ours were a world of human beings cast on the scale of Johnson, we do not know that this rolling thunder would even seem too grandiose. At all events, what can have more of the intense compression which marks a vivid inward fire than the fine close to his "Vanity of Human Wishes?" —

> "Where then shall Hope and Fear their objects find?
> Must dull suspense corrupt the stagnant mind?
> Must helpless man in ignorance sedate,
> Roll darkling down the torrent of his fate?
> Must no dislike alarm, no wishes rise,

No cries invoke the mercies of the skies?
Inquirer, cease; petitions yet remain
Which Heav'n may hear, nor deem religion vain.
Still raise for good the supplicating voice,
But leave to Heav'n the measure and the choice:
Safe in his power, whose eyes discern afar
The secret ambush of a specious pray'r!
Implore his aid, in his decisions rest,
Secure, whate'er he gives, he gives the best.
Yet, when the sense of sacred presence fires,
And strong devotion to the skies aspires,
Pour forth thy fervours for a healthful mind,
Obedient passions, and a will resign'd;
For love, which scarce collective man can fill;
For patience, sov'reign o'er transmuted ill;
For faith, that, panting for a happier seat,
Counts death kind Nature's signal of retreat:
These goods for man the laws of Heav'n ordain,
These goods he grants, who grants the pow'r to gain;
With these celestial Wisdom calms the mind,
And makes the happiness she does not find."[8]

It would be hardly possible to find a truer and yet a more caustic expression for the true agnostic theory of life than that contained in the couplet, —

"Must helpless man, in ignorance sedate,
Roll darkling down the torrent of his fate?"

'Sedate' ignorance is the very attitude of mind in which clearly "the Unknown and Unknowable"[9] ought to be approached, and yet it expresses, as it would be otherwise difficult to express, the revolt of human nature against the creed it implies. Again, what can express more grandly the helplessness and the dreariness of the "stream of tendency"[10] of which, on that theory, we are the sport, than the line in which those "darkling" rapids are described?

On the whole, though there is no flexibility in Johnson's poetry, and no variety, though the monotony which often wearies us in Pope and Dryden would have wearied us still more in Johnson if Johnson had been anything like as voluminous a poet as Pope or Dryden, yet no poetry of that order, neither Pope's nor Dryden's, seems to us to contain so much that is really majestic in it, so much that portrays for us a great mind and a glowing heart, groping its way painfully through the darkness of the world, by the help of a vivid but distant gleam of supernatural light, and intent on 'making' — by that aid — 'the happiness it could not find.' Johnson was too intent on great ends for a satirist; his mind was too stiff for the poetry of ordinary sentiment or ordinary reflection; but for the rare occasions on which you want in poetry what we may call the concentrated pressure of many atmospheres,[11] — whether for the purpose of expressing the vastness of Shakespeare's genius, or the sorely hampered life of human short-sightedness and want, or the secret store of power to be found in human self-abnegation, — we know of no English poet like Dr. Johnson.

The Hero of "Daniel Deronda"

We quite agree as yet with Sir Hugo Mallinger, when, looking "at men and society from a liberal-menagerie point of view," he piques himself on the difficulty of classifying his adopted (or possibly his own) son, Daniel Deronda, and describes the young man, to himself at least, in words like these: — "You see this fine young fellow, — not such as you see every day, is he? — he belongs to me in a sort of way; I brought him up from a child, but you would not ticket him off easily; he has notions of his own, and he's far as the poles asunder from what I was at his age."[1] It *would* be very difficult to ticket off Daniel Deronda; and it would do a certain amount of credit to the classifying power of the men of science attached to the "Liberal menagerie" if they could give any clear account of him. And yet it is not for want of study on the part of the great writer who has chosen him for her hero. He is much the most-described young gentleman with whom we have ever had to deal in her stories. We suspect he is still a bit of a problem to the author herself. She can't study him enough, and almost always leaves us with the feeling that there was something behind which she wanted to say of him, and had not been able quite to find the right word for. No doubt the chief feature of his character is intended to be a warm sympathy and receptiveness, much enhanced by reflecting on his own ambiguous position in the world, and by a sense of wrong diverted by an intense natural generosity into an eager desire to enter into the sufferings of others, instead of to resent or revenge his own. Already this high chivalry of nature has found four objects on which to lavish sympathy, — the poor artist fellow-student whose studies Deronda helped at the cost of his own chance of a scholarship; the despairing Jewess, whom he saved from drowning herself in the Thames; the spoiled girl whom he first saw gambling at Leubronn, and afterwards finds betrothed, and later, married to the cold and cruel Grandcourt; and finally, the consumptive Jewish poet, or thinker, or both, who, in his *tête-exaltée* dreams, fastens on Deronda as the man who may inherit his ideas, and thus rescue his thoughts from the grave, in which they might otherwise be buried with him. To struggling art, to hopeless misery, to sin touched with any gleam of remorse or regret, and to the enthusiasm of pure intellectual passion, Deronda is painted as extending with equal readiness his ardent and tender sympathy, and yet as feeling a certain irritation when people look upon him as so purely disinterested that they cannot even impute to him selfish hopes of his own, in connection with any of his chivalric enterprises. Thus Hans Meyrick's mode of regarding Deronda as if he were quite out of the field when speaking of his own love for the pretty Jewess, Mirah Cohen, rouses a deep feeling of annoyance in the chivalric young hero, whose character had hitherto been painted as having almost too conscientious a tolerance for all courses of action which might seem likely to interfere with his own views. But barring this little touch, and, of course, the high morale which makes him turn in disgust from forms of evil in which there is no sign of relenting or remorse, the difficulty of catching the character is the difficulty of getting any distinct impression of wax, or any other substance which takes any mould impressed upon it. It is not easy as yet to see exactly, what he is, on any of the sides on which he is so lavish of his heartfelt sympathy. His views on art are tentative and very undefined; his attitude towards the beautiful little Jewess he has saved from drowning is uncertain, and even in carrying out her own wish to discover her mother and brother, he is reluctant and hesitating; his moral help to Gwendolen, in her errors and sins, cordially as it is given, is of the very vaguest character; and whether or not he has any convictions of his own which will prevent him from taking the impress of Mordecai's musings, and attempting to expound and publish them to the world, is as yet as great a question for the reader as it ever could have been for the man himself. George Eliot has rarely spent more pains on any character, but except its disinterestedness, its large receptiveness, and its moral elevation, we find, as yet, little or no individuality in it. We have not been told what Mordecai's ideas are, and of course, therefore, we could not, even in any case, – even if Deronda had been ever so clearly defined, – know whether or not they would have any fascination for him. But we have so little notion of Deronda's own intellectual nature that, as far as we know, he might be accessible to any Neo-Jewish or other theosophic ideas, which had on them a clear impress of moral grandeur, no matter what they were.

And it is the same with his ethical notions. When Gwendolen, smarting under the sense that she had done a great wrong to Grandcourt's mistress, Mrs. Glasher, in marrying Grandcourt with the full knowledge of the poor woman's claims and the claims of her children upon him, appeals to Deronda for help in atoning for the wrong in any way she may, his counsel is of the vaguest. In a former conversation, he had told her that "affection is the broadest basis of good in life," and that the objects of all deep affections are generally not exactly real persons, but "a mixture, half-persons and half-ideas," – by which, we suppose, he meant that idealised persons, – persons regarded in the light of the highest characteristics they are capable of *suggesting*, — are the true objects of the highest affection.[2] When afterwards the question is put more directly what one who has never been "fond of people," — as poor Gwendolen confesses that she never has been, except of her mother, — can do to atone in any way for a great wrong, Deronda's only advice is to enlarge her knowledge, and with her knowledge, her sympathy with the world. "It is the curse of your life, — forgive me, — of so many lives, that all passion is spent in a narrow round, for want of ideas and sympathies to make a larger home for it." Gwendolen objects that she is "frightened at everything," "at herself," and Deronda replies, "Turn your fear into a safeguard. Keep your dread fixed on the idea of increasing that remorse, which is so bitter to you. Fixed meditation may do a great deal towards defining our longing or dread. We are not always in a state of strong emotion, and when we are calm, we can use our memories, and gradually change the bias of our fear, as we do our tastes. Take your fear as a safeguard. It is like quickness of hearing. It may make consequences passionately present to you. Try to take hold of your sensibility, and use it as if it were a faculty, like vision."[3] Both bits of advice, — both that as to extending the range of knowledge, and so of her sympathies, and that as to making her fear of herself and her own rash acts a new power to appreciate the possible consequences of action, — are certainly good, so far as they go, but they do strike one as of the nature of the present of a stone to one who asks for bread. It was not want of knowledge which led Gwendolen wrong; and even if a fuller sensibility to the consequences would have kept her right, her want of sensibility was not due to any deficiency of selfish fears; indeed, the only tangible good that advice so vague and abstract could do her was, we suspect, the confidence its earnestness gave her in Deronda's sympathy, and the tendency it might have, therefore, to put before her mind an image of a nature, — half-personal, half-ideal, as Deronda himself had put it, — of a nobler kind than any to which she had accustomed herself. So far as specific moral direction was wanted by her, we fear there was none.

No doubt the noble vagueness and wax-like tentativeness of Deronda's character, — the vagueness and tentativeness which make him shrink from even choosing as yet any profession for himself, — is meant to be specially contrasted with Grandcourt's sterile, inert, and stony selfishness of imagination, and to suggest to the reader that there is something absolutely good in the plastic moral temperament, and absolutely evil in the impenetrability which shuts out with a sort of rigid snap all purposes but its own. In the fourth book, George Eliot has given us one of her subtlest sketches of Grandcourt, in his inert musings:

"He spent the evening in the solitude of the smaller drawing-room, where, with various new publications on the table, of the kind a gentleman may like to have at hand without touching, he employed himself (as a philosopher might have done) in sitting meditatively on a sofa and abstaining from literature – political, comic, cynical, or romantic. In this way hours may pass surprisingly soon, without the arduous, invisible chase of philosophy; not from love of thought, but from hatred of effort – from a state of the inward world, something like premature age, where the need for action lapses into a mere image of what has been, is, and may or might be; where impulse is born and dies in a phantasmal world, pausing in rejection even of a shadowy fulfilment. That is a condition which often comes with whitening hair; and sometimes, too, an intense obstinacy and tenacity of rule, like the main trunk of an exorbitant egoism, conspicuous in proportion as the varied susceptibilities of younger years are stripped away."[4]

All that Grandcourt does, whether in relation to Lush, or to Mrs. Glasher, or to Gwendolen, is illustrative of this tenacious purpose and of this sterility of imagination which accompanies it. His slow and low sentences give all who have to deal with him the sense of "as absolute a resistance as if their fingers had been pushing at a fast-shut iron door,"[5] – and it is this dull fixity of purpose, as much almost as his utter selfishness, which is brought into contrast with Deronda's wide, and plastic, and ready sympathies. Grandcourt cannot even sympathise with poor Sir Hugo Mallinger's efforts to make the best of his not very fine stud of horses, and remarks that he does not call it riding, "to sit astride a set of brutes with every deformity under the sun;"[6] – which, indeed, we suspect Mr. Grandcourt was too much of the conventional gentleman to *say*, under the circumstances, in Sir Hugo's presence, though he might have said it in his absence. Still, no doubt, the author attributes this insolent remark to him to make clearer his absolute incapacity to sympathise with any human being in the world; and she illustrates the same incapacity in the masterly sketch of the scene with Mrs. Glasher, as well as in the fine scene where he forces Gwendolen to wear the diamonds. Deronda, who is receptive towards every genuine feeling, and especially to every form of keen suffering, is painted as the very antithesis to Grandcourt, who is receptive only towards impressions which anyhow affect himself, and in regard to these is quick enough in his perceptions. Of course, the latter is ignoble, cruel, iron-hearted, generous in nothing but in money-giving where the conventional feelings of a gentleman are supposed to require it; while the former is noble, generous, self-sacrificing. But the contrast is meant certainly to be not simply moral, but intellectual, and we cannot help fancying that the drift and suggestion of the story are, — that plasticity and receptiveness of nature are the root of the higher temper, while sterility, rigidity, and impenetrability of nature are the root of the lower temper. However that may be, it is certain that Grandcourt, though his insolence impresses us as exaggerated, — and affects us more as the insolence of a bad woman, than as the insolence of a bad man, — is much the more definite picture of the two; and that Daniel Deronda runs the risk of appearing to the end as little more than a wreath of moral mist, — a mere tentative, or rather group of tentatives, in character-conceiving, which the author may find it exceedingly difficult to crystallise into a distinct form. Is not this to some extent the result indeed of George Eliot's philosophy, which has parted with all the old lines of principle, except the keen sympathy with every noble sentiment which she always betrays, and imported nothing new and definite in their places, except the vaguest hopes and aspirations? We do not think that the higher class of characters, though they may well *begin* like Daniel Deronda's, can ever ripen into any high type, without far more power of rejecting the multiplied solicitings of all sorts of sympathies, and far more also of definite conviction, than anything we have as yet seen in the picture of her new hero. Possibly, however, Mordecai's teaching is intended to crystallise the young man's mind into clear and vigorous purpose; and we shall be eager to withdraw anything depreciatory in the present criticism, if that result should be achieved.

The Cultus of Impressionability

Mr. Pater, — the well-known writer on Art, — has written in the new number of *Macmillan* an imaginary portrait of a child, "Florian Deleal," which is intended as a contribution to the study of "that process of brain-building by which we are, each one of us, what we are." He makes Florian Deleal meet accidentally an inhabitant of the place in which he had passed his childhood, and on the following night Florian dreams of his early home so vividly that it comes back to him with "a finer sort of memory," "raised a little above itself and above ordinary retrospect." In that half-spiritualised house, it is said "he could watch the better, over again, the gradual expansion of the soul which had come to be there, — of which, indeed, through the law which makes the material objects about them so large an element in children's lives, it had actually become a part; inward and outward being woven through and through each other into one inextricable texture, — half, tint and trace and accident of homely colour and form, from the wood and the bricks of it, — half, mere soul-stuff floated hither from who knows how far? In the house and garden of his dream he saw a child moving, and could divide the main streams, at least, of the winds that had played on him, and study so the first stage in that mental journey."[1] And the paper, which, as is usual with Mr. Pater's papers, is very well written, — though diversified with just such quavering, emotional emphases as are indicated, for instance, by saying "the wood and the bricks of it," like Carlyle, instead of "its wood and bricks," like other human beings, an idiom no doubt used to notify the reader that he is reading something to the form of which he is bound to pay attention, as well as to its substance, — gives a very subtle and delicate picture of the various objects and events which took effect on the nature of a very impressionable child, and tended, according to the author's view, to make him sympathetic and imaginative in times to come.

But the paper, whether meant to have any other drift or not than to give us a psychological study of the story of a sensitive child, certainly will have to most who read it another drift, namely, to glorify afresh the impressionable nature which feels so deeply and vividly all the external forms and colours and sympathetic savours of the "environment," as the new psychology delights to call it, in which it is placed.[2] Florian Deleal's childhood would hardly be thus carefully painted at all, if there were not in the author a considerable admiration for such temperaments as Florian Deleal's, and a wish to make them seem even more admirable to the world at large than they seem now. The tacit assumption of the paper is that it is a very fine thing to be able to recall poignantly the cry of an aged aunt come to announce a father's death, – to realise so vividly, as Florian Deleal realised, "that little white room with the window, across which the heavy blossoms could beat so peevishly in the wind, with just that particular catch or throb, such a sense of teasing in it, on gusty mornings;" – and to rehearse so well how on one evening of his life, a gate usually closed stood open, "and lo! within, a great red hawthorn in full flower, embossing heavily the bleached and twisted trunk and branches, so aged that there were but few green leaves thereto, – a plumage of tender crimson fire out of the heart of the dry wood."[3] Nor do we wish to deny that so far as it is good to multiply such experiences at all, it is good to know precisely what they were in all faithfulness and accuracy. But the drift of Mr. Pater's paper goes far beyond this. For instance, we are told of Florian Deleal that, in consequence of this delicate susceptibility to material impressions, "he became more and more to be unable to care for or think of soul but as in an actual body, or of any world but that wherein are water and trees, and where men and women look so or so, and press actual hands. It was the trick even his pity learned, fostering those who suffered in anywise to his affections by a kind of sensible attachment. He would think of Julian fallen into incurable sickness, as spoiled in the sweet blossom of his skin like pale amber, and his honey-like hair; of Cecil early dead as cut off from the lilies, from golden summer days, from women's voices; and then what comforted him a little was the thought of the turning of the child's flesh to violets in the turf above him."[4] We suspect that what comforted him much more, was the thought that he had such a sweet and tender imagination as to take comfort in the notion of "the turning of the child's flesh to violets in the turf above him;" but be this as it may, it is clear that the tendency of Mr. Pater's study, for all who read it with sympathy, will be to make them ask themselves if they had ever thought, when lamenting the sickness of a child, of thinking of him "as spoiled in the sweet blossom of his skin like pale amber, and his honey-like hair," or of deploring especially that another, cut off in early youth, was cut off "from the lilies, from golden summer days, from women's voices;" and if they have not felt that, or anything very like that, they will reproach themselves as deficient in the sweet susceptibilities of Florian Deleal. The tendency, then, of Mr. Pater's study is clearly to make each of us cherish, and foster, and congratulate ourselves upon, our sweet physical susceptibilities, to go to bed with a better aesthetic conscience when we have luxuriated in the soft perfume of a clematis under the stars, or to feel that we have discharged our duty better to a dead friend, if we have had strongly impressed on us the velvet touch of her hand, or the soft brilliance of her hair, and if we mix our sorrow with a special yearning after something sweet and physical which is associated with her presence. That Mr. Pater's study carries this drift with it, whether intended to carry it or not, there can be no doubt.

And though, as we said, we have no objection at all to the assumption that it is far better to have true and keen impressions of the things around us, than to have faint and blunt impressions, — supposing, that is, that it is a question merely between the two, and not rather between having the former without any active principle that makes use of them, or the latter *with* some active principle, which helps us both to direct our life better and to imagine it more truly than the mind of fluctuating, sensuous susceptibility generally can direct and imagine it, — still, as a rule, it is not a question merely between the two. As a rule, the sensuous susceptibilities are a sea of restless waves which, in a mind more than usually subject to them, foster a certain pride of receptivity, while confusing or breaking the stronger purposes to which nine men out of ten owe their usefulness. The devotees of the new cultus of Impressionability seem to forget that there is no more real merit in having a profound feeling of the glory of sunset or the exquisiteness of dawn, than there is in the facility with which a bed of wax takes off an impression of the form that is left upon it. No doubt, the mind adds something in the one case, which, — as far, at least, as we know, — the wax does not add in the other. The mind feels the beauty, as well as retaining a trace of it. The wax only retains the trace of what impresses it. But is there more merit in the one than in the other, apart from the use made of the impression? If the mind is not merely impressed, but uses the impression so made to make clear to other minds, as a poet often makes clear, something which brings them into closer communion with the mind of the Creator; or if it ultimately uses the impression to diminish greatly the total sum of human misery; or still better, to increase greatly the total sum of human virtue; or if it uses the impression to widen greatly the total sum of human knowledge, — then indeed, in any or all of these cases, the fidelity, the depth of the impression is worth something, and deserves to be recorded as part of the education of the poet or philanthropist, the prophet or the lover of wisdom. But if the impression is the beginning and end of the matter, — if the flux of impressions, as so often happens, makes up the man, — if a man goes about glorying in his susceptibility, hugging himself because he has had that delicious sense of languor as he gazed on the daffodil sky, — feeling himself but a little lower than the angels because he was sensible of the glory of the Alpine storm, while so many others never even interrupted their *table d'hôte* to glance at it, — recording every shade of namby-pamby tenderness in which his unreal passion for some rural beauty died away, — preening his susceptibilities as a bird preens his plumage, — enshrining himself in his aesthetic exclusiveness of feeling as a god in the golden cloud of Olympus, — then we assert that he is going the straight road to cast himself, — we will not say to the dogs, — but to the Zephyrs, which are a great deal more prone than the dogs to make spoil of that in life which is most worth living for, the strongest and the manliest part of human nature. For all this sensuous experience is only useful to one who has been given either a high poetic imagination, or some high and ardent practical purpose which is not in danger of being despoiled by the luxury of sensuousness of any of its nerve. For ordinary creatures, it is a vast deal better not to be so constantly tossed on the waves of sensuous susceptibility, as to be robbed of those high ambitions, or even of those relatively low ambitions, which give a unity to life, and which, by increasing the jar and conflict of human purposes, lead to the ultimate victory of those purposes which are noblest and most capable of raising men to a higher level. It is better far for ordinary boys to be hungering after the world of independent action for which they are not as yet mature enough, than to be tossing about on the ripple of small susceptibilities and emotions, without either a great ambition or a high aspiration to guide them. The merit which appears to be claimed by the modern devotee of sensitive impressions for appreciating duly the flux of phenomena, is a curious contrast to the far higher aspiration of the old Stoics, to find in themselves a strength which would raise them above the influence of that flux; and still more to the infinitely higher aspiration of the Christian, who learnt to despise even his own susceptibilities, if only he might thereby come into communion with the unchangeable purposes of God.

Mr. Henry James's Tales

These tales will increase, rather than diminish, Mr. Henry James's reputation as a student of human nature, though they are all short, and all, after his usual habit, sketchy. They are all studies, taken from the point of view of what may be called a refined neutrality, of the unsatisfactory aspects of human destiny. What interests Mr. Henry James is, – we think we may say exclusively, – any absolute misunderstanding and misfit between character and circumstance. He delights in analysing the seeming perversities of the human lot, – the critical failures of the higher genius, – the miserliness of fortune just when even the most sparing gift would be enough to secure a great wealth of happiness, – the mysterious recoils of feeling which cause so many cups of joy to be dashed voluntarily from the very lips, – the tyrannies of the past over the present. Mr. Henry James's subjects very often remind us of Mr. Clough's *Amours de Voyage*, though that exquisite literary gem is a poem, and Mr. James's tales are all, in form at least, prose.[1] Mr. Clough was the first to introduce the practice of making the insufficiency of emotion for its own purposes a separate subject of critical study, and to accompany his picture by indications of all that wealth of inherited culture and delicate criticism which are needful to make you understand how the springs of the emotions had been weakened by the rarified intellectual atmosphere in which they grew. In *Amours de Voyage* you see perfectly mirrored the great store of influences – critical, poetic, artistic, ethical, historical – which make up the culture of our age, and the effect which these have on a mind of high calibre in implanting a deep distrust of its own feelings, and a tendency to acquiesce in every check which they receive from fortune. Mr. Henry James is always taking up the same theme, and indeed very often he takes it up in the same outward world, – the world of Italian art and English culture. In the first of these tales, he shows us how the genius of an American artist just great enough to enable him to execute something great where the pressure of a momentary emergency was at hand to help him, yet failed in adequate stimulus for the creative life, and left a wreck and a failure, where nature had given every element of success except self-confidence, and that initiative which self-confidence ensures. In the second – the weakest tale in these volumes, and the weakest we have seen from Mr. Henry James's pen—he paints a perverse caprice of nature's, in making the wounded pride caused by a beautiful woman's rejection of the hero, effect a cure in an apparently dying man, and then causing the woman to pine away and die for the want of the love which she had rejected and could not recover. This is much the feeblest and least natural of the tales, and seems to be rather a *tour-de-force* in presenting the pessimist view of human destiny, than a serious composition. In the third tale, we have a very subtle study of the contrast between a pure American girl's idealistic view of the old French *noblesse*, and her actual experience of a selfish and worthless French husband of long descent, whom she has married out of the depths of her girlish enthusiasm,—the contrast being pointed, of course, by the appearance of the right man on the scene when it is too late to have any effect on the development of the story, except by eliciting a deeper shade of depravity in the husband, and a finer shade of moral idealism in the wife. In the fourth tale, Mr. Henry James studies the passion of an ingenuous, utterly inexperienced, American youth for a clever Prussian adventuress, whose only interest in him is her perception that he keeps back something from her which stimulates her sense of intellectual curiosity, and induces her to lead him on with a false hope till she has solved her problem. In the fifth tale, he describes to us how a man of fifty finds out that he had been wrong in distrusting the woman he had loved thirty years before,—a fact which he discovers as a consequence of warning a young friend against the daughter of this woman, so finding that his warnings are needless, and the young man's confidence better founded than his own former diffidence. And in the last tale, Mr. Henry James gives us a study of a poet who loves two women at the same time, one in one mood, and one in another, and discovers that to marry, or be perfectly devoted to, either, is to lose the spring of his imaginative passion, by losing the contrast which is needful to its highest fire.

In all these stories there is the same bent for discovering and analysing, not the harmonies, but the discords, of the world. Mr. Henry James loves torsos. His favourite theme is not what used to be called poetic justice, but rather the poetic injustice of life. A woman who deserves to be most happy and is unhappy, on account chiefly of the purity of her own girlish enthusiasm,—an artist who has had everything given him but the initiative and audacity needful to succeed,—a faithful lover, who has ruined his highest hopes by a mistake of judgment,—or to go back to former tales of his, a girl too frank for the conventional modesty, and too modest for the reputation she unfortunately gains by her singular frankness,—a simple American, who falls in love with the mellow beauty of the older world, and who finds the prejudices and traditions of that older world all combining to rob him of the prize he has half-won,—such are the themes in which Mr. Henry James chiefly delights, and in the perverse turns of which he finds his keenest intellectual stimulus.

And yet you can hardly say that Mr. James is a pessimist, though there is pessimism in all his plots. He does not so much seem to indict the scheme of Providence, – to reproach the destinies with wilfully punishing the noble-minded, and wrecking the high aims of genius, – as to note these shortcomings with a refined kind of neutrality, even intimating that these apparent blots in life are, after all, very endurable, and due, perhaps not unfrequently, to some deep reserve or self-restraining strain of temperament in man, that may, after all, be better than happiness itself. Thus his last tale in the first volume of this book ends with the death of Madame de Mauves' bad husband; whereupon the young American, who had felt that she was his highest ideal of womanhood, hears of this, but does *not* return to Europe. He was at first strongly moved to do so, "but several years have passed, and he still lingers at home. The truth is, that in the midst of all the ardent tenderness of his memory of Madame de Mauves, he has become conscious of a singular feeling, – a feeling for which awe would hardly be too strong a term."[2] But evidently Mr. Henry James is not here quite sincere with us. There is no excuse for awe at all. Madame de Mauves had behaved just as any woman of true purity of mind and heart would have behaved, and not otherwise. What was restraining the young man was not awe of Madame de Mauves, but a secret doubt whether his own feeling for her was adequate to her ideal of what this kind of devotion ought to be, and a secret distrust of the depth and intensity of his own feeling. Indeed, though Mr. Henry James's heroes are generally, on the whole, good, he very often almost apologises for their goodness, or at least admits that he can find no better explanation and justification of it, than a lingering asceticism, inherited from the old Puritans, which had survived the moral logic of its origin. His tastes are much finer than his principles – so far, of course, as he develops them dramatically in these stories – ever appear to be. The self-abnegation, of which his favourite characters are generally capable, is due more to a fastidious taste, than to a deep conviction of right and wrong. And as their moral taste is more fastidious than their principles, so their love is apt to be more refined than earnest. They often find it fade away when it comes to the final test. In the last tale, the poet cannot bring himself to sacrifice his imaginative life to his affection for either of the young ladies between whom his heart is divided, just as, in "Madame de Mauves," Longmore finds himself disposed to linger in the United States after every obstacle to his avowal of love for the lady appears to have been removed. The moral background of Mr. Henry James's novels is a refined criticism of the emotions, which results in a conviction that they will not bear very much strain upon them, and which tends, of course, to produce the result which it thus anticipates. He sometimes describes even the higher morality as due to nothing better than a half-intelligible "asceticism" of feeling;[3] and certainly, if men are like the creatures of Mr. Henry James's fables, so it must often be, for this asceticism of feeling, or at least that reluctance to act upon the promptings of feeling which he attributes to this "asceticism," continues after the moral restraints which made such "asceticism" coincident with virtue are withdrawn. On the whole, Mr. Henry James's world is very like the world depicted in Mr. Clough's fine poem, a world in which all the principles and all the affections are so much diluted with a fine speculative doubt, that neither are the principles strong enough to rule the character, except when they survive in the form of fastidious tastes, nor are the affections strong enough to win their own happiness, unless, — which rarely happens, — the hand of destiny pulls along with the too faint promptings of the heart.

Carlyle as a Painter

Carlyle will live in literature as a painter, rather than as a thinker. Of all our literary artists, he is the greatest of the school, – of Rembrandt we were going to write, – but Rembrandt is too sharp and narrow in his contrasts of light and shade, to suggest the literary effects in which Carlyle most delights. It is not light and shadow merely, but chaos and order, that he loves to paint; nor even chaos and order only, but all the great paradoxes of human nature, fiery passions struggling with stiff conventions, panic with purpose, vague, smouldering discontent, with shrill, confident, punctual precisianism. Nay, he loves all sorts of vague cumulative effects, – will crowd on his canvas the stupidities and frenzies of the multitude, the thin rhetorical melodrama of the self-conscious orator, and the grim democratic audacity of the born leader. But the contrasts he most loves are the contrasts between passion and purpose, – on the one hand, the seething, fermenting yeast of a chaotic mass of human fears and hopes; on the other, the deliberate purpose, good or bad, of a potent mind, able to impress upon this chaos its own drift. This is what made the "French Revolution" Carlyle's masterpiece. The subject exactly suited him. He had there an almost indefinite scope for the painting of all sorts of human force and feebleness, in every stage of gathering and declining power. And he made of it such a series of dissolving views of vivid scenes as no man ever before painted in this world, and perhaps no man will ever paint again. Take, for instance, the terse sketch of Louis XV's death-bed, at the very opening of this great story: – "There are nods and sagacious glances; go-betweens, silk dowagers mysteriously gliding, with smiles for this constellation, sighs for that; there is tremor of hope or desperation in several hearts. There is the pale, grinning Shadow of Death, ceremoniously ushered along by another grinning Shadow of Etiquette; at intervals, the growl of Chapel-organs, like prayer by machinery; proclaiming, as in a kind of horrid, diabolic horse-laughter, *Vanity of Vanities, All is Vanity.*" "Yes, poor Louis, Death has found thee. No palace walls or life-guards, gorgeous tapestries or gilt buckram of stiffest ceremonial, could keep him out; but he is here, here at thy very life-breath, and will extinguish it. Thou, whose whole existence hitherto was a chimaera and scenic show,

227

at length becomest a reality; sumptuous Versailles bursts asunder like a Dream, into void immensity; Time is done, and all the scaffolding of Time falls crushed with hideous clangour round thy soul; the pale kingdoms yawn open; there must thou enter, naked, all unking'd, and await what is appointed thee."[1] That is the opening of the great drama, and prefigures, with the power of a great dramatist's prelude, the story that is coming. But as that story gathers meaning and force, Carlyle's power of painting grows. Open the book almost at random, and you see him painting the results of the great collapse, — the gradual break-up of all those simulated beliefs which, even when true, are more destructive to those who simulate them than unbeliefs themselves, because they end in more violent reaction: — "Looking into this National Hall and its scenes, behold Bishop Torné, a Constitutional prelate, not of severe morals, demanding that 'religious costumes and such caricatures' be abolished. Bishop Torné warms, catches fire, finishes by untying, and indignantly flinging on the table, as if for gage or bet, his own pontifical cross. Which cross, at any rate, is instantly covered by the cross of *Te-Deum* Fauchet, then by other crosses and insignia, till all are stripped; this clerical senator clutching off his skull-cap, that other his frill-collar, — lest Fanaticism return on us. Quick is the movement here! And then so confused, unsubstantial, you might call it almost *spectral*, pallid, dim, inane, like the Kingdom of Dis. Unruly Linguet, shrunk to a kind of spectre for us, pleads here some cause that he has; amid rumour and interruption which excel human patience; he 'tears his papers' and withdraws, the irascible, adust little man. Nay, honourable members will tear their papers being effervescent; Merlin of Thionville tears his papers, crying, 'So the people cannot be saved by *you!*' "[2] What a powerful picture is this of the deliquescence not only of beliefs, but even of the patience which rests on beliefs, patience which is rendered possible only by belief alike in God and in man! And so the story goes on to tell of Paris patrolled in the Terror, like "a naphtha-lighted city of the dead, with here and there a flight of perturbed ghosts," of Robespierre, "with eyes red-spotted, fruit of extreme bile," as perchance walking "like a sea-green ghost through the blooming July," and proclaiming to his "Jacobin House of Lords" "his woes, his uncommon virtues, his incorruptibilities," and his readiness to die at a moment's warning; whereupon the painter David cries, "Robespierre, I will drink the hemlock with thee," — "a thing not essential to *do*," remarks Carlyle, "but which in the fire of the moment can be said;" and then of the last moment, when Robespierre appeals to the "President of Assassins" in vain, when "his frothing lips are grown 'blue,' his tongue dry, cleaving to the roof of his mouth," and the mutineers cry, "The blood of Danton chokes him."[3] Such a series of pictures of national fermentation, national anarchy, national blood-thirst, with here and there the temporary rise and setting of some stronger controlling mind, as Carlyle has crowded into these three small volumes, could not be found in all the remainder of our national literature.

Nor is the secret of the spell hard to find. No one knows as Carlyle does how to contrast the uncertain, and at most only guessable, store of forces at work in human nature, with the certain and historical result, so as to fill up the interstices of our knowledge with a clear indication of our vast ignorance. Observe how powerfully Carlyle always puts in the element of hesitation and vacillation which marks the growth of every popular movement: — "Reader, fancy not in thy languid way," he says, "that insurrection is easy. Insurrection is difficult; each individual uncertain even of his next neighbour; totally uncertain of his distant neighbours, what strength is with him, what strength is against him; certain only that in case of failure his individual portion is the gallows. Eight hundred thousand heads, and in each of them a separate estimate of these uncertainties, a separate theorem of action conformable to that; out of so many uncertainties does the certainty and inevitable net result never to be abolished, go on at all moments, bodying itself forth, leading thee also towards civic crowns, or an ignominious noose. Could the reader take an Asmodeus' flight, and waving open all roofs and privacies, look down from the tower of Notre Dame, what a Paris were it! Of treble-voice whimperings or vehemence, of bass-voice growlings, dubitations; Courage screwing itself to desperate defiance; Cowardice trembling silent within barred doors; and all round Dulness calmly snoring; for much Dulness, flung on its mattresses, always sleeps; Oh, between the clangour of these high-storming tocsins and that snore of Dulness, what a gamut, of trepidation, excitation, desperation; and above it mere Doubt, Danger, Atropos, and Nox."[4] That passage tells at once Carlyle's great strength as a painter of social emotion. He always indicates how much of the field is unseen; and by taking care to make us aware how much we cannot in any way fill in, as well as how much we can, he enormously heightens the truthfulness and vividness of the effect. The whole of his "Clothes Philosophy," — of "Sartor Resartus," — is a variation on this theme, of the enormous effect produced by our voluntary disguises, our voluntary ignorance, on the imagination and practical actions of men: — "When I read," he says, "of pompous ceremonials, Frankfort coronations, royal drawing-rooms, levées, couchées, and how the ushers and macers and poursuivants are all in waiting...on a sudden, as by some enchanter's wand, the clothes fly off the whole dramatic corps, and dukes, grandees, bishops, generals, Anointed presence itself, every mother's son of them, stand shuddering there, not a shirt on them, and I know not whether to laugh or weep."[5] There is not one great picture in Carlyle where you cannot trace the influence of this idea that men's imaginations are as much and as practically influenced by the deficiencies of those imaginations, as by the positive force they exert when moving in the narrow grooves in which imagination tells most powerfully; that their inability to strip off the various husks and veils with which men signalise and indefinitely magnify the differences which they discover between man and man, like all their other uncertainties and ignorances, is one of the great factors in human action, tending sometimes to multiply indefinitely the effect of any skilful initiative, and sometimes to deaden or paralyse the force of even a very sagacious initiative which does not happen to have taken enough account of the unfathomable inertia and indolences of the race. Most painters of men forget the curious influence of the dark rays of the spectrum on life. Carlyle never does. Half the effect of his most glowing pictures is due to the influence he allows for half-known or latent causes, of the existence of which we are all aware, but which, simply because they are half-known or latent, are so seldom taken into account by graphic writers. Carlyle knew better. He knew that in the picturing of human things, graphic power is gained, not lost, by suggesting how much is dark, how much is vague, how much is known only in general outline or in net result, how confused are the elements out of which such lurid effects proceed, — how far above our measuring is the cloud from which the lightning flashes, — how unfathomable is the sea which bounds our active life. It is the touch of mystery in life of which this great painter makes the most effective use; and by mystery, we mean not only the infinite power behind life, but also the inscrutable elements within it, — the inscrutable apathies, no less than the inscrutable passions of our race; the inscrutable obstinacies, no less than the inscrutable pliancies of the people; the inscrutable long-suffering, no less than the inscrutably sudden impatience of blind guides. Carlyle's effects are all vivid, but none of his effects are presented more effectively than his cold, grey, formless mists behind his rising or setting sun.

The Weak Side of Wordsworth

"If we want to secure for Wordsworth his true rank as a poet," says Mr. Arnold, with his usual critical discrimination, "we must be on our guard against the Wordsworthians."[1] But ought we, or ought we not, to be on our guard against so cultivated and shrewd a critic and woman of the world as Mrs. Oliphant, who, in her literary history of England, from the end of the last century to the close of the first quarter of the present century, gives us a very interesting chapter on the authors of the "Lyrical Ballads?"[2] Is she, too, in this sense a Wordsworthian, or the reverse? Is she, too, in league with Wordsworthians to lay stress upon the points on which Wordsworth is weakest, and to ignore many of those on which he is strongest? Certainly, Mrs. Oliphant believes herself to be amongst the discriminating few who can magnanimously consent "to lose both 'Excursion' and 'Prelude,' rather than consent to part with the 'Leech-gatherer,' and that great Ode which also belongs to these peaceful, prefatory years," who can speak with something like dread of "the waste of sonnets," of which she would desire to save only about "a dozen" from absolute oblivion. She speaks loftily of "Peter Bell" as mere "dullness and failure," though she admits it to be fitted with a powerful and striking preliminary sketch of the wandering vagrant himself. She lays it down that "Laodamia perhaps shows none of the characteristic qualities of Wordsworth." She gently depreciates the "Prelude," his poem on the growth of his own mind, and hushes up the "Excursion" with a compassionate judgment of "long, monotonous, and unequal," describing it as a composition which, "though it contains many passages of the noblest poetry," contains only "here and there a note to which the heart could respond."[3] Taking this entirely un-Wordsworthian view of Wordsworth, as Mrs. Oliphant does, we were certainly prepared to find her more fully alive to Wordsworth's true weakness than, as a matter of fact, she seems to us to be. She is, indeed, not at all disposed to cast in her lot with those "bold, bad men," to use Mr. Arnold's happy phrase, who quote the dullest Wordsworth at Social-Science Associations, and use him to make enlightenment soporific, and even a poet's "moral being" leaden.[4] Mrs. Oliphant is painfully conscious of Wordsworth's want of humour, of his rather "solemn egotism," and of his undeniable disposition to preach;

231

and, so far, she may be trusted not to guide the unwary student to the flat passages in Wordsworth, of which discriminating critics well know that there are but too many. But while it is plain enough that Mrs. Oliphant looks at Wordsworth with the shrewd, bright eye of a very keen literary taste, and that anything which she does speak well of is sure to be fairly good of its kind, we are unable to trust her judgment in the criticism of Wordsworth's weak side. Mrs. Oliphant, in her criticism of Wordsworth, is at bottom the woman of society. She is not only a little ashamed of Wordsworth's want of humour, of his almost pedantic simplicity, of the great weight of his moralities, of his earnest disposition to improve the occasion, — in all which she is quite right, — but she is disposed to direct attention as much as possible away from anything that can give rise to ridicule. She even seems to "give place by subjection" to the critics of Lord Jeffrey's type, who, though they detected truly where some of Wordsworth's weaknesses lay, were so absorbed in wonder at the baldnesses which they exposed, as to miss altogether the distinguishing traits of power in the poems of which they had laid bare the weakness.[5] In fact, Mrs. Oliphant seems to us not only quite guiltless of being a Wordsworthian in Mr. Arnold's sense, but hardly enough of a Wordsworthian in any true sense, to appreciate perfectly either the great strength of Wordsworth, or his chief weakness. For instance, when she speaks of the "Anecdote for Fathers" as one of the poems in the "Lyrical Ballads" which indicated Wordsworth's true power,[6] she seems to us to go sadly astray, selecting rather one of those poems which, under some lighter and more playful form, Cowper might have given us, and given us better than Wordsworth, than one which struck in any sense the key-note of Wordsworth's genius. This poem, headed, in its later editions, with the quotation, "Retine vim istam, falsa enim dicam, si coges," in other words, "Don't press heavily on me, for I shall only give you false replies, if you do," is as follows: —

"ANECDOTE FOR FATHERS.

I have a boy of five years old;
His face is fair and fresh to see;
His limbs are cast in beauty's mould,
And dearly he loves me.

One morn we strolled on our dry walk,
Our quiet home all full in view,
And held such intermitted talk
As we are wont to do.

My thoughts on former pleasures ran;
I thought of Kilve's delightful shore,

Our pleasant home when Spring began,
A long, long year before.

A day it was when I could bear
Some fond regrets to entertain;
With so much happiness to spare,
I could not feel a pain.

The green earth echoed to the feet
Of lambs that bounded through the glade,
From shade to sunshine, and as fleet
From sunshine back to shade.

Birds warbled round me — every trace
Of inward sadness had its charm;
'Kilve,' said I, 'was a favoured place,
And so is Liswyn farm.'

My Boy was by my side, so slim
And graceful in his rustic dress!
And, as we talked, I questioned him,
In very idleness.

'Now tell me, had you rather be,'
I said, and took him by the arm,
'On Kilve's smooth shore, by the green sea,
Or here at Liswyn farm?'

In careless mood he looked at me,
While still I held him by the arm,
And said, 'At Kilve I'd rather be
Than here at Liswyn farm.'

'Now, little Edward, say why so;
My little Edward, tell me why.' —
'I cannot tell, I do not know.' —
'Why, this is strange,' said I;

'For, here are woods, and green hills warm:
There surely must some reason be
Why you would change sweet Liswyn farm
For Kilve by the green sea.'

At this, my Boy hung down his head,
He blushed with shame, nor made reply;
And five times to the child I said,
'Why, Edward, tell me why?'

His head he raised — there was in sight,
It caught his eye, he saw it plain —
Upon the house-top, glittering bright,
A broad and gilded Vane.

> Then did the Boy his tongue unlock;
> And thus to me he made reply:
> 'At Kilve there was no weather-cock,
> And that's the reason why.'
>
> O dearest, dearest Boy! my heart
> For better lore would seldom yearn,
> Could I but teach the hundredth part
> Of what from thee I learn."

That is a pretty little poem enough of the anecdotic kind, which any one
would praise as graceful, if it were not for the too ecstatic delight of the
concluding verse, where the poet has, as it seems to us, extracted, as he
often did, *more* in imagination out of a trifle than there really was in it to
be extracted. It was not such a very wonderful lesson of wisdom for the
child to give, that if you extorted a reason for a preference which he could
not analyse, he would be sure to invent the first that came to hand; and
the "hundredth part" of what this respectable father learned from the
child who fastened eagerly on the weathercock as the objectionable
feature of Liswyn Farm, seems to us a truly infinitesimal dose of wisdom,
which no homoeopathist could underbid.[7] The poem is pretty in a style
in which Wordsworth is never very great, but the only essentially
Wordsworthian thing in it is the undue emphasis, the almost artificial
ecstacy of the last verse, — where you see the poet squeezing his almost
dry sponge with a dithyrambic rapture for which you can hardly account.
It reminds one of the poem on the Gipsies whom the poet accused of
having been utterly idle for twelve hours, and whom he addressed in
language of extravagant reproach, as follows: —

> "— Better wrong and strife,
> Better vain deeds, or evil, than such life!
> The silent heavens have goings-on,
> The stars have tasks, — but these have none."[8]

That, as Coleridge remarked, was making a great deal more of the twelve
hours of rest which the weary wayfarers had taken, than the occasion
justified.[9] As a rule, in all poems on incident Wordsworth squeezed his
moral a great deal too dry; and, as it seems to us, that is the only *specially*
Wordsworthian touch in the poem of the "Weathercock," a poem which
Cowper would have chiselled out with far more delicate touch than
Wordsworth. But Mrs. Oliphant chooses this otherwise happy trifle,
weighted with the unjustified ecstasy of the closing verse, for the highest
panegyric she bestows on any one of Wordsworth's slighter poems: — "No
one till then, not even Shakespeare himself, had so revealed that simplest,
yet most complex germ of humanity, separated from us by a distinction

more subtle than any which exists between rich and poor, yet entirely intelligible to us, — the mind of a child."[10] Well, we should say of that criticism just what we should say of the poem which calls it forth, — that it presses the subject harder than it will bear. Wordsworth got up a rapture over the child's happy fib, which the happy fib did not justify. Mrs. Oliphant gets up a rapture over the poet's delineation of the happy fib, which the delineation will not justify. She is so glad to direct attention to a graceful popular poem which almost any one might rather like, that she misses the fact that the most Wordsworthian feature in this poem is its heavy rapture, where no rapture is properly justified.

Mrs. Oliphant's want of true Wordsworthianism not only renders her disposed to be too kind to poems deficient in the real Wordsworthian genius, except, indeed, where they display special Wordsworthian defects, but makes her much too contemptuous of poems which have some of the true Wordsworthian genius, in case they are disfigured, as they often are, by the sort of fault to which the public common-sense is most sensitive. Mrs. Oliphant has scarcely words adequate to express her contempt for "The Idiot Boy," — her chief, and so far as it goes, very just objection, being to the artificial simplicity of the subject, and especially of the names "Betty Foy" and "Susan Gale."[11] We quite admit the validity of the criticism; the poem, as a whole, is undoubtedly ostentatiously simple. Betty Foy and Susan Gale are rather ludicrous *dramatis personae*. The whole style of treatment is unfortunate, is that, namely, in which a poet destitute of humour writes *down* to the level of his not very sound theory; but still, when Mrs. Oliphant speaks of the "wordy foolishness" of this poem, and declares it to have been a failure, and an utter failure, she seems to us to show that excessive shame for one of Wordsworth's weaknesses which blinds her to Wordsworth's strength. The poem is certainly far from an utter failure. It is greatly injured by this affectation of simplicity; but the assertion of an "absolute insignificance" in the incident on which the poem is founded, — that incident being really the evidence of that excess of maternal passion which idiocy so often excites in the genuine mother's heart, — is to our minds an utter blunder. The core of the poem is full of significance, and of significance of Wordsworth's highest kind. The deep, homely passion of a mother for her half-witted son is painted on a fine background of natural scenery, and though there are many trivial and feeble verses, in which Wordsworth talks elaborately *down* to his theory, there are also several from which any critic of insight would have discovered at once that here was a great poet, who understood at once the homely passions of human nature, and the grandeur of the theatre in which they play their part. Take the following, for instance: —

"She listens, but she cannot hear
The foot of horse, the voice of man;
The streams with softest sound are flowing,
The grass you almost hear it growing, —
You hear it now, if e'er you can.

The owlets through the long, blue night
Are shouting to each other still;
Fond lovers, yet not quite hobnob,
They lengthen out the tremulous sob
That echoes far from hill to hill.

. . . .

And Johnny burrs, and laughs aloud;
Whether in cunning or in joy,
I cannot tell; but while he laughs,
Betty a drunken pleasure quaffs
To hear again her idiot boy."

We do not defend the form of the poem, or assert that there is beauty or power in the majority of its stanzas; but in these three stanzas alone there is more of the essence of Wordsworth's genius, of the lonely rapture[12] of vision, and the strong human grasp of the ground-passions of our nature, than in twenty such poems as "The Anecdote for Fathers." "The Idiot Boy" has much more of Wordsworth's special weakness than the latter poem, but much more of his fundamental imaginative strength of conception, too. The last line but one of those which we have quoted is instinct with the genius of Wordsworth, in spite of the appearance in it of the needlessly objectionable name to which Mrs. Oliphant directs her ridicule.

Wordsworth's weak side, as a poet, was his great difficulty in perceiving when he had and when he had not succeeded in fusing the language which he used with the fire of his own meditative passion. Sometimes, in the midst of a passage of the truest rapture, he will descend suddenly upon a little bit of dry, hard fact, and not be at all aware that the fact remains like an irregular, unlovely stone pressing down a group of flowers, a monument of the sudden failure of the power of his emotion over his language. Thus, in the lovely lines, "She was a phantom of delight," the reader is suddenly oppressed by being told that the poet at last sees, "with eye serene the very pulse of the machine," — as if a phantom of delight could possibly have been a machine, or even, like a waxwork figure, contained one. There is the same fault in one of the finest of the original "Lyrical Ballads," — the one called "The Thorn," of which Mrs. Oliphant, by the way, who does not seem to have written with a copy of the "Lyrical Ballads" before her, makes no mention, but which Lord

Jeffrey epitomised, if we remember rightly, as describing how a woman in a red cloak went up to the top of a hill, and said, "Oh, misery!" and then came down again.[13] The greater part of the ballad, Lord Jeffrey "to the contrary in anywise notwithstanding,"[14] as the lawyers say, is penetrated through and through by the most genuine imaginative passion; but when, in the form in which the poem originally appeared, Wordsworth specified the dimensions of the little muddy pool by the infant's grave, —

> "I've measured it from side to side;
> 'Tis three feet long, and two feet wide,"[15]

he suddenly precipitated, as it were, into the midst of his poem a little deposit of ugly clay, which made his readers change the sob which the finer parts of the ballad excited, into an hysterical giggle. Wordsworth's weakness — especially in the earlier part of his career as a poet — was this, that he never knew how far his imagination had transmuted, or had failed to transmute, the rough clay of rude circumstance into the material of his plastic art. *He* was not awakened from his dream by such a descent as we have just quoted, and he did not know that his readers, who did not fully enter into his ecstacy, and probably did see, what Wordsworth could not see, the ludicrous contrasts and inequalities of his mood, would be awakened from their dream by these shocks. We find fault with Mrs. Oliphant, not for seeing how puerile and dull Wordsworth often is — that we frankly admit — but for giving up so much that was penetrated with his highest genius, only because it is injured by flaws of puerility and dullness, and yet at the same time greatly over-praising, as it seems to us, somewhat conventional poems, which, pretty and pleasing though they be, have more in them to remind us of other poets than they have to remind us of Wordsworth. She speaks of Coleridge as having produced much the greatest poem in the "Lyrical Ballads," and, as far as popularity goes, she is right.[16] The "Ancient Mariner" is a glorious dream, which will always fascinate those who care for an eerie conception magnificently expressed. But the "Ancient Mariner" has nothing in it to compare in force and passion with the "Lines written a few miles above Tintern Abbey," the "Mad Mother," "The Thorn," "Ruth," and "Michael," all of which appeared among the "Lyrical Ballads," and to none of which does Mrs. Oliphant make the slightest reference, when she is criticising them. Yet these are pieces which found out the source of rapture in many a heart, which sprang a well of living water never reached before, a feat which we venture to think that the splendid dream of the "Ancient Mariner," far more superficially captivating as it is, rarely, if ever, accomplished; and these pieces of Wordsworth's achieved this unique triumph simply because the fountains of Wordsworth's poetry sprang from so much deeper a source in his nature, than did the pictures of Coleridge's gorgeous dream.

Thin Pessimism

Mr. Henry James, Junior, in his very interesting paper on "The Correspondence between Carlyle and Emerson," published in the June number of the *Century*, remarks that Emerson was by nature an optimist, with a high and noble conception of good, but without any definite conception of evil; while Carlyle was a pessimist of pessimists, with a vivid conception of evil, but no corresponding perception of good. Further, he remarks that Emerson's genius, like the genius of the whole of the New-England literature of his day, had "a singular thinness, an almost touching lightness, sparseness, transparency, about it;" while Carlyle's was full of the dense, warm life of his London atmosphere. Emerson's mind was full of ghostly hopefulness, Carlyle's of passionate and wrathful despondency. "No one," says Mr. Henry James, "maintained a more hospitable attitude than Emerson towards anything that any one might have to say. There was no presumption against even the humblest, and the ear of the universe was open to any articulate voice. In this respect, the opposition to Carlyle was complete. The great Scotchman thought all talk a jabbering of apes, whereas Emerson, who was the perfection of a listener, stood always in a position of hopeful expectancy, and regarded each delivery of a personal view as a new fact to be estimated on its merits."[1] Mr. Henry James regards both the eminent correspondents as eccentric to the verge of madness, Emerson in a gentle fashion, with a mild and moonlight madness of his own; Carlyle with a moody madness as exemplified in the fierce and violent gesticulations with which he made his mock at the universe, and flouted "the Dead-sea apes" of whom he conceived the human race to consist.[2] Mr. Henry James himself evidently stands between the two men. He is struck by the whimsical spectacle of Emerson's transcendental hopefulness and optimism. It amuses him to think that so clear-minded and painstaking a man should have been so sanguine and so deferential to the fellow-creatures with whom he lived. On the other hand, Carlyle's convulsive agony under the spectacle of human folly and misdoing seems to him profoundly irrational. If all the world is out of joint what is the good of trying to set the innumerable dislocations of limb? "Pessimism, cynicism," says Mr. Henry James "usually imply a certain amount of indifference and resignation, but in

Carlyle these forces were nothing if not querulous and vocal." "Other persons have enjoyed life as little as Carlyle, other men have been pessimists and cynics; but few men have rioted so in their disenchantments, or thumped so perpetually on the hollowness of things, with the view of making it resound."[3] Mr. Henry James hardly knows which of the two makes him smile most, Emerson's mild and urbane infatuation of hope, or Carlyle's fury of despair. One can well understand his embarrassment. All his own works breathe, not Emerson's thin optimism, nor Carlyle's murky and chaotic pessimism, but, on the contrary, a thin pessimism of his own, as mild, quiet, and observant as Emerson's optimism, but as free from anything like satisfaction in what he observes as Carlyle's pessimism. He does not toss his arms about, and fret or fume, like the imprisoned Scotch Titan under his pile of mountains, — that would only be consistent, he thinks, with some substantial hope of making the world the better for these gigantic struggles, — but he combines the twilight calm of Emerson's impassibility with the "current contempt," as he calls it, of Carlyle's attitude towards the universe in which he lived.[4]

What Mr. Henry James would regard as the most defensible attitude towards the universe is a smiling acquiescence in the shallowness and poverty of things, from which nothing short of Emerson's moon-struck exaltation could expect infinite good; while to wrestle furiously and wildly with its evil seems to him, no doubt, to imply a great deal more bottom of belief than is consistent with the "Dead-sea ape" view of human life and action. The genuine optimist must be gifted with a singular reticence and self-distrust, if he does not fling himself into the most conspicuous movements of his day, if he does not adore the Zeit-geist[5] as a sort of divine oracle. The genuine pessimist must be overborne by a singular sense of fatality, if he takes any very great trouble to row against a stream which he believes to be irresistible. But what can be more suitable than for a pessimist who is a pessimist in truth, to be quiet and acquiescent, to smile, when it is possible, at the inevitable mishaps which overtake men, and to dry his tears as soon as may be when smiling is not possible; to offer no vain resistance to the confusion in which he sees human affairs more and more inextricably involved, but to avail himself of every little opportunity of saving what may be saved from the abyss, and to ignore, as far as possible, the cries of helplessness and terror proceeding from the various wrecks which sink into it. This, or something like this, we should gather from Mr. Henry James's various books, is the attitude which he would take, in preference to either the thin optimism of Emerson, or the yeasty fury of Carlyle; for he cannot really understand either the modest infatuation of hope with which Emerson watches for the oracles that he cannot himself hear, or the convulsive wrath with which Carlyle rages against the Destinies which he himself recognises as wholly uncontrolled and uncontrollable, when he declares God's creatures to be mostly fools or Dead-sea apes, for whom he finds no salvation in their theoretically divine origin. Mr. James blames Emerson for being deficient in the salt of "current contempt" for the manifest tendencies about him. He blames Carlyle for sighing after "so crude an occurrence" as the return of Oliver Cromwell's Ironsides to authority in any modern realm.[6] 'Despise the present, and hope nothing from the future, but, above all, don't hanker after the past,' appears to be the sort of attitude of mind which Mr. Henry James would inculcate in the reader alike of his novels and his criticisms. 'The world is getting into a hopeless tangle,' he seems to say, 'but at least you cannot use the old world shears to divide the threads. Probably the tangle cannot be disentangled at all, but whether it can or cannot, it is but a mad aspiration to yearn after anachronisms in the hope of severing the knot.' With the equanimity of Emerson, Mr. James would combine a good deal of the pessimism of Carlyle, and blend the two into a principle of calm acquiescence even in a destiny that merits little except to be seasoned with what he calls "the salt of current contempt."

We believe that the fierce pessimism of Carlyle, the thin optimism of Emerson, and the thin pessimism of Mr. Henry James, represent in a descending scale the creed inherited from the old Puritanism, as it comes out after the dropping of all faith in revelation. Carlyle's Puritanism was not quite emptied of all its faith. It is perfectly true that he was, as we may say, always virtually quarrelling with God, finding fault with him, just as Mr. Ruskin also does, for not having created a very different being from man; finding fault with him for making man so disposed as he is to fall into mechanical habits; to vegetate with but a small share of spiritual life; to drone out the thoughts of his ancestors instead of thinking fresh thoughts for himself; to interest himself so much in commerce, and to attach so much importance as modern man does to what he calls freedom. Against all these conditions, concerning which Carlyle knew as well as any one that they arise from the constitution of human nature, and not from any abuse of human nature, he raged as if he were raging against mere mendacity and wickedness, and, indeed, was never weary of calling all language that did not please him "jabber," and all laws and constitutional customs that did not please him mere formulas. But, with all this fury against the constitution of the universe, Carlyle had at heart a belief that honest and true men might find power in God to alter things for the better, and this was the one living ember of the old Puritanism which still burnt vividly in his mind. Emerson snatched eagerly at Carlyle's transcendentalism, which was in Carlyle rather the product of his wonderfully vivid imagination than due to any deep intellectual conviction, but at once separated it from Carlyle's belief that God forms true heroes, and does not care for the "dim, common populations,"[7] except so far as they can be stirred by true heroes into giving them a loyal and passionate support; and in Emerson's hands, this transcendentalism became, as he himself remarked, a mild optimism, that was disposed to accept almost anything as divine, and to treat almost all ills, physical, spiritual, or moral, with an almost ignoble patience, – the one exception being in Emerson's case the evil which seemed to Carlyle almost a positive good, slavery. For the rest, Carlyle's deep belief that in some true sense God does bring to naught all insincerities and consumes them with his wrath, hardly reappears in Emerson at all, who regards the great source of life as too sublime for any share in the passions of the prophet. Practically, Emerson's transcendental optimism, which shows little sympathy with Carlyle's view of God as a God of battles, was, we think, a very inferior form of Puritanism even to Carlyle's, – a form which held fast to the purity of Puritanism, but not to its internecine war with evil. No doubt, it took up the divine benevolence which Carlyle almost rejected, but it dropped altogether that potent belief in the spiritual interventions of God in human affairs, which gave to the old Puritanism all its power, – a power which can never long survive the faith in divine revelation, but which did survive that faith in Carlyle. In Mr. Henry James's view of life, if we may trust his melancholy though wonderfully subtle novels, and the hints thrown out in this delicate criticism, we have the lowest form of the rapidly dwindling Puritanic faith, a thin sort of pessimism which recognises the taint in human things without recognising any divine remedy for that taint, which believes in no real power to fight against the inevitable evolution of things, which believes in nothing, indeed, except the importance of critical lucidity in contemplating the facts of life, and in the mild despondency which that contemplation is apt to inspire. He likes Emerson's tranquillity, but he would base it on a gentle pessimism rather than a gentle optimism. Optimism might lead to enthusiasm, pessimism never can; and yet pessimism, unless it is profound enough to make the world unendurable, and an exit from the world imperative, ought to extinguish the fiercer passions. If evil, and especially a growing confusion of evil, is inevitable, a spirit of toleration, and of ever-growing toleration, is necessary, too. You cannot train yourself too soon to be amused with the evils which no one can uproot. Adapt your eye, then, to the twilight; learn to smile at that which it is useless, and therefore unbecoming, to storm at; teach yourself to look for nothing excellent, but to recognise that which is not excellent, – which is, indeed, even less and less excellent, as probably our lot in life. Such is, we should say, Mr. Henry James's inner creed. Such, at least, is the temper of his many delicately painted pictures of life, and of his criticism of the two great men whose correspondence he so well describes. 'Most life is superficial, all life is a tangle; nothing, then, should put us out; but it is an intellectual duty to expect little, and not to fret, even when we get less than we expect.'[8] The duty of lucid observation and of a low tone of expectation, is almost the only duty which, so far as we can see, Mr. Henry James thoroughly and universally approves. A sadder remnant of the old Puritanism it is not easy to conceive.

Mr. Trollope as Critic

In Mr. Trollope's "Autobiography" he gives us a brief estimate both of his own works of fiction, and, to some extent, at least, of the novels of his contemporaries. What does one gather from these chapters of his own power as a critic? Certainly this, – that his critical powers did not in any degree approach the calibre of his creative and constructive powers. That he had a substantially sound judgment on such matters is a matter of course, for the great characteristic of all his novels is knowledge of the world; and a perfect knowledge of the world, even taken alone, implies that there could not have been in him any wide deviation from the healthy taste of cultivated Englishmen. Mr. Trollope's taste in novels was doubtless a sound one. Especially in relation to the novels of domestic life he was an admirable judge. He thought for a long time that Miss Austen's "Pride and Prejudice" was the best novel in the English language. Then he placed "Ivanhoe" above it. Then he accorded the highest position to Thackeray's "Esmond."[1] Whether the finest critical judgment would endorse these views we greatly doubt, but they are sufficiently in accordance with the average judgment of educated men to show the thorough sanity of Mr. Trollope's taste. Again, of the novelists of his day, he puts George Eliot second to Thackeray, and greatly prefers the novels of her first period, those down to and including "Silas Marner," to her later tales. He has no high estimate of Dickens's knowledge of human nature, thinks his pathos somewhat false in ring, and cannot even justify to his own judgment the vast popularity of Dickens's humour. Of Bulwer, Mr. Trollope's estimate is altogether low, and though he recognises his great talent, he finds mannerism and affectation in all his works. Of Wilkie Collins and his school, again, Mr. Trollope speaks with great frankness and good sense. It vexes him that "the author seems always to be warning me to remember that something happened at exactly half-past two o'clock on Tuesday morning; or that a woman disappeared from the road just fifteen yards beyond the fourth milestone."[2] Again, on his own works, – whether he judges with delicacy, or not, – Mr. Trollope's judgment is thoroughly sane. He prefers the Barsetshire series to any other class of his novels, and thinks "The Last Chronicle of Barset" the best of the series. He could remember less, he said, of "The Belton

Estate" than of any book he had ever written, and doubtless there was
less of his own mind in it than in any book he ever wrote.[3] All these
opinions show Mr. Trollope's judgment, we do not say to be of the highest
kind, — his estimate of Dickens's humour seems to us palpably and
absurdly defective, — but thoroughly healthy and marked by the right
tendencies. But there was very little of the finest elements of the critic in
him. No great critic, we take it, could possibly have preferred Thackeray's
"Esmond," with all its skill and fineness of texture, to the overflowing
wealth and power of "Vanity Fair." In "Esmond," Thackeray's creative
power was certainly much less prodigal, much less magnificent in its
effects, than it was in "Vanity Fair." Again, even in "Esmond," Mr.
Trollope does not single out anything like the finest scene, when he selects
Lady Castlewood's defence of Henry Esmond to the Duke of Hamilton,
as the scene of the book. Thackeray rose far higher in the passion of the
scene in which Lady Castlewood welcomes Henry Esmond back from the
Continent, after the Evensong in Winchester Cathedral, than in that of
the scene with the Duke of Hamilton.[4] Indeed Thackeray is almost always
much greater when he paints the unchecked overflow of a woman's love,
than when he paints her in a dramatic position addressing herself to a
number of hearers. His passion is tender and deep; in the scenes of social
effect he cannot help showing that he is not only a painter of the heart,
but a satirist of the weaknesses of men.

The truth was, as is evident from his "Autobiography," that Mr.
Trollope, knowing how inferior is the function of criticism to the function
of creative genius, never recognised the distinction between the two, and
was not aware that, as a rule, vast creative power is too active, too positive,
to be receptive and to discriminate very finely the shades of effect in the
works of other authors. It is comparatively seldom that redundant
creative power is accompanied by fine critical power. Sir Walter Scott,
the most powerful by far of all English novelists, was, like Mr. Trollope
himself, a sound and sensible, but by no means a fine critic. Sir Walter
was too much occupied by the hardy and teeming life in his own brain to
lend fully his imaginative life to the service of others. It is the same with
Dickens, and apparently even with George Eliot. What is wanted for truly
fine criticism is the receptive side of the poet, without an imagination so
teeming as to interfere with the fullest exercise of the receptive powers.
Some of the best criticisms of our century have been the criticisms of
Goethe and of Matthew Arnold, both of them fine poets, but both of them
poets without hurry of creative impulse, without imaginative idiosyncracy
so preponderant as to prevent them from fully submitting their minds to
the influence of other men of genius of whose work they desired to form
a true estimate. Nothing can be less like such a temperament as this than

the temperament of Mr. Trollope. Let us see how he himself describes his own creative power, and the manner in which it worked: —

> "I had long since convinced myself that in such work as mine the great secret consisted in acknowledging myself to be bound to rules of labour similar to those which an artisan or a mechanic is forced to obey. A shoemaker, when he has finished one pair of shoes, does not sit down and contemplate his work in idle satisfaction. 'There is my pair of shoes finished at last! What a pair of shoes it is!' The shoemaker who so indulged himself would be without wages half his time. It is the same with a professional writer of books. An author may, of course, want time to study a new subject. He will at any rate assure himself that there is some such good reason why he should pause. He does pause, and will be idle for a month or two while he tells himself how beautiful is that last pair of shoes which he has finished! Having thought much of all this, and having made up my mind that I could be really happy only when I was at work, I had now quite accustomed myself to begin a second pair as soon as the first was out of my hands."[5]

And yet though Mr. Trollope has almost always begun one novel on the day succeeding that on which the previous novel was finished, he has, he tells us, been entirely wrapped up in his creations, and has lived his life with them as if they were the inhabitants of his own world:

> "But the novelist has other aims than the elucidation of his plot. He desires to make his readers so intimately acquainted with his characters that the creatures of his brain should be to them speaking, moving, living, human creatures. This he can never do unless he know those fictitious personages himself, and he can never know them unless he can live with them in the full reality of established intimacy. They must be with him as he lies down to sleep, and as he wakes from his dreams. He must learn to hate them and to love them. He must argue with them, quarrel with them, forgive them, and even submit to them. He must know of them whether they be cold-blooded or passionate, whether true or false, and how far true, and how far false. The depth and the breadth, and the narrowness and the shallowness of each should be clear to him. And, as here, in our outer world, we know that men and women change, — become worse or better as temptation or conscience may guide them, — so should these creations of his change, and every change should be noted by him. On the last day of each month recorded, every person in his novel should be a month older than on the first. If the would-be novelist have aptitudes that way, all this will come to him without much struggling; — but if it do not come, I think he can only make novels of wood. It is so that I have lived with my

characters, and thence has come whatever success I have obtained. There is a gallery of them, and of all in that gallery I may say that I know the tone of the voice, and the colour of the hair, every flame of the eye, and the very clothes they wear. Of each man I could assert whether he would have said these or the other words; of every woman, whether she would then have smiled or so have frowned. When I shall feel that this intimacy ceases, then I shall know that the old horse should be turned out to grass."[6]

Is it possible that an author who has lived this sort of imaginative life for day after day during thirty years, giving himself no rest, but entering a new imaginary world on the very morrow of the day on which he quitted the world which had just grown familiar to him, should be capable of that fine receptivity of mind which is requisite to appreciate with any delicacy the productions of others? It seems to us quite certain that neither Sir Walter Scott nor Mr. Trollope, — both of whom, in their very different spheres, led this kind of imaginative life, — did appreciate with any delicacy the productions of others. Nor could Mr. Trollope give us better proof of this than his very unhappy remark in relation to Lady Eustace of "The Eustace Diamonds." "As I wrote the book, the idea constantly presented itself to me that Lizzie Eustace was but a second Becky Sharpe; but in planning the character I had not thought of this, and I believe that Lizzie would have been just as she is, though Becky Sharpe had never been described."[7] Mr. Trollope need not have given us this assurance. He might almost as well have warned us that Archdeacon Grantley was not taken from Shakespeare's "Wolsey." Becky Sharp, — he spells her wrongly, as he does also Colonel Newcome, whom he repeatedly calls Colonel Newcombe, — is a type of the infinite resource and unscrupulous genius of feminine intrigue, — a type of audacious craft as rich and humorous, and as full of the buoyant energy of selfishness, as Iago is rich and unscrupulous and full of buoyant malignity and evil. Lizzie Eustace is a treacherous, cunning little drawing-room woman, of no humour, no great power, and far, indeed, from the dimensions of Becky Sharp. If Mr. Trollope had compared Lizzie Eustace to Thackeray's Blanche Amory, he would have been nearer the mark. Becky Sharp is one of the greatest creations of Thackeray's genius. Lizzie Eustace is not even one of the best creations of Mr. Trollope's.

Indeed, one of the best evidences that Mr. Trollope's power is not in the main of that receptive kind which makes the critic, is the great inferiority of his women to his men. We agree with him that Lily Dale is a good deal of a prig. But we do not agree with him in any depth of admiration for Lucy Robarts, or indeed for any other of his heroines, though we like Grace Crawley the best.[8] The feminine essence is beyond the reach of men unless they be true poets, and never was there a man of great creative power who had less of the poet in him than Mr. Trollope. He speaks of the necessity of a certain rhythm and harmony of style, but his own victories were achieved in spite of a style that was almost painfully devoid of grace or inward expressiveness. He has what we may call a bouncing style, — not, of course, a style of bounce, but the style of a bouncing ball, — one not ineffective to produce the impression that the events narrated by Mr. Trollope are real events, happening to real people, and reported by a real observer, — but effective rather because it is the style of a reporter hurrying on with the chronicle of matters which he has undertaken punctually to note down, than because it reflects any profound impression made on the feelings and imagination of the narrator. His style is clear, business-like, rapidly moving, noisy, and a little defiant, as if the writer would be beforehand with you, and wished to assert his own right to be heard before you had had time to dispute that right. It is a hard and rather dictatorial style that does not seem so much to come from deep-felt impressions as from certain knowledge. That is a good style to produce the sense of reality but it is not the style of a fine critic, and though Mr. Trollope was a sensible critic, — as indeed he was sensible in everything, — a fine critic, even of his own writings, he was not. And for the same reason, probably, he was not a successful editor. His editing of the *St. Paul's Magazine* was conventional.[9] He did not really know how to use contributors, how to make the most of them. Mr. Trollope's stories were well spun out of the imagination of a keen and vigilant observer; but all his observing power was assimilated in the work of creation, was used-up as the flax is used up in the making of linen, and apparently he had little opportunity left for reflecting on the works of others, and for discriminating the fine threads and delicate colours by the use of which they had made their work characteristic and unique.

Mr. Morris's "Odyssey"

Mr. Morris's *Odyssey* is completed in this volume, and completed, we need hardly say, in the same fashion in which the task was commenced. It is definitely an attempt to make the *Odyssey* read as quaintly and as little in keeping with modern conceptions, whether as regards thought or language, as it is possible to make it consistently with a tolerably intelligible style. For this purpose, all kinds of odd-sounding composite words are coined even where the original does not give us any equally grotesque phrase, but in place of it either a very ordinary word, or two ordinary words not in any way interlocked as Mr. Morris loves to interlock them. Thus, ἐπίνεον, which merely means, we suppose, "assented," and is in no respects an odder word in Greek than "assented" is in English, Mr. Morris translates in Book xiii., l. 47, by "yea-said:" —

"So he spake; and all yea-said him, and bade the thing to be,"

where Mr. Morris deliberately makes, to English ears, his translation much more quaint and grotesque than the Greek word would be to Greek ears. And so, again, in the same book, where Athene addresses Ulysses, as "insatiate of deceits" (δόλων ἆτ'), Mr. Morris invents as the equivalent the very unjustified quaintness "guile-greedy," though "greedy of guile" would have been far nearer to the mechanism of Homer's phrase. So, again, he translates ἀλήτης, which surely is not at worst at all quainter than "vagrant," by "gangrel," a word entirely foreign to any classical English, though ἀλήτης is not at all foreign to classical Greek. The same thirst for archaisms, — jarring and misleading archaisms, as we maintain, — pursues Mr. Morris throughout his *Odyssey*. Λελασμένος ἱππονάων becomes "all thy horse-lore heed gone by;" θάρσει, "be of good cheer," becomes "heart-up;" νεφεληγερέτα Ζεύς becomes "Zeus the Cloud-pack's Herder;" χειρὶ χαταπρηνεῖ, "with a stroke from the palm of his hand," becomes "with a stroke of his hand laid flatling" (where there is no conceivable excuse for the "ling," except the malice prepense of a theory that Homer should be made grotesquely quaint). When Euryclea anoints Ulysses with oil, Mr. Morris gives it "with oil she *sleeked* his skin;" and when Ulysses comes out from his bath "with a form like to the immortals," Mr. Morris says, —

"And as he went up from the bath-vat, like the deathless his body did show."[1]

When Athene spreads a mist round Ulysses so that he does not recognise the localities of his own Ithacan home, since it is the natural effect of a concealing and magnifying mist which shuts out all that is not close under the eye, and magnifies what is close under it, that the roads appear to have no turning, and to be quite continuous, the harbours to be all that one could wish, the rocks steep, and the trees luxuriant, – Mr. Morris gives us the following, –

"Therefore all things about him the King as strange did see,
The uncrooked ways far-reaching, the all-safe havens there,
The steep, high rocks, and the trees, well-growing, leafy-fair."[2]

"Uncrooked" is a vile phrase for "without turnings," and hardly suggests the true meaning; it was not that the roads looked "uncrooked," but that they did not look crooked, as they would have done if Ulysses could have seen further. Then ερπάζων παρὰ θῖνα πολυφλοίσβοιο θαλάσσης comes out

"As along the shore of the wallow of the washing seas he crept,"[3]

where "wallow" is, we think, a pure superfluity of grotesqueness for which there is no excuse; nor do we think "washing" at all a good translation for a word which is used to express the roar of a great multitude of men, as well as the roar of the ocean. It is not the washing sound that the word must indicate, not the gurgle of the breakers on the beach, but the indistinct tumult of the distant waters.

On the whole, we like Mr. Morris's translation less in this second volume than we did in his first, because there are fewer passages of the idyllic sort such as rather beguiled the poet from his theory. In his picture of Circe and Calypso in their different island homes, Mr. Morris to a certain extent forgot his theory, and painted, with the genuine zest of a poet, a beautiful idyllic subject. But here there are fewer passages of that description, nor is his style at all suited to the grander bits of this portion of the *Odyssey*, like the bending of Ulysses' bow and the slaughter of the suitors. Unlike Homer as Pope cannot help being, we infinitely prefer Pope's rendering of the bending of Ulysses' bow to Mr. Morris's. There is far more fire in it, more motion, more menace, more triumph. Here is Mr. Morris's: –

"And silently forth from the house meanwhile had Philoetius sped,
And therewith he bolted the gate of the well-walled forecourt there;
But there lay beneath the cloister a curved ship's mooring-gear,

A flag-wrought rope, and therewith he bound o'er the gate of the
  close,
And then gat him aback and sat down on the bench whence he
  erewhile arose,
And set his eyes on Odysseus, who as now the great bow bare,
And was turning it over on all sides, and trying it here and there,
Lest the worms its horn should have eaten while long was its
  master away,
And one would be eyeing his neighbour, and thuswise would he
  say:
'Lo here, a lover of bows, one cunning in archery!
Or belike in his house at home e'en such-like gear doth lie;
Or e'en such an one is he minded to fashion, since handling it
  still,
He turneth it o'er, this gangrel, this crafty one of ill!'
And then would another be saying of those younglings haughty
  and high:
'E'en so soon and so great a measure of gain may he come by
As he may now accomplish the bending of the bow.'

So the Wooers spake; but Odysseus, that many a rede did know,
When the great bow he had handled, and eyed it about and along,
Then straight, as a man well learned in the lyre and the song,
On a new pin lightly stretcheth the cord, and maketh fast
From side to side the sheep-gut well-twined and overcast:
So the mighty bow he bended with no whit of labouring,
And caught it up in his right hand, and fell to try the string,
That 'neath his hand sang lovely as a swallow's voice is fair.
But great grief fell on the Wooers, and their skin changed colour
  there,
And mightily Zeus thundered, and made manifest a sign;
And thereat rejoiced Odysseus, the toil-stout man divine,
At that sign of the Son of Cronos, the crooked-counselled Lord;
And he caught up a swift arrow that lay bare upon the board,
Since in that hollow quiver as yet the others lay,
Which those men of the Achaeans should taste ere long that day,
And he laid it on the bow-bridge, and the nock and the string he
  drew,
And thence from his seat on the settle he shot a shaft that flew
Straight-aimed, and of all the axes missed not a single head,
From the first ring: through and through them, and out at the
  last it sped,
The brass-shod shaft; and therewith to Telemachus spake he:
'The guest in thine halls a-sitting in nowise shameth thee,
Telemachus. I missed not thy mark, nor overlong
Toiled I the bow a-bending; stark yet am I and strong.

> Forsooth, the Wooers that shamed me no more may make me
> scorn!
> But now for these Achaeans is the hour and the season born
> To dight the feast in the daylight, and otherwise to be fain
> With the song and the harp thereafter that crown the banquet's
> gain.'
> So he spake; and with bent brow nodded, and Telemachus the
> lord,
> Dear son of the godlike Odysseus, girt on his whetted sword;
> His dear hand gripped the spear-shaft, and his father's side
> anear,
> He stood by the high-seat crested with the gleaming brazen
> gear."[4]

One sees here how Mr. Morris's effort to be quaint spoils the directness
and rapidity of Homer, – "with *no whit* of labouring" is the equivalent of
the simple ἄτερ σπουδῆς, "without effort;" "*fell* to try the string" is the
equivalent of πειρήσατο νευρῆς, "tried the string." Ἡ δ' ὑπὸ χαλὸν
ἄεισε χελιδόνι εἰχέλη αὐδην, "But it sang beautifully under his hand, like
in voice to a swallow," is weakened both by the introduction of the epithet
"fair" for the swallow's voice, and the substitution of the quaint adverb
"lovely" for "beautifully," for it surely is not meant that the note was
intrinsically beautiful (indeed, the swallow's cry is somewhat shrill), but
that the bow sang beautifully to the ear of the grim warrior who knew what
he was about to do with it. That the sound was not beautiful to the suitors,
the next lines tell us. Again, the cold irony of the invitation to the suitors
to begin feasting, and feasting to the sound of music, while such a fate was
preparing for them, is lost in the dreadful archaism of the couplet: –

> "To dight the feast in the daylight, and otherwise to be fain
> With the song and the harp thereafter that crown the banquet's
> gain."

Pope's version, –

> "Ill I deserved these haughty peers' disdain,
> Now let them comfort their dejected train,
> In sweet repast the present hour employ,
> Nor wait till evening for the genial joy;
> Then to the lute's soft voice prolong the night,
> Music the banquet's most refined delight," –[5]

is three times as nervous and disdainful.

Mr. Morris seems to us to make a great mistake when he treats the
extremely germinal character of Homer's conceptions of such matters as
geography, history, natural laws, and domestic civilisation, as suggesting
that the *language* in which these matters are treated should also be of that
half-developed kind proper to a society which is groping for utterance.

Homer was master of one of the most splendid forms of speech which have ever been at the command of man. Look carefully at Mr. Morris's selected phraseology for the rendering of Homer, and we find that it abounds in such words as "gangrel," "sleeked," "heart-up," "bath-vat," "toil-stout," "Cloud-packs Herder," "flatling," "uncrooked," "guile-greedy," &c., – that is, in clumsy compound words which have either been devised for the particular occasion and jar on the ear, or which must be supposed to have dropped out of use because they produced an effect in excess of that which they were intended to produce, and so diverted the attention of the reader from more important points. Now, this we may safely say, – that Homer's expressions never produce this effect of clumsy tentativeness or of spotty impressiveness. There never was a form of speech more full of harmony, less marked by disagreeable singularities, than Homer's. If he is antique in his knowledge of the universe, as, of course, he is, he is up to the highest mark we can conceive in the fine tone of his phraseology, the perfect blending of his tints, the general harmony of his effects. Mr. Morris's *Odyssey* makes one shrink at every page from the oddity of the combinations which he invents, of the patches of effect which he grafts upon his author. To translate νεφεληγερέτα Ζεύς, "Cloud-pack's Herder;" to translate διάχτορος Αργειφόντης (epithets of Hermes), "the flitter, the Argus-bane," instead of "the Messenger, the slayer of Argus," produces much the same sort of grotesque effect as would any sixteenth-century historian who should have called Henry VIII. "the wife-ridder, the Pope-bane." In a word, Mr. Morris makes us stare, where Homer makes us quite at home. We do not think that Mr. Worsley's *Odyssey* is at all like the original, for, with all its beauty, it has lost Homer's simplicity, and we are sure that Cowper's *Odyssey* is as much too dull and flat as Mr. Worsley's is too rich and complex.[6] But either the one or the other seems to us to be a less misleading rendering of Homer's *Odyssey* than Mr. Morris's, which, in spite of some beautiful passages, is limping, grotesque, and destitute of the mellow beauty of Homer.

The Genius of Tennyson

Those who, in 1842, when Tennyson's first important poems were published, were just old enough to love poetry, and yet young enough to have no prepossessions or prejudices against poetry of a new type, probably owe more to the great poet who is just dead, than either his own contemporaries, whose taste in poetry was formed before his poems were published, or those younger generations which have grown up to find Tennyson's fame well established and taken for granted by the whole world around them.[1] An original poet is usually more or less unwelcome to those who have formed their own taste on older models; and yet there is something in the young which rather resents the conventional praise of the society in which they live, and delights to discover a literary hero for themselves. The death of the Poet-Laureate has brought a severe shock to those whose earliest intellectual youth was saturated with admiration for his rich, grave, measured, and elaborate genius, who in their College days declaimed to themselves the stately rhetoric of "Locksley Hall," brooded over the glowing pictures of the "Dream of Fair Women" and "The Palace of Art," wandered at will into the Palace of the Sleeping Beauty, followed all the windings of the subtle controversy between "The Two Voices," accompanied Sir Bedivere to the lake into which he was so reluctant to plunge Excalibur, and gazed at their own College friendships through the same "vinous mist" which coloured so charmingly the "lyrical monologue" of Will Waterproof at the 'Cock;' and all this, long before they had any opinion on the comparative merits of the many great English poets. Those who were growing up, but not yet grown up, in 1842, can hardly know how much of their ideal of life they owe to Tennyson, and how much to the innate bias of their own character. They only know that they owe him very much of the imaginative scenery of their own minds, much of their insight into the doubts and faith of their contemporaries, much of their political preference for "ordered freedom," and much, too, of their fastidious discrimination between the various notes of tender and pathetic song. But they will find some difficulty in determining what it is that Tennyson has most effectually taught them to enjoy and dread, where he has enlarged to most purpose the range of their love and reverence, and stimulated most powerfully their recoil from ugliness and evil.

We should say that perhaps the most distinctive, though not the most striking and impressive characteristic of Tennyson's genius, was the definitely artistic character of his poetry. There is not a single one of his greater poems which does not bear the signs of careful thought and meditation, not to say study. There is both care and ease in every line, — the care of delicate touches, the ease which hides the care. Tennyson is not a poet whose poetry bubbles up and flows on with the superfluous buoyancy and redundancy of a fountain or a rapid. It is inlaid with conscious emotion, saturated with purpose and reflection. Its grace and ease, — and it is almost always graceful and easy, — are the grace and ease of a flexible and vigilant attention. There is what theologians call "recollection" in every line.[2] He is as much artist as poet. Nothing that he says seems to be unconscious. Even his passion is deliberate and more patient than stormy: —

> "Dear mother Ida, hearken ere I die,
> I waited underneath the dawning hills,
> Aloft the mountain lawn was dewy-dark,
> And dewy-dark aloft the mountain pine;
> Beautiful Paris, evil-hearted Paris,
> Leading a jet-black goat, white-horned, white-hooved,
> Came up from reedy Simois, all alone."[3]

What a richly painted picture is there, and that is Tennyson's usual style. Every verse of "The Palace of Art," every verse of "The Dream of Fair Women," is a separate work of art, a separate compartment of a great whole. Consider only the rich workmanship, the masterly concentration of care on such a pair of stanzas as the following in the picture of Cleopatra:

> "Her warbling voice, a lyre of widest range,
>   Struck by all passion did fall down and glance
> From tone to tone, and glided through all change
>   Of liveliest utterance.
>
> When she made pause, I knew not for delight;
>   Because with sudden motion from the ground
> She raised her piercing orbs, and filled with light
>   The interval of sound."[4]

That is no ripple of artless eloquence. It is the very opulence of richly wrought imaginative speech.

And Tennyson's art is as signal in the careful ordering and evolution of his *thoughts* as in the painting of his pictures. Examine the structure of "The Two Voices," or of the argument with Scepticism, in "In Memoriam," and you will find how carefully the evolution of the whole is planned, how the simple and more obvious difficulties are dealt with first, the larger and wider further on, and how the whole presents the effect of a fully studied and gradually developed plan. Tennyson was evidently one of those

"Who rowing hard against the stream,
Saw distant gates of Eden gleam,
And did not dream it was a dream,"[5]

as he himself describes them. And yet he was willing to listen with rapt attention to all who did dream it was a dream, that he might fully read all that was in their heart, and bring it to the judgment of his own larger and wider and richer experience.

Great as Tennyson was as an artist, he not unfrequently erred on the side of redundancy in the use of light and colour. His richly jewelled speech, – as in "Enoch Arden," – sometimes distracted attention from the substance of his narrative. He occasionally filled his canvas too full of glowing and enamelled fancy. His poems, especially in the middle period of his genius, are almost too much concerned with the pageantry and sentiment of life, so that the outline is lost in the richness of the detail. Sometimes, too, he harps too much on the minor key, – as in that reiterated refrain, "Dear mother Ida, hearken ere I die," which overloads the beauty of "Oenone" with its plaintive wail, or on the over-wrought pathos of "The May Queen," or "Mariana in the Moated Grange." This is the chief defect of his art. But it is a fault wholly absent from those studies in which he assumed voluntarily and even something of the severity of the classical models. In poems like "Tithonus" or "Ulysses" his art rises to its highest perfection: –

"I ask'd thee, 'Give me immortality.'
Then didst thou grant mine asking with a smile,
Like wealthy men who care not how they give.
But thy strong Hours indignant work'd their wills
And beat me down and marr'd and wasted me,
And though they could not end me, left me maim'd
To dwell in presence of immortal youth,
Immortal age beside immortal youth,
And all I was, in ashes. Can thy love,
Thy beauty make amends, tho' even now
Close over us, the silver star, thy guide,
Shines in those tremulous eyes that fill with tears
To hear me? Let me go; take back thy gift."[6]

There we see the artist at his highest point, – the intensity of the feeling not allowed to overflow into any excess or redundancy of expression, but restrained with something of the severe simplicity of the Attic genius, while yet the passion of the rhythm, and a note or two of modern despair, betray the depth of self-conscious anguish that beats beneath the surface of the antique legend. In many of the finest cantos of "The Idylls of the King,"—especially in "The Coming of Arthur" and "The Passing of Arthur,"—there is the same refined intensity, kept strictly within the severest limits. And where this is so, we recognise in Tennyson one of the greatest artists of all time. His modernness, however, too often betrays itself by a reiteration, an emphasis of expression,—especially where the mood is one of pathos,—that verges on the morbid vein of our own too plaintive and garrulous generation.

This tendency, however, to be too microscopic and elaborate in the structure of his poems of pathos, is itself the secret of his strength when he takes a theme like that of "In Memoriam," and devotes all his great powers to the task of delineating the various phases of human grief, when he confronts us with the dismay and doubts to which it gives rise, and shows us the conviction that springs ultimately out of them, if they are fairly faced, that the deeper affections have a future before them of which death is only the beginning. In a poem of this kind, great delicacy and minuteness of treatment, and great power of expatiating on all the various phases of doubt and faith, is absolutely necessary, if the poem is to be a perfect one. And probably no poem of the kind has ever been written which succeeds so completely in throwing a glorious rainbow upon the black cloud. "In Memoriam" would have lost half its value if it had not struck all the chords of a profoundly patient and tenacious sorrow, and dwelt on the blank despair, the tremulous hope, the humility of love, the tyranny of the senses, the insurrection of the conscience against that tyranny, the testimony of the spirit, the indomitable elasticity of faith, with all the vividness and freshness of a great imagination and an intellect of a candour and courage of something like prophetic calibre. When has the humility of love, in dwelling on a friend's higher state of being, ever before been painted with such strength and tenderness as in itself to more than compensate the supposed inequality of the two natures so compared? —

"He past; a soul of nobler tone;
   My spirit loved, and loves him yet
   Like some poor girl whose heart is set
On one whose rank exceeds her own.

In mixing with his proper sphere,
   She finds the baseness of her lot,
   Half jealous of she knows not what,
And envying all that meet him there.

The little village looks forlorn;
    She sighs amid her narrow days,
    Moving about the household ways,
In that dark house where she was born.

The foolish neighbours come and go
    And tease her till the day draws by;
    At night she weeps, 'How vain am I!
How should he love a thing so low?' "[7]

And where in all Literature has the protest of the spirit against the triumph of physical Nature over its higher life, been conceived and expressed with so much intensity as in this great poem, of which even the following splendid lines are hardly more than an average specimen: —

"And he, shall he,
Man, her last work, who seem'd so fair,
    Such splendid purpose in his eyes,
    Who roll'd the psalm to wintry skies,
Who built him fanes of fruitless prayer,

. . . .

Who lov'd, who suffer'd countless ills,
    Who battled for the True, the Just,
    Be blown about the desert dust,
Or seal'd within the iron hills?"[8]

How many of those who followed Lord Tennyson to his grave in the great Abbey on Wednesday must have been haunted, as was the present writer, by the deep passion of that indignant question! It took all Tennyson's pertinacious fidelity, all the passion of his devoted love, all the patience of his plaintiveness, to give to the world such a poem as his "In Memoriam" on the early death of Arthur Hallam. His favourite minor key, swelling at the close into the exultation of victorious faith, was the true setting for that rosary of grief.

There is a good deal more difference of feeling about the spiritual element in "The Idylls of the King." King Arthur has not been a favourite with many of the best critics, though it is easy to discern that it was half in memory of the glorified friend of his youth, and only half in honour of the hero of the Round Table, that Tennyson's Idylls were conceived and executed. It is very difficult to delineate a perfect nature, — at least, in a mere man, — without exciting the grudging spirit which takes umbrage at any assumption of sanctity; and it may perhaps be admitted that in the closing scene of "Guinevere," Arthur does assume too much of the stainlessness and sinlessness which belonged only to one who was more than man. But even with this admission, we believe that "The Idylls of

the King" contain a wonderfully fine "romance of eternity," to use an
expression of M. Renan's,[9] which he misapplies to something much
greater than any romance, — and that the picture of the faith and failure,
and especially of the faith *in* failure, of the King, contains one of the
noblest of the many noble though imperfect poetic ideals of our day. The
warnings with which Arthur opens the quest for the holy grail, and the
foreboding vision of the collapse of his kingdom with which he sums up
the story of these self-consuming or defeated hopes, seem to us the finest
possible comments on the craving of enthusiasts for religious excitement,
which the spiritual wisdom of man has ever uttered. We quote the closing
words of the passage in which Arthur insists that the excessive enthusiasm
of mystics has wrecked the reign of law and righteousness, and yet claims
for himself visions more than they all, — but visions meant to strengthen
for, not to distract from, the true work of life: —

> "And some among you held that if the King
> Had seen the sight, he would have sworn the vow:
> Not easily, seeing that the King must guard
> That which he rules, and is but as the hind
> To whom a space of land is given to plough,
> Who may not wander from the allotted field
> Before his work be done; but being done
> Let Visions of the night, or of the day
> Come as they will; and many a time they come
> Until this earth he walks on seems not earth,
> This light that strikes his eyeball is not light,
> This air that smites his forehead is not air,
> But vision, — yea his very hand and foot —
> In moments when he feels he cannot die,
> And knows himself no vision to himself,
> Nor the high God a vision, nor that One
> Who rose again; ye have seen what ye have seen."[10]

That, we have the means of knowing, was more or less a transcript of
Tennyson's own experience.[11] It witnesses to something like the same
experience of the nothingness of all material things which Wordsworth
claimed for himself in the great "Ode on the Intimations of Immortality."
And the picture of the impending moral catastrophe in "The Last
Tournament" is still grander. There we see the moral analogue of
"ragged rims of thunder brooding low, and shadow streaks of rain."[12]
Whatever may be the shortcomings in the picture of Arthur, "The Idylls
of the King" seem to us to contain a most powerful delineation of the
various conflicts between earthly passions and spiritual aims. If the
literary perfection be less complete than that of "In Memoriam," the
design was richer, and covered a much wider field.

And Tennyson's ideal of spiritual life included not only the individual, but the nation. No one can read these visions of the Arthurian kingdom without being conscious that the poet's eye was fixed on the spiritual ambitions and the spiritual shrinkings and timidities of his own country and his own day. Indeed, he expressly says so in his epilogue addressed to the Queen. His sympathy with deeds of valour makes the English heart beat higher. His dread of anything like national insincerity or unmanly self-distrust raised the courage and daring of his fellow-countrymen to their proper level. And he ended his Idylls with one of the finest exhortations to his own people which our language contains: —

> "The loyal to their Crown
> Are loyal to their own far sons, who love
> Our ocean-empire with her boundless homes
> For ever-broadening England, and her throne
> In our vast Orient, and one isle, one isle
> That knows not her own greatness; if she knows
> And dreads it, we are fall'n."[13]

Never was Tennyson greater than when he spoke for the nation with something like the authority of one conscious of the nation's reverence and trust.

But perhaps the highest point which Tennyson's poetry ever reached was in those exquisite little lyrics which test the inspiration of a poet more even than more massive structures. He was not great in drama, though his insight into ruling passions and purposes, especially when dealing with the simpler and rougher and more massive character of half-developed natures, was profound, as is shown by his sketch of the "Grandmother," of the two "Northern Farmers," and of the "Northern Cobbler," who conquers his passion for drink by boldly confronting the tempter day after day in the shape of a great bottle of gin. But these were the incidental triumphs of a great poet. For the most part, his concrete characters are not powerful. His figures have no wealth of life in them, and their actions do not carry you on. But though on ground of this kind he could not touch the hem of Shakespeare's garment, the little songs with which the dramas and the longer poems are interspersed are, for beauty, tenderness, and sweetness, quite Shakespearian. And they have, moreover, very frequently a singularly dramatic effect, — Fair Rosamond's little song, for instance, in *Becket:* —

> "Rainbow, stay,
>   Gleam upon gloom,
>   Bright as my dream
> Rainbow, stay!
> But it passes away,

> Gloom upon gleam,
> Dark as my doom —
> O rainbow stay."[14]

It is the same with the lovely song, "Come into the garden, Maud," — perhaps the most perfect of its kind in English literature, — and Enid's song, "Turn, fortune, turn thy wheel," and with Maid Marian's song, "Love flew in at the window," in his *Foresters*. There is singular beauty and even dramatic effect in that song, as there is in all Tennyson's songs, — only they are all the songs of a musing and meditative fancy, not of a wild and free imagination. Milton spoke of Shakespeare as "Sweetest Shakespeare, Fancy's child," warbling "his native wood-notes wild."[15] That description would never have applied to Tennyson. His wood-notes are not wild. They are, perhaps, even more beautiful, but they are also less simple. They are, to Shakespeare's songs, what the garden rose is to the wild rose, — richer, fuller, more wonderful works of art, but with less of that exquisite singleness of effect which conquers by its very modesty. Tennyson's songs are miracles of gaiety or pathos, or wonder or grief; especially of grief. Our language has never elsewhere reached the special beauty of his "Tears, idle tears," or his "Break, break, break;" nor for magic of sound has the spell of his "Blow, bugles, blow" ever been commanded by another. But even these perfect blossoms of song are all the growth of highly complex conditions of thought or feeling, which show themselves in the elaborate delicacy and harmony of their structure. High culture is of the very essence of Tennyson's poetry, be it picture, or playful reverie, or love, or sorrow, or self-reproach. He is, indeed, the living refutation of Carlyle's theory that genius is never self-conscious.[16] Without clear self-consciousness, there could never have been a Tennyson, and therefore, without clear self-consciousness, one of the highest types of genius would be impossible.

An Illustrated "Pride and Prejudice"

Mr. Hugh Thomson is not as successful with Miss Austen as we had ventured to hope. For one thing, he is not careful to impress the same stamp on all his various sketches of the same person, and yet Miss Austen herself never loses that happy knack of impressing the personality she intends upon her characters, which makes it impossible to mistake who is speaking and in what mood. Mr. Thomson's Elizabeth Bennet is often almost indistinguishable from his Jane, and his Darcy is hardly ever to be recognised as Miss Austen's Darcy at all. Lydia is not half giddy or vulgar enough, and Jane has not that deeply impressed mildness and sweetness which saves her from being insipid. Mr. Collins is often presented as a stupid young Pecksniff, as if a Pecksniff or a Tartuffe could ever be stupid,[1] – instead of as the pompously servile clergyman, as proud of his servility as if it were the very bond of peace and of all virtues. Again, the meddling and ill-tempered self-importance of Lady Catherine De Bourgh is extremely inadequately rendered, and she is generally presented as having no neck at all, whereas to our mind she ought to have had one that would have reared her arbitrary and blundering head into all sorts of inappropriate and undignified attitudes of arrogant meddlesomeness. The lady who, when bent on a scolding mission, could find time to throw open the doors of the dining and drawing rooms at Longbourn, and to pronounce them very decent rooms, before attacking Elizabeth as to her suspected engagement with Darcy, could hardly have been without a scraggy and restless neck. Worst of all, perhaps, is the conception of Darcy, who has only in one scene that air of haughtiness which gives its name to the book. Generally, he is presented to us as something of a fop, and with no touch in him of grand or resolute nobility; and we venture to affirm that there is no authority in Miss Austen for the eye-glass with which Mr. Hugh Thomson has endowed him. Indeed, there is one passage in which he is stated to have directed his eyes with a very serious expression towards Bingley and Jane, where Miss Austen would have naturally mentioned an eye-glass, if she had intended him to have one. To our minds, Mr. Bennet is almost the only successful sketch in the book, unless we except the figure of Mr. Collins in the one scene in which he is trying to show both his pique at Elizabeth for her refusal and his determination to resist Mrs. Bennet's solicitations that he should persevere. That is something like Mr. Collins, though it shows us hardly more than his back; but in almost all the other scenes Mr. Collins is presented as an ordinary booby, and not as that peerless booby, as full of self-satisfaction as he is empty of brains, whom Miss Austen had the genius to conceive. And Mrs. Bennet, though she is made as foolish and vulgar as she really was, is given without any of those remains of her former beauty to which Mr. Bennet pays so exaggerated a compliment. Mr. Hugh Thomson has not made *Pride and Prejudice* his own before attempting to illustrate it, or if he has, it may certainly be said of him, as Goldsmith recommends us to say of other designers, that the pictures would have been better if the painter had taken more pains.[2]

Mr. Saintsbury, in his preface to *Pride and Prejudice*, dwells on the variety of tastes amongst Miss Austen's admirers as to which of her novels shall be called the best, and quite rightly, we think, gives the primacy to *Pride and Prejudice*, though we do not like the touch of flippant familiarity with which he terms Miss Austen's admirers "Austenians or *Janites*."[3] As if any worthy admirer of Miss Austen would call himself by the latter title. Elizabeth Bennet was, no doubt, meant to be occasionally pert; but Miss Austen herself is never pert, and Mr. Saintsbury is injudicious in suggesting that her true admirers could patronise her in that pert fashion by enrolling themselves under her as "Jane." The very notion of so talking of her is repulsive. Half of the charm in her writings is that tinge of modest dignity which so delightfully qualifies her delicate playfulness and humour. We can fully understand those who cannot admire and enjoy Miss Austen, though we think it a great deficiency in intellectual sympathy not to do so; but we cannot understand those who, admiring and enjoying her as Mr. Saintsbury does with a really fine discrimination, are yet disposed to make free with her, and almost to patronise her for taking life so lightly. Miss Austen is no doubt wanting in idealism. She has little or no passion in her. She cannot rise above a tame kind of sweet and refined tenderness. She cannot descend into anything like those depths of self-abasement of which the soul is capable. The great charm of her writing is that in every phase of human life she always finds something to amuse her. She is more amused than shocked even with human vices. She can see the folly of them even more clearly than she sees their wickedness. She pardons any true wit, like Mr. Bennet, even for the ill-breeding and the cold-heartedness which can enjoy making a butt of his wife and of the stupider of his daughters. She does not shrink even from Wickham's falsehood and wantonness. She is more than lenient to Henry Crawford's adultery. She enjoys Mrs. Norris's stinginess so much that we cannot conceive her even wishing to convert her to a more generous frame of mind. Miss Austen would hardly know how to enjoy a world in which there was no empty-headed vanity, and no malicious envy that overreaches itself. With very few exceptions we may say that she makes a great deal more of her poorest characters than she does of her best. In *Persuasion*, much as we admire Anne Elliot's tenderness and refinement, what we dwell on with most enjoyment is probably Sir Walter Elliot's cold-blooded selfishness and his gradually growing hallucination that the designing Mrs. Clay's freckles are disappearing under his favourite Gowland wash, or old Mrs. Musgrove's noisy domesticities and family egotisms. In *Emma* we care more for Miss Bates's little weaknesses than even for her inexhaustible kindness of heart, and remember Mr. Woodhouse and his gruel far oftener than Mr. Knightly's generous and self-forgetful nature. What would the otherwise rather dull *Mansfield Park* be to us without Mrs. Norris to laugh at? Should we be delighted with either Eleanor or Henry Tilney if we had not John and Isabella Thorpe for the butts of *Northanger Abbey*, and Catherine Morland's romantic dreams of a secret tragedy blossoming into the dark revelation of a washing bill? No doubt Miss Austen's great power is that she is always amusing, that she makes us laugh even at her most sentimental heroine's premature despair, and still more at her designing adventuresses and conceited worldlings. Whatever else she fails in, she never fails to be amusing, because she herself is always amused. Nothing in the world, not even its sins and vices, move her to the depths. There appears to be hardly any room in her world for a *de profundis*. And that seems to us the true reason why so many thoughtful people cannot endure her stories, — feeling that they attenuate the whole scope of human nature, and eclipse its heroisms and its sins by the overpowering interest of its follies. We are not going to deny that there is a real truth in this charge. At the same time there is a sort of reserve in Miss Austen which renders it impossible to think of her as seeing no more in the world than she thus exhibits to us. She never goes deeper, but she not unfrequently seems almost to suggest that if it is not in her to go deeper, it is because her own power of drawing is too limited, and not because there is nothing deeper to draw. For example, in dealing with Mrs. Rushworth's shame and misery in *Mansfield Park*, she seems purposely to fight shy of it because it is beyond her range, and there is a modesty about her representations of life which seems to deprecate the notion that there is no deeper world, though she may be incompetent to delineate it. Miss Austen never claims that she can touch the springs of the deeper life. She can draw delightfully wherever she herself is amused, but she never ventures beyond the range of the lighter comedy. It is a great art to be so easily amused and therefore so very amusing; but it is not the kind of art which pretends even to hold the mirror up to human nature. There are greater things in literature than this quite unrivalled power of amusing us; but then, no one knows better than Miss Austen that there are greater things in literature, and that she herself would be unwise to attempt them.

Notes

Much of Hutton's voluminous work is listed in two bibliographies by Robert H. Tener: "The Writings of Richard Holt Hutton: A Check-list of Identifications," *Victorian Periodicals Newsletter*, No. 17 (September, 1972), entire issue, and "R.H. Hutton: Some Attributions," *V.P.N.*, No. 20 (June, 1973), 14-31. Because these bibliographies may not be readily available to readers, we indicate in the heading to the notes for each article reprinted here whether the authorship has been identified or simply attributed. And because many of the books that Hutton commented on ran to more than one edition, we locate the sources of his quotations and allusions by chapter numbers, putting the page numbers of the actual editions he used in parentheses. In nearly all cases, of course, Hutton reviewed the first edition of the works he cited. Where a work had only one edition we use page numbers only.

'Mr. Grote on the Abuses of Newspaper Criticism'
Originally published in the *Spectator*, June 29, 1861, pp. 696-97, as a subleader on John Grote's pamphlet, *A Few Words on Criticism* (Cambridge and London, 1861), issued the day of Hutton's article. [Attributed.]

1. The "able contemporary" was the *Saturday Review* as the subtitle of Grote's pamphlet makes clear.

2. Hutton corrected this mistaken identification in the *Spectator* of July 6, p. 717. John Grote was not George Grote, the historian of Greece, but the Professor of Moral Philosophy at Cambridge.

3. Matthew Arnold, *On Translating Homer* (London, 1861), pp. 63-64.

4. Arnold first used the phrase, the "grand style," in the "Preface" to his *Poems* of 1853, p. xiii.

5. Virgil, *Aeneid*, Bk. IV, ll. 176-77: "Soon she lifts herself into the air / And walks along the ground, hiding her head in the clouds." (The editors are indebted to Dr. Barry Baldwin of the University of Calgary for identifying this and other Latin quotations. The translations are the editors').

'Tom Brown at Oxford'

Originally published in the *Spectator*, November 23, 1861, pp. 1288-90, as a review of Thomas Hughes's three-volume novel of that title published in London in 1861. In *Thomas Hughes: The Life of the Author of 'Tom Brown's School Days'* (London, 1953), p. 95, E.C. Mack and W.H.G. Armytage declare this review to be "the most interesting of contemporary analyses of Hughes' writing...." [Attributed.]

1. Ovid, *Epistulae ex Ponto*, Bk. II, No. 9, l. 48: "He makes manners more relaxed without permitting men to become beasts."

2. I Corinthians 1.17, a favourite Biblical quotation with Hutton.

3. Hughes, Vol. I, Ch. 15 (pp. 296-98).

4. Hughes, Vol. II, Ch. 13 (pp. 252-53).

5. Hughes, Vol. II, Ch. 2 (pp. 42-44).

6. William Caldwell Roscoe, *Violenzia*, II. i. 62-68; for "nature" read "spirit," and for "the weary war" read "his weary war" (cf. Roscoe's *Poems and Essays*, ed. by his brother-in-law, R.H. Hutton, 2 vols. (London, 1860), I, 243-44.) Hutton once referred to Roscoe as "more than a brother to me."

7. The "truly great man" was Frederick Denison Maurice who had recently weaned Hutton away from Unitarianism and into a belief in the Incarnation.

'Ineffectual Novels'

Originally published in the *Spectator*, February 22, 1862, pp. 218-19, as a review of Mrs. Latham's *Baronscliffe; or, The Deed of Other Days* (London, 1862). [Attributed.]

1. Hutton was a student of natural philosophy (physics) at University College London, in the early 1840's. In his identified leading article, "Sir W.V. Harcourt at Oxford," *Spectator*, December 16, 1874, p. 1625, he wrote, "There is, as the old philosophers used to call it, a 'want of sufficient reason' why Sir William Harcourt should be trying for the lead in either party rather than in the other."

2. Although a few other contributors to the journals for which Hutton wrote occasionally quoted this saying by Napoleon III, Hutton made use of it eighteen times in his identified writings, and also quoted it several times in articles attributable to him.

3. Meg Merrilies is the famous gipsy in Sir Walter Scott's *Guy Mannering*.

4. "Conspicuous by its absence" is an adaptation of a phrase in an 1859 political speech by Lord John Russell. Hutton uses this adaptation a dozen and a half times in his identified writings, and more than a dozen times in attributed ones.

'Mr. Arnold's Last Words on Translating Homer'
Originally published in the *Spectator*, March 22, 1862, pp. 328-29, as a
review of Arnold's *On Translating Homer: Last Words* (London, 1862),
his second attack on F.W. Newman's version of the *Iliad*. This is the
earliest of Hutton's *Spectator* articles on Arnold, on whom he wrote
twenty-seven identified articles (plus three more in other journals) and
twenty-nine attributable to him, all but three in the *Spectator*.
[Attributed.]

1. Arnold, p. 10.
2. P. 10.
3. Arnold first introduced his concept of the "grand style" in the
"Preface" to his *Poems* of 1853, p. xiii.
4. In the Authorized version Arnold's lines from the Vulgate's Psalm
119, l. 157, read, "Many are my persecutors and mine enemies; yet do I
not decline from thy testimonies."
5. John 8. 24.
6. Arnold, p. 64. Hutton moved Arnold's translations from the
footnotes into the text, and placed square brackets around a comment by
Arnold.
7. Arnold, p. 63.
8. In the *National Review*, 9 (October, 1859), 447-74, Hutton
published his essay, "The Poetry of the Old Testament."
9. As in "Ineffectual Novels," Hutton in this image draws upon his
knowledge of science. Imagery involving atmospheric pressure may be
found in many of his articles, for example in the concluding sentence of
"Johnsonese Poetry" in this collection.

'Miss Mulock's Fairy Book'
Originally published in the *Spectator*, May 9, 1863, pp. 1985-86, as a review
of Dinah Maria Mulock's *The Best Popular Fairy Stories Selected and
Rendered Anew* (London, 1863). Hutton consistently misspells Mulock's
name with an "h" throughout his review. [Attributed.]

1. Hutton quotes Johnson's remark seven times in his identified
writings, and six times in attributed ones. Its original appearance was in
Johnson's *Journal of a Tour to the Hebrides* in the entry for September 29,
1773. For its aid in attribution see Robert H. Tener's "R.H. Hutton and
Samuel Johnson," *The New Rambler* (1975), pp. 16-19.
2. Dinah Maria Mulock published *A Woman's Thoughts about
Women* in 1858.
3. Some Victorian theologians foolishly defended the scientific
accuracy of Leviticus 11.6. which states that the hare chews its cud (and
therefore being a ruminant must have a second stomach).

4. In "The Limits of Illustration," *Spectator*, December 11, 1875, p. 1552, Hutton declared that Cruikshank was "born to make the marvels of German fairy tales visible to the eyes of children."

5. Cruikshank's illustration of this scene was a favourite with Hutton because it had been a favourite with his beloved brother-in-law, William Caldwell Roscoe (1823-1859). See Roscoe's *Poems and Essays*, ed. R.H. Hutton, 2 vols. (London, 1860), II, 512.

6. Hutton's amused contempt at this time for the phenomena of spiritualism may be seen in his essay, "The Unspiritual World of Spirits," *Victoria Magazine*, 1 (May, 1863), 42-60.

7. Hutton intensely disliked the priggish and didactic Agnes Wickfield in *David Copperfield* who is often depicted as "pointing upward," a phrase Hutton repeats in half a dozen identified articles.

8. Richard Owen's *Classification of Mammalia* appeared in 1859.

'Mr. Kingsley's Water-Babies'
Originally published in the *Spectator*, May 23, 1863, pp. 2037-38, as a review of Charles Kingsley's *The Water-Babies: A Fairy Tale for a Land-Baby* (London, 1863), which was earlier serialized in *Macmillan's Magazine*. [Attributed.]

1. This "warning to the critics" does not appear in the 1863 book edition.

2. The dedication in the book edition reads: "To my youngest son, Grenville Arthur, and to all other good little boys." The motto which follows reads: "Come read me my riddle, each good little man: / If you cannot read it, no grown-up folk can."

3. Most of these supposedly amusing circumlocutions are explained later in Hutton's review.

4. Kingsley, Ch. 3 (p. 128).

5. Hutton had a sharp eye for such variations: see in this collection his review of Matthew Arnold's 1867 poems.

6. Kingsley, Ch. 3 (pp. 114-15).

7. Kingsley, Ch. 4 (pp. 169-70, 173).

8. See "Miss Mulock's Fairy Book" in this collection.

9. Kingsley, Ch. 8 (pp. 340-41).

10. This sentence is a reminder that Hutton was a prize-winning student of mathematics at University College London, in the 1840's and a Professor of Mathematics at Bedford College when he wrote this review.

'Mr. Browning's Poetry'
Originally published in the *Spectator*, September 5, 1863, pp. 2460-62, as a review of *The Poetical Works of Robert Browning*, Third Edition, 3 vols.

(London, 1863), Vols. I and II. Hutton's major essay on Browning reviewed all three volumes of the same edition the next month in the *National Review*. He wrote sixteen additional identified articles on Browning, and ten more that may be attributed to him. [Attributed.]

1. Wordsworth, "Three Years She Grew in Sun and Shower," l. 29.

2. Lieutenant R. Morrison, late of the Royal Navy and proprietor of *Zadkiel's Almanac*, brought an action for libel against Sir Edward Belcher who accused him of taking money from the credulous who looked for visions in Morrison's crystal ball. Morrison denied charging members of the public, and early in July, 1863, was awarded one pound in damages. See "News of the Week," *Spectator*, July 4, 1863, p. 2190.

3. Adapts l. 126 of "One Word More."

4. "Flight of the Duchess," ll. 112-23.

5. "The Last Ride Together," ll. 23-24.

6. "Love and Duty," ll. 35-44.

7. Adapts *The Prelude*, V. 383.

8. The concept of the Renaissance as a distinct historical period was only beginning to emerge in mid-Victorian Britain. See Matthew Arnold's note on "Renaissance" in Ch. IV of *Culture and Anarchy* (1869).

9. "Saul," ll. 296-323.

'A Luckless Poet'

Originally published in the *Spectator*, May 28, 1864, pp. 615-17, as a subleader on the lately dead John Clare. [Attributed.]

1. "Clare's Poems," *Quarterly Review*, 23 (May, 1820), 166-74. The reviewer was William Gifford.

2. John Henry Newman, "The Call of David" (from poem LVII in the *Lyra Apostolica*, 1836). In a letter to Newman of February 28, 1864, Hutton said that he had known this poem by heart since he was in college. See *The Letters and Diaries of John Henry Newman*, ed. C.S. Dessain and E.E. Kelly, 31 vols. (London, 1971), XXI, 68.

3. Hutton's garbled version of Matthew Arnold's "The Youth of Nature," ll. 51-52. On the significance of this misquotation for attribution see Robert H. Tener's "Five Hutton Attributions, an Arnold Quotation, – and Carlyle," *Newsletter of the Victorian Studies Association of Western Canada*, 5 (Spring, 1979), 7-8.

4. "Address to Plenty: In Winter," ll. 37-40.

5. In "What Endures in Poetry?" *Spectator*, August 24, 1889, p. 237, Hutton declared that Cowper's poem, "The Castaway," would live as long as the English language.

6. "The Morning Wind," ll. 13-14. Hutton has "Ere" for "Till."

7. "The Flitting," ll. 57-60.

8. "Impulses of Spring," ll. 41-48.

9. Unlike the passage from "The Flitting," Hutton gives another version of this poem in his 1865 review of Frederick Martin's biography of Clare.

10. William Wordsworth, "Resolution and Independence," ll. 48-49.

'Mr. Bagehot on Tennyson'

Originally published in the *Spectator*, November 26, 1864, pp. 1355-57, as a subleader on Walter Bagehot's essay, "Wordsworth, Tennyson, and Browning: or, Pure, Ornate, and Grotesque Art in English Poetry," *National Review*, New Series, 1 (November, 1864), 27-66. Hutton regarded Bagehot as his most intimate friend. They had met as fellow students in University College London, where they competed for prizes, and where both (in different years) had been awarded the Gold Medal with the M.A. They later contributed to and edited various journals together, the two of them being founding editors of the *National Review* from which Hutton resigned in 1862 after serving for seven years. [Attributed.]

1. Hutton was always a great admirer of Bagehot's writings, even in his college days (Mrs. Russell Barrington, *Life of Walter Bagehot* (London, 1914), pp. 151, 169). Later, after Bagehot's death, he edited three collections of his writings.

2. Tennyson published *Enoch Arden and Other Poems* by the middle of July, 1864. "The Northern Farmer" was the fifth poem in the collection.

3. In the review, "Mr. Longman's Illustrated New Testament," in the *Spectator* of the previous week, the writer (probably Hutton) had declared on p. 1334 that Raphael "had never reached a height above his 'Madonna di San Sisto'."

4. Francis Jeffrey made this comment when reviewing Crabbe's poems in the *Edinburgh Review*, 12 (April, 1808), 135. See in this collection "The Weak Side of Wordsworth," n. 5.

5. "Will Waterproof's Lyrical Monologue" was from his early college days one of Hutton's favourite Tennyson poems, as may be seen in this collection in his 1892 memorial summing-up, "The Genius of Tennyson." He quotes from this poem ten times in his identified articles.

'Atalanta in Calydon'

Originally published in the *Pall Mall Gazette*, April 18, 1865, p. 11, as a review of Swinburne's poem of that title published in London in 1865 by Edward Moxon. Hutton contributed a number of political sketches to the *Pall Mall* in the same year, collecting them as *Studies in Parliament* (London, 1866). In the *Spectator* he published four identified articles on

Swinburne and ten attributable, including a review of *Atalanta in Calydon* on April 15, 1865. [Attributed.]

1. Hutton uses this wild flower/garden flower comparison elsewhere to contrast simplicity with complexity: see "Mr. Matthew Arnold on the Modern Element in Literature," *Spectator*, February 20, 1869, p. 223, reprinted in the present collection, and "The Genius of Tennyson," *Spectator*, October 15, 1892, p. 524, also in this collection.

2. The famous first chorus near the opening of Swinburne's poem, ll. 65-120.

3. Aeschylus, *Prometheus Bound*, l. 90.

4. Hutton was a student of mechanics and other branches of physics at University College London, in the early 1840's. He often employed imagery drawn from the sciences.

'The Reporter in Mr. Dickens'

Originally published in the *Spectator*, May 27, 1865, pp. 575-76, as a subleader on Dickens's address at the Newspaper Press Fund dinner on May 20. [Attributed.]

1. Dickens began his parliamentary reporting in the *Mirror of Parliament* early in 1832, his work for *The Morning Chronicle* in August 1833, and resigned towards the end of 1836.

2. This was said by Walter Bagehot in "Charles Dickens," *National Review*, 7 (October, 1858), 466.

3. For many readers *A Christmas Carol* contains the most memorable preparations for Christmas. The Cratchits' feast occurs in Stave Three. Perhaps in referring to the dismal wet Sunday near the Saracen's Head on Snow Hill Hutton is conflating the beginning of Ch. 4 of *Nicholas Nickleby* and the beginning of Bk. I, Ch. 3, of *Little Dorrit*.

4. *Martin Chuzzlewit*, Ch. 51 (p. 581).

5. *Martin Chuzzlewit*, Ch. 36 (pp. 419-22).

6. *Martin Chuzzlewit*, Chs. 45 and 53 (pp. 514-15, 608). The phrase, "damned iteration," appears in another article on Dickens attributable to Hutton, "Great Expectations," *Spectator*, July 20, 1861, p. 784.

7. *Our Mutual Friend*, Book the First, Ch. 2 (pp. 7-8).

8. Hutton frequently criticized this feature in Dickens, for instance, in "Miss Honeywood's Lovers," *Spectator*, October 16, 1875, p. 1296.

9. *Dombey and Son*, Ch. 60 (p. 610).

'Clarissa'

Originally published in the *Spectator*, September 9, 1865, pp. 1005-7, as a review of the four-volume Tauchnitz edition published in Leipzig in 1862. The evidence for attribution is given in Robert H. Tener's "The

Authorship of a Neglected Appraisal of *Clarissa*," *English Language Notes*, 24 (December, 1986), 58-66. [Attributed.]

1. In the same issue of the *Spectator* as this "Clarissa" review is the travel article, "Nuremberg," pp. 998-1000, and in the issue for the previous week (September 2, pp. 978-79) is a review of Trollope's *Can You Forgive Her?*

2. Hutton's political sketch of Lord John Russell, Britain's Foreign Secretary during Prussia's 1864 invasion of Denmark, appeared in the *Pall Mall Gazette* on July 25, 1865, pp. 1-2, and leads off the sketches in his *Studies in Parliament*, 1866.

3. Richardson, Vol. I, Letter XCI (p. 421).

4. Richardson, Vol. IV, Letter CXLVI (p. 371).

5. Richardson, Vol. IV, Letter CXLVI (p. 365).

6. Genesis 37.7.

7. Richardson, Vol. II, Letter XLIX (p. 168).

8. Johnson compares Lothario with Lovelace in his life of Rowe in *The Lives of the English Poets*.

9. Richardson, Vol. I, Letter XLVI (p. 223).

10. Hutton should have said "eighteenth century."

'Mr. Carlyle and his Constituency'

Originally published in the *Spectator*, November 18, 1865, pp. 1281-82, as a subleader on Carlyle's election to the Rectorship of the University of Edinburgh. Hutton wrote twenty-nine identified articles on Carlyle (the major essay appearing in 1887 in his *Modern Guides of English Thought*), and nine more attributable to him of which this is one of the earliest. [Attributed.]

1. "Phantasm Captain" is a term Carlyle uses often in *Latter-Day Pamphlets*.

2. Teufelsdröckh describes his education in the Hinterschlag Gymnasium in *Sartor Resartus*, Bk. II, Ch. 3. The reference to the *Saturday Review* is to "The Edinburgh Rectorship," November 11, 1865, pp. 606-7.

3. Hutton describes his own days in the early 1840's at University College London, in very similar terms. See his memoir of his great friend, Walter Bagehot, which prefaces his edition of Bagehot's *Literary Studies*, 2 vols. (London, 1879), I, xiii-xvii.

4. Not identified.

5. Matthew Arnold, "The Youth of Nature," l. 54.

6. *Sartor Resartus*, Bk. I, Ch. 3.

7. Probably the best-known location for Carlyle's recurrent — and false — etymology of "king" is *Sartor Resartus*, Bk. III, Ch. 7. See also *The French Revolution*, Vol. I, Bk. I, Ch. 2, and *On Heroes, Hero-Worship, and*

the Heroic in History, Lecture VI. Lindley Murray (1745-1826) was known as "the father of English grammar."

8. Notorious for repeating his favourite ideas and expressions, Carlyle incorporated many found in this list in works stretching from *Sartor Resartus* to *Frederick the Great*. Most of them appear in *Latter-Day Pamphlets*.

'An Intellectual Angel'

Originally published in the *Spectator*, February 3, 1866, pp. 125-26, as a subleader on Matthew Arnold's essay cited in n. 1 below. [Attributed.]

1. "My Countrymen," *Cornhill*, 13 (February, 1866), 153-72, and reprinted in Arnold's *Friendship's Garland* (London, 1871), pp. 115-62.

2. Shelley, "Prometheus Unbound," Act I, ll. 437-38.

3. "Heine's Grave," ll. 88-89.

4. [James Fitzjames Stephen], "Mr. Matthew Arnold and his Countrymen," *Saturday Review*, December 3, 1864, p. 684; *Morning Star*, December 2, 1864, p. 4 (see *Friendship's Garland* in *The Complete Prose Works of Matthew Arnold*, ed. R.H. Super, 11 vols. (Ann Arbor, 1965), V, 5-6, 364).

5. *Cornhill Magazine*, p. 155. Revelation 22.11.

6. *Cornhill*, p. 170.

7. *Cornhill*, p. 159. The phrase, "Mr. John Parry's amusing entertainment," refers to Parry's performance in "Mrs. Roseleaf's Little Evening Party" then running at the Royal Gallery of Illustration.

8. Hutton was himself not at all averse to using "the true means" for opposing "a gigantic moral iniquity" — slavery — for again and again the political pages of the *Spectator* during the American Civil War attempted to stir up English moral feeling against those who defended the South and its "peculiar institution."

9. "dim common populations" — Carlyle's *Life of John Sterling*, last paragraph; "till the breaking of the day...let me go, for the day breaketh" — Genesis 32. 24, 26.

' "Get Geist" '

Originally published in the *Spectator*, July 28, 1866, pp. 828-29, as a subleader on the first of Matthew Arnold's Arminius letters in the *Pall Mall Gazette* (July 21). [Attributed.]

1. Matthew Arnold's first letter embodying the opinions of his fictitious Prussian friend, Arminius Von Thunder-ten-Tronckh, appeared in the *Pall Mall Gazette*, Saturday, July 21, 1866 (letters which in 1871 were collected in Arnold's *Friendship's Garland*). Two days later, a large crowd, headed by leaders of the Reform League — the lawyer, Edmond Beales, and others — sought to hold a meeting in the park to agitate for

franchise reform, but found that the Cabinet had ordered the gates to be locked. Beales and the other leaders quietly left, but hundreds of disappointed followers, impatient with the snail-pace of franchise extension, proceeded to tear down 1,400 yards of metal railings, trample the flowers and shrubbery, and do other minor damage. The public afterwards felt that the Home Secretary, Spencer Walpole, was much too lenient with the perpetrators.

2. Arminius Von Thunder-ten-Tronckh.

3. Lord John Russell's unsuccessful reform bill of 1866 had proposed extending the franchise to urban householders paying an annual rent of seven pounds.

4. Arnold in his essay, "My Countrymen," in the *Cornhill Magazine* in February, 1866, had invented the "Spotted Dog" pub as the site of his imaginary speech proffering unwanted Socratic commonplaces to his imaginary political followers.

5. Proverbs 4. 7.

6. Under Bismarck's policy of blood and iron, the Prussians on July 3, 1866, had utterly defeated the Austrians at Sadowa.

7. Napoleon III.

8. "Heine's Grave," ll. 88-89.

9. For four years in the 1860's Bismarck, contemptuous of liberal reforms, governed Prussia without a parliament and without a legal budget.

10. These were stops on the railway line that Hutton took to get from London to his home at Englefield Green.

'Mr. Arnold on the Enemies of Culture'

Originally published in the *Spectator*, July 6, 1867, pp. 746-48, as a subleader on Matthew Arnold's final lecture as Professor of Poetry at Oxford, "Culture and its Enemies," later published in the *Cornhill*, 16 (July, 1867), 36-53. In 1869 Arnold reprinted it without its title as the first chapter in *Culture and Anarchy*. [Attributed.]

1. Hutton was for the whole of his adult life a great admirer of Newman, but not an entirely uncritical admirer.

2. The *Nonconformist* was founded and edited for many years by Edward Miall who sought to show that an Established Church was vicious.

3. Matthew 5. 58.

'Mr. Arnold's New Poems'

Originally published in the *Spectator*, September 7, 1867, pp. 1003-5, as a review of Matthew Arnold's *New Poems* (London, 1867). Hutton was not only an early admirer of Arnold's verse, but also, it would appear, one of his first reviewers: see Robert H. Tener's "Hutton's Earliest Review of Arnold," *English Language Notes*, 12 (December, 1974), 102-9, which makes a case for Hutton as a reviewer of Arnold's *Poems* of 1853. [Attributed.]

1. Hutton, of course, means *The Strayed Reveller, and Other Poems*, by "A", published in 1849.

2. By "the first or second series of Mr. Arnold's acknowledged poems" Hutton means *Poems*, 1853, with its famous "Preface," the first collection published under Arnold's name, and *Poems*, Second Series, 1855, also a signed volume.

3. "My Countrymen," *Cornhill Magazine*, 13 (February, 1866), 153-72.

4. Adapts Wordsworth, "Yarrow Unvisited," l. 51.

5. Hutton means "Obermann Once More."

6. Ll. 81-136.

7. Ll. 161-88.

8. Ll. 323-24.

9. In "The Poetry of Matthew Arnold," *British Quarterly Review*, 55 (April, 1872), 347, revised for *Essays Theological and Literary*, 1877, Hutton asserted that though no Christian can agree with Arnold's religious views, "his poetry is no more the worse, as poetry, for its false spiritual assumptions, than Drama is the worse, as drama, for delineating men as they seem to each other to be and not as they really are to the eye of God."

10. "Heine's Grave," ll. 67-96.

11. "Heine's Grave," ll. 97-102, 129-51, 206-11.

'Mr. Emerson's Poems'

Originally published in the *Spectator*, October 19, 1867, pp. 1174-75, as a review of Ralph Waldo Emerson's *May-Day, and Other Poems* (London, 1867). [Attributed.]

1. Hutton borrowed this phrase from Matthew Arnold's *On Translating Homer: Last Words* (1862), p. 60, and used it more than two dozen times in his identified writings, and frequently in articles attributable to him. See Robert H. Tener, "An Arnold Quotation as a Clue to R.H. Hutton's 'Spectator' Articles," *Notes and Queries*, New Series, 18 (March, 1971), 100-1.

2. "I Wandered Lonely as a Cloud," ll. 19-24. For "That" read "Which."

3. "The Harp," ll. 41-106.

4. "The Harp," ll. 1-10. Instead of "Nor" Hutton gives "Or"; instead of "windy," "inward."

5. Hutton liked to use the image of capillary repulsion from time to time; see the following identified writings: "The Hard Church Novel," *National Review*, 3 (July, 1856), 133; "Dr. Newman's Apology [Second Notice]," *Spectator*, June 11, 1864, pp. 682, 683; "Earl Grey," *Pall Mall Gazette*, July 10, 1865, p. 2; "Nathaniel Hawthorne's Note-Book," *Spectator*, January 2, 1869, p. 15.

6. Hutton quotes the entire poem.

7. In a letter dated "March 1850" to James Martineau in Manchester College, Oxford, Hutton states that he has been reading Emerson's *Representative Men*. The image involving incarnate chlorine which he took from that book he recalled not only here in this attributed 1867 review but also in his identified subleader, "Ralph Waldo Emerson," *Spectator*, May 6, 1882, p. 591.

8. Although others called him a Unitarian, Hutton's father always liked to refer to himself as an English Presbyterian. For an explanation of the term, see Hutton's brief review of an issue of *Blackwood's Magazine* in the *Spectator*, April 12, 1884, p. 496.

9. Hutton quotes Ward's saying several times in his identified and attributed writings alike, for instance, in "Exaggeration and Caricature," *Spectator*, August 31, 1895, p. 263.

'Professor Huxley's Hidden Chess-Player'
Originally published in the *Spectator,* January 11, 1868, pp. 41-42, as a subleader on Thomas Henry Huxley's lecture, "A Liberal Education and Where to Find It," delivered the previous week to the South London Working Men's College. Hutton often wrote about Huxley, producing fifteen identified articles on him, and thirteen more that may be attributed to him. [Attributed.]

1. Hutton always greatly admired this passage, as much for its style as for its challenge to his ideas: see his memorial subleader, "The Great Agnostic," *Spectator*, July 6, 1895, pp. 10-11, and his essay, "Professor Huxley," *Forum*, 20 (September, 1895), 23-32.

2. In 1769 Wolfgang von Kempelen invented a so-called automaton chess player, a life-size figure of a Turk. For years well into the nineteenth century the automaton beat all opponents, including Napoleon, when it performed in major centres in Europe and Britain. In actuality it was operated by a small man hidden inside.

3. Hutton employs this Darwinian phrase seventeen times in his identified writings, and almost as frequently in his attributed work.

4. John MacLeod Campbell, *The Nature of the Atonement*, Second Edition (London, 1867), p. xxvii.

'The Darwinian Jeremiad'

Originally published in the *Spectator*, October 17, 1868, pp. 1215-16, as a subleader on the controversy referred to in n. 2 below. Several articles and reviews on Darwin may be attributed to Hutton, two of them mentioned in n. 1. The two-part review of *The Descent of Man, Spectator*, March 11 and 18, 1871, is Hutton's major assessment of a book by Darwin. [Attributed.]

1. In the second edition of *The Descent of Man* (1874) Darwin speaks (p. 133, n. 9) of "two remarkable essays" in the *Spectator*: "Natural and Supernatural Selection," October 3, 1868, pp. 1154-55, and "The Darwinian Jeremiad." Darwin took cuttings of these subleaders which are now in the Darwin Papers in the Cambridge University Library.

2. W.R. Greg published his anonymous article, "On the failure of 'Natural Selection' in the Case of Man" in *Fraser's Magazine*, 78 (September, 1868), 353-62. Hutton commented on this in "Natural and Supernatural Selection," his *Spectator* subleader of October 3rd. Greg replied with his unsigned letter, "Natural *versus* Supernatural Selection," in the *Spectator* of October 17, pp. 1220-21, and Hutton's subleader on this letter was "The Darwinian Jeremiad" in the same number.

'Dr. Newman's Oxford Sermons'

Originally published in the *Spectator*, December 5, 1868, pp. 1436-38, as a review of seven of the eight volumes of John Henry Newman's *Parochial and Plain Sermons*, New Edition (London, 1868). Although Hutton's admiration of Newman grew into hero-worship as the years went by, it was never a blind admiration. [Attributed.]

1. Hutton may have known some of these sermons in the mid-1840's during his college days; he did know Newman's poems in the *Lyra Apostolica* at that time, and had read *Loss and Gain* shortly after it was published in 1848 (*The Letters and Diaries of John Henry Newman*, ed. C.S. Dessain and E.E. Kelly, 31 vols. (London, 1971), XXI, 68, 120).

2. "thus I will, thus I command."

3. "Holiness Necessary for Future Blessedness," *Parochial and Plain Sermons*, I, 5-6.

4. The "very remarkable parable" appeared in the last column of "The Archbishop of York on the Limits of Philosophical Inquiry," *Pall Mall Gazette*, November 26, 1868, pp. 11-12. The "parable" is presented as an allegorical dream of a ship voyaging in perpetual darkness to an unmapped, unknown port while passengers and crew dispute the direction in which they ought to travel. The phrase, "neither clear nor dark," is a misquotation from the fifth stanza of John Keble's *Christian Year* poem, "Twenty-first Sunday after Trinity," a phrase that Hutton misquotes in exactly the same way when introducing the stanzas

containing it in his major essay on Newman: *Contemporary Review*, 49 (March, 1886), 353.

5. Vol. IV, p. 299.

6. Newman's sermon on "Unreal Words" preached on June 2, 1839, was crucially important to Hutton as "one of the greater influences" governing the conduct of his life (*Cardinal Newman*, London, 1891, p. 102). Not surprisingly, Hutton quoted from this sermon or referred to it pointedly on many occasions.

7. Vol. V, p. 43.

8. Vol. III, pp. 202-3, 217.

9. Vol. III, p. 195.

10. Next to "Unreal Words" this sermon was of chief importance to Hutton. He quotes from it nearly a dozen times.

11. Vol. IV, pp. 261-62.

'Mr. Matthew Arnold on the Modern Element in Literature'
Originally published in the *Spectator*, February 20, 1869, pp. 222-23, as a subleader on Arnold's essay, "On the Modern Element in Literature," *Macmillan's Magazine*, 19 (February, 1869), 304-14. This article is identified as Hutton's in the January 30, 1905, letter by his niece, Elizabeth M. Roscoe, to the Macmillan Company, Macmillan and Company Correspondence, British Library.

1. *Macmillan's Magazine*, (1869), p. 306.

2. *Macmillan's*, p. 311.

3. *Macmillan's*, p. 305.

4. *Macmillan's*, p. 309. The tribute to Sophocles occurs in Arnold's sonnet, "To a Friend," l. 12.

5. Arnold, "Memorial Verses," ll. 27-28.

6. Tennyson, "In Memoriam," Epilogue, ll. 143-44.

7. See, for example, Robert Buchanan's "Liz" and "Nell." Hutton seriously overrated Buchanan's talent.

8. Hutton did not need to apologize; the *O.E.D.* records the word's use as early as 1802, and "integrate" much earlier. Perhaps Hutton was thinking of its mathematical meaning.

9. Hutton's major essay on Goethe is "Characteristics of Goethe," *National Review*, 2 (April, 1856), 241-96.

'Weighing Tennyson'
Originally published in the *Spectator*, May 1, 1869, pp. 535-36, as a subleader on two anonymous articles: J.R. Mozley's "Modern English Poets," *Quarterly Review*, 126 (April, 1869), 328-59, and Alfred Austin's "The Poetry of the Period: Mr. Tennyson," *Temple Bar*, 26 (May, 1869), 179-94. [Attributed.]

1. *The Winter's Tale*, IV. iv. 120-22.

2. *Temple Bar*, (1869), p. 193.

3. Chaffanbrass (Hutton misspells his name) is the Old Bailey barrister in Anthony Trollope's *The Three Clerks, Orley Farm*, and *Phineas Redux*.

4. *Temple Bar*, p. 180.

5. *Temple Bar*, p. 191.

6. *Temple Bar*, pp. 184-86.

7. Hutton used the image of a microscope three and a half years later in his identified major essay on the poet, "Tennyson," *Macmillan's Magazine*, 27 (December, 1872), 150, 152: "He has a striking microscopic faculty on which his poetic imagination works...Unquestionably there is much of the microscopic naturalist in the spiritual as well as the physical part of Mr. Tennyson's musings. Any mood, however subtle, when submitted to his eye, grows large beneath that close and minute scrutiny, and reappears on a new and magnified scale..."

8. *Temple Bar*, p. 182.

9. "Ulysses," ll. 19-21, 30-32, 39-43. For "admiration" in l. 42 read "adoration."

10. In the essay cited in n. 7 above Hutton asserted that in "Break, Break, Break" Tennyson found a voice "indescribably sweet" for "dumb, wistful grief...No poet ever made the dumb speak so effectually..." (p. 147) And in "The Genius of Tennyson," reprinted in the present collection, he stated, "Tennyson's songs are miracles of gaiety or pathos, or wonder or grief; especially of grief. Our language has never elsewhere reached the special beauty of his "Tears, idle tears," or his "Break, break, break...."

11. Percy Bysshe Shelley, "When the Lamp is Shattered," ll. 1-4. Hutton misquotes the last word: it should be "shed."

12. This was one of Hutton's best-loved Tennyson poems; he had loved it since his college days. See n. 5 for "Mr. Bagehot on Tennyson" in this collection.

'The Worship of Children'

Originally published in the *Spectator*, November 6, 1869, pp. 1298-1300, as a subleader on the recent increase in publications for children. [Attributed.]

1. In "Miss Mulock's Fairy Book," *Spectator*, May 9, 1863, p. 1985, a review included in the present collection, Hutton pointedly objected to the editor's phrase, "child-heart," repudiating it as an example of "modern sentimentalism."

2. Hutton's father, the Reverend Joseph Hutton, was Irish; round-towers are conspicuous in Ireland's historic landscape.

3. William Brighty Rands was the author of *Lilliput Levee*, 1864.

4. Hutton's signed article, "St. Paul," had recently appeared in *Macmillan's Magazine*, 20 (October, 1869), 509-18.

5. Hutton was certainly aware of Dr. Aikin and Mrs. Barbauld's book from his early days, for in "Bogus Butter," *Spectator*, July 26, 1884, p. 976, he recalled reading as a child a startling story in *Evenings at Home*, while in "A Danish Parsonage," *Spectator*, August 30, 1884, p. 1144, he remarked that the conversations in the book he was reviewing were "a little too much in the old style of didactic dialogue between 'Tutor, George, and Harry' in the *Evenings at Home*."

6. Christian Gotthilf Salzmann, *Elements of Morality, for the Use of Children*, [translated and adapted by Mary Wollstonecraft], 3 vols. (London, 1791). The illustrations were engraved by Blake, not designed by him. In his identified article "What is Priggishness?" *Spectator*, June 11, 1892, p. 807, Hutton declared that the period "which gave to the world...'Elements of Morality' (by Rev. C.G. Salzmann), the book which Blake illustrated so quaintly and so vividly for the little prigs of the last decade of the last century, was in the highest degree a priggish period," and just as Hutton then quoted at length from Salzmann's book so the writer of "The Worship of Children" quotes at length from it, too.

7. *Elements of Morality*, Ch. 5 (pp. 50-52).

'The Memoir of Miss Austen'
Originally published in the *Spectator*, December 25, 1869, pp. 1533-35, as a review of J.E. Austen-Leigh's *A Memoir of Jane Austen* (London, 1870). [Attributed.]

1. Matthew Arnold, "Stanzas in Memory of the Author of 'Obermann'," ll. 69-72.

2. Austen-Leigh, Ch. 1 (p. 10).

3. Austen-Leigh, Ch. 5 (pp. 112-13).

4. Austen-Leigh, Ch. 5 (pp. 121-22).

5. Austen-Leigh, Ch. 6 (p. 134).

6. Austen-Leigh, Ch. 7 (pp. 162-65).

'Pope Huxley'
Originally published in the *Spectator*, January 29, 1870, pp. 135-36, as a subleader on a dispute between Huxley and a correspondent calling himself "A Devonshire Man." For the evidence that Hutton wrote this subleader see Robert H. Tener's "R.H. Hutton and 'Agnostic'," *Notes and Queries*, New Series, 11 (November, 1964), 429-31. [Attributed.]

1. Hutton and Huxley were founding members of the Metaphysical Society in the Spring of 1869. This is why Hutton can say later in "Pope Huxley" that his anonymousness "will be no veil to Professor Huxley."

See Alan Willard Brown, *The Metaphysical Society: Victorian Minds in Crisis, 1869-1880* (New York, 1947), pp. 25, 318.

2. According to the *Oxford English Dictionary* this is the first appearance of "agnostic" in print. On the origin of the term, Hutton wrote to the editors of the *Dictionary* on March 13, 1881: "Suggested by Prof. Huxley at a party held previous to the formation of the now defunct Metaphysical Society, at Mr. James Knowles's house on Clapham Common, one evening in 1869, in my hearing."

3. Huxley's lecture on Basques, Celts, and Saxons, entitled "The Forefathers and Forerunners of the English People," was delivered on January 9, 1870, the second in a series of Sunday Evenings for the People sponsored by the National Sunday League. A report of the lecture was published the next day by the *Pall Mall Gazette*: "Professor Huxley on Political Ethnology," Monday, January 10, 1870, p. 8, col. 5; p. 9, cols. 1-3. For a reprint of the report and the letters by "A Devonshire Man" and others see the *Anthropological Review*, 8, no. 29 (April, 1870), 197-216.

4. *latae sententiae*: excommunications which take effect the moment the act which incurs them is committed (cf. "Papal Infallibility and the 'Latae Sententiae,'" *Spectator*, January 1, 1870, p. 8).

5. For weeks preceding "Pope Huxley" virtually every issue of the *Spectator* reported on the Ecumenical Council on Papal infallibility, and as late as 1876 Hutton devoted much of the preface he wrote for the second edition of his *Essays Theological and Literary* to this question. Monseigneur Dupanloup, a leader of the Gallican party, opposed the concept of Papal infallibility, as did the excommunicate, Père Hyacinthe, who in protest resigned as Superior of the Carmelites in Paris ("News of the Week," *Spectator*, September 25, 1869, p. 1113; December 11, 1869, p. 1145).

'Mr. Arnold on God'

Originally published in the *Spectator*, July 8, 1871, pp. 825-27, as a subleader on Matthew Arnold's "Literature and Dogma (Part I)," *Cornhill Magazine*, 24 (July, 1871), 25-47. The authorship of this subleader is discussed in n. 1 below. [Identified.]

1. See Hutton's signed article, "Mr. Arnold on St. Paul and his Creed," *Contemporary Review*, 14 (June, 1870), 339-41. The statement by the writer of "Mr. Arnold on God" that "we commented" on Arnold's phrase, "a stream of tendency" "at the time he first published it" proves that Hutton wrote this subleader, for no such comment occurs in the *Spectator*'s review of Arnold's *St. Paul*; the comment does appear, however, in Hutton's signed *Contemporary* article on the pages given.

2. *Cornhill Magazine*, (1871), pp. 36-37, 39.

3. The Rev. Dr. John Cumming of the National Scottish Church, Covent Garden, made himself ridiculous with his prophecies based on the Apocalypse. Wilhelm De Wette and Daniel Schenkel were, respectively, earlier and later nineteenth-century German Biblical scholars.

4. *Cornhill*, p. 40.

5. *Cornhill*, p. 32.

6. Arthur Hugh Clough, "Come Back Again, My Olden Heart!" ll. 5-8. Hutton quotes the same four lines in his identified subleader, "Arthur Hugh Clough — In Memoriam," *Spectator*, November 23, 1861, p. 1286.

7. *Cornhill*, p. 42.

8. Hutton and James Martineau studied Hegel together in Berlin in the winter of 1848-1849. In a letter to Martineau, dated "March 1850," in Manchester College, Oxford, he asked, "What could poor Hegel's reine Seyne...do...?" And the College's *Proceedings in Connection with the Retirement of the Rev. James Martineau* (London, 1885), p. 39, record him as recollecting humorously those early days with Martineau: "I remember the search after Hegel's pure being and pure nothing."

9. Psalm 36, ll. 5-7, 9; John 12. 27-28.

'The Tension in Charles Dickens'
Originally published in the *Spectator*, November 16, 1872, pp. 1456-58. The *Spectator* review of vol. 3 of Forster's *Life of Dickens* — February 7, 1874, pp. 174-76 — is identified as Hutton's in his *Contemporary Thought and Thinkers*, 2 vols. (London, 1894), I, 94-102. There can be little doubt that this subleader on vol. 2 is his as well. At any rate, he wrote nine identified articles on Dickens, and twelve more that may be attributed to him. [Attributed.]

1. The "great sculptor" was most probably Thomas Woolner who carved a marble bust of Dickens in 1872 (Amy Woolner, *Thomas Woolner* (London, 1917), p. 341).

2. Forster, *Life*, Vol. II, Ch. 2 (p. 40).

3. Forster, Vol. II, Ch. 3 (pp. 61-62). For " 'Mrs. Gamp,' she says to me" read " 'Mrs. Gamp', she says in answer;" for "cretur" read "creetur." This speech by Mrs. Gamp in *Martin Chuzzlewit* was a favourite of Hutton's; in identified articles he quoted from it as early as "The Genius of Dickens," *Spectator*, June 18, 1870, p. 750, and as late as "The Superfine View of Dickens," *Spectator*, January 26, 1895, p. 128.

4. Forster, Vol. II, Ch. 3 (p. 43).

5. Forster, Vol. II, Ch. 3 (p. 63).

6. Forster, Vol. II, Ch. 4 (pp. 75-76).

7. Forster, Vol. II, Ch. 7 (p. 148); Ch. 9 (pp. 189-90).

8. Forster, Vol. II, Ch. 4 (p. 79). Taine's blunder about Augustus Moddle and his perception of Dickens's skill in dealing with the madness of fixed ideas appear in his *Histoire de la Littérature Anglaise*, 1863-1864, translated by H. Van Laun, 2 vols. (Edinburgh, 1872), II, 343-44, 356.

'The Humour of Middlemarch'

Originally published in the *Spectator*, December 14, 1872, pp. 1582-83, as a subleader surveying this aspect of George Eliot's novel which was published the previous week in four volumes after having appeared over the course of a year in eight parts. When Hutton wrote to Henry Allon, the editor of the *British Quarterly Review*, on January 14, 1873, to express some dismay that Allon was counting on him to write a review of *Middlemarch*, Hutton stated that he "had written such a lot about it" that he needed a holiday (*Letters to a Victorian Editor, Henry Allon*, ed. Albert Peel (London, 1929), p. 189). Seven articles in the *Spectator* on this novel may be assigned to Hutton, two of them positively identified. His phrase, "written a lot," would therefore seem to include "The Humour of Middlemarch." Because he studied the part-form of *Middlemarch* so closely the page numbers given in parenthesis below are keyed to the parts. In any case, the four-volume edition of 1872 was bound up from the same sheets. Altogether Hutton wrote twenty-four identified articles on George Eliot, and twelve more that may be attributed to him. His major essay on George Eliot had appeared early: "The Novels of George Eliot," *National Review*, 11 (July, 1860), 181-219, substantially enlarged after her death for his *Modern Guides of English Thought in Matters of Faith* (London, 1887), pp. 147-258, which was followed (pp. 261-99) by his appraisal of J.W. Cross's *George Eliot's Life*, 3 vols. (Edinburgh and London, 1885). [Attributed.]

1. Bk. VII, Ch. 64 (pp. 19-20).

2. Bk. I, Ch. 2 (pp. 23-24), etc.; Bk. I, Ch. 2 (pp. 18-19); Bk. VIII, Ch. 72 (p. 184); Bk. VIII, Ch. 84 (p. 329).

3. Bk. I, Ch. 2 (p. 17) — "some" is Hutton's addition; Bk. I, Ch. 6 (pp. 83-84).

4. Hutton encountered this allusion in James Martineau's essay on Joseph Priestley in the *Monthly Repository* of 1833, and made use of it on several occasions in identified writings — for instance, "Jelly-Fish Opinion," *Spectator*, March 1, 1884, p. 278, and "Two Notable Poets," *Spectator*, May 2, 1896, p. 635.

5. Bk. I, Ch. 2 (p. 17); Bk. I, Ch. 4 (p. 63); Bk. VIII, Ch. 84 (p. 330). "Chettam" is Hutton's addition.

6. Bk. VIII, Ch. 84 (pp. 334-35). Hutton adds "but that" and "the way."

7. Bk. I, Ch. 6 (p. 87); Bk. IV, Ch. 38 (pp. 288, 290).

8. Bk. V, Ch. 51 (pp. 139-44).

9. Hutton often makes use of imagery drawn from astronomy — for instance, in his signed article "St. Paul," *Macmillan's Magazine*, 20 (October, 1869), 509, he states that Renan's saying that he "persists" in finding St. Paul's role in the creation of Christianity to be inferior to that of Christ's would be like the astronomer who "persists" that in the constitution of the solar system "the part of the planet Jupiter ought to be accounted very inferior to that of the sun."

10. Bk. I, Ch. 12 (pp. 182-83, 186, 187-88).

11. Bk. VIII, Ch. 71 (p. 157 ff.); Bk. V, Ch. 45 (p. 23); Bk. VII, Ch. 71 (pp. 162-63).

12. Bk. IV, Ch. 40 (p. 327). What George Eliot wrote was "Like Cincinnatus — hooray!"

13. Bk. V, Ch. 53 (p. 171); Bk. VII, Ch. 71 (p. 149); Bk. V, Ch. 45 (p. 46). "Toft" is a misprint for "Taft."

'Mr. John Stuart Mill'

Originally published in the *Spectator*, May 17, 1873, pp. 631-32, as a subleader assessing the works of the great Utilitarian thinker who had died on May 8. [Attributed.]

1. Mill served from 1865 to 1868.

2. John Locke, *An Essay Concerning Human Understanding*, Bk. II, Ch. 10. (R.H. Carnie of the University of Calgary kindly tracked this down for us.)

3. *An Examination of Sir William Hamilton's Philosophy* (London, 1865), Ch. 7. Hutton devoted three reviews to it in the *Spectator* in 1865: May 27, and June 3 and 10.

4. *Dissertations and Discussions*, 2nd ed., 3 vols. (London, 1867). The first edition appeared in two volumes in 1859.

5. *Principles of Political Economy*, 2 vols. (London, 1848); *A System of Logic*, 2 vols. (London, 1843). Hutton reviewed the second edition of the *Logic* in the *Prospective Review* in February, 1850; Mill, in a footnote to the third edition, referred to him as an intelligent reviewer.

6. "Coleridge" (1840) was reprinted in *Dissertations and Discussions* (1867), I, 393-466; "Alfred de Vigny" (1838) was reprinted in the same place, I, 287-329; Hutton fails to state which of the four essays Mill wrote on Grote he is referring to.

7. *Utilitarianism* (London, 1863). Hutton reviewed it in the *Spectator* on April 11, 1863.

8. Carlyle referred to political economy as the "dismal science" in the first of his *Latter-Day Pamphlets*. Hutton's knowledge of the science (one of the disciplines for which he was awarded the Gold Medal when he took his MA in 1849) enabled him to join the staff of the *Economist* and later

to become an Examiner in Political Economy for the University of London.

9. Adam Sedgwick, a geologist and a divine, had his misrepresentations of Utilitarianism exposed by Mill in the April, 1835, number of the *London Review*.

10. "Thoughts on Poetry and its Varieties" (1833) was reprinted in *Dissertations and Discussions* (1867), I, 63-94.

11. Robert Lowe supported the 1866 bill to compensate cattle owners whose animals had died or been destroyed because of rinderpest; Mill opposed the bill, arguing that the owners were sufficiently compensated by the greatly increased prices paid for beef.

12. Mill's defeat in the 1868 election was caused not so much by his advocacy of Edwin Chadwick, the sanitation reformer, but by his public support of the atheist, Charles Bradlaugh — Hutton's "other candidate"?

'Johnsonese Poetry'

Originally published in the *Spectator*, May 13, 1876, pp. 619-20, as a subleader on the choice by one of the universities of Samuel Johnson's Juvenalian satires as a subject for examination in the state-supported schools. In 1970 in their *Samuel Johnson: A Survey and Bibliography of Critical Studies*, James L. Clifford and Donald Green described this subleader as "very possibly the most acute criticism of Johnson's poetry before T.S. Eliot's famous essay of 1930..." (p. 9). [Identified.]

1. This opening sentence is a good illustration of the structural clumsiness of which Hutton was occasionally guilty.

2. Boswell, *Life of Johnson*, April 27, 1773.

3. "Prologue Spoken by Mr. Garrick, at the Opening of the Theatre in Drury Lane, 1747," ll. 3-6.

4. Juvenal, "Satire X," ll. 188-95. In the early nineteenth century, William Gifford provided this verse translation:

" 'Life! Length of life!' For this with earnest cries,
Or sick or well, we supplicate the skies.
Pernicious prayer! for mark, what ills attend
Still on the old, as to the grave they bend:
A ghastly visage, to themselves unknown,
For a smooth skin, a hide with scurf o'ergrown,
And such a flabby cheek, as an old ape,
In Tabraca's thick woods, might haply scrape."

5. Johnson, "The Vanity of Human Wishes," ll. 255-66.

6. Johnson, ll. 143-64.

7. Johnson, ll. 211-22.

8. Johnson, ll. 343-68.

9. T.H. Huxley's adaptation in "On the Advisableness of Improving Natural Knowledge," *Fortnightly Review*, January 15, 1866, of a phrase by Sir William Hamilton. Hutton borrowed Huxley's adaptation on more than three dozen occasions, often in connection with "agnostic."

10. A truncated version of Matthew Arnold's phrase, a "stream of tendency by which all things seek to fulfil the law of their being," from *St. Paul and Protestantism*.

11. See this same image in "Mr. Arnold's Last Words on Translating Homer" in this collection.

'The Hero of "Daniel Deronda"'

Originally published in the *Spectator*, June 10, 1876, pp. 733-34, this subleader appeared after the publication of Book V of George Eliot's novel. [Identified.]

1. Bk. IV, Ch. 28 (p. 215).
2. Bk. V, Ch. 35 (pp. 30-31).
3. Bk. V, Ch. 36 (pp. 95-96, 98-99).
4. Bk. IV, Ch. 28 (pp. 209-10).
5. Bk. IV, Ch. 30 (p. 259).
6. Bk. V, Ch. 35 (p. 38).

'The Cultus of Impressionability'

Originally published in the *Spectator*, August 10, 1878, pp. 1010-11, as a subleader occasioned by Walter Pater's "Imaginary Portraits – No. I: The Child in the House," *Macmillan's Magazine*, 38 (August, 1878), 313-21. [Attributed.]

1. *Macmillan's Magazine*, (1878), p. 313.
2. Herbert Spencer in 1855 had used the term in his *Principles of Psychology*.
3. *Macmillan's*, pp. 315, 317.
4. *Macmillan's*, p. 318.

'Mr. Henry James's Tales'

Originally published in the *Spectator*, November 1, 1879, pp. 1379-80, as a review of *The Madonna of the Future, and Other Tales*, 2 vols. (London, 1879). Hutton wrote six identified articles and reviews of James, and six that may be attributed to him. [Attributed.]

1. Hutton served under Clough as Vice-Principal of University Hall, succeeded him as Principal, published an obituary assessment on him in the *Spectator* in 1861, and from this and two other *Spectator* articles produced in 1871 in *Essays Theological and Literary* one of the finest Victorian criticisms of Clough's poetry, including two or three acute pages on "Amours de Voyage."

2. James, "Madame de Mauves," Vol. I (p. 288). Hutton changed the final word in the quotation from "name" to "term."

3. James introduced the concept, "asceticism," in "Benvolio," Vol. II (p. 245): "He [Longmore] had in his composition a lurking principle of asceticism to whose authority he ever paid an unquestioning respect."

'Carlyle as a Painter'

Originally published in the *Spectator*, March 19, 1881, pp. 373-74, as a subleader following Carlyle's death the previous month and Hutton's review of the sage's *Reminiscences* the previous week. [Identified.]

1. Not quite "the very opening," but Vol. I, Bk. I, Chs. 3 and 4 (pp. 23, 25).

2. Vol. II, Bk. V, Ch. 7 (pp. 292-93).

3. Vol. III, Bk. VI, Chs. 6 and 7 (pp. 340-41, 344, 346-47).

4. Vol. II, Bk. VI, Ch. 6 (p. 355).

5. Bk. I, Ch. 9 (p. 60).

'The Weak Side of Wordsworth'

Originally published in the *Spectator*, May 27, 1882, pp. 687-88, as a subleader on the chapter on *Lyrical Ballads* in Margaret Oliphant's *The Literary History of England in the End of the Eighteenth Century and Beginning of the Nineteenth Century*, 3 vols. (London, 1882). Hutton stressed the strong side of Wordsworth in his major essay on the poet, "William Wordsworth," *National Review*, 4 (January, 1857), 1-30. [Identified.]

1. Matthew Arnold, "Wordsworth," *Macmillan's Magazine*, 40 (July, 1879), 201. Hutton not only reverses the order of the clauses in this sentence, he also substitutes "true" for Arnold's "due."

2. Vol. I, Ch. 7.

3. Oliphant, I, 317, 323-24, 330-31.

4. Arnold, *Macmillan's Magazine*, (1879), p. 202.

5. Francis Jeffrey, for instance, wrote of the tragic figure in "The Thorn" that Wordsworth "has contrived to tell us nothing whatever...but that her name is Martha Ray; and that she goes up to the top of a hill, in a red cloak, and cries 'O misery!' All the rest of the poem is filled with a description of an old thorn and a pond, and of the silly stories which the neighbouring old women told about them" ("Crabbe's Poems," *Edinburgh Review*, 12 (April, 1808), 135).

6. Oliphant, I, 283.

7. The homeopathist attempts to cure a disease by administering minute quantities of the substance that in a healthy person would produce symptoms of the disease.

8. "Gipsies," ll. 21-24.

9. *Biographia Literaria*, Ch. 22.

10. Oliphant, I, 283.

11. Oliphant, I, 280-87.

12. This is part of a phrase — "the lonely rapture of lonely minds" — by Hutton's great friend, Walter Bagehot, when writing of the appeal of Wordsworth in "The First Edinburgh Reviewers," *National Review*, 1 (October, 1855), 274-75. Hutton quoted the phrase on several occasions in identified and attributed articles alike. Here he applies it to ll. 282-91, 377-81, of "The Idiot Boy."

13. See n. 5.

14. For the use of this phrase in an attributed article see "Science and the New School of Poetry," *Spectator*, November 2, 1867, pp. 1225-26.

15. Hutton fails to point out that Wordsworth altered these lines to "Though but of compass small, and bare / To thirsty suns and parching air" after Coleridge objected to them in Ch. 17 of *Biographia Literaria*.

16. Oliphant, I, 292-95.

'Thin Pessimism'

Originally published in the *Spectator*, June ?, 1883, pp. 702-3, as a subleader on Henry James's "The Correspondence between Carlyle and Emerson," *Century Magazine*, 26 (June, 1883), 265-72. [Identified.]

1. *Century Magazine*, pp. 269-70.

2. *Century Magazine*, p. 271. The "Dead-sea apes" is an allusion to passages in *Past and Present*, Bk. III, Ch. 3 and 13.

3. *Century Magazine*, p. 271.

4. *Century Magazine*, p. 269.

5. In his 1863 essay, "Dr. Stanley's Lectures on the Jewish Church," Matthew Arnold reminded the English reading public of this German expression for the Time-Spirit. It is possible that he borrowed it from Goethe, but more likely he found it in Carlyle's "Characteristics" or in *Sartor Resartus*.

6. *Century Magazine*, p. 269.

7. This quotation from the last paragraph of Carlyle's *Life of John Sterling*, was used by Hutton thirty-six times in his identified writings, and fifteen times in attributed ones.

8. Hutton's formulation of James's philosophy.

'Mr. Trollope as Critic'

Originally published in the *Spectator*, October 27, 1883, pp. 1373-74, as a subleader occasioned by the appearance of Anthony Trollope's *Autobiography*, 2 vols. (London, 1883). Hutton reviewed the book in the same issue. [Identified.]

1. Trollope, Vol. I, Ch. 3 (p. 55).

2. Trollope, Vol. II, Ch. 13 (pp. 81-82).
3. Trollope, Vol. I, Ch. 10 (p. 259).
4. Trollope, Vol. II, Ch. 12 (p. 42). A few years later Hutton described the scene where Lady Castlewood welcomes Henry Esmond back from the Continent as "the most pathetic passage known to us in our modern fiction..." ("Pathos," *Spectator*, August 13, 1887, p. 1083).
5. Trollope, Vol. II, Ch. 17 (pp. 168-69).
6. Trollope, Vol. II, Ch. 12 (pp. 49-51).
7. Trollope, Vol. II, Ch. 19 (p. 196).
8. Lily Dale first appeared in *The Small House at Allington*, Lucy Robarts in *Framley Parsonage*, and Grace Crawley in the same novel.
9. Trollope's editorship was short-lived – October, 1867, to July, 1870.

'Mr. Morris's "Odyssey" '
Originally published in the *Spectator*, December 17, 1887, pp. 1742-44, as a review of William Morris's *The Odyssey of Homer Done Into English Verse*, 2 vols. (London, 1887), Vol. II. Hutton wrote a subleader on the first volume some months earlier – see "The Dignity of Homer," *Spectator*, April 30, 1887, pp. 587-88. [Identified.]
1. Morris, Bk. XXIII, l. 154 (Hutton confuses Eurynome with Euryclea); Bk. XXIII, l. 163 (Hutton should have capitalized "deathless").
2. Morris, Bk. XIII, ll. 194-96.
3. Morris, Bk. XIII, l. 220.
4. Morris, Bk. XXI, ll. 388-434.
5. Morris, Bk. XXI, ll. 429-30; Alexander Pope, trans., *The Odyssey of Homer*, Bk. XXI, ll. 469-74.
6. William Cowper, *The Iliad and Odyssey of Homer, Translated into English Blank Verse*, 2 vols. (London, 1791). Hutton quoted two passages from Cowper's *Odyssey* in his identified article, "The Poetry of the Old Testament," *National Review*, 9 (October, 1859), 453-54, 465. Philip Stanhope Worsley translated the *Odyssey* into Spenserian stanzas, 2 vols. (Edinburgh and London, 1861); the review of it in the *Spectator*, December 21, 1861, pp. 1398-99, may be attributed to Hutton.

'The Genius of Tennyson'
Originally published in the *Spectator*, October 15, 1892, pp. 522-24, as a subleader assessing the poet's achievement nine days after his death. Hutton published thirty identified articles and reviews on Tennyson in the *Spectator* and about a dozen attributable ones, but his major essay appeared in *Macmillan's Magazine*, 27 (December, 1872), 143-67. [Identified.]

1. When Tennyson's two volumes of *Poems* were published on May 14, 1842, Hutton was not quite sixteen. Tennyson's poetry was clearly a significant ingredient in the young Hutton's developing outlook.

2. The theologians define "recollection" as a religious or serious concentration of thought; as being abstracted from the creature and turned towards God.

3. "Oenone," ll. 45-51.

4. "A Dream of Fair Women," ll. 165-72.

5. "The Two Voices," ll. 211-13.

6. "Tithonus," ll. 15-27.

7. "In Memoriam," Section LX.

8. "In Memoriam," Section LVI, ll. 8-12, 17-20.

9. In his obituary subleader on Renan in the *Spectator* of the previous week (October 8, 1892, p. 492) Hutton had translated Renan's expression as "The Romance of the Infinite."

10. "The Holy Grail," ll. 899-915.

11. Hutton and Tennyson became personally known to each other as members of the Metaphysical Society (Alan Willard Brown, *The Metaphysical Society: Victorian Minds in Crisis, 1869-1880* (New York, 1947), pp. 25-27). On at least one occasion the two men talked about the *Idylls of the King*: see *The Diary of Alfred Domett, 1872-1885*, ed. E.A. Horsman (London, 1953), p. 79.

12. "The Palace of Art," ll. 75-76, slightly misquoted.

13. "To the Queen," ll. 27-33.

14. *Becket*, III, i.

15. John Milton, "L'Allegro," ll. 133-34.

16. Carlyle presented his theory most explicitly in his essay, "Characteristics" in 1831. Hutton was raising questions about this theory as early as December, 1853: see James Drummond and C.B. Upton, *The Life and Letters of James Martineau*, 2 vols. (London, 1902), II, 340.

'An Illustrated "Pride and Prejudice" '
Originally published in the *Spectator*, November 10, 1894, pp. 644-45, as a review of an edition of Jane Austen's novel illustrated by Hugh Thomson and supplied with a Preface by George Saintsbury, and published in London in 1894. [Identified.]

1. Pecksniff appears in Charles Dickens's *Martin Chuzzlewit*, and Tartuffe, another hypocrite, in Molière's comedy of that name. But in "The Genius of Dickens," *Spectator*, June 18, 1870, p. 751, Hutton declared, "Molière's Tartuffe is poor and thin compared to Dickens's Pecksniff."

2. Oliver Goldsmith, *The Vicar of Wakefield*, Ch. 20. Hutton's great friend, Walter Bagehot, had cited this remark in "Shakespeare,"

Prospective Review, 9 (August, 1853), 414, an essay which Hutton included in his edition of Bagehot's *Literary Essays* in 1879.

    3. "Preface," p. ix.